GROMBRINDAL
CHRONICLES OF
THE WANDERER

Other great stories from Warhammer Age of Sigmar

GROMBRINDAL
CHRONICLES OF THE WANDERER

DAVID GUYMER

BLACK LIBRARY

A BLACK LIBRARY PUBLICATION

First published in 2022.
This edition published in Great Britain in 2023 by
Black Library, Games Workshop Ltd., Willow Road,
Nottingham, NG7 2WS, UK.

Represented by: Games Workshop Limited – Irish branch,
Unit 3, Lower Liffey Street, Dublin 1,
D01 K199, Ireland.

10 9 8 7 6 5 4 3 2 1

Produced by Games Workshop in Nottingham.
Cover illustration by Christian Byrne.

A CIP record for this book is available from the British Library.

ISBN 13: 978-1-80407-299-8

See Black Library on the internet at

blacklibrary.com

Find out more about Games Workshop
and the worlds of Warhammer at

games-workshop.com

Printed and bound in the UK.

The Mortal Realms have been despoiled. Ravaged by the followers of the Chaos Gods, they stand on the brink of utter destruction.

The fortress-cities of Sigmar are islands of light in a sea of darkness. Constantly besieged, their walls are assailed by maniacal hordes and monstrous beasts. The bones of good men are littered thick outside the gates. These bulwarks of Order are embattled within as well as without, for the lure of Chaos beguiles the citizens with promises of power.

Still the champions of Order fight on. At the break of dawn, the Crusader's Bell rings and a new expedition departs. Storm-forged knights march shoulder to shoulder with resolute militia, stoic duardin and slender aelves. Bedecked in the splendour of war, the Dawnbringer Crusades venture out to found civilisations anew. These grim pioneers take with them the fires of hope. Yet they go forth into a hellish wasteland.

Out in the wilds, hardy colonists restore order to a crumbling world. Haunted eyes scan the horizon for tyrannical reavers as they build upon the bones of ancient empires, eking out a meagre existence from cursed soil and ice-cold seas. By their valour, the fate of the Mortal Realms will be decided.

The ravening terrors that prey upon these settlers take a thousand forms. Cannibal barbarians and deranged murderers crawl from hidden lairs. Martial hosts clad in black steel march from skull-strewn castles. The savage hordes of Destruction batter the frontier towns until no stone stands atop another. In the dead of night come howling throngs of the undead, hungry to feast upon the living.

Against such foes, courage is the truest defence and the most effective weapon. It is something that Sigmar's chosen do not lack. But they are not always strong enough to prevail, and even in victory, each new battle saps their souls a little more.

This is the time of turmoil. This is the era of war.

This is the Age of Sigmar.

CONTENTS

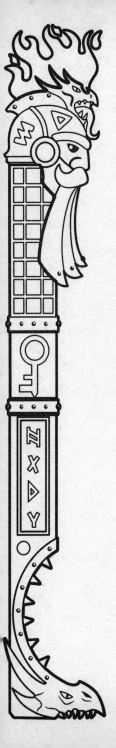

MOTHER
OF FIRE

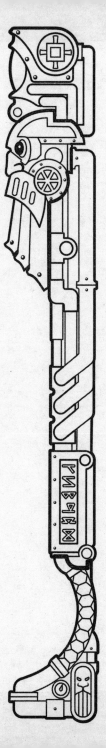

'Duardin, as all peoples of the Mortal Realms know, are a proud and insular folk, as reluctant to ask for a stranger's aid as they are to freely offer their own. And yet, in all duardin traditions, there is a similar legend, an aged traveller by whose timely arrival calamity will be averted or intractable wrongs righted. Who is this white-bearded wanderer? From whence does he come, that all duardin peoples recognise and know him? And where does he go when his act of charity is done…?'

Heat steamed from a giant crack in the earth, its roar akin to that of a godbeast giving birth to fire. The air was languid and molten. From rocky walls the graven idols of Grimnir in all his aspects sweated. The golden lines of his many mouths moved with silent utterances, eyes alive with the wit of ages and the wisdom of stone-sleep. Feeling that warm, wrathful gaze upon her, Helka Hravnsdottier bore her unnamed son to the ledge of rock overlooking Mothirzharr.

She smiled as the flameling punched at her arm with tiny fists, protesting the heat, the noise, or any of the dozen or so confused urges that could stir a month-old infant to ire.

So young, and already a fighter.

Murmuring a lullaby about blood and gold, she drew him to her breastplate, soothing his temper with the blistering touch of hot metal. The child looked up, mesmerised by her face, entirely disinterested in the wealth of brooches and jewels that framed it. Helka felt her own ambitions melt in the forge-heat of his regard.

The child was just beginning to bulk out with muscle, and already Helka could discern the warrior he would become; the battles he would win, the glory he would claim, the foes he would slay. Nor did her heart shy from envisioning the manner in which he would one day die, for they were children of Grimnir, and a violent death was as inevitable as the *drip-drip-drip* surrender of rock to Mothirzharr. Helka's father was long dead. Her brothers were all fallen in battle. They were at Grimnir's side now, awaiting the call to the final battles of the doomgron, their deaths celebrated in the hearts of all who had witnessed or heard the battlesmiths' tales. If she mourned their passing at all it was that she alone remained to have grown old.

Three Fyreslayers awaited her at the precipice, a nation's wealth in gold and fyresteel shimmering against Mothirzharr's sulphurous breath. To the left was an elderly duardin, streaks of ash-grey in the fire of his beard. Shadows wavering along deep crags in his face pooled into the bowls of his eyes. Ur-gold runes bulged from shrunken muscles, but his grip on his runestaff was strong, both it and he enveloped by the runes' golden glow. His eyes were tight shut as he muttered invocations under his breath, teeth gritted against the occasional cough brought on by the gorlbrost from which he suffered in his dimming years. His name was Morthrun Bloodsmith. Power rolled off the ancient runemaster like a second source of heat, and Helka could almost feel Mothirzharr tremble at having its temper stayed.

To the right was Tangrorn. The battlesmith was as broad and strong as any rendering of the Shattered God he might forge. The icon of Grimnir he held in one hand had been fashioned from ur-gold and fyresteel, with a beard of magmadroth-hide straps studded with sapphires and blue spinel. The eyes were shadowed and grave –little more than hollows in the metal – yet they were at once somehow joyful. Grimnir in his aspect of the Father.

Tangrorn struck the icon pole rhythmically on the baked rock, beard straps jingling, almost perfectly in time to the grumbling of the earth, the chanting of the lodge's mustered fyrds, and the beating of Helka's heart.

Between them stood Jord-Grimnir: her husband. Runefather of the Skarravorn lodge.

'From the fires of breaking are we made,' he intoned, his voice betraying a lifetime spent inhaling smoke and drinking fire.

He was clad for the naming ceremony in a kilt of golden scales, a large buckle bearing the image of Grimnir, and a set of crossed keys in white gold, fyresteel and Skarravorn sapphires. His helmet was a whorl of knotwork and zharrgrim runecraft, funnelling his hair into a crest that echoed the wall of heat rising from the chasm behind his back. Smoke rose from his beard. His expression, such as Helka could read of it, was one of excitement. They had both reached an age where neither had expected to see this day.

'By the fires of making are we made strong.'

Raising one hand, he half turned, holding it out over the heat of the chasm. He grimaced, but made no other sound. The ur-gold embedded in his forearm began to hiss and sputter.

'By the fires of our own deaths do we return.'

He withdrew his hand, flexed his fingers, then made a fist. The skin wheezed where it had reddened and cracked, but the runes remained aflame, as though the runefather had been cut open, baring the fire that burned within them all.

'And from the fire do we rise to fight and die again!'

Bending to the ground, Jord-Grimnir scooped up a handful of grit and tossed it into the chasm. Smaller pebbles popped the moment they were free of his hand; the larger stones burned for longer, creating a brief, brilliant sheet of rain over the crack in the ground. He bowed his head.

Tangrorn beat his pole against the rock to the same steady beat.

The watching fyrds rumbled their unspoken approval as, marching in time, Kazrigar-Grimnir of the Unbrogun lodge left their ranks for the Long Walk to Mothirzharr. Brostur-Grimnir followed him. Then Rorvik-Grimnir and Vulgun-Grimnir. With them went their runesons, the priests of the zharrgrim, the battlesmiths and karls and thegns of the fyrds. No order of precedence was observed. They were Fyreslayers, united as much by temperament as by tradition, and by the spirit of their law as much as its letter. There, by the mouth of the fire, they clapped Jord-Grimnir on the back, congratulated him in terms ranging from the solemn to the ribald depending on their familiarity, tossing their own fistful of gravel into Aqshy's furnace before making the return. Many had words too for Helka, of congratulation and commiseration, others simply touching her hair or her armour or smiling at the child in her arms as they passed.

Anticipation became as raw as burned skin in the heat. Pockets of song broke out as those who had paid their respects to Jord-Grimnir and the fire and then returned to their fyrds began to outnumber those who had not. Jord-Grimnir broke his dignified observance to bawl for silence, and Helka felt herself smile. *I am*, he had said earlier that day, the final preparations for the Rite of Naming frustrating him as such duties always had, *too old for fatherhood to temper me now*.

Last of all to the ledge were the lodges' Hearthguard. They came as a respectful throng, leaving Helka and Jord-Grimnir unmolested in order to offer their tokens to Mothirzharr and depart.

Amongst the last group to make its walk was a warrior made striking by the white crest of hair pluming from his helmet, a beard of the same colour dressed in gold rings reaching well past his ankles. His face was old, and yet unlike Morthrun, the runemaster, he seemed stronger for his years. The way that lava will thicken and harden over time to become rock. His eyes were older yet, but at the same time harboured such a capacity for mirth that Helka could not meet them without feeling the solemnity of the occasion slipping from her. Ur-gold studded his leather-hard torso, but the runes they described were unfamiliar. His wargear, too, was exceptionally fine for a warrior of his rank.

'A strong-looking lad,' he muttered in passing.

'Thank you, hearthkarl,' she said, bowing her head in reply. The duardin grinned fire-blackened teeth at her and continued on his way. Helka soon lost him to the throng.

When it was done, the last warriors drifting back to their fyrds, Jord-Grimnir turned to Helka. Tangrorn pounded out the steady rhythm. Morthrun's strained voice matched it with his incantations, and compelled the unruly earth to be still. Arguably, the task of shackling Mothirzharr for the ritual's duration should have fallen to one of the runemaster's undersmiters. But Morthrun had overseen Jord-Grimnir's own naming, and that of his father, and the runefather would have no other for his own son.

The runefather extended his arms to his wife. Fire wreathed him. He glowed with it, his immensely muscled torso twisted by the heat. Behind him, and despite Morthrun's best efforts, an inferno fire roared.

'When I went before your father to claim your hand, I promised him gold and a grandson.' Jord-Grimnir regarded the ill-tempered bundle in Helka's arms, pride briefly unmasking the father behind the king. 'I had come to fear that I would next stand beside him in the doomgron fyrd as an oathbreaker.'

'I could always use more gold, husband.'

The runefather grinned as Helka handed him his son. The fyrds, never comfortable when restrained, gave such a roar of approval that the heat rising from Mothirzharr fluttered like a curtain of smoke.

'We *are* the fire!' Jord-Grimnir yelled at them. 'In our birth. And in our death. We are the lords of our own lives. We fight so that we may die. And join the fire willingly when it is our time.' He turned fully to face the boiling chasm, the young runeson held firmly between his giant fists. 'And not before!'

He thrust the child into the heat, the ur-gold studding his fore-arms flaring within the acrid smoke.

Helka watched, open-mouthed.

The fyrds fell silent.

Tangrorn beat his staff upon the ground.

Once.

Twice.

'Your great-great-grandfather, who was Baeldrun, son of Baelash the Sunderer, lasted a nine-beat before crying out,' said Tangrorn as his staff struck a fourth, a fifth, a sixth.

'Do you hear that?' Jord-Grimnir shouted, fierce with affection. 'Do you hear, runemother? Our son is too stubborn to cry.'

Seven.

'Had you been present for the birth then you would know from which of us that comes.'

Eight.

'The name you have chosen for him had best be a hero's,' said Jord-Grimnir.

'I've one in mind.'

Nine.

Jord-Grimnir started to laugh. 'My mountain is not hot enough for this boy!'

'That's enough,' said Helka.

'He cannot be named before the fyrds until Mothirzharr hears him cry.'

'Your arms are burning.'

'I'll not be shamed by my own child.'

'Jord!' she yelled as the ground trembled, hot gases boiling from the fissure. The runemaster continued his chant, but the strain on his face was telling.

'The fyrds gather to hear him cry!' said Jord-Grimnir.

'Then let them depart having seen him refuse.'

The runefather gritted his teeth. 'No.'

The shelf trembled again, unbalancing Tangrorn and breaking the battlesmith's rhythm.

Fifteen.

'Morthrun!' Helka snapped, turning to the runemaster.

Gold flared from Morthrun's staff in undirected bursts, the elder folding to the ground with a wracking cough and a cry of what must have been agony. Fire shot from Mothirzharr's jagged mouth, scorching the high ceiling, and driving Jord-Grimnir from the ledge with a shout of pain. His arms were black and steaming, except for where ur-gold burned like the bruises left after a beating from a god.

His hands were empty.

Helka looked between Morthrun and Jord-Grimnir. Her expression was volcanic. And with a strangled yell, she started towards the crevasse after her son.

'Easy, lass,' said the voice attached to the restraining hand on her shoulder. 'That'd be the last unwise thing you ever do.'

'*Unhand me,*' Helka snarled.

'I will. When you stop pulling so hard to go over.'

Helka whirled, one hand raised into a fist, finding herself face to face with the white-haired hearthkarl she had traded pleasantries with earlier. She would have knocked down her own father had he been stood behind her then – even Grimnir himself, and without care for the consequences – but something about the duardin's expression stayed her temper. The certitude of years radiated off him like warmth from a stone.

'Wait,' he said.

'For what?'

'*Listen.*'

'For wh–?'

'You'll know it when you hear it.'

And then she heard it: a thin and frail cry, almost buried under the infernal, never-ending outbreath of volcanic sound.

'Now...' Jord-Grimnir was on his back, arms black and bleeding gold. Tangrorn crouched over him. Morthrun was a few paces away on his hands and knees, overlooking the edge. '*Now* he cries.'

Helka flew at him, and it took all the hearthkarl's considerable strength to restrain her.

'You dropped him!' Helka snapped.

'He lives,' said Jord-Grimnir. With a slow hiss of rising pain, he laughed. 'And he will be a legend.'

Morthrun turned from the ledge, his long face drawn. 'It is not the runefather's fault.'

'It is not *only* the runefather's fault,' said Helka.

'It was Grimnir who handed you so fearless a son,' said Tangrorn sternly. 'As it is his stirrings that quicken Aqshy's molten heart.'

'I will not have you defend me, battlesmith,' said Morthrun. 'The fault was mine. I failed to control the fire's wrath.'

'I have heard enough from both of you,' said Helka. 'Lest I throw you in as well.'

'I do not know what *I*–' Tangrorn began.

'Goading him always with feats of the past that might be bettered.' Before the battlesmith could speak again, Helka turned to the stunned fyrds to shout. 'Fetch hooks and lines.' The Fyre-slayers milled uncertainly, held back from the edge by their priests and runesons. 'Now!' she yelled.

'I will retrieve him,' said Jord-Grimnir, pulling himself upright as warriors hastened to obey.

'You have done enough for one day, husband.'

'It is my shame to amend.'

'Yes, it is.'

'You are impossible, woman,' he snarled, but not without affection.

'Can Mothirzharr be scaled?' said the white-beard, in a voice so level that it gave the arguing Fyreslayers pause.

'What is your name, hearthkarl?' Helka asked.

'Around here, I've always gone by Azkharn.'

'With which runefather do you travel?' said Jord-Grimnir, struggling to sit up with Tangrorn struggling equally to restrain him and tend his burns.

'I came alone. I'd heard of Mothirzharr and the Rite of Naming and came to witness it.'

'Mothirzharr breathes hot,' said Morthrun, supressing a cough to answer the hearthkarl's earlier question. His limbs shone golden as he tapped his runes for the strength he needed to stand. 'Grimnir tosses in his slumber. The mountain feels it, and I fear the eruption from Shyish brings worse yet in store.' He coughed again, the gorlbrost afflicting his lungs flecking the back of his fist with gold. It was difficult to remain furious with him. 'The Mother of Fire has been explored in ages past, but not for a hundred years.'

'And yet my son lives,' said Helka.

'Aye,' the runemaster conceded with a glance at Jord-Grimnir. 'He'll grow to be a rare one.'

As he spoke, Fyreslayers clad in baked leathers and gold, with the blue ornamentation of the Skarravorn, returned bearing climbing tools and harnesses.

'I will go down,' said Helka.

'Those days are behind you, runemother.' Tangrorn made to lay a consoling hand on her shoulder, only for the look on her face to dissuade him of it.

'I will go,' she said again.

The battlesmith threw his hands up in aggravated surrender. 'Then I will go too, and Grimnir's best wishes to any who would try and stop me.'

'And I,' Morthrun wheezed.

'You can barely stand, let alone climb,' said Helka.

'I will go,' he insisted. 'I will quell the mountain as I should have or neither of you will get near the bottom.'

'One of your undersmiters can do that,' said Helka.

'Don't disdain him his age,' said Azkharn and, with all eyes on him again, gave the same fire-dark grin that Helka had seen first in passing. 'Aye, maybe he's not so mighty as once he was, but who here is? And if nothing else then he's old enough to know what he's talking about.'

'The fires of Aqshy erase all deeds in time,' said Tangrorn.

'Aye,' said Azkharn. 'I'd wager they do at that.'

Helka turned to him. She was not sure what compelled her to ask, or why his presence walked goosebumps along her spine. 'Will you come?'

'Aye, lass. If you'll have me.'

The air was smoke. Breathing it in through the nose left even the tough skin that lined a Fyreslayer's nostrils stung and raw. Drawing it instead through the mouth scalded the back of the throat, drying the lips and the inside of the mouth so hard it felt as though teeth would come loose from gums. It did not smell of anything, nor taste of anything. The heat was so total, there was nothing else. The way that Hysh light was white. Or fyresteel was fyresteel, regardless of the iron, silver and gold that went into its making.

There was no part of herself that Helka could see. Smoke boiled across her, as though she descended the chimney of a working magmaforge. The power of it was appalling. It buffeted her body, strong enough almost to force her back without any active participation on her part. Only the faint, frail cries of her son guided her deeper.

Fyreslayers were supremely resistant to heat. They did not feel it. Rarely suffered it. But delve deep enough, and fire could be found that would burn even their flesh. The walls of the chasm were too hot to climb. The rock would have been liable to collapse or simply explode if Helka had attempted to grip it. Instead, the Fyreslayers descended by line, feeding out fyresteel chain from a spool at their hips. This Helka did continuously, she might almost have said monotonously, but for the jolt her heart gave with every length of chain she ran out through her palm, dreading the snag or the jam that would leave her helpless and dangling. In her left hand, gripped like a talisman too dreadful to ever be used, was a snap-hook that would allow her to graduate her descent. But she would not. Deep down, like all Fyreslayers, she exulted in her peril. She let the chain run out as quickly as it could be unspooled, listening out for the tell-tale creak that would be her first and last warning of death. As with Fyreslayer flesh, fyresteel too had its melting point.

'How far to the bottom?' she called out.

Smoke answered her, the rippling laughter of the mountain's depths. She strained, but could hear no other voice but her son's cries, nor the creak of other harness chains. For a moment she feared that she was alone, that her companions had surrendered to Mothirzharr and returned to the surface without her knowledge, or that the earth had somehow devoured them whole.

Or had the heat addled her senses? Had she been alone all along?

'I do not know.' Morthrun's belated answer was distorted by the boiling fumes, seeming to bounce at her from all sides, making it impossible to tell how far the runemaster was from her, or whether he was even above her or below. 'The zharrgrim holds no lore of successful expeditions in my lifetime. And the fire is changeable. What was true a half-millennium past is true no longer.'

'Might the runeson have landed on some kind of ledge before reaching the bottom?'

Again, that arduous wait, as though the smoke separated them in time.

'There's no way to say.' The fumes muffled the sounds of coughing, but not the hard consonant curse of the zharrgrim's secret *rhun* tongue that the runemaster managed to get out. Light bloomed about twelve beard-lengths below Helka's feet. The fire caged within Morthrun's runestaff, the smallest ember of the Skarravorn Master Forge, itself the smallest ember of the eternal firestorm ignited by Vulcatrix's death throes, snapped at the smoke and for a moment forced it to recoil. With a sultry *crack* the rocks flanking their descent began to cool. Like skin going blue in the cold. Mothirzharr was still hot enough to melt tin, but Helka shivered all the same.

Morthrun coughed again, more clearly now with the fumes' clearance.

'I cannot hold the fires of Aqshy at bay forever,' he said. 'Even as a younger duardin my rune-might was not so great.'

Helka would have praised him for his efforts, consoled him with the proof of their progress thus far, but that stung with a defeatism she would not countenance. Defeat was a concept she did not acknowledge. Even death, honourably claimed, was victory of a sort. It was the guarantee of a place in Grimnir's final fyrd, and a triumph over any consequence of failure. And so instead she barked at him to grow a beard and stop his whining.

'No one asked you to hold it forever. Just long enough to reach the bottom.'

'Aye, runemother.'

Helka strained her ears to fix again on her son's cries when she caught the final bars of a song.

> *Karaz Ankor krunked,*
> *a khazakendrum zharr,*
>
> *Bin rikkuz loz grungned,*
> *Angrung kan binazyr,*
>
> *Kharadron binskarren,*
> *Drengizharr a galaz,*
>
> *Azka duardrazhal,*
> *Karaz Ankor grungnaz.*

Her lips mimicked the shape of the words, despite the unfamiliarity of the dialect and the verse, calling as they did to something fundamental in her beneath the heat and the wrath. It spoke to her of ancient sagas, of times lost, legends of yesteryear and a future that might yet be as golden. Azkharn was well ahead of them all. As badly as Helka suffered, she could imagine how fierce the conditions must be for him, beyond the shielding influence of Morthrun's powers. What strange gifts did the runes in that Fyreslayer's body provide, she wondered? A resilience to heat that surpassed even that of a master of the zharrgrim? Immunity to fire and pain?

Who was this Fyreslayer? What runefather beyond the legendary Fjul-Grimnir himself could command the axe of such a karl in their Hearthguard?

'What is this verse that you sing?' Tangrorn called, yards from death, and yet unable to resist the glimmering of a nugget of ancient lore.

The hearthkarl was silent a while, as though he genuinely struggled to recall. 'A ditty I once heard.'

'It is not one I have ever heard sung,' said Tangrorn. 'And I have travelled throughout this realm and the realms beyond, and consulted with the battlesmiths of many lodges.'

'Yours is an old tradition, lad. *Ours*,' Azkharn corrected himself. 'Older than the zharrkhul and the forge fires of the first lodges. It begins before the death of Grimnir. With those duardin who aided him in his quest for Vulcatrix or who, inspired by him, pledged oaths to destroy evils of their own. Aye, oldflame, you could say that ours is the oldest tradition of them all, except, perhaps, the Khazalid empires of old.' He chuckled, idly letting out chain from his spool. 'But you'd be wrong, of course.'

'Then how–' Tangrorn began, before Helka shushed him. 'But I–'

'*Shhh.*'

Heart suddenly strident in her chest, she strained her hearing against the venting force of furnace smoke. She listened until she could convince herself that she could hear almost anything.

Except for the one sound she was desperate to hear.

'He has stopped crying...'

Outstretched toes touched ground.

The rock had been baked by forces far beyond those of mere heat. It was no longer entirely solid, nor exactly liquid. It gave under the pressure of Helka's descending weight like a sponge swollen with sparks. She struggled to free herself from her descent chain. Haste made her hands clumsy. Clumsiness made her angry. With a curse on all smiths and makers she succeeded in unhooking herself from the spool mechanism latched to her belt and then threw it to one side, sprinting to where Morthrun, Tangrorn and Azkharn were already waiting for her.

Smoke veiled their broad, rune-studded backs from view. Compared to Mothirzharr's higher reaches the smoke was insubstantial and without direction, but it remained thick enough to choke on and hot enough to ignite ur-gold without the need for a zharr-grim's command.

Morthrun and Tangrorn were both standing.

Azkharn knelt. Steam rose from his knee where it sank into the ground, the scent of burned meat and soldered metal mingling with the sulphuric fumes.

Given strength in exchange for a terror she would not name, she barged between Morthrun and Tangrorn, casting the latter to his face, before throwing herself to the ground beside Azkharn, drawing up hot sparks with both knees.

A bowl-shaped depression had been dug out of the hot earth, large enough to install a magmic battleforge with all its smiths and priests in attendance. Huge, clawed feet had been employed to drive out the semi-molten spoil, banking it to make high sides that contained and aggravated the heat. The inside was littered with plates of mottled eggshell, thicker than Helka's hand was wide. The pieces varied in size. The smallest were fingernail-sized. The largest were broader than a volkite slingshield.

Eggs. She was looking at a nest.

She looked over its entirety, a feeling in her breast that was altogether too cold to have been called rage, regardless of how it made her body quiver.

'I'm sorry, my lady,' Azkharn mumbled.

Helka glared at him, but he gave no suggestion that he had ever intended to say more.

'A magmadroth,' said Morthrun.

The runemaster pulled off his helmet, silver and red hair spilling from its flute neck and tumbling over his broad shoulders. No Fyreslayer ever looked more forlorn than one geared for battle, but with their head undressed. It was the garb of the walking wounded and those in mourning. He tugged on his beard with a clank of gold braid, cleared his throat with a crackling wheeze.

'Big one too,' said Tangrorn, nudging the banked sides with a bare toe, looking not at Helka but at the miniature landslide of sizzling sand he had caused. 'Going by the hole she's dug.'

'Aye,' said Morthrun.

'Aye,' said Azkharn.

Helka picked up one of the larger eggshell pieces. It was heavy. 'My son...'

She could imagine only too easily what must have happened. The magmadroth would not have ventured far from her nest. They were territorial. As were the Fyreslayers. She would have heard the young runeson's cries just as Helka had from the mouth of Mothirzharr. She would have returned to her nest to find–

Helka killed the thought, turning her face from her companions, grateful, if only for that moment, for the heat that scorched every drop of moisture from her eyes.

Azkharn put a hand on her shoulder. 'Aye,' he said.

'It's a wonder he survived his fall,' said Morthrun. As if that changed anything, or helped anyone.

'What now?' said Azkharn, with tenderness enough to startle her from her grief.

What now?

She wanted her son back. Alive. But she was a Fyreslayer. Their god had destroyed himself in battle, and ever since they had been forced to make do without recourse to miracles.

So what now...?

She turned back to the nest. Closer inspection revealed four or five smaller sets of tracks scattered lightly over the top of the very much larger and deeper set that had excavated the nest. She pointed to them.

Azkharn nodded, as though there had been a right answer to his question and this was it.

'I grieve with you, runemother,' said Tangrorn. 'I grieve *for* you. But it is time for us to return, that Jord-Grimnir might be told of what happened here and grieve also.'

'We swore oaths,' said Azkharn, runes glowing bright with sudden anger. Fully helmeted and wreathed in golden fire, the hearthkarl seemed for a moment to be twice his usual size. 'To see the young runeson returned.'

'The runeson is dead,' said Morthrun.

'Then it is Grudgement that is called for,' said Azkharn.

Morthrun looked at him without comprehension.

'You mean vengeance?' Tangrorn scoffed. 'That is an Ulrung's game.'

'And what of our own failures?' Azkharn tapped on the golden rings that sheathed his beard. 'Do they demand no penance?'

Helka looked down at her hands. Through them. Into herself, where she could feel something long inert touched by the hearth-karl's talk of oaths and vengeance.

'Runemother,' said Morthrun. 'Jord-Grimnir can send an entire fyrd to capture the magmadroth. As he will need to do in any case should we fail to return soon.'

Azkharn dipped his head in acknowledgement.

'You agree with him?' said Helka.

'What is there to disagree with?' the hearthkarl shrugged. 'If Grimnir had ever heeded a priest he'd likely still be here now.'

'He did not though, did he?' said Helka.

Azkharn's moustaches hiked in what might have been amusement. 'No, lass. I don't imagine he ever did.'

A series of loud, crackling booms echoed through the labyrinth of branching tunnels. Fire sprites, pin-sized elementals of bright magic, drawn to the sound like scavengers to soured meat, formed whirlwind constellations of fire. Morthrun sat back against a stalagmite and let rip another resounding cough, sending swirls of confused sprites chasing after the ever-splitting echoes. He cleared his throat of dust and gunge, until the muscles of his chest ached, before raising a hand to show he was able to continue. Tangrorn shook his head and walked on. Helka made a disgusted noise in the back of her throat before following. Only the outsider hearthkarl stopped.

'Are you well, oldflame?'

'Aye,' Morthrun answered with a wheeze, his lungs crackling like the burning of cheap candles.

'Something ails you.'

'You think so, do you?' Morthrun tempered his sharpness with a chuckle that soon brought on another cough. 'Gorlbrost. The gold-lung. The fire of this place aggravates it, I think.' He took a deep breath to allow for another deliberate cough. 'It would seem that it is my fate to perish of old age's accumulated ills rather than to die in battle.'

'The young of today don't appreciate the old as they once did.'

Morthrun frowned in remembrance. 'And when was it that they did?'

Azkharn's response was a faint smile and a faraway look. 'Are you recovered enough to walk?'

'Aye.'

The hearthkarl helped him to stand, but was wise enough to withdraw his aid immediately thereafter. Side by side, they continued on.

The rock at that depth was of an odd material: glassy, and veined with metamorphic crystal that flickered and faded like some mineralised form of fire. In spite of their peril, the runemaster still yearned to take a hammer to it, break a piece open, pestle it into the mortar of the palm of his hand and smell it, taste it, subject it to fire, note the colour of its flame. No Fyreslayer had delved this far into Mothirzharr since the spiritquake. Who could say how far this arcology might extend, what monsters and miracles it might harbour, and which distant cousins might warm their hearths from its same fire.

'Wait...' said Azkharn.

Morthrun winced as he dropped into a crouch. The joints. It was the joints that age took first, and the joints that a duardin missed most, even after everything else started to fail. Azkharn waved at something ahead.

'Aye,' Morthrun muttered, watching from the partial cover of another flickering stalagmite as Helka and Tangrorn walked ahead. The effervescent rocks bathed the runemother in gold, colouring her cuirass and skirt and shoulders of mail. Her hair had been elaborately dressed for the Rite of Naming, but had freed itself in the travails since. Shod in fyresteel, she did not move quietly. He smiled to himself, envying the runemother her brashness. He had earned the name 'Bloodsmith' as a young runesmiter for a similar abandon in battle. The name had outlasted the fire that had given it to him.

Preceded by the echo of the runemother's own footsteps, Helka and Tangrorn passed across the gaping maw of an old lava tube. It was gnarled and craggy. Lumps of stone protruded like teeth from an old orruk's mouth. A deep growl, low and trembling, ran through the rocks. Morthrun tensed. His palm, suddenly moist, went to the grip of the handaxe that swung by a thong from his belt. Tangrorn looked nervously up at the tunnel mouth. Helka ignored it, walking on past the larger branch as if drawn by some instinct towards another that lay further ahead.

'We are not equipped to bring down a magmadroth ancient,' Morthrun muttered to himself, although he did not care who heard. 'We've no pikes or javelins. No nets, bait or lures.'

Azkharn chuckled, still watching the other Fyreslayers. 'Oh, we've bait right enough.'

'Is that why you stay back with the old runemaster?'

'When did you last hunt a magmadroth, oldflame?'

Morthrun sighed. 'Not since I was an undersmiter, tasked by the lord of the lodge klinkin to join a fyrd of youths led by Rune-son Bjard.' He smiled in reminiscence. 'That was Jord-Grimnir's father. We were to retrieve the body of a hale beast, that we might feed its heart to the forge fire and nourish the Master Flame.' He sighed again. 'A long time ago.'

The hearthkarl briefly touched his shoulder. 'Not *so* long ago, oldflame.' He turned to where Helka and Tangrorn continued to move away. 'The lines of Vulcatrix and Grimnir are two peaks of the same range. Sometimes it's hard to know where one ends and the other begins. Both have always been drawn to the hottest blood and the fiercest challenge, to strive against an equal and perish whilst we burn at our brightest. My blood isn't nearly so hot. There are times, like now, I think I might wish it otherwise, but there are too many ties for me in the realms for me to go out as Grimnir did.'

'You speak of responsibilities.'

'Aye.'

Morthrun snorted. 'And what are the responsibilities of a karl without a hearth?'

Azkharn supressed a fuller laugh. 'You've got me there, oldflame. By Grimnir, you've got me there.'

'You may stop calling me *oldflame*.'

'It's a term of respect.'

'I know. Though I suspect you mock me with it, for we both know that you are by far the elder of me.'

Azkharn's expression became sober. He dipped his head. 'I meant no insult.'

'Come on then,' said Morthrun, feeling faintly embarrassed to have mentioned it at all. 'The runemother gets ahead of us.' Hands flat against the stalagmite, he pushed himself upwards. Azkharn followed in wary silence.

The opening to the tunnel yawned over them, never more like a giant mouth than as the two Fyreslayers passed across it. After a short distance, the tunnel plunged down towards depths unfathomable, waves of dry heat blowing out and then fading back like breaths. Beholding it from up close, Morthrun noticed something unusual that he had failed to mark before. While the near side of the mouth was thoroughly gnarled and warted with rocky protrusions and bulges, the other side of the half-circle was smooth, blasted clean by the same magmic processes that had carved the rest of the tube. He puzzled for a moment as to why one half of the opening had been left so uneven before moving on.

Another deep, tectonic growl trembled under his feet.

Close now. Whatever it was.

He paused halfway across the tunnel mouth, an old warrior's senses screaming for him to turn around. He did, jaw dropping open as the contours of the opening's rougher side rippled, optical illusions breaking down before his eyes. Rocky outgrowths became armour plates. Stalactites became claws, protective spines the length of pike blades. The magmadroth that had been warming herself against the curvature of the lava tube dropped the chameleonic pigmentation of her scales, sliding from gold to bronze to black as she moved.

'Grimnir...' he breathed.

All magmadroth had the ability to alter their colouration, and could be trained to do it by a Fyreslayer of adequate patience, but he had never seen a wild magmadroth mask themselves so completely. He was awed. There was no place in his heart for terror.

Eyes the size of clenched fists and the colour of lava-crust blinked, shattering the last traces of disguise as two heavy forelegs crashed into the ground before him. A sledgehammer head, armoured and scaled, ridged and rimmed with spines, peered down at the two duardin. A tongue of living fire pressed against the backs of long, black teeth, spraying the two Fyreslayers with sparks.

Azkharn drew his axe.

If that blade was to be the last thing Morthrun ever witnessed then he would go to Grimnir gladly.

'Khazuk!' he bellowed gladly, as the world turned to fire.

Helka spun around just as the molten stream went over Morthrun with a sound like a thousand gallons of liquid rock forcing a crack in the earth. There was a flash of gold, runic protections flashing and failing at the same time. A splash sent Azkharn flailing, covering his beard and his eyes, the force of the eruption punching the runemaster back through a stalagmite and into a wall that turned instantly to broken glass. The magmadroth had more to come, the soft, unprotected skin of its throat ribbing as it brought up lumps of molten rock from its belly. Helka whirled as Azkharn hefted his axe and barrelled towards the titanic beast.

'Khazuk!' he roared, his helmet and beard chain bloodshot with reflected fire, his beard turning briefly orange as he brought his axe down.

Even a fyresteel grandaxe would have bounced off the rock-hard skin of an elder magmadroth, unless driven with the runehanced strength of a grimwrath berzerker, but Azkharn's runeaxe cleft her bottom lip neatly and deep. Sparks flew in place of blood, and the hearthkarl shook his head as sizzling motes rained across his crest. A Fyreslayer's hair would smoulder, but it would never burn. He ducked a swiping foot, back-pedalled beyond the reach of a lunging bite, countered with an uppercut, but the magmadroth

34

had already pulled back. It growled, wary beyond its immense size, eyeing the hearthkarl the way an emberfox would eye a spring-trap baited with fresh coal.

With a wild yell, Helka sprinted back towards them. Her heart pounded with the thrill of battle and the hot closeness of death. Tangrorn followed on stout legs, slowed by the bead-book rolls that fell from his belt and the heft of the icon in his hand.

'See first to Morthrun,' she shouted.

'But–'

'He's a warrior of the Skarravorn. He's earned the right to have his last words recorded by a battlesmith.'

'Aye,' he said reluctantly, peeling off to allow Helka to proceed alone.

She bared her teeth and willed herself to go faster, ruing the fact that as a runemother her body carried little ur-gold to lend her speed or her muscles strength. And yet she was unafraid. She charged the beast just as Azkharn recovered his poise. Its attention was fixed entirely on the hearthkarl. And that, Helka would not allow. It offended the blood of the godly many-times-great grandsire that burned through her veins.

'Runk-ha!'

The magmadroth twisted its neck towards her, distracted, as Azkharn buried his runeaxe in its shoulder. The monster belched fire in pain. Hurdling the last yards of broken rock and blistered glass, Helka leapt onto the magmadroth's side, hand burning where she found a hold between two spines, axe coming down hard. The blade skidded off marble-like scales. Pain rang through Helka's arm. Holding firm to her grips she wound back and struck again, this time aiming for the overlap between the rows of scales. The blade wedged in to the join but caused no obvious damage. She cursed, feeling rock-hard muscles bunching beneath her as the monster reared onto hind legs. Ignoring the meat-smoke spilling from her left-hand grip Helka held grimly on to the magmadroth's spines.

The beast took another lumbering swipe at Azkharn, who skipped out of the way, but it was a ruse only, and it turned its neck adder-swift to snap for the irritant clinging onto its back. No time to do anything but react, Helka let go. She rolled down the monster's flank, hot air displaced from the magmadroth's champing jaws propelling her on her way to the ground. She landed in an awkward tangle on top of her axe. Joints ground with chalky *pops* as the magmadroth turned towards her.

'Over here!' Azkharn bellowed. 'Fight a duardin nearer your own age.'

The hearthkarl ran at the beast at an angle intended to catch the magmadroth's eye and draw it from the runemother. And it did, but with an old beast's wiliness it flicked out a disguised foot to sweep out the Fyreslayer's legs. Azkharn's face slammed into the rocks and he slid across the monster's underbelly. The magmadroth set its foot onto his back and, with the immense satisfaction of one unwittingly reprising ancient battles, applied her colossal body weight to the leg.

Metal crunched.

Helka rolled onto her back just as the magmadroth swung her head back towards her, spines scraping dust and sparks from the rock walls. The monster's head hovered over her like an anvil. Azkharn's exhortation returned to her then; about right, about honour, about standing by what was grudged regardless of how little it was worth.

'For my son!' she yelled, and hacked her axe into the side of the magmadroth's head.

She had been aiming for the beast's eye, but her target was obscured behind smoke from its nostrils and protected by ridged flesh and armour. She missed. Her blade bounced off.

The magmadroth breathed its mockery into Helka's face. With a scream of defiance she dropped her axe to take hold instead of the knobs of bone that protruded from the thing's jaws, duardin strength enough to guide them away from her face, but nothing more. The snout struck Helka's breastplate like a hammer into a nail. Metal groaned. Bones creaked. Hot air blasted across her, everything that was not metal or of Grimnir's blood curling off her in smoke. Her mouth formed a wide 'O' in lieu of the scream she no longer held the breath for. Magmic saliva dribbled into the etchings of her plate, pooling in the runic motifs of her lodge.

She felt herself dying.

'Gorzharr!' came Azkharn's voice, from beyond the grave most certainly, for even the most strident of doomseekers would have surely perished against what he had suffered. It rose into a battle-chant, and then into a song. 'Afurk a Grimnir, uzkul!' Morthrun's smoke-thin wheeze rose to join it, and Helka's heart rejoiced to hear the war-song of the doomgron from the valorous dead who arose to lead her to Grimnir's fyrd. Only then the runemaster's voice fell silent, and Tangrorn's rose in timbre to take its place. 'Afson a Grimnir, uzkul!'

Realising that she yet lived, Helka gritted her teeth and stared the magmadroth in the eye. 'Not today. Today the children of Grimnir live.'

The magmadroth bellowed as Azkharn hewed into its hind-quarters with a sound like a miner breaking stone. The beast spun to face him, and Helka rolled to avoid being crushed between the rock and its tail. The beast's throat hitched, scales ribbing, a retching sound rumbling from deep within her gorge as she dropped her jaws and vomited forth a stream of molten-red rock over Azkharn and Tangrorn.

The eruption shook the foundations of the cavern, bringing

cascades of cinders from the ceiling and turning great swathes of the ground into a molten lake. The battlesmith reeled back from it, but Azkharn somehow found a way to skip through, not merely holding his ground but advancing, and for a moment Helka thought that she could see many duardin in place of one. Different lengths of hair. Different cuts of beard. Some wore armour of various styles. Some were draped in a warm red cloak with a golden, runic trim. But all had the same good-humoured face, the same timeless eyes. As soon as she attempted to focus on one of these different duardin he became fixed again, a Fyreslayer in his powerful entirety as his axe descended, roaring with rune-struck might as the blade gouged deep into the magmadroth's flank.

The beast arched its back and bellowed. Lava flowed in rivers from the wound, pooling under Azkharn's bare feet. He heeded it not. His axe came down again, met by another shriek, weaker and more plaintive than the one before; like that of a warrior whose prior courage has taken flight and who now cries impotently for their mother. Helka wondered if such thoughts had entered her own child's mind as he had called for her. Her hands balled into fists, only then to loosen as Azkharn's axe arced to smite the beast a third and final time. The hearthkarl planted a foot onto the magmadroth's stricken hide, wheezing like a forge bellows.

It was over.

But beyond that, the monster's final moments had stirred something in her that she would not have expected she possessed. Pity. One grieving mother to another. But then the children of Grimnir and Vulcatrix shared a bond of gold *and* fire.

She could almost still hear the creature's cries.

'Runemother.'

Coughing as harshly as Morthrun had through his final years, Tangrorn staggered from the smoke and the fire. His beard and hair were asmoulder. His icon glowered like a star impaled on a magmapike. He was looking at something other than Azkharn or her.

Helka turned towards it. The smaller tunnel that instinct had drawn her to, before the magmadroth's ambush.

She *could* hear cries.

Before she knew what she was doing she was running, axe on the ground somewhere behind her, mail skirts drawn up in both hands. The tunnel swallowed her. Inside, it was darker, the fire in the stones hot but steady. A chorus of belligerent chirps assailed her as her eyes adapted. Five hatchling magmadroths made uncertain moves towards her, snapping jaws filled with pale, still-soft teeth, flicking tails, all the while mewling for their absent mother.

And with them…

Heedless of the infant reptiles, Helka snatched up the child and crushed him to her chest. Tiny hands knotted themselves in her hair. A broad, chubby face rubbed itself against her breastplate. The child continued to cry, and Helka unconsciously began to rock him in her arms, singing Azkharn's battle-song under her breath. '*Drengizharr a galaz, Azka duardrazhal…*' Dry tears stung her eyes.

'New-hatched,' said Tangrorn, behind her. 'The magmadroth we slew must have mistaken the runeson for one of her own.'

'Maybe,' said Azkharn. He walked to the tunnel's mouth bearing Morthrun's body. 'Or maybe the daughters of Vulcatrix seek to dominate the sons of Grimnir, just as you would conquer them in turn. Grudgement begets Grudgement. As it ever was, so must it always be.' The hearthkarl nodded towards the clutch of hatchlings. 'A fine stable to gift a young runeson, eh, lass?' He looked up, something combustible, almost ephemeral about him in the aftermath of battle. 'Promise me you teach him something other than war, though. The Fyreslayers deserve more than their god's worst hour.'

'I swear it,' Helka murmured, her attention fully on her son's face, slack now in exhausted slumber against his mother's breast-plate. 'I would have abandoned him to a magmadroth if not for your insistence. If this is all you ask in payment then it is yours.'

She looked up. The hearthkarl fizzed around the edges of her tired eyes.

'Why did you come here this day? Why did you aid us?'

Azkharn shrugged. 'Why do the matrons of the Skarravorn wear armour?'

'The warriors might say it is to protect us.'

'I'd wager they do. What do you say?'

She thought about it. 'I'd say that someone has to.'

With a knowing look, the hearthkarl turned as though to leave.

'Wait,' said Tangrorn. 'Where are you taking Morthrun's body?'

Azkharn smiled, his eyes glimmering with familiar mirth. 'To his maker.' With that he did turn, and he did leave, the smoke and embers folding in to envelop and scatter him to the eight winds as though neither he, his axe, nor Morthrun Bloodsmith had ever been real at all.

For a long time, neither Helka nor Tangrorn felt that there was anything more to be said.

'Where did he go?' the battlesmith asked, at last.

Helka did not answer. All she could do was take the hearth-karl at his word. He had taken Runemaster Morthrun back to their maker.

'Have you a name for him?' said Tangrorn as the silence stretched.

'I do.'

Helka looked down at her sleeping child.

'A hero's name.'

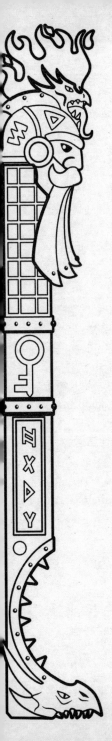

OLD
WHITEBEARD'S
SPECIAL

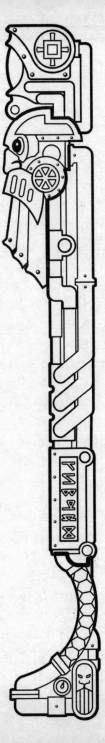

'The Bearded Dragon had been in the keeping of the Edrundour duardin for three hundred years. The eldest longbeard who drank there would remark with approval that naught about it ever changed but that year's signature brew and the sawdust on the floor. Those with longer memories still would recall too that it was Brognor Edrundour who, having led the return of his folk from Azyr, had built an exact replica of the one kept by his distant forebears on the same site. Those grey hills, irrevocably tainted by the occupation of Chaos, were a hard place to make any kind of living. But they were duardin lands, and it is often rightly said of the Dispossessed that they would sooner be poor in the homes of their ancestors than be rich elsewhere.

'But the Edrundour were not poor. Indeed, with the occasional guidance of one white-bearded patron of extraordinarily lengthy memory, they prospered...'

Brida Edrundour padded down the stairs barefoot. It was late, well past time for beardlings to be abed, but the nightmare that had wakened her wouldn't let her fall back to sleep. In it, she had seen the moon transformed into a leering skull, growing larger in the sky and darkening the hills around it as it leaned towards her room. Now, the bars of moonlight that fell around the curtains into the living quarters became a source of horror, and the windowless dark of the stairwell strangely welcoming. At the bottom, she crossed the small landing and pushed against the taproom door. Light streamed through the joins. The wood trembled with the noise. She pushed it wide.

As usual, it was standing room only in the Bearded Dragon. Duardin from all over the Copperback Hills packed round its tables. Human travellers from further afield drank and laughed under the beams. Two roaring hearths banished thoughts of *outside* to the corner snugs. A half gross of musical instruments and several competing strains of song filled the air. The dream made it all seem surreal. Clutching the small ironoak hammer that her mother had carved for her as a Grungni's Day gift, she ventured from the safety of the dark.

The rain spattered against the leaded glass where a troupe of travelling aelves sat. The Wanderers were garbed in drab greys and cold browns, and spoke amongst each other in voices as weary as old wood and as musical as rain on the brewery roof. The aelves, too, were a familiar sight, if not regular patrons. The Bearded Dragon had once, long ago, sat on the trade road between Barak Zilfin and Barak Urbaz, but as the land had altered, so too had its great cities and the nature of the routes that linked them. Such was the character of the realm and its peculiar magicks. Nevertheless, the more experienced traveller allocated their journey the extra days required to make a stop at the Bearded Dragon. Bjarn, her father, had never hidden his dislike for aelvenkind – or humanity, for that matter. This was partly on principle, for they could not match a duardin's appetite for food or ale and, in his words, *they brought down the mood*. By way of redress he billed them treble for stabling. If they ever knew, they clearly felt the warmth and fine food of the Bearded Dragon a price worth paying.

But even the sharp eyes of the aelves slipped over her as she shuffled by their table.

'Crowded tonight,' grumbled Druri, the wagoner, standing with arms crossed, heavy coat stinking of pipe smoke and horse.

'Not like in my day,' said Gudruntarn.

'Wouldn't have seen a longbeard standing while an aelf sits in Brognor's time,' added Dain, a duardin of no particular employ who made a living out of performing odd jobs for younger and less able duardin.

'Shouldn't you be on the road by now anyway?' said Gudruntarn to Druri. 'Bjarn's ale won't deliver itself.'

Druri chuckled. 'It'll deliver me, one way or another.'

Leaving the longbeards to their grouching, Brida picked her way through the throng towards the bar. Her face brightened as she saw her father. Bjarn was as broad as the barn door, but his build was workmanlike rather than that of a warrior, built through lugging barrels instead of swinging the ancestral greataxe, Reliable, which was mounted above the bar. His shoulders were huge, his hands big and scarred, and his belly round to match. His beard had the scruff of a recently widowed father. The face it covered was mottled red, from the warmth of the hearth and too much drink, but also from his permanent state of near breathlessness. Brida's first instinct was to run straight towards him, but something held her back. He was polishing a metal tankard and chatting distractedly with Thodrun, the local constable. The true object of both duardin's attentions however, and indeed that of most of the brewery's clientele, was sat alone, a few empty stools from them down the bar.

The old duardin's hair was as white as the snow on a mountain top and he wore it long. So long in fact that it flowed into his white beard, which itself lapped over his knees and fell well past the soles of his boots on the stretcher of his stool. His cloak was travel-worn. His trousers were muddy. Silver mail and the occasional jewel twinkled below the outer layers. Brida, with the insight of one as yet clear of the grudges and oaths of later life, had the strongest impression that if she could look even deeper she would find something worth more than silver and gems. She wondered if he might be a descendent of the kings of the Khazalid Empire. The fortunes of the duardin were such that it was not uncommon to see kings and thegns drinking in the Bearded Dragon alongside goatherds. And even aelves.

He was nursing a tankard of the Bearded Special.

The annual tradition of *The Special* was one that the Edrundour line had always observed. Even in their long exile in the star-halls of Azyrheim they had continued to craft their commemorative ales, although the Specials of those years were known for being sorrowful and bitter.

Whitebeard raised the tankard to his lips. To Brida's astonishment, she saw that he was drinking from the metal tankard that Bjarn normally kept in pride of place on the mantle by Reliable. The quart tankard was pewter, with a hinged lid and a golden rune in old Khazalid that no one in the Edrundour line could still read, but which looked to Brida like two mountain peaks stacked on their sides. Whitebeard dampened his moustache as he took a considered sip. He smacked his lips thoughtfully. The circle of duardin and men around him grew hushed. Bjarn stood at the far end of the bar with his elbow in the air as though frozen mid-polish. Whitebeard nodded to himself and muttered as he lowered the tankard to the counter. The watching longbeards leaned in.

Oblivious, Whitebeard lifted the tankard and took another sip.

Half the taproom sighed, and Brida giggled despite herself.

Whitebeard turned on his stool, hearing what even the aelves had failed to, and gave her a crooked smile. His eyes sparkled like jewels in ancient treasures, and Brida felt her earlier unease lift from her at once.

'You're up early, lass,' he said, gesturing one-handed towards her woollen nightdress and bare feet. 'Or up late.' He winked and beckoned her towards him. 'Come, girl, and help me, for I'm as yet undecided on this year's Bearded Special.'

Brida glanced to her father. She was expecting a stern look and the promise of strong words to follow after closing, but he looked stunned that this stranger had spoken to her and waved her towards the empty stool beside him. Whitebeard bent down, displaying surprising flexibility for one so long of beard, and hoiked her onto the seat beside him. Brida became very aware of the hubbub dying around her. She swallowed and turned to Whitebeard as the old traveller leant in towards her. His beard smelled of her father's beer and the Copperback Road. His face, for all its twinkling good humour, looked worn.

'Are they still watching, lass?'

Brida looked over her shoulder. 'Yes.'

Whitebeard chuckled, and then pushed his tankard across the counter towards her. 'Go on. Take a sip. Tell me what you think.'

Brida did as she was asked. Despite not yet being ten she was a brewer's daughter and a duardin to boot, and knew her way around an ale.

Whitebeard nodded approvingly as she took a taste, leaning back from the counter to fish in his travel bags for tobacco and pipe. 'Go on then, lass. Speak up.'

'It's nice.'

Whitebeard laughed until his mail rustled against his chest. 'I suppose you'd have to say that. What with your father hovering over my shoulder like the ghost of Grimnir.' He tamped a pinch of dried leaves into the bowl of his pipe and lit it. Shaking off his fingers, he took a sup on the stem, still chuckling to himself. 'Aye, I know who you are, and I know whose blood runs in your veins. So, tell me what you really think.'

Brida took another sip. She concentrated hard.

'It could be sweeter.'

'Spoken like every beardling who was ever asked about anything. Have another go.'

Brida supped again. 'This has been a good year. The beer is too bitter for it. It should be… brighter.'

'And when the Bearded Dragon prospers so too does the Copperback, eh?'

'That's what my father says.'

'And you always heed your father?'

Brida looked shocked. 'Of course.'

'Good.' Whitebeard chewed thoughtfully on his pipe. 'A duardin should always heed their elders. Master their ways and learn from their mistakes.' He puffed a moment longer. 'If it were me… The Dregsons who work the valley over yonder hill have cultivated a fine crop of klinkinberries this year. Storing this beer in old klinkinberry barrels will stand it in fine stead, and spread your good year a little wider to those as have need of a little fortune.'

Ignored by Whitebeard himself, the taproom set itself to muttering, Bjarn hauling Druri the wagoner over from his grumbling to arrange for the purchase of all the klinkinberry barrels that the Dregsons would be able to sell. Whitebeard took his beer back and proffered his pipe. Brida screwed her face up at the smell.

The duardin laughed. 'Quite right, lass.' He puffed amiably. 'Quite right.' Sinking the rest of the tankard in one gulp, he replaced the pipe in his mouth and drew up his hood. Then he stood, bending to pick up the large rune-axe that stood propped against the bar.

'You're leaving already?' said Brida.

'Aye. I must.'

'Why?'

Whitebeard gave her a tired grin. 'Been a while since anyone's asked me that.'

'You look tired.'

Whitebeard sighed as he adjusted his cloak over his armour, then he winked at her, and the sadness she had thought she'd seen disappeared into the lines of his smile. 'Maybe I'll pass this way again some time. Mine is thirsty work.'

Indeed, Brida saw the old Whitebeard many times thereafter.

She never knew how he managed to always appear at the same time each year, just as the nights were drawing in and Bjarn brought out the first samples of Bearded Special for tasting. The old calendar of her ancestors was the one piece of ancient craft that Brognor Edrundour had reluctantly set aside (though he had put it in a chest rather than throw it away). In the Spiral Crux, even time was changeable. And yet, somehow, in the handful of days between the tester cups going out and the barrels being passed on to the traders, Brida would wander into the taproom and see him sitting in the same stool, supping the Special from the old tankard.

'What is the story behind that cup?' she asked her father during one visit. She was nineteen. Old enough, so he said, to wait tables as well as sweep floors and muck out stables. If it had anything to do with the worsening wheeze of his lungs then neither of them said so, and no duardin patron ever made mention of his cough, however severe it got. 'It looks rather plain apart from the old rune.'

'It's a Klinkerhun letter,' said Bjarn. 'From the old empire. Brognor knew that much, but even he wasn't old enough to remember the ancestors' language.'

'How did he get it?'

Bjarn nodded towards Whitebeard where he sat, sampling that year's Special as he had every year since Brida had been nine, and long before. 'The first year after Brognor reopened the Bearded Dragon *he* came in through that door, sat in that very stool, gave it to your grandfather and asked for a taste of the Special. He gave Brognor some suggestions, which my father was not too proud to heed, and when he was finished the old Whitebeard asked him to keep the tankard for his next visit. Said he'd be doing him a favour, taking it off his hands, and that it'd bring the brewery luck. And it did. After a hundred years or so, Brognor started displaying it up there on the mantle next to Reliable.'

'What was he like back then?'

Bjarn coughed into his hand and thought a moment. 'I can only tell you what he was like when I was young.'

'Which was?'

He nodded again towards the old duardin. 'Like that.'

'You mean he's not aged in three hundred years?'

Bjarn shrugged. 'Maybe it's because he drinks Bearded Special.' He coughed some more, wiping the blood on a rag before Brida could see.

But she was too old now not to notice.

The years went on, and even in the absence of a working calendar Whitebeard marked them with his regular but infrequent visits. The duardin of the Copperback Hills observed it as religiously as their ancestors had Grungni's Day. Every winter's night they took to gathering in the warmth of the Bearded Dragon to wait for his arrival and then to watch the ritual sup and eventual, almost casual mutter of 'might have been a tad stronger' or 'bit hoppy this year, wouldn't you agree?' For a few weeks each year it brought the disparate communities of the Copperback and its neighbours under one roof, and for a long while they all prospered. The fortunes of the Bearded Dragon grew beyond those enjoyed in Brognor's day, as did its fame, built on the popularity and constant renewal of its Bearded Special. And if the nights seemed darker and the winters colder, then it was so gradual as to only have become apparent to Brida in hindsight. And if the taproom never again seemed quite as full as it had been, then it was with the eyes of a matron looking back at the golden years of a girl.

'Has the trade road moved further to the north?' Bjarn asked one year of a human caravan master, having not seen another of his race from beyond the hills in months.

'What trade?' the man snorted. 'It's become too expensive to move goods by road. Too dangerous. The number of mercenaries we need to hire, would you believe it's cheaper to commission a Kharadron skyship these days?'

Even the aelves (beholden to ancient ways, to Bjarn's grudging respect, they continued to frequent the Bearded Dragon as they ever had) spoke of dead things abroad and the stirrings of evil. Their talk, from what little Brida could pick up of the Wanderers' lilting tongue, was of omens and portents and of reckonings brought forward from their proper time.

'You should leave this place,' their chieftain said to Brida one time, using the common language of Azyr, sipping at a narrow glass of the old klinkinberry vintage as she did so. 'A dark power stirs. His curse weighs heavily upon the roots of the elder hills.'

Brida simply shook her head.

It seemed to please the aelf, who smiled into her glass. Her resignation reminded Brida of any longbeard, except that no longbeard ever smiled.

'Then I congratulate you, Lady Edrundour. If only my people had had the foresight to stay and die.'

Druri burst through the stout wooden door, waving his torn hand above his head for all the room to see, not that there were too many there to care. Brida had, by then, graduated from waiting tables to serving at the bar. Bjarn spent most of his time in the big chair that a couple of the younger duardin had helped carry down for him from the living quarters upstairs. The handful of grim-faced stalwarts grumbled about ghosts and aelven curses as Druri stomped up and planted his axe across the bar, as one might present their landlord with a rat. Brida filled a mug of Bearded Special from one of the early-tapped kegs and poured it over Druri's injured hand. Crystals of what looked like amethyst buried in the cuts hissed as the beer ran over them.

'Chainrasps,' Druri muttered. 'And not five miles from this door.'

Brida didn't answer. Silently, she marvelled at Whitebeard's foresight.

The previous year he had suggested sprinkling in a few Capilarian flameseeds, commenting that the year to come was 'looking nippy'. Flameseeds were a well-known spice, even in Ayadah. They were much lesser known as a medicament against supernatural chills.

'What's the realm coming to?' Druri complained.

Later that year, the Bearded Dragon saw its first alterations since the original had been burned to the ground untold centuries before. Bjarn sat in his chair and directed as strapping duardin lads fitted sturdy shutters to the ground floor windows and braced the old oak door with brass. He even offered old Dain (the failure of so many farms of late leaving him begging for work, had he not been so proud) a permanent job as a doorman. The longbeard brought his own family axe, and Bjarn further furnished him with a pot helm, a leather cuirass and his own father's shield.

'Could you spare nothing for the protection of the road?' asked Thodrun.

'The roads are your affair,' Bjarn answered gruffly.

Thodrun had wanted to argue, but Bjarn fell to coughing and cut the argument short.

'Shouldn't we help him, father?' Brida asked later. 'We need the roads as much as anyone. More, since we're the last ones here doing any real business.'

'Look first to your own.' Bjarn took her hand in both of his as though he were imparting her something of import. 'Build your walls high and sink your foundations deep. That is the way the duardin have always done things. That is the way we will endure.'

* * *

The next time that travellers darkened Bjarn's doorstep on the way to Barak Zilfin he sent them away with gold for a blunderbuss from the Kharadron skyfort. They returned with it about six months later. In years past they might have returned with change. Bjarn was just glad to have received it at all, and had wealth enough yet to be careless if he chose, much to the grumbling of Thodrun and Druri and those few still present whose fortunes had not weathered the downturn as comfortably as the Bearded Dragon. He took to falling asleep in his big chair with the gun across his lap. It brought him comfort, and so Brida said nothing of it.

'I'm... too old... for... Reliable... now,' he wheezed. He beckoned for water, preferring it of late even to ale, and gestured to the axe above the bar. She saw the shame in his eyes. The frustration of a duardin being failed by his body. 'It's... yours... now.'

No one said a word as Brida lifted him from his chair, so thin had he become, and carried him upstairs to his bed.

Druri pulled his cap from his head and muttered into his beer.

That year, Whitebeard visited early.

The taproom was as full as it had been in many years. Every duardin still in the Copperback Hills was there, but though both fires had been lit for the first time in decades, the mood was grim.

'How did you know to come?' she asked.

Her eyes were raw from the conscious effort of *not* weeping. Her hair was braided in the way her father had done it when she was a girl, as her mother had worn hers. Whitebeard sat across from her, drinking alone as he almost always did, except for the odd occasion when a human or aelf who did not know him would join him at the bar, invariably departing with a tall tale and words of wisdom they would not soon forget. That had not happened in years. Too early in the year for the Special, instead a quart of the perennial favourite, Dragon's Hoard, filled his usual tankard.

Despite sipping at it for well over an hour, it seemed no closer to emptying.

'I always know where I'm needed,' he said, his voice assuming a sympathetic gruffness. He looked down into his tankard. 'I warned your grandfather not to build here. All of them that returned with him from Azyr. There's Chaos in the rocks here still, and in the water, but they wouldn't hear me.'

'This is where our ancestors built,' said Brida. 'It's where we'll build.'

Whitebeard snorted, without humour. He looked tired as always, but now there were bags under his eyes so deep they seemed to draw down the longbeard's face. 'That's what they said.' With one hand – the other still wrapped around his tankard – Whitebeard fished a small bottle from his cloak pocket and set it on the bar.

'What's this?' Brida picked it up. The glass was too dark for her to make out what was inside, beyond that it was liquid.

'A good beer's all about the water. Brognor knew that, and so did his ancestors when they first brewed beer here.' He shrugged. 'I thought that if he made good enough beer, nobody would drink the water. And there's a kind of power in good beer. Duardin will fight over it, aye, but they'll be best friends afterwards.'

'You won't make much beer with this water.'

'I should hope not,' Whitebeard chuckled. 'This is water from Lake Lethis, from the underworld of Stygxx in the Realm of Death. Drink even this much and you'll wake up sometime next century wondering where you are and what your name is. But add a few drops to the barrel...' He shrugged, sipped his cup of Hoard as though the suggestion was hers to take or leave. 'It'll bring who-ever drinks from it a sense of peace.' He looked upwards. 'And when they do, through the waters of Lethis, they might feel the dead of the Ancestors' Hall stirring to join the round by their side.'

Brida's hand closed around the little bottle. Duardin were not known for carelessness, but she was absurdly terrified she might drop it. 'I've never heard of this *Lethis*. From Shyish? It must have taken you months to get it here. If not years. It must have cost you a fortune.'

He sighed, 'It always comes down to cost with the Edrundour, doesn't it?'

Brida's grip on the bottle tightened in anger. 'How long have you known my father was going to die?'

Whitebeard regarded her from beneath bushy white brows, and despite her hundred years Brida suddenly felt very young and foolish for having raised her voice in anger. What he said however, when he decided to, unnerved her even more.

'You think he was the only one?'

Brida poured a tankard of Black Beard from the tapped keg above the bar, circling the mug around the flow to create a swirl in the head. She passed it over the countertop. Faregun, the farmhand from over the Greyfold, grunted as he took it, leaving a smattering of faintly greened coinage on the bar, and retreated, drink in hand, to a corner snug. Half the tables were empty. Of those that were not, few seated more than a single duardin, or two at best, brooding in one another's company. The brewery's timbers spoke louder than its occupants, creaking under the onslaught of wind and rain. Humans, in times of trial and privation, would flock to their temples and fill the air with prayer. The Dispossessed turned instead to their brewery, and instead of song and prayer they bent their bar steward's ear with grumbles about the price of barley and the state of the weather.

Mentally, Brida totted up the coins that Faregun had left to her and, to her mild surprise, found that they came more-or-less right. She scraped them into the front pocket of her apron.

She would not say anything of the sort, but she missed her father. And she longed for Whitebeard's return. After Bjarn's burial, the old longbeard had started to appear every other year. Then every third. Always looking older and more haggard than he had the time before. It had been five years now. Privately, she had resigned herself to the fact that he was not coming back. Travel was hard these days. The Wanderers had not been seen in nigh on a decade either. And Whitebeard was very old.

'Another sign of the times,' she had said once, realising that she had become old when the taproom, her temple, responded with consenting nods and many an approving 'Aye.'

She swept up a rag to polish Faregun's ale ring from the counter when a moan, like a trapped breeze from outside, sounded through the beer cellar.

The trapdoor rattled under her feet.

'There's that sound again,' said Thodrun, as though laying out a long-held and oft-quarrelled position on the hardness of stone. The old constable was semi-retired these days. Hardly anyone ventured abroad at night any more unless sorely pressed, but he still went nowhere without the brace of heavy pistols that now sat on his table and the notched battle-axe across his back. He was sitting facing the door, so as to eye up or give welcome, depending on their aelvishness or demeanour, to those coming through. His companion, Vagnar, a barley grower from across the valley, sat across from him, saying nothing and looking sour.

'Don't tell me you can't hear it,' he said.

'Sounds like rats,' said Vagnar.

'There are no rats in Brognor's cellar,' said Brida. 'And shame on you, Vagnar Ungulsson, for suggesting it.'

The duardin looked duly abashed. He tugged on his beard and mumbled an apology.

Brida stamped on the trapdoor. 'He dug out that cellar himself.

Walled it in stone this thick.' She spread her hands wide. 'Had it quarried to order from the Sidereal Mountains in Azyr by master miners of the Starhammerer's Guild. Every stone he had etched with runes to keep the beer fresh and my ancestors quiet in their tombs.'

'Forgive the words of an old fool,' said Thodrun. 'He means nothing by them. Except, perhaps, to say that he needs more beer.'

'Well, since he no longer speaks for himself, would you mind telling him that a *please* or even a *thank you* now and then is more likely to earn him a refill.'

The odd creaking sounded again from the cellar.

'Maybe it's the pipes,' said Vagnar.

'It's not my pipes,' Brida snapped, and Vagnar dutifully raised his hand in surrender.

The front door opened and all present started.

Brida went for Bjarn's old blunderbuss where it lived under the counter.

'*Whoah!*' Druri held up his hands, shivering rain off his cloak and stamping anxiously on the floor.

Brida lowered her gun to the bar. 'Easy now, Dain,' she said. 'Back off.'

The burly, but now veritably ancient longbeard was sitting on his stool by the door, a cloak wrapped tightly around Bjarn's rune-scored leather cuirass, in no obvious peril of standing up any time soon. 'Close the door behind you, wagoner,' he said. 'You're letting the rain in.'

Druri kicked the door to without so much as turning his head and hastened towards the bar.

Brida poured out a tall flagon of last year's Bearded Special as Druri took a seat by the bar. He took up the tankard and downed a long, deep swallow.

'Cold out,' he muttered, after setting his tankard back down.

'Did you bring in the hops and barley we need?'

Druri shook his head. 'Had to go the long way around. More than once I heard what sounded like hooves on the road behind me, only when I turned there was nothing following but mist. Could still hear them, though.' He shuddered. 'Those farmers as will still come to their doors when a longbeard knocks speak of strange lights over the hills, and of black coaches on the old trade-way. Hexwraiths and dreadblade harrow share the roads with the living now, they say, and claim a toll on any who dare to move about the hills by night. Versaldus is besieged by a legion of the numberless dead and soon to fall, or so I hear from those who flee it, and those on our roads are mere outriders for the hosts of Shyish. Is it a wonder we've seen nary a hair of an aelf or a human traveller in all these years?'

'Good riddance, I say,' said Thodrun. 'To each of us our own.'

'And what of Whitebeard?' said Druri.

'He's from faraway hills,' Thodrun mumbled, but he was grumbling for grumbling's sake and his heart was no longer in it.

The taproom fell to sombre reflection.

'Aye,' said Druri. 'I thought so. The old longbeard has with-drawn his blessings from this place. Whatever fortune he set over these four walls in Brognor's day has surely passed.' He swirled his tankard of Special. 'This is good, but it's far from your finest. When was the last time a trader from Barak Zilfin or Merchants' Mouth or even from free cities beyond the realm came for a taste of Bearded Special? When?'

Brida glared. 'I'll take it off you and pour it down the basin if you find the taste so off.'

Druri drew it protectively towards him. 'I said it was good, didn't I?'

'Whitebeard will be back. See? He has left his cup.'

Druri muttered, but said nothing. A duardin could set great store by the smallest of things.

'Will you need Kimli stabling for the night?' Brida asked.

'Aye,' said Druri, looking down as though addressing someone at the bottom of his tankard. 'I parked the wagon round back, and took the liberty of bolting the stable gate behind me too. I'll not be heading out again this night. There are times when I think about just upping and leaving in the night, like Gudruntarn. Taking Kimli, loading up my wagon with all I have left and leaving these accursed hills. But where would I go? I've a cousin still in Azyrheim. But if Versaldus really has fallen then what hope is there that the Gates of Azyr still stand.' He shook his head, falling back to every longbeard's familiar grumble. 'These are dark days, worse even than those endured by our far ancestors with the first rising of Chaos.'

The faint wind rattled again from the cellar.

Vagnar muttered grumpily into his tankard. 'Sounds like rats.'

'For the last and final time.' Brida undid her apron strings. 'There are no rats in Brognor Edrundour's cellar.' She hoisted the apron over her head and slapped it on the counter beside Druri. He was so tightly wound that he jumped. 'Mind the bar for me.'

'Dain's the one you're paying.'

'Don't remind me.'

Squatting down beside the trapdoor she took the brass ring handle in one hand, twisted, and pulled.

Cool air gusted out. It was cool and dry, tasting of stone and smelling of starlight. Nothing kept beer cool and dark magic at bay like Azyrite stone. But Vagnar was right. It did feel unnaturally cold down there. Rolling her sleeves down over her goosebumped arms, she walked down the steps.

No dank human cellar this, the steps were of finely carved stone. Glimstones set into the corner seams between the ceiling blocks gave off a low, blueish light that would not disturb the beers. They rested in tun barrels in great racks thrice her height.

The tinted light turned those barrels grey. Hot breaths rose from Brida's mouth as she waited at the bottom step. *Listening.* She could hear the murmur of conversation from the taproom. The patter of rain and the drone of wind outside. Nothing to suggest either was getting into the cellar somehow. She was about to turn and head back up when she heard what sounded like a scratching. As though someone further in was sanding stone. A faint moan followed it, a shiver and a dull creak running through the pipes overhead. She swore under her breath.

Vagnar was right after all. It *was* the pipes.

She padded further in, absurdly reminded of the night that she had crept downstairs, barefoot and in her nightdress, to see Whitebeard for the first time. She shook her head. She had not thought herself a child in a hundred years. Halfway along the run of pipes, directly underneath Brida's living rooms two storeys up, the ranks of barrels parted respectfully around the arch of a doorway. Its stone lintel was engraved with runes of permanence. The Edrundours' ancestral tomb. With a wary look down the length of the beer cellar, Brida went inside.

The hairs on the back of her neck bristled as she passed under the warded threshold. It was even colder in the crypt than it had been in the beer cellar. The runes written on the walls and into the lids of the tombs shone like frost in moonlight.

A dozen stone tombs filled the modest crypt. Three had carved lids representing the ancestors they held. Brognor. Brunhilda. Bjarn. The rest were unsealed and empty, waiting for ancestors yet to come. She brushed her hand reverently across the carved likeness of Bjarn Edrundour.

'I've let Thodrun and Vagnar make a fool of me,' she whispered.

There was nothing here. A draft, nothing more.

Brida had made the decision to head back and say nothing more of it when she heard the noise again. A rubbing and a patting and a scratching. And what sounded like a breath. Very close. The pipework immediately on the other side of the threshold behind her vibrated.

She whirled as the partially mummified corpse of a duardin staggered out of the beer cellar, where it must have been stumbling backwards and forwards for days, and into the light of the crypt. 'Brognor...' she mumbled, fumbling behind her over her father's tomb for anything she might be able to wrench loose and use as a weapon. But there was nothing. 'No.'

The mummy lunged for her, arms outstretched and fingers grasping. It bundled her towards Bjarn's tomb, its mouth creaking open and shut as it strained for her face. Gritting her teeth against the embalmed stench, Brida pushed the heel of her palm up under its jaw. It worked its mouth, not yet realising that its teeth were not sunk into living flesh.

'Druri!' she yelled, punching the corpse of her grandfather repeatedly in the ribs. The muscles of its chest squelched and caved under her blows. Meat strung away on her knuckles. Acting to some kind of fighting instinct, the mummy slid both hands around her throat. Her back hit the wall. 'Thodrun! Dain!'

Spilling loose coins over the floor, she pulled the ring on which she kept the brewery keys from her trouser pocket. The back-door key was a jag-toothed beast of Azyr-made bronze. Finding it on the ring, she rammed it into the mummy's belly. Already-dried blood oozed from the wound. She stabbed it again and again and again. Blood tarred her arm to the elbow. But it couldn't cut deep enough.

The duardin corpse pushed against her restraining hand, buckling her elbow, and it snapped towards her. Its breath on her face was like a damp cloth soaked in grave mould. 'Help!' she screamed again as its teeth gnashed nearer towards her face. 'Anybody!' She turned her head aside. Dry lips sanded her cheek. She rammed her key into the side of its neck and sawed frantically, as though with infinite time and a patient foe she might sever its head from its body. Tubes and gristle frayed from its throat, but no blood gushed over her, no air whistled over her face.

It bit, pulling away a mouthful of her cheek.

She screamed.

Suddenly there was a *thunk* of a sharp blade hitting meat. The mummy spasmed. It released its chokehold and collapsed on top of her. Lifeless again. She gasped and rolled it off her, struggling to get out from underneath it and upright with her back secure against Bjarn's tomb.

Whitebeard stood over her. He looked bone tired, leaning on his axe with both arms crossed over its bloodied head, his long beard tumbling over the ornate blade, past the haft, and to the floor. Even so, he found it in him to smile like a beardling who had just helped his grandmother to find a lost coin.

'I heard you shouting.'

Brida's mouth worked, but no sound seemed to come out of it. Her head rolled until it was staring at the corpse on the ground.

'Brognor Edrundour,' Whitebeard sighed. 'He deserved better.'

'How did this happen?' Brida said. 'The runes on the tombs are supposed to keep the bodies from being tampered with or their spirits disturbed. They were written by runelords in Azyrheim over three centuries ago.'

Straightening with some clear discomfort, Whitebeard took the cheek of his axe like a crutch and ran his spare hand across Bjarn's tomb. It might have been the sudden rush of air to her brain making her vision blurry, but the runes appeared to glow faintly, as though newly struck, as his hand passed over them. 'You might want to renew these, if you've inherited any of Brognor's rune-skill. If not...' He frowned, and gestured back over his shoulder. 'If not then I'd double the locks and put something stout and heavy on top of that trapdoor.'

'But…' she trailed off, turning again to look at her grandfather, strewn and ruined on the floor of the crypt.

'I know, lass, but when you grow a beard as long as mine you get a keen sense of what can and can't wait until morning.'

'You look exhausted.'

'You're not exactly skipping about yourself.'

'No. I suppose not. But then some of us are older than we used to be.'

'We're all a little bit older, lass. That's just the way of things.'

'You've not aged an hour since I was a girl.'

'Then you're not looking close enough,' he snapped. The long-beard's brow prickled, until his flush of temper seemed to subside. 'Forgive me, girl. It's been a hard road getting here, and a long night. It's been a year of long nights, and then some. I've a lot of work to do in the realms and those I do it for have a habit of making it harder for me, and themselves.'

'Then won't you stay this one night?'

Whitebeard lowered his head and sighed. 'How many times have you asked me that over the last hundred-odd years? How many ways can a duardin come up with of saying no? If I'm here, then I'm not out there.'

'Don't you need to rest?'

'Even Grungni needs to down tools every once in a while. Or so I'm told.' His moustaches twitched in what, had he been less weary, might have become a smile. 'But then he's a god and he has that luxury.'

'What about a home?'

'Once.' For a moment he looked wistful. 'In that, at least, I'm not so estranged from my people. Few of us have one in these times. And that's why I can't stay. But I wouldn't say no to a swift half of the Bearded Special for the road.' He turned to lead her back upstairs, when Brida reached out to touch his arm.

A tingle ran down her fingers, as if from touching a great weight of gold, and not unlike the first time she met the old duardin she had the sense of something deeper and greater than the stone under the hills.

'Rest,' she said. 'Just for one night. If not for yourself, then for me.'

He turned back. 'For you, you say?'

'The dead assail my door if you'd listen to Druri. My own ancestor stirs beneath my house.' She shivered and hugged herself. 'I doubt I will have any rest myself tonight, but having you and your axe under my roof will do my chances no harm.'

Whitebeard opened his mouth, but she saw his protestations crumble under the weight of a sigh. His brow unfurrowed. His stern jaw unclenched. Whatever had busied him for the last half decade, it had left him too weary to argue any more about it.

'Well… if it's for you. It would be nice to feel the comfort of a bed, I suppose. And to look forward to a proper breakfast in the morning.'

'You will have both,' Brida promised. 'And first thing in the morning I will have Druri prepare his wagon to take you wherever you need to go.'

'That does all sound appealing, lass. Though someone will have to pay for it in the morning I don't doubt.'

'Oh no. After all you've done for my father and my grandfather, I'll not take a penny from you now.'

Whitebeard's face again tested that almost smile.

'I wasn't thinking about myself.'

Eventually, the runes on the door failed. But they did not fail all at once. The bladegheist fell partway through the door before becoming stuck around its middle, its upper body and the scythe blade throwing a greenish pulse over the Bearded Dragon's threshold. Brida lifted Bjarn's blunderbuss. The gun was heavy in her old hands. Muttering a prayer to Grungni and to her ancestors, ignoring the beating and scraping of the dead on the shuttered windows, she took aim and fired.

Lead shot whizzed through the spirit and drummed the solid oak-and-brass door behind it. The pellets had been cast by the Kharadron, however, relations of the Dispossessed in distant times, and Brida liked to think that the intercession of her ancestors added further efficacy to her shot.

The bladegheist thrashed, stuck fast in the solidity of the door and dispersed with a silent wail.

There was no time to celebrate.

The shutter to her left splintered. Glass crashed over the taproom floor as a skeletal arm clothed in a mist of greenish robes pushed through. Heedless of broken glass, the hexwraith climbed inside.

Another shutter gave.

Then another.

And another.

The dead spilled in, all hellish eyes and grinning skulls. Their whisperings beckoned to her. They looked almost happy.

Brida swung her blunderbuss towards the hexwraith on the left, but there were too many for her to make any difference now and she hesitated over her shot. The trapdoor beside her feet gave an urgent rattle against the heavy barrel she had rolled on top of it. She scrunched her eyes shut. She wished Dain was here to stand beside her, but he had died in his sleep years ago. She had burned his body and buried the ashes in the lake in a lead casket. Druri had taken the wagon out one night and had, as he had said he would, simply never come back.

The farms were gone.

The duardin were gone.

Only Brida was left.

Opening her eyes, jaw set with hardened resolve, she sent a blast of shot into the horde. Shifting aim to the right, she fired again. Spirits cursed her as Kharadron shot tore them to aether. And still they came.

Throwing down the blunderbuss, she reached up behind her to pull the ancestral greataxe, Reliable, from its mount on the wall. As far as she knew it had never been taken down. Even Brognor had never spoken of having wielded it on the return from Azyr. Where it came from, and who it had originally belonged to, was a mystery. And yet it seemed to welcome Brida's grip as much as she did its weight in her hand. Wraith-light shimmered across its blade. The centuries had blunted its edge somewhat. But these were foes without form to cut. She did not expect its physical sharpness to be of any consequence here.

'I am Brida Edrundour, daughter of Bjarn, son of Brognor. You may take these hills for your master in Shyish, but only when the last daughter of the duardin fails.'

She turned with a roar as a leering hexwraith drifted through the counter. She knocked aside its sword on the head of her axe, the ancient runes stamped into the blade head pulsing as she reversed the swing to carry the axe blade through the death knight's spectral chest. It grasped and wailed as its body dissolved into the pervading gloom.

Another revenant came around the side of the bar. She swung at it. Reliable clove through its shoulder as though it were fog. The spirit's body turned to mist behind her axe even as the blade passed through it. She moved quickly to engage another. A swirl of green light and shadowed folds, a barbed helmet so aethereal she could see the ghostly skull inside. At the same time as she and it crossed blades, two more wraiths floated through the bar to attack her from behind. She had been thinking of it as a barrier, but to the dead it was nothing of the kind. At best it was worthless. At worst it was an impediment to her axe.

She cut down the helmeted wraith, turning to fend off the other two while more closed, looking desperately around the taproom. There had to be a better place to mount a last stand. One of the broken windows caught her eye. It was a few yards away from her, a handful of spirits between her and it. Even then, she hesitated, taking a last despairing look around the Bearded Dragon. She saw Whitebeard's tankard on its mantle, and something made her reach up and grab it. If she could not save the brewery, she could at least honour her grandfather's oath to Whitebeard and save this. Clutching the tankard to her breast, she ran towards the window.

The dead veered to intercept her, but they were slow to react and slower to move, and most were still drifting towards the bar as she hurled herself bodily through the broken window.

Duardin were infrequently acknowledged for their agility. Even as a beardling girl she doubted she would have emerged from such a leap with dignity. But what the duardin were, and what was often said, was rugged, proud, and stoic to the point of disaffecting pain. Her joints might have niggled, her hearing, like Reliable, had lost some of its sharpness over the centuries, but her bones were still hard, and her skull blessed with duardin thickness.

Barely bruised, she checked first that the tankard was undamaged before attending to herself, dragging herself up off the ground.

It had been years since she had last stepped outside of her home. She had almost forgotten what the Copperback Hills looked like. It had not been a conscious decision to remain inside and look to her own walls, merely a culmination of choices that had felt right to her at the time. The wind was jagged against her cut face, and cold. It carried no smell. Tattered scraps of cloud raced across the huge, skull face of a moon. Her breath misted in front of her, but not enough to hide that horror in the sky.

She could hear the panicked babbling of the stream. The whispers of the dead.

Behind her, the Bearded Dragon was thoroughly ablaze. Or so it appeared. It was no earthly fire that consumed it, but the flickering manifestations of hexwraiths and bladegheists and chainghasts, their bodies merging and splitting like the tongues of a spectral pyre as they tore the brewery apart. A few lonely spirits wandered mournfully around the front yard and the stables, or milled mindlessly on the little stretch of moon-silvered road that was visible before it wound into the Copperback Hills. Others drifted past her, more intent it seemed on the destruction of the brewery and whatever stamp of permanence it represented to them than they were on her.

'You came,' said a voice from the road behind her. 'Good. There's clearly hope for you yet.'

Whirling back from the burning inn, she lowered Reliable in astonishment at the sight of Whitebeard. Nighthaunt gloam haloed his unruly mane of white hair. His cloak was flung back over his shoulder, gromril scales and bright gems shining by witch-fire and fell moonlight. His axe rested idle on his shoulder, but from the slump in his posture and the drawn look to his face he had been fighting hard. The dead seemed to avoid him, flowing around him or fleeing outright to the hills rather than approach too near.

'What do you mean?'

He gestured towards the brewery. 'You could have died for it. But what would that have achieved? The Dispossessed cleave to the old ways, but don't forget, your ancestors are those who had the good sense to up and run when all was lost. This land of yours...' He stamped his boot on the ground. 'This is just stone. You will find it anywhere.'

'But...'

Squinting into the haze of ghosts at Whitebeard's back she caught a few of prouder aspect and duardin shape. They appeared to be with him. Duardin with tall draconic helms. Duardin with cropped beards and strange suits of armour. Others that looked like…

Her knees felt weak and she sank to the ground.

'Mother. Father. My ancestors.'

'I warned Bruni not to build here,' said Whitebeard. 'Chaos in the rocks and in the water, I told him. But he wouldn't listen. Too proud. Your father was the same. For the obvious want of a Special on which to pass comment this year, let me pass on this wisdom instead.' He tilted his head back, looking up as the brewery's roof slowly collapsed. 'This is what will always happen when the duardin seal themselves away behind their gates and wait out the darkness. You asked me to stay and watch over your hall. In a moment of weakness for the hearth I once knew, I agreed. But what is the brewer without the farmers and millers and carters, without the merchants and buyers in distant lands? What are any of us without our fellow duardin? Without the humans and the aelves who'd join us in shunning the darkness if we let them? The shadow will pass, aye. But it must be made to.'

Brida listened to every word, but she was no longer looking at him. The ghost of Brunhilda Edrundour smiled at her from Whitebeard's halo. She was wearing the wooden hammer that she had made for Brida's sixth birthday gift. She looked proud. She looked entirely untroubled by the defilement of her tomb. Despite the destruction of her world, Brida felt freer at that than she had in a long while. Since she had been a girl.

Brida lifted the tankard. She had held on to it without thinking.

'This is yours,' she said.

'Keep it. Build again somewhere else. Anywhere else. If the beer is good enough then the duardin will come. And perhaps others too. Turn no one away.'

She looked at the tankard, studying the ancient Klinkerhun character on its metal face. 'Why me?'

'An ancestor of yours held something for me once. Long ago. As I told your grandfather, you do me a favour by keeping it for me.'

'I will do as you ask.'

She looked up to thank him, but Whitebeard had already turned from her and was walking away into the mist. He seemed to sink into the stone of the hills as the ranks of the ancestral dead closed around him and then themselves faded into the wind. Shivering from its touch, she turned, taking one last look at her ancestral home as it disintegrated in cold fire.

Then she took up Whitebeard's tankard, shouldered Reliable, and walked away.

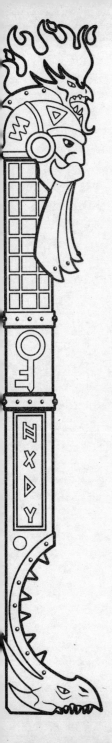

THE MAKER'S
MARK

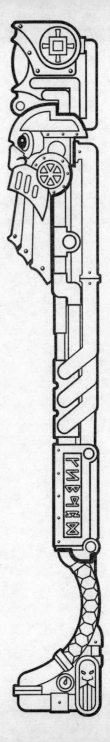

'One can hardly speak of the duardin without remarking on their tenacity and stubbornness, their reverence for past deeds or their love of gold. But to those with more than a passing familiarity with legend, and to any who have been blessed with cause to venture into the grand halls where they dwell, it is their skill at artifice that defines them. Masters of stone and metal and the makers of intricate machines are they. The Khazalid Empire of old was the home of a thousand wonders, with colonies in all eight Mortal Realms and untold sub-realms beyond, many of which were conjured by the realm-craft of the duardin themselves. Places where rare gems ran like water or where the clockwork of the Cosmos Arcane could be accessed and amended to their needs. Sigmar had little to teach the forefathers of the duardin when it came to the art of building. Indeed, had he half the wisdom back then that he has since been forced to acquire, perhaps he would have learned a thing or two from the duardin, and the sad history of that time would have been different.

'The passing of Myth and the touch of Chaos has left many races diminished in their crafts, but not so the duardin. Their skill is all that it once was and in many cases furthered by privation and need. It is only the means and the materials at their disposal that are lesser now than in the days of their glory...'

Rikkorn Mikazrin let the lead ball of the arcendulum drop from his fist, the chain-link arm snapping taut. After a few seconds, the lodestone began to drift.

The mountainous landscape before him was one of fractured geometries, an endless maze of conundrums long sundered from their solution. The duardin squinted in the direction that the instrument was being pulled. His eyes were furnished with goggles. His beard was wrapped around his face like a headscarf, for the light of Hysh burned as well as blinded. The beard's tawny ends flapped in the wind, shining like copper.

He made a minute adjustment to his goggles, narrowing the apertures of the lenses. Then he reeled in the arcendulum and stuffed it back into his pack. He scratched a note of the reading with a graver into his log, then stowed the string of copper plates and hoisted the heavy pack over his shoulders.

He took a deep breath.

And then struck out into the maze.

The mountains of Syar, one of the Ten Paradises of Hysh, were not like those of home. The great wars of the aelves that had precipitated the Age of Chaos in that realm had broken them, and had obfuscated by violence the symbolism of their placement and form. What remained of the range was a taunt, a fragment of something profound that could not and would never be pieced together again. Those peaks that still reached, unbroken, for the realm's zenith were possessed of a koanic beauty. They were rugged and yet delicate, sculpted like tohnasai trees. Realm ice shone from their high peaks, wreathed in arcanocirrus and the gemstone glitter of the multiple rainbows that sprang from great waterfalls. The wind crafted patterns in the clouds. The passage of time was a puzzle. The play of light on every rock and flower and flake of snow hinted at a deeper meaning. Mikazrin could have spent an eternity here without realising it, without putting one foot in front of the other. He grunted, narrowed his lenses further still, and turned to the old duardin exercise of counting gold in his head.

The sciences of navigation had always fascinated his ancestors. And him. He would defeat this maze. He pushed on.

Low clouds and deep snow blocked passes that from afar had seemed clear, while cliffs that had looked unassailable and sheer would, in moments of inspiration, present winding trails to the next summit or vale, bypassing the ancient rockfalls and the ruins of elder peaks whose symbolism led nowhere but deeper into the maze. There was no single way through the mountains. It had to be *felt*, and it differed for everyone who made the attempt. Kharadron pioneers from Xintil and even further afield would often attempt to overfly the ice-bound summits instead, but the spirits of Mountain and Zenith would invariably confound and deny them. And punish them if they persisted. Even Swifthawk princes, assuming an aelven heritage would grant them a freer passage to Ar-Ennascath, learned to swallow their pride and walk if they meant to cross at all. The ruins of several sky vessels formed a number of abstract symbols on the backs of distant peaks; cyphers in iron and gold.

Mikazrin took several readings over the course of several days. One day they had him scrambling through cloudbark copses. The next might pull him in the opposite direction entirely, wading up to the roots of his beard in fast-running water with his pack and its precious wares on his head, skidding over loose scree or chasing after ever-distant rainbows. There was no 'day' here. No 'night'. He walked on the source of all daylight in the Cosmos Arcane. Even that was a challenge, a test for the mind and the will and the worth of the individual to go on. It had defeated his ancestors, but Mikazrin had not come unprepared.

He diligently recorded the latest set of readings in his log, and went on.

There was, unsurprisingly, no shade to be had. Even amongst the mountains there were no shadows. Everything emitted light of some kind or degree, even if it was only the pale radiance of a grass-blade or a worm. Nor was there any shelter to be found from the elements, for if the realm sought to freeze or douse you then it would do so, for reasons that a traveller would be better off attempting to interpret than resisting. His log – the first few plates of which had been chiselled by his great grandfather, before being added to by closer ancestors – did, however, speak of predators. Mikazrin had already spotted a few that even they had failed to catalogue: ravenous promises, predatory hopes, creatures that wore light like a camouflage and hunted through time as well as physical space.

Only when doughty duardin endurance failed him did Mikazrin risk stopping to make a camp, and despite the lack of obvious shelter he nevertheless chose his ground with care.

Setting up on a rocky outcropping overlooking a green valley and surrounded by tall pines, he carefully unpackaged and laid out traps. Few of them looked like anything that an orruk or a Kurnothi would catch their foot in, but the arcanomechanical contraptions, the spools of silver wire and spinning discs of lead and mercury, were, according to his father's notes, quite lethal in their own way.

Taking a last reading with the arcendulum before allowing himself to rest, he looked up. The preternaturally blue sky winked occasionally. In any other realm he might have taken it for a comet shower or a shooting star from Azyr. But here it was the Hyshian realmstone, in its natural state as a form of magical light, shooting from one end of the realmsphere to the other, deflecting off the Perimeter Inimical as if from the surface of a mirror and firing back. Random and forever. Unless caught by the arts of the Lumineth.

As he laid out his bedroll for the 'night', Mikazrin found himself thinking long about what a master engineer of the Ironweld might accomplish with such lore. He smiled, like a beardling indulging a favourite fantasy, and set a small pewter ancestor figurine by his stony pillow. The ancestor was male but the features were too idealised and generic for him to say that they resembled anyone in particular. Nevertheless, when he touched its metal bust and gruffed his short, nightly prayer to Grungni the Maker, it was his father, grandfather, and the great-grandfather he had never met whose likenesses were in his mind.

'I'll see out the family dream,' he muttered to them all. 'I'll be the Mikazrin whose work sees the other side.'

Then, ensuring his volleypistol was fully loaded and underneath his pillow, he slotted the thickest and blackest lenses that Ironweld craft could cut into his goggles and fell straight to sleep.

In Hysh there was no such thing as a dreamless sleep and the nights there were seldom restful, except for the deeply contented and the very wise. Since Mikazrin was neither of those things his dreams were filled with strange imagery.

In them, the ancestor figurine beside him stirred and came alive and began to jabber riddles in ancient tongues, resorting to drawing increasingly obscure pictograms on the ground as its frustration with him grew. And all the while the spirit of the stone rumbled its displeasure. The mountain across the vale grew a full beard of gold-coloured leaves and white snow, the earth rising to hold the peak aloft as if on the back of a shield. His dreaming consciousness assumed the ancestor to be his father, white-bearded, disappointed and stern, but it spoke urgently in languages he could not comprehend.

The sky split as though enraged by his failure to understand.

'*What are you doing here?*' the mountains demanded.

Mikazrin sat bolt upright. The thunder from his dream continued to ring out through the copse of silently knowing trees. He swore under his breath and rolled onto his beard, reached under his pillow for the volleypistol and pulled it out. He aimed the compact four-barrelled gun into the woods.

The clash came again.

He swung his gun towards it. A shout this time, he was sure of it; then a strange growl and the *clang* of metal against stone.

Stuffing his pistol into his belt and unclicking the thick night lenses from his goggles, Mikazrin quickly set about disarming his traps and packing his gear. He had studied the notes left to him by his forebears and he knew that there could be absolutely no guarantee of his ever finding this campsite again if he left it in haste now. Without his gear he would be as good as dead. Or worse than dead.

Beaten.

The shout came again. The *clang*.

Mikazrin pulled the straps of his pack tight and drew the

volleypistol from his belt. Last of all he snatched up the ancestor figurine, holding it out like a miner's lantern, and lumped into the woods towards the sounds of battle.

He would not walk on and leave a fellow traveller in danger. He'd been raised better than that. Honour wouldn't allow it.

He crashed through the thin copse and, after several minutes of running flat out, onto a high mead of waving grass.

A duardin in cunningly wrought armour, a mail coat made of interlocking gromril cogs rather than the usual rings, stood in the light of the clearing. He was laden with packs and baggage, and over it all he wore a red coat stuffed with pockets. His long white beard was girded in glimmering gromril plates with the golden stamp of the Ironweld on each one, though of which city's school Mikazrin could not make out over that distance. In his gauntleted hands was a large double-bladed axe. It was a simple weapon, ill-suited to an Ironweld forge master, but at the same time the most singularly beautiful piece that Mikazrin had ever seen. It was as though Hysh again spoke to him in riddles and double-meaning, but there was little about the axe that was not plain and deliberately made so. The blade was deeply incised with gold lettering, the intense and unforgiving light of Hysh finding in its metalwork no fault or flaw as it flashed and glittered, chopping deeply into obstinate stone.

The mountain aelementor bellowed and drew back.

Its form resembled that of a broken wall, given accidental animus by some kind of rogue spell. Its humanoid shape was cobbled together from loose rocks, two lumps of stone pressed together at the top of its brick-solid body made a head, and a beard of short grass and snowdrop flowers swayed from it as it moved. It was fifteen beards high, and furious.

With a ululating war cry, the duardin looped his axe overhead and brought it crashing down into the spirit's leg. The monster raised its chipped knee high and bellowed, though if and how it felt pain Mikazrin did not know. The foot came down to flatten the old master where he stood, but the duardin sprang back, light on his toes for one so lengthy of beard. The spirit's arm was already swinging like an aethervoid pendulum.

Solid Hyshian rock crunched into gromril scales.

The duardin flew through the air and landed like a felled tree. His packs tore open, shedding complicated looking gears and gizmos as he rolled through the long grass.

'Over here!' Mikazrin yelled, and raised his volleypistol. He aimed for the solid stone mass of chest as the aelementor turned towards his shout.

Just like he had been taught. Nothing fancy.

He squeezed the trigger.

A punishing few seconds of shot from all four barrels drilled a hole the size of a duardin's fist into the spirit's chest. Its body swayed back under the deluge of honest Chamon lead and almost fell until a stone foot stamped into the ground like a foundation pile and steadied it.

It fixed its blank, solid gaze on Mikazrin. The assortment of anemometers and oscilloscopes strung about his person began variously to spin, whistle and chime in the build-up of elemental light magic. Mikazrin threw himself to one side as the ground beneath him crumpled. Grass and flowers sank underground while jagged blades of white stone thrust up to the surface like spears.

He heard a gruff-voiced roar as the old master ran back in. He looked up from the ground to see the duardin hacking and chipping away at the wild aelementor's turned back. Mikazrin quickly got himself back up and reloaded, the volleypistol making a complicated crunching and grinding noise as its inner workings drew more round shot from the storage drum under the barrel and into the cylinders. He was just swinging it up, sighting down the pin, when the old duardin delivered what turned out to be the telling blow.

His great-axe found a plane of weakness exposed by Mikazrin's shot and clove along it, its runes glowing like an impossible alloy of sunmetal and celestium as the duardin carved the giant stone spirit in two.

As Mikazrin ran towards him, the aelementor piled itself into a cairn of its constituent rocks as it died. The old duardin lowered his axe. When Mikazrin reached him, he brought his volleypistol around, fully intending to empty it into whatever spirit animus the creature had left. If his ancestors' logs had taught him one thing, it was never to underestimate the fauna of Syar.

'Don't, youngling.'

The grip that appeared around Mikazrin's wrist was unbelievably strong. Enough for Mikazrin to let the *youngling* slide. The old duardin forced his aim aside from the crumbling mound of stone.

'The Realm-lords prefer to let their predators be, as annoying as that might be for the rest of us. If you're looking to cross their mountains and earn their favour then honouring their ways is as good a place to start as any.'

Mikazrin nodded his thanks and holstered his pistol. While the old duardin watched in apparent bafflement, he took off his pack, pulled out the log and graver that he was always careful to pack last, and scratched the engineer's advice into the marginalia.

Only then did it occur to him what else the old master had said. His gaze shot up. The duardin was looking at him wryly from under prickly white brows.

'What makes you think I'm looking for the Realm-lords?'

The old duardin puffed on a long-stemmed pipe, the smoke curling into curious and meaningful shapes as it climbed. As with all things in that place it sought to draw the eye thither and make the mind wander, but never quite succeeded, not with that old duardin sat beneath it, eased back on the grass with a contented scowl and his pipe. Mikazrin had never seen anyone, in Hysh or elsewhere, so casually, obstinately *solid*. He was as potent a curative to the mysteries of the realm as any of the gold-counting exercises or repetitive games that Mikazrin had brought with him from Chamon. Mikazrin poured them both a small measure of ale from the flask in his pack. The old duardin took it gravely.

'Thank you, lad.'

'I haven't much, but I'm happy to share it.'

The old duardin's brow crinkled under a heavy smile. 'It was *you* who ran to *my* aid, as I recall.' He took a sip, made a face, but was evidently too honourable to say what he thought of Mikazrin's well-travelled brew. 'Not that I needed the help, mind. I think you'll find I had that little beastie well in hand.'

'I don't doubt it,' Mikazrin said, too polite himself to argue the point with an elder. If a duardin with a beard that long and white said he could battle the mountain alone, then battle the mountain alone he could.

'But be that as it may,' the old master went on, 'it's a rare duardin in this fallen age who'll sup with a stranger in the wild lands of the Mortal Realms.' He stuffed his pipe back into his mouth and raised his half-emptied cup. 'And for that may you count Gormdal the Wanderer your honoured friend.'

Mikazrin raised his cup and they clanked vessels. Gormdal pulled the pipe from his mouth and slugged down what was left. He made another face.

'You know… I could teach you how to make a barrel that'll keep a beer fresh weeks after broaching, and keep it cool whether you're traipsing through a Ghyranic jungle or the Flamescar Plateaux of Aqshy.'

'Thank you, old master, but I think I'll hold you in debt a little longer yet.'

The duardin laughed. 'A wise lad. They still teach that in the schools of Chamon then, do they?'

Mikazrin emptied his own cup. It tasted perfectly fair to him. 'I have a little food to share as well, if you're hungry.'

Gormdal slapped his thigh and gestured expansively to the grass. 'A veritable banquet it'll seem to me after my own adventures, I'm sure.'

Mikazrin unpacked the few wax-wrapped parcels he kept in his pack amongst his tools and wares and set them on the grass. The old duardin smacked his lips happily, but his eyes glittered as he beheld the curious assortment of instruments, and Mikazrin had to ply him with more ale – better on a second tasting, it seemed – before he would touch the spread.

'How did you know I was seeking the Realm-lords?' Mikazrin asked again, while the elder crunched on a salted cake.

'It's the time of the contest, unless my sense is way off, so it was no great guess on my part. You seem well prepared for the journey. Better than most who make it. Have you ventured to the Syari capital before?'

Mikazrin shook his head. 'My great-grandfather was the first to attempt the journey, but he didn't make it across the wastes. My grandfather made it to the mountains only to be bested by them.' He pulled the logbook from his pack and opened it, simultaneously displaying it while holding the precious thing closer to his lap. 'Whenever one of them made the attempt they took this with them, making particular note of what they learned of the journey and how they failed.'

Gormdal nodded sagely. 'Good and methodical.'

'My ancestors were well-known masters of the Greenfire Ironweld in their time. You could call it the family obsession. Plenty in the Arsenal do.'

'Well you might just be the one to prove them wrong. You're not far off the city now, and I judge the worst of the mountain's trials to be behind you.'

'You have been to Ar-Ennascath?'

'Aye,' said Gormdal, his heavy face deep with reverie. 'Many times. The first time I beheld it was long ago, when the aelves in this realm were fewer and, may my own kin forgive me for uttering it, its beauty was the poorer for it. Nowadays it's a true wonder of the Mortal Realms, and I say that not lightly, but as one who's laid his eyes on the Forge Eternal of Sigmaron and even the great works of Elixia before Grungni's city was lost to our kind.'

Mikazrin was no callow youngling, but his mouth had fallen wide. 'What was it like?'

'That, lad, I'll never say, and nor count it against the tally of favours I owe. One day, perhaps one day soon, you might see it for yourself, but you might not, and I'll not haunt your remaining days with the knowledge of what can never be again, however poorly a duardin's words can serve the Maker's wonder.'

'Is it so glorious?'

'Aye. It is that, and then some.'

Mikazrin looked at the elder with awe. 'From what school do you hail, longbeard? It must be famous indeed.'

'No school, lad.'

'You must have been trained somewhere.'

'I don't stick "the Wanderer" after my name for nothing, you know.'

'How is it that I've never heard of you? As journeyed a cogsmith as you claim to be must be renowned the realms over.'

'My claims, as you call them, are all true, if a trifle exaggerated in the telling, but even a duardin's legend can't endure the test of time.' He drew the pipe from his mouth and tapped the bowl on the axe resting on the grass by his side. 'But the work, now…'

He gestured to the pack where Mikazrin had carefully put away his more delicate gear. '*That's* what'll outlive us both, what your descendants will know when they speak your name. As duardin all over the realms do today when they invoke the names *Alaric*, *Bugman*, or *Makaisson*, celebrating their works with daily use without ever knowing ought of who those duardin once were. That's what you'll be, lad, if you work hard and you're lucky, long after your deeds in life are dust.'

'This I know well enough. Even in my own lifetime, long enough as it's been, though short perhaps by your reckoning, I've seen my grandfather's work become forgotten. Particularly amongst my human apprentices.'

'Humans have shorter memories than most, though we duardin are not without our faults. Better hidden though they are.'

Mikazrin nodded. 'All in Greenfire will know my family's name when I reach Ar-Ennascath.'

Gormdal leant forward, a light in his eyes that was somehow all his own and owing nothing to that of Hysh. 'So... when do I get to see what's in the bag?'

Mikazrin hugged the book and pack in his lap aggressively.

'Come on, lad. You've been lugging your work all this way. You're going to have to show it to someone eventually.'

To Mikazrin's surprise, he did almost ease his grip on his pack and open it, allowing the old master a peek inside. Despite being nigh two hundred years old himself, and a recognised master of his forge for the past thirty, he felt a tingle in the roots of his beard at the thought of earning this duardin's approval. But the Ironweld had not been founded to share its knowledge: it had come together in the wake of the Age of Chaos, a reaction to all that had been destroyed and lost, in order to hoard that which remained. Secrets were passed, and even then often grudgingly, from master to apprentice and from the cold dead grip of father to son.

'You can see it along with everyone else when I present it at the festival at Ar-Ennascath.'

The old duardin chuckled. 'If that's your wish then I'll respect it. But another set of eyes seldom go amiss. And I'll warn you – the Syari aren't easily impressed by craft that's not their own.'

'That's because they've not yet seen Ironweld work.'

Gormdal raised his pipe in salute. 'All the best to you then, young master, and on that note I'll bid you good night and impose on your kind heart no more.' He spread out as if to lay himself out where he sat. 'I've a walk ahead of me yet, and battling that stone spirit didn't half take the breath out of me.'

'I've only just woken,' said Mikazrin, worried suddenly that he had offended the old white-beard. 'But I'll stay just the same and sit watch if you'll let me.'

'You're really banking these favours, aren't you, lad?'

Mikazrin smiled, relieved to see the irreverent gleam returned to the longbeard's eye. 'It'll be good to just sit and have some-body nearby while I rest.'

Six hours later, according to the timepiece he carried in his fob pocket, the sky still bright and preternaturally blue, Gormdal stirred from his deep, fretful slumber, and told Mikazrin to get some rest.

He did.

He was not at all surprised to find the old master gone by the time he awoke. There was no one way to Ar-Ennascath, and it had to be walked alone.

Ar-Ennascath.

At first, and for the longest while, Mikazrin thought that he was again dreaming. The golden city appeared so suddenly, and so miraculously, on the flank of the mountain overlooking the

Luminaris Sea, and in no less spectacular a fashion than any of the sights that had descended on his imagination while dreaming in the Realm of Light. A road paved with glass and set at intervals with variously coloured gemstones appeared under his feet as though it had been with him every step of the way from Greenfire. It led towards a stupendously high gate that, as Mikazrin drew closer, he found to be made not of wood or stone, or even the precious metals of some strongholds of Chamon, but of gossamer-thin cloth picked out with auralan runes. It was the soaring confidence of the Syari, more than any particular artistry, that took Mikazrin's breath, that they could entrust themselves wholly to their craft and fear no adversary here at the centre of their own power.

Unchallenged by any of the glittering spear-wielding aelves that guarded passage through the gates, Mikazrin passed under the breeze-thin walls, stumbling out of a dream and into a song. He fumbled with the leather straps of his goggles and pulled them from his face, leaving them to hang against his beard as he stared dumbly about him.

The city was set upon the shoulder of a great and beauteous mountain, overlooking the bright, sapphire blue vista of the Luminaris Sea that encircled the Ten Paradises of Hysh and bordered Syar to the north. Every building was its own singular marvel, elegant and plain, but also glorious, with its own enlightenment to share if one would only dwell long enough to puzzle on its promise. But while each structure was a work of high art, each masterpiece blended harmoniously into the symmetry of the greater whole, and in such a way as detracted nothing from the natural beauty and innate symbolism of the mountain itself.

The architecture of the Syari did not seek to impose on the landscape as did the structures of Chamon or Azyr. It complemented it.

From what he could see once he was able to tear his gaze away from the astounding beauty of a joiner's shop's front wall, the festival was already well under way. Aelves in luminous attire glided through the wide boulevards of their home city like winsome ghosts. In small groups they lingered around the countless stalls, chatting gaily over any small thing that delighted them, eviscerating with kind words and bright smiles the hopes of those whose works they deemed to have fallen short of the Syari ideal of perfection. Most of the craftsfolk were aelven, but Mikazrin could see a few other races represented amongst the stalls. A pair of Fyreslayers with bleached hair and white-gold runes stamped into their muscles stood with their arms crossed over a table laden with fyresteel axes. Elsewhere, a group of humans ran a demonstration of their exotic firearms for a party of smiling aelves who indulged their work as one might a picture drawn for them by a child.

Mikazrin barely even noticed them. Still less, their wares.

Like a thief who had set it upon himself to break into the Celestial Palaces of Sigmaron only to find himself unexpectedly in the Throne Room of the God-King himself, he clutched the arm straps of his pack, blinded and dizzied by the terrible wonders that surrounded him. Swords more perfect than anything he had ever seen on an Ironweld forge. Fine armours that looked as though they weighed nothing at all. And it was not just weaponry. All forms of craftsmanship were on display there, and the crowds of Ar-Ennascath seemed to take joy in it equally. There was jewellery such as would have shamed an empress; drinking cups, clothing, and many works of pure art as well, although the craft of the Syari seemed to effortlessly blur the lines between the functional and the merely beautiful.

'Are you in need of some direction, friend?'

An aelf in a shimmering gown of yellow suncloth embroidered with rows of white chequers approached from the crowd.

He wore an elaborate fanlike headpiece adorned with jewels and glass and an aetherquartz splint that made the whole ensemble glow. Mikazrin was attired in perfectly serviceable travelling gear and mail, and had never wanted for better, but he felt suddenly rough and unpolished in this aelf's company.

He smoothed out his beard and scowled. But he could not seem to think of anything to say.

The aelf smiled. On a face less surpassingly beautiful than his it might have been mistaken for a smirk.

'You are here for the craft fayre, I presume. Just looking at you I can tell that you must have travelled far, and endured great hardships, for the privilege of attending the fayre.' He gestured to himself with a jewelled fan that looked as though it could also function as a superlative blade should the need arise, in the unlikely event that the aelf had nothing better to hand. 'I am Anasrith Athaer, a simple metalsmith from the Ithalin Province on the southern coast. I too am arrived but recently after a long and arduous journey.' Mikazrin took in the aelf and his flawless attire. 'Perhaps we might find ourselves adjoining stalls and display our wares together?' He smiled again.

The aelf's companions, who seemed to have emerged from the delighted throngs behind, laughed. If there was a deeper meaning to their mirth then it was painfully obscured to Mikazrin.

'No,' he gruffed, clutching the packs of his straps tightly. 'No *thank you,*' he added, shocked by the crudity of his own words, and turned away, trying hard not to run as the light laughter of the aelves rang in his ears.

Mikazrin sat at an out-of-the-way table, under the corner vaults of the high-ceilinged drinking house. Light fell through windows of stained and brilliantly coloured glass. There was no speck of dust in the common lounge to dance in the rays, and instead the colours formed artful rainbows that wobbled into the likenesses of exalted beasts or great aelf heroes of myth as horse-drawn carriages and pedestrians passed across the window outside. There he sat, bent, burying his shame in scowls and glowers for the occasional aelf who would risk his temper to enquire as to whether he would inspect the menu, and engraved his latest, and last, entry into his log.

The trials of a craftsman's worth did not, it would seem, conclude at the city's gate.

He shook his head as the graver moved across the copper plate. How could he display such tawdry wares as he had borne with him from Chamon? The shame of it would surely surpass any that mere failure could have outdone, and better the sneers of the Arsenal masters of Greenfire than the gentle mockery of the Syari. That would be more disgrace than he could bear, and more by far than his forebears in the craft shops of the Ancestors' Hall deserved to witness.

A pair of aelves at the next table looked over, intrigued by the tapping and scratching of his letters. He discouraged their interest with a scowl and continued.

But maybe *his* son could still learn from his father's failure, and would know to craft something even finer. Of how the youngling, an apprentice still, six decades old and barely grown into his beard, would accomplish such a feat of craftsmanship Mikazrin had no guidance to write down. The work he had brought with him was already the finest he knew how to produce.

Nevertheless, his son would have to do better.

At the sound of footsteps approaching his corner table, he looked up.

'I'll look at the menu when I'm damn well good and ready to–'

The words dried up in his mouth. Gormdal, the old master from the mountains, stood across the table from him with his thumbs in his belt. His coat was open and his armour was shining in the varicoloured light. His head was shining white, in spite of the full colour spectrum falling across him from the windowpanes, as pure in its own straightforward way as the Lumineth themselves. But sturdier somehow. More *real*.

'Is this seat taken?'

'Old master,' said Mikazrin, standing, bowing his head and tugging lightly on his beard, just the slightest twitch of his jaw to suggest that company would be very much unwelcome.

'Good,' said Gormdal, and planted himself down in the chair opposite. Almost at once he began fishing in his various pockets, pulling out a tinderbox, pipe, and a small aromatic parcel of dried leaves, which he proceeded to remove a pinch of and tamp into the bowl of his pipe. 'Good to see a familiar face around here. The Lumineth are friendly enough, in the manner of aelves of course, but altogether too *tall* for my liking.'

He proffered the now-lit pipe across the table. Mikazrin waved it away.

'A duardin ought to smoke,' said Gormdal, puffing contentedly and ignoring the quizzical looks of the aelves at the neighbouring tables. 'It's good for the lungs. And the act of doing so of course makes him look older and more venerable than he truly is, even though he be more than adequately old and venerable enough.' As if to demonstrate the virtue, he took a long draw on the stem and blew out a smoke ring. It drifted teasingly into the form of one of the Lumineth's eight mandalic runes before a passing aelf pulled it apart.

The serving aelf returned. Gormdal ordered something incomprehensible but beautiful sounding for them both before Mikazrin could intervene. The aelf glimmered back to the kitchens.

Mikazrin chewed on his beard. Even the servants were dazzling.

'What are you doing here?' said Gormdal.

Mikazrin blinked. The question sounded like one he had heard before. In a dream, perhaps.

Yes, in a dream.

'Shouldn't you be out there?' The old master jerked a thumb towards the window.

Mikazrin shook his head to clear it of the eerie sensation of reprising a dream. He knew it would probably be best to say nothing, particularly to an itinerant stranger of no school, however learned and venerable he might seem, but come the moment he found his embarrassment was simply too great not to share. And better to share it with an elderly stranger, he supposed, than any of his own peers at the Greenfire Arsenal.

'I was so arrogant,' he muttered. 'I thought that all I had to do was get here and the Lumineth would fall over themselves in awe of Ironweld work. But you've seen what it's like out there. I can't show what I've brought here, against *that*. For as long as there are aelves still living in the Mortal Realms the Mikazrin name would be the laughing stock of Syar.'

Gormdal stroked his beard thoughtfully. 'It was arrogant, I'll grant you, though you're hardly alone in that.' He leant over the table and dropped his voice, gesturing furtively with his eyes as if at something over his shoulder that he would rather not alert with a more obvious gesture. 'Don't look now, lad, but you're in the capital of the *aelves*.'

Mikazrin fought with a smile, and Gormdal leant back again as the server returned.

The younger duardin watched, feeling faintly disoriented as if by a street magician's sleight-of-hand, as plates were laid out across the table, a symmetry of glistening seafood and colourful vegetables that would have been a work of art even if every dish that composed it had been less perfect.

'You see the jewels they all wear?' said Gormdal, watching

him as the server departed. 'Aetherquartz. They all carry it. High and low, if there is such a thing as low amidst the Realm-lords. It lends inspiration and insight, and the Syari in particular use it in their crafting.' He picked up a lightly grilled piece of tentacle. 'All their crafting, in fact, because why make something excellent when you can make something unique and perfect every single time you pick up a hammer? Some of us might call that cheating, but it's a poor workman as blames his tools, as the old saying goes, so you can't well look in envy at the tools of a great one, can you?'

'There is nothing wrong with my tools.'

'I didn't say there was.'

'Then it's with my work.'

Chewing on his squid, Gormdal rapped his knuckles on the table. 'Get it out then, youngling, and let's have a look at it. You wouldn't show me before, but you may as well show me now.'

Nodding, resigned, Mikazrin turned to the chair beside him where he had sat his pack and delved inside. He withdrew a number of small pieces: the arcendulum, a hextant, a chamonite compass that floated on a small cushion of aether-gold when unwrapped, and set them out on the table. He pulled the goggles from around his neck and set them down too. Last to emerge was a bundle of soft fleece which, when unfastened, revealed a brass cylinder about six inches long. He let it rest on his palm for a moment, the weight of it soaking into his hand, feeling the cool of the metal and the rivets in his skin, re-enacting in his mind the act of casting and setting each and every piece by hand. Then, and only then, he opened it, releasing silver clasps and unpackaging sliding segments to produce a tube closer to three feet in length.

'The other things are trinkets compared to this. The Ironweld is most famous for its war machines, of course, but my family's main concern has always been navigation. We have crafted the tools by which the armies of Sigmar march across the Spiral Crux for nigh on six hundred years.' With one large, calloused hand near to the eyepiece, he ran his fingers along the main tube in search of imperfections in the metal, and found none. 'Optics has always fascinated me. When I was an apprentice my father would tease me for playing with glass and lenses when I could have been working metal. And I even found myself in trouble once or twice, as respectable as I look now, for stealing time at the forge here and there to craft a fine piece like this for a rich noble or a scholar in between the spyglasses I would produce by the gross for the Arsenal's artillerists. See here.'

He lifted the ornate telescope and, with his hands, he described the piece.

'The casing is brass. It's more functional than gold, of course, and it's harder wearing. The rings are steel, for strength when extending or collapsing the tube. But the real wonder is inside.' He swivelled the instrument about to show Gormdal the eyepiece. 'The lenses aren't glass as you might find in common telescopes, but a crystal of quartz that can be quarried only from the Patina Peaks in Gazan Zhar, and from which chamonite has first been cut. There are a hundred of them inside the tube. Each one refines the light a little more and a little more before permitting the light to touch your eye.'

He tapped on the eyepiece, and then abruptly collapsed the tube.

He sighed. 'A duardin could glimpse the most distant constellations of Azyr and see the face of Celemnar in the Zenith of Hysh. A better telescope there never was in all of Chamon.'

'I don't doubt it,' said Gormdal quietly, his food entirely forgotten in favour of the instruments laid out across the table.

Mikazrin looked up. For a moment he had forgotten he was talking to anyone other than himself. He looked down to the newly truncated cylinder in his hand.

'Maybe if I were to rework the tube in gold after all, add some jewels or inlay, a carving perhaps.' He scowled, wrapping the instrument again in fleece and returning it to his pack. The rest he left strewn across the tabletop, shamed by the effortless dignity of the repast. 'No. Not even then. I can't compete with the artisanry of the Teclian aelves. Perhaps I'd be better off destroying my log when I return to Greenfire, and save my son and those who come after him this thankless task.' He sighed. 'If not for the hard work of my ancestors I'd toss it into the Luminaris Sea right here.'

'It's right that you honour the work of your ancestors,' said Gormdal, 'but if I might make a small suggestion?'

Mikazrin gave an impatient nod.

'You've focused so much on the task of just getting here, there's barely one thing here that you've made for the simple joy of just *making*.' He raised his hand as the engineer began to protest. 'The telescope is very fine, but you told me that this was your forefather's work. As was this notion of having your work shown at the annual festival at Ar-Ennascath. My suggestion, then, is this – that it's possible to venerate your ancestors without being forever beholden to their work.'

'What do you mean?'

Gormdal gestured to the dishes around him. 'First get something in your belly, for no masterwork was ever fashioned by a duardin on an empty stomach, and then you can come with me.' He grinned as he stuffed something gelatinous into his mouth and then spoke around it. 'I'm going to show you something.'

Gormdal led him down a flight of stairs that ran behind the back of a farrier's shop and towards a cellar. The sound of struck hammer and the blast of furnaces rang through the stones. It was a comforting and familiar din that, despite the Syari reputation and all the evidence of their craftsmanship, had been strangely absent from Ar-Ennascath until then. However they shaped the work of their hands and their hearts, it was in some other fashion to the heat and beating of the Ironweld. This, however, felt familiar. In spite of the light that, even as they ventured underground, beat from every surface, it felt like coming home.

They came to an iron-bound door. The air was warm. Gormdal pushed the door open and entered.

A huge golden forge spitting fire was set into the far wall. Its bell-shaped central body was in the shape of an ancestor's head similar to that which Mikazrin carried with him, albeit on a much grander scale and with small differences in style. The beard was emblazoned with glowing runes and framed the furnace in the figure's mouth. Black smoke rose like a crest from the chimney in its crown.

A single well-muscled duardin, naked from the waist up, tended the flames. With a curt nod to Gormdal that looked almost like a bow, and a most curious look, he withdrew without a word.

'A magmic battleforge,' said Gormdal, sticking his thumbs under his belt and rocking back onto his heels. 'It belongs to the battle-smiths of the Thungur lodge. You may have seen them at the festival. The Lumineth do love Lunarest fyresteel. They think it quaint, but don't tell the Thungur I said so or they might not let us borrow their forge.'

'Borrow?' Mikazrin backed away from the fire-breathing idol, so different from the precision furnaces and kilns of the Ironweld Arsenal. 'Why would one of Grimnir's sons loan you a forge?'

'Because I asked.'

'And who are you to them?'

'Much as I am to you. No more and no less.' The old duardin gave a strange smile, all black teeth and orange shadows in the flickering light. It was the first time Mikazrin had seen shadows since he had left Chamon, and the sight of them startled him. 'Do you find that odd?'

'The Fyreslayers and the Ironweld may share an ancestor, but there's no kinship between us.' Mikazrin looked up at the glowering godhead. The heat of it, greater than any forge in his home city, made his eyeballs ache and the ends of his beard curl. 'We're cousins who seldom speak and have nothing left in common.'

'But we're all of us duardin. We've a way of remembering that when the moment is right.'

'And that moment is now?'

Gormdal laughed and clapped both hands on Mikazrin's back. 'To get one over on the *elgi*, it is always that moment.'

'I don't know that word. What does it mean?'

'It's very old. But don't think on that now.'

Gently but inexorably, both hands still on Mikazrin's shoulders, the old master guided the engineer towards the bright, hot mouth of the magmaforge.

'Take out your handicraft, youngling.'

As though hypnotised by the roaring flame and the old duardin's voice, Mikazrin unpacked his telescope. He looked down at it. Then up into the blistering heat of the forge.

'This is too delicate an instrument for such a workplace. It won't be bettered by the heat of a forge, nor by hammer and tongs.'

Gormdal smiled. His face shone red in the furnace heat and his eyes gleamed like precious metals. 'You spoke before of jewels, of gold and ornament. You'll not better this work with those either. There's beauty to be had in such things, but only in the proper place, and nothing conveys beauty to a duardin than a thing built to do a task and do it well. A shirt of mail that won't break under a blow. A perfectly cast cannon that will never mischarge in a thousand firings. Those things are beautiful, if you know your craft, and trust me, the Syari do know their craft. But they take their inspiration from their realmstone and from their light. We're duardin. The spirit of our craft comes from some-place much deeper.'

He tapped on his beard where it smothered his broad chest. 'It's in our blood and it's in our bones. The pure need to *make* things. It's in our soul. Isn't it? Go on, youngling, feel it. Don't look to imitate the aelves with their fancy stones and their pretty metals. *Better* them. Amaze them with something they've never seen before, and with all the aetherquartz of the Ten Paradises can scarce imagine. You're a duardin engineer. Impress the Syari with what that really means.'

As he spoke he turned fully to the forge.

'Think, youngling. Find the purpose in what you mean to create and bring it out. Forget what your ancestors did or what you think they might wish of you now, and feel what *you* would have the Maker fashion through your hands.'

Mikazrin looked down into his hands. The tube's brass casing rippled red in the flames. The outermost lenses in the aperture glinted.

He felt a stirring in his chest. Something almost spiritual. An enlightenment, but one that was all his own and beholden to no one else, captured not from light and realm magic but from some quintessence of his own heritage. His beard tingled as if with a divine charge as he looked up into the fire.

The fire of making.

'Yes. I think I see it.'

Gormdal clapped him on the back. Mikazrin barely felt it. He was too deep in thought.

The old duardin asked him a question.

'Not long,' he muttered, scarcely listening as he bent to work. 'This won't take long at all.'

* * *

Several dozen aelves crowded around the table. Those at the front leant forwards to examine the object more closely, those at the back standing to their fullest height on tip-toes to see over their heads.

'What is it?' asked one. 'In its clarity and elegance it speaks to me of the Zenith.'

'But see,' argued his companion. 'See how the light moves through. It does not simply pass through unhindered but is borne and changed by its journey – plainly it is the very embodiment of the River.'

'Clearly it bears the character of both. An element of the Wind, then, is what it must be.'

'And yet it is solid,' a third aelf mused. 'A crystal offered up from the heart of the Mountain, although of a kind I have never before seen in Syar or heard of existing anywhere in the Ten Paradises. Please tell me, Master Mikazrin, from which exotic lands do you find your stone?'

Mikazrin stood with his arms folded over his beard, too proud to beam as broadly as he might have liked, but well pleased regardless as the Lumineth took their turns to *oooh* and *aaah* over the array of polished crystal lenses that he had set across his table.

'May I hold it, Master Mikazrin?' asked one.

Mikazrin nodded gravely.

The aelf picked up the lens with inordinate care, marvelling at the interplay of Hyshian light with worked Chamonic crystal. 'Is it jewel or instrument?' he wondered. 'Art or craft? I know not.'

Beside him, standing over an entirely neglected display of ornate metalwork and decorative blades, Anasrith of Ithalin crossed his arms over his gilded robes and glowered.

'It looks like a simple thing to me.'

'And therein lies its beauty,' said its admirer, turning the lens under the light, before a growing crowd of impatient onlookers forced him to surrender it back to the table.

Mikazrin turned to Anasrith and grinned. 'I should probably thank you for helping me secure this stall next to yours,' he said, unable to resist. 'You might learn something.'

The artisan bristled. 'Perhaps. If the odour of your soot and toil were not such a distraction to learning. But then, perhaps not, I say. There are not the words in your tongue to describe what aelven minds might think and their hands work. I could learn more of worth by waiting on the enlightenment of the Wind.'

'I hear a great number of fancy words, and naught in them but the soreness of a bad loser.'

'If there was less hair in your ears then perhaps you would understand simple speech better. But to look at the carpet growing from your face it is clearly too vain a hope.'

Mikazrin pulled the volleypistol from his belt and snarled. 'Leave the beard out of it.'

With a flick of the wrist, Anasrith snapped out his gold-leaf fan. The sharpened points of its sunmetal ribs glinted in the Hysh light.

The watching Lumineth murmured excitedly, as though this was a tremendous diversion to an otherwise tedious annual festival. From across the street, an incredibly muscular pair of Thungur Fyreslayers bellowed encouragements.

'Now, now,' said Gormdal, appearing from the crowd behind them both, putting one tanned, fatherly hand on Mikazrin's shoulder and the other on Anasrith's back. 'The aelves have quick hearts as are too readily aggrieved, unlike the duardin who will shrug off most any insult, unless they are determined to be affronted, and so are wont to speak idly in jest. Naught was meant by it, Master Athaer.'

The aelf hesitated, as though searching for the hidden slight or alternate meaning in the old duardin's words and appearing quite flummoxed at discovering none.

He snapped his fan blade closed. Mikazrin grumbled and

holstered his pistol. Half the crowd muttered in disappointment. The other half whispered its approval.

'Good,' said Gormdal, and chuckled. 'Always have duardin and aelves found ways to make less of one another. Which is as it should be. Grungni and Teclis are as alike to one another as any good rival ought to be. Where would any of us, fighter or maker or thinker, be without someone to better?' He glanced up to the taller aelf. 'Without another rung on the Teclian Ladder to climb?'

'Who are you, duardin?' said Anasrith. 'So wise in the hearts of aelves?'

'Just a wanderer,' said Gormdal.

'In Ithalin I am considered a master of my art. But with you I almost feel the thrill of being a new apprentice, starting anew on my journey of enlightenment. There is so much I could learn from you.'

'Aye, I'd wager there is.' He picked up one of the lenses from Mikazrin's table and presented it to the artisan. His eyes twinkled with Hysh light, shone and infinitely refracted through Chamonic crystal. 'I'd wager you've a lot to learn from each other.'

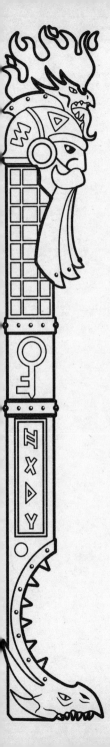

PROTECT
WITH HONOUR

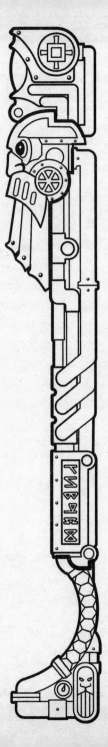

'In the ember days of the Age of Myth, the forefathers of the Kharadron turned their backs on the old ways. They forsook the mountain fastnesses that their old gods had taught their ancestors how to keep, and instead sought prospects and safety in the infinite skies of the Mortal Realms.

'Many of those old strongholds fell to Chaos in their time, but a few, a handful, better and more cleverly concealed from the foe, survived. So it was too for their gods. They still walked the Mortal Realms that their children had abandoned, and they never turned their backs on the Kharadron...'

In spite of the threat of attack, Admiral Trem Brokkenthrom expected the fleet captains and the representatives of its guilds and unions to join him at his table. It was a tradition, and so he insisted upon it. Tradition, insofar as Brynt Gambsson could reckon the admiral's worldview, was not merely something the admiral respected: it was something he was owed.

Metal clanked dully onto metal, the magnetic surface of the admiral's table grabbing on to the base of the tankard as he concluded another lengthy and unprompted toast to himself. The admiral grinned expansively over the dented ancestor masks and wheezing arkanaut suits gathered about his table, settling on the one unfamiliar mask in his company. There was a malicious twinkle in his eye.

'Gambsson, is it?' His voice was cracked and low, the growl of an old model endrin with something dangerously out of alignment.

Brynt drew the tubing from his own tankard and slotted it back into his skysuit's fluid pouch in the proper way. 'Brynt Gambsson,' he replied. 'Grundpilot First Rate, Captain of the *Sistromm*.'

Unthinkingly, he neglected to add *admiral* or *sir*. Trem was no admiral. Not in any properly Codified sense. Scuttlebutt was he'd been passed over three times in a row at Musterpress, and had gone on to command an aether-tanker that he'd since bolted a couple of great skyhooks to, painted gold, and reclassed as a dreadnought. He wore the sky-blue undersuit and golden armour of Barak-Zilfin with an overbearing pride, while the Sky-Fleets Guild citations drilled into his breastplate – according, again, to ship rumour – had been stolen from the wreckage of a Barak-Zon ironclad beached on a mountainside on the borders of Ayadah. His hair – for he made a point of never covering his head while aboard his own ship, regardless of altitude – was a shocking, almost painful white. There was a joke around the fleet that he bleached it every day under powerful aether-lamps so as to appear older and more distinguished than he truly was. This was something his cabin mate would neither confirm nor deny.

Brynt did not know if any of it was true, but he knew that everyone in the fleet believed it.

The admiral smiled, like someone killing time while they interpreted a joke. 'That's a little grand, isn't it, *captain*? What do you call the other duardin on that tub?'

'I call him Hikkram,' said Brynt, straight-faced behind his ancestor mask. Several of the captains produced short rumbles of laughter from theirs.

The admiral gave a crooked grin. 'And what's become of Grund-Commander Strond? Should I be concerned?'

'He said I could do with a proper meal.'

'Another duardin might be offended at having a lieutenant sent to his table.'

'He wanted to be on deck. Just in case.'

'I can't argue with that, I suppose. It is what I'm paying him for. I worried for a moment that a table full of sky-captains was too poor a company for him.'

Brynt frowned. 'I don't follow you.'

'The Grund-Commander is a wealthy duardin.'

'I'm sure you've a share or two stashed away with the Union of Usurers and Bankers.'

'I don't like to boast,' said the admiral, implicitly adding that Hysh was gloomy at that moment and Aqshy wet. 'But I'm not a senior commander of the Grundstok Company. Why, if I had a garrison in every port and the full monopoly over the fleet protection business then I'd be scouring the sky-lanes for Grungni. I'd be looking to buy him out.'

'If you're implying the Company's fees are anything but competitive–'

The admiral laughed. It was a bitter laugh, the kind that always came at someone else's expense and this time it was Brynt's. The admiral never paid for anything from his own pocket.

'I'm just teasing you, Gambsson. Where's your sense of humour? As a matter of fact I heartily approve of the Grundcorps' business practices. There are times even I look back at my younger self and curse the beardling for pursuing the dream of a career in the sky-fleets instead of enlisting with the Company. That's where the real rewards are, eh? Better than chasing the mother lode at the end of the strahlstrom.'

He chuckled, stroking the bleached white strands of his beard.

'The perfect hindsight of old age. You can train your nose, hone your instinct, learn how to read the signs. You can haggle yourself a controlling share in the fastest ship, recruit an eager and experienced crew, and more often than most times you'll still come up with naught. Except perhaps an angry harkraken for your troubles.' The admiral gave another laugh. 'Which goes to prove my point, doesn't it, Gambsson? Win or lose, we still need to pay the Grundcorps.'

He reached across the table for the iron-bodied pitcher and poured himself another full measure of beer.

'Has the Grundcorps ever considered adding a clause to its contracts – indemnity against angry shareholders?'

Genuine laughter rumbled around the table at that. Even Brynt found himself smiling at the image the admiral conjured.

'You'd make a killing,' he added.

'I doubt you've had much need for that particular clause,' said Brynt.

'I've made some good investments, it's true. It's more than just luck. The real trick was realising early on that aether-gold is for fools. There are fortunes to be made, don't get me wrong. I'll harvest the seam if I should happen upon it. But the risks, the chances, the competition… better to be chasing your riches where no other Kharadron is looking.'

Tankard in one ostentatiously begemmed gauntlet, the admiral settled the other over the strongbox unsubtly positioned on the table before him. The hubbub of conversation that had been the background to their meal until then fell suddenly away. To Brynt, the silence seemed to be filled with threats and whispers, all of them emanating from that box. Arkanaut suits rumbled. The converted tanker's endrins chuntered and iron bones creaked. Shadows brushed against the hardened glass of the porthole covers and slid across, but all eyes were for the box. *Don't count your shares until they're weighed* was a well-known saying. But the admiral had an abiding need for his cleverness and wealth to be recognised by those he wanted very much to think of as his peers.

'Who here wants to see it? Who wants to see what it's all about? What the *drakking* aelves won't let us have away?'

The captains traded looks. One, the captain of the *Klinkharn*, about whom the best that could be said was that he was more trust-worthy than his half-brother who profiteered for Barak-Urbaz, raised a gauntleted hand. Others followed suit. Not wanting to be the odd one left out, Brynt grunted and added his vote.

'The ayes have it.' The admiral grinned, and beckoned to his lodemaster, a hefty old sailor with a ring of keys dangling from an ample gut that strained in turn against his vulcanised skysuit.

The duardin stepped forward and unlocked the box. He opened it.

Brynt joined every Kharadron around him in leaning across the table to see what was inside.

'What is it?' asked the *Klinkharn*'s captain.

'By all means, Thorngrume, have a closer look.'

The sky-captain looked uncertainly around him, then reached his hand into the box. *'Draz!'* He pulled his hand back as though it had been bitten or stung. Several of the other officers startled. A few pulled weapons and trained them on the box. One had his volleypistol pointed at Thorngrume, just in case.

Brynt felt a whispering in his skull and a curious itch under the skin of his hands. To his surprise, his own sidearm was drawn and in his hand. He felt a terrible urge to discharge it, and he did not really mind at whom. He stared at it for a moment, and then with a great effort slid it back into its holster.

The admiral laughed. Never at his own expense.

Brynt peered into the box. Inside, nestled in a bed of wire wool and padded gauze, was a roughly triangular piece of ruddy brass or copper. It was difficult to tell which without touching it and Brynt had decided that he did not want to touch it. It looked as though it had been ripped violently from some larger piece. Stress marks and deformations accounted for the entire sliver. A single droplet of duardin blood now covered most of its surface. For a moment, the imperfections in the surface seemed to cause the blood to flow into a shape. Lines split off from the centre and curled. Like a hieroglyph. Or an aelven rune.

Brynt raised his hand to adjust the lenses in his helmet, sensitive to aether disturbances and Ulguanite anomalies, but before he was lowering his hands again the shape was gone. Just a bloody thumbprint on an otherwise unspectacular lump of metal. And a thumping in Brynt's head. He looked around the table. He wondered if the other Kharadron felt it too.

Thorngrume, meanwhile, had torn off his gauntlet and was staring at his hand. In spite of armour and undersuit, a thin line of blood crossed his palm from thumb to little finger. He turned the hand over, horror rasping through the tubes of his breather mask.

'What is this?'

'I know what the aelves think it is,' said the admiral. 'Superstitious freaks. But I found it first and if they want it then they and their queen are going to have to come find me in Barak-Zilfin and pay through their dainty little noses for it.'

'We should toss it overboard,' said Thorngrume with unusual vehemence, nursing his bloodied hand.

The admiral snorted. 'Don't you start as well. The navigators will have found the final lighthouse in a day or two, I'm sure of it. Any day now and we'll be back in the sky-lanes of Chamon. Perhaps even as early as tomorrow. In the meantime, I don't need to remind anyone here that you're all under contract.' He reached across the table and closed the strongbox.

Brynt could still feel it there.

While the lodemaster dutifully locked the box and secreted away the key, the admiral clapped his hands together as if to forcibly alter the mood. 'Now!' He grinned. 'Who's ready for pudding?'

The *Han-Gorak*, as Admiral Brokkenthrom's flagship was registered with the fleetmaster's office in Barak-Ziflin – though Brynt was aware of at least one other name – was a pregnant whale of a ship. Her pot belly enclosed vast cargo holds, originally for the transport of volatile aether-gold, but now for whatever commodity her master saw profit in. Every one of her three stout masts and the thrumming endrin orbs mounted atop them was needed to keep her buoyant. She could have been the match of any ship of the line that sailed under Barak-Zilfin colours except, of course, in manoeuvrability and speed. Great skyhooks had been installed forward and aft, and sky cannons were fixed to the gunwale every gross of beard-lengths. Her iron skin was thick, her crew strength was twice that of any other ship in the fleet.

Most of that crew was up on her deck, standing at the rails with scopes and glasses and searching for a glimmer of a lighthouse beacon or a star to guide them. A few had climbed to the crow's nests atop the endrins for a better view, but it was a curiosity of the realms that magic became more forceful and volatile the further one went from its centre. This was as true of the realm's zenith as it was of realm's edge, and the spotters' view of the shadow-paths of Nakarth was, if anything, even worse than that of their crew-mates on deck.

Brynt clumped onto the mooring prongs where a handful of Company machinesmiths had their work cut out beating the battle damage out of a pair of gunhaulers. The rest were all out on patrol.

Sistromm bobbed under line in one of the flagship's slipways. The gunhauler was a stocky little craft with the pilot's seat recessed under the main gun and the gunner's cupola. It didn't leave a lot of room for a Kharadron on top, but duardin had a famously high discomfort threshold. And it wasn't built to be flown for more than an hour or two at a stretch.

Brynt clambered up to the cockpit and wriggled his way in under the support housing of the aethershot carbine. He strapped himself in and powered up the endrin. Where the *Han-Gorak*'s buoyancy furnaces emitted a tectonic, deck-rattling rumble, *Sistromm*'s was a sweet purr. Gem lights flickered to life across his dashboard, the shade of Ulgu banished from the cockpit by Kharadron science. He ran his gauntlets lovingly over the dashboard. Like all Kharadron things it had been made with practicality in mind. The back panelling was brushed steel and aluminium: lightweight, clean and strong. The dials were brass, sturdy but simple to work, and thus simple as well to replace without need for specialist tools and forges should the need arise. The colour contrast also made it easier for a pilot to read them at a glance, a feature that had been further improved upon with the addition of tiny bulbs illuminated by cells of aether and plated with thin layers of quartz. It had not been made to be beautiful, but it was beautiful, simply by being what it was.

Brynt looked up from his pre-flight reveries as a duardin he did not recognise, wispy white hair poking out from behind his helmet's beard shield, stomped across the weather deck, past the machinesmiths, and made for *Sistromm*'s air slip. He had, of all the outdated kit he might have boasted, an axe strapped across his back and was eating flaked lumprey from a tin with his fingers.

'Who are you?' said Brynt.

'Wytskarn,' belched the other, tossing the tin over the side and licking the metal fingers of his gauntlet.

'Where's Hikkram?'

Wytskarn shrugged. 'Grounded for the rest of the day. He's overrun his guild-allowed flying hours for the week.'

'Is this a joke?'

'I never joke about Company regulations,' the older duardin grunted. 'That would be a violation of sub-artycle eighteen.'

'Wytskarn's an odd name.'

'My mother gave it to me. Or was it my father?' The Kharadron shook his head, then shrugged. 'I've been billeted on Jonti's bucket to now. You know old Jonti. Anyway, it's all been arranged with the Grund-Commander.'

'I thought I knew all the Grundcorps in Brokkenthrom's fleet.'

'I have one of those common faces. I look like everyone.' Without waiting on ceremony, the duardin clambered up and squeezed his greater bulk into the elevated gunner's cupola. An arm thrust out over the sky cannon and waggled an unstoppered flask half-filled with some astringent grog. 'Quick nip before we're off?'

Brynt recoiled from the smell. 'I took on enough at the admiral's table to fill an ironclad. If only to bear his company. But I'd rather keep the last of my wits about me now.'

'Suit yourself.'

'Buckle in,' said Brynt. 'We're already overdue on patrol.'

The shadow-paths were formless and grey. The air that penetrated the imperfect seals of Brynt's helmet felt like nothing. It tasted of nothing. A stringy umbral substance cobwebbed his lenses, up until the moment he made any kind of decision to look at it directly whereupon it evaporated like mist. He was accustomed to it by now. They had all become experts. The gunhaulers and frigates flew with their running lamps lit and the shields drawn from their endrins so that they glowed.

It was a flotilla of lanterns that sailed through the mists of Ulgu.

With a firm hand on the stick, Brynt swung the gunhauler to starboard. The little ship veered over the lead ship's dorsal axis, levelling out a few hundred yards off her starboard side and under her keel line. Wytskarn tracked the darkness with the cannon, back and forth, on its narrow forward arc.

'Anything?' Brynt yelled.

'What?'

Brynt puffed out his cheeks. 'I said, do you see anything?'

'Nothing I'd be prepared to swear to before an admiral's court with my hand on the Maldralta Code.'

Brynt nodded to himself, saying nothing. He knew exactly what the other duardin meant. He pulled back on the stick and played with the foot pedals. The endrin sputtered and the gunhauler felt briefly weightless as they lost speed. The wind dropped away, and they were scudding backwards as the great behemoths of the fleet ground across their eyeline.

'I wish they'd just come and try something,' Brynt muttered loudly.

'Careful what you wish for,' said Wytskarn.

'Is that a ratified amendment I'm unfamiliar with?'

'Would be. If I'd had any hand in drafting the Code.'

'When the aelves attack I at least know for certain that we *are* somewhere.'

'We're somewhere. Stands to reason.'

'The admiral hasn't a clue where we are.'

'That's a worry for the Nav-League.'

Brynt snorted. 'If you'd seen the thing that Brokkenthrom pulled out of that castle in Nakarth you'd be worrying too.'

'Then I'm glad I didn't. I disapprove strongly of worrying where it's not my business to.'

'The admiral thinks it's going to make him rich.'

'Good on the admiral!'

'But I'm with Thorngrume. I'd toss it right over the sterncastle rail and cut my losses here.'

'What?'

Brynt took a deep breath. 'I *said*–'

He paused as the dials on his dashboard nudged their needles into higher ranges. The endrin noise increased noticeably in pitch. The sky rumbled.

'Weather coming in?' he wondered aloud.

'Pfft,' said Wytskarn, and Brynt knew his gunner was right.

He turned to port, orienting himself by the position of the *Han-Gorak* as Wytskarn suddenly cried out '*Drakkol!*' followed by the hard, hammer-pulse report of a sky cannon opening fire.

Brynt hadn't yet glimpsed what his gunner had seen. The pulse of the aethershot was all the confirmation of danger he needed. He pulled the stick hard to the left. *Sistromm* banked so sharply she almost capsized and stalled. At the same time a mouth larger than the gunhauler's entire body chomped down where the endrin had just been. Displaced air, foul with smoke, rocked the little ship and almost tipped her over again. Brynt stabilised with a firm hand on the rudder and some quick work with the pedals.

'Dragon!' he yelled.

'I can see it's a bloody dragon!' Wytskarn barked back.

The dragon's jaws slammed shut a second time. A turbine tore away from the side of the endrin. Teeth sank into the metal casing. The support stanchion squealed and bent. Wytskarn pulled out a sidearm and blazed away at the monster's head. He was aiming for its eyes, but the salvo chipped and sparked harmlessly off black scales.

The stanchion snapped, and suddenly the gunhauler was free. Brynt's stomach rolled. He threw *Sistromm* into another turn, this time to starboard, and the dragon's bulk swept over them.

It went on sweeping for half a minute.

'Have us about it,' Wytskarn yelled.

'We're hanging on to our endrin by half a rig and a prayer. Push it too hard now and we'll lose it.'

The gunhauler shook into a wide turn, coming back onto the dragon's tail. An aelf lord, armoured all in black and with a fluttering cape, sat bestride the monster's long neck. The aelf looked over his shoulder. He appeared to sneer.

'Not on my watch, you don't,' said Wytskarn, and stitched the air with aethershot bursts.

The aelf lord ducked back, and the dragon rolled across the bullet hose and out of their arc. The beast was agile, in spite of its ungodly size.

Brynt took *Sistromm* after it. They swept under the missile pods and bay doors of the *Han-Gorak* and up the other side. The running lamps of the fleet wheeled across the sky.

A brighter flash, a sudden *boom*, aether-gold igniting and something massive exploding. A second dragon roared. Gunfire blossomed in the darkness.

Sistromm complained as Brynt pushed her to match the dragon's turns. Wytskarn fired again.

'Stay on the beast!' he yelled.

'I'm doing my best! We have to keep in sight of the flagship.' Behind them, the *Han-Gorak* was just then running out her guns and scrambling the last of the gunhaulers not yet aloft. 'We'll never find her again if we don't.'

'What?'

'I said–'

'Never mind that now. Bring us atop the drake and drop a Grudgesettler on its spine.'

Brynt gritted his teeth. What was it with gunners? They always expected miracles of their pilots.

'I'm taking us back.'

'Hold her steady!'

'We're too far from the fleet already.'

'One more shot!'

The aelf lord glanced over the fluted pauldron of his shoulder armour. The dragon bellowed, trimmed a wing, and then swept across to ram them. Had the monster hit then, it would have surely smashed the gunhauler with ease. Brynt slammed his feet down on the pedals, shuddering the gunhauler into an ungainly climb that lifted her over the dragon's back.

'Now!' Wytskarn bellowed. 'Now! Bombs away!'

'Too late!' The dragon was already flapping ahead of them and roaring.

Wytskarn shouted in frustration and opened up with one last burst from his cannon. The hail of aethershot punched through the dragon's hard black scales, glittered through meat and muscle, and then puffed out the other side of its enormous body as if from a large cloud. The dragon and the aelf lord upon its back came apart like a cloud shape in a strong wind.

Wytskarn gawped.

Brynt felt cold. Cursing, he broke them off.

'That's it, we're heading right...'

His words trailed off. He stared into the vast night, the endless cloud and dark of the shadow-paths that now lay between them and realm's edge. The fleet was gone. There was no fleet.

'...back.'

Brynt shut everything off but the endrin. It grumbled with just enough power to achieve buoyancy in the thin air. The stricken gunhauler bobbed like an ocean buoy with every breath of wind. The running lamps were off. The dashboard controls were dark. Ulgu was already starting to creep back into the cockpit. His own endrin, not twelve beard-lengths up, was a vague orb and a metallic hum. With everything off, he pulled himself out of the cockpit and climbed the undamaged stanchion to the endrin.

There, he secured his skysuit to the circumference rail with a length of thick rope and some heavy-duty clips. With the gauntleted tips of his fingers he inspected the damage to the endrin. One finger disappeared into an enormous puncture in the metal casing. When he withdrew it, it shimmered, brighter than gold. He cursed.

No worse than he'd expected. No better than he'd hoped.

'The endrin's leaking all right.'

Disconnecting the safety harness, he free-climbed the rest of the way up the rig, using bolts, rivets and tooth-gouges for hand-holds until he reached the top. There, he sat, clips and line clattering, his heart thumping from the hard climb and the danger, and peered into the darkness around him. He'd been hoping for a better view. But there was nothing there to see. Just cloud and shadow. He cursed again.

'Anything?' Wytskarn called up.

'Nothing.'

'Can you fix the endrin?'

'Wouldn't do us any good. We've enough aether left to hold us steady here for a day or two. We could fly for a bit if we don't push too much speed out of her.' Brynt scowled. 'What I wouldn't pay for an endrinrigger's first year apprentice right now.'

'Maybe we ought to put down?'

'We'll never get up again.'

'Any idea where we are?'

'I couldn't tell you where we *were*.'

There came a rustle from the cupola as Wytskarn unfolded a large map.

'Put that away,' Brynt yelled down. 'You've not been certified.'

'Are you worried we'll get more lost?'

Climbing back down as quickly as he could, hooking himself back up once he was as far as the guide rail – he was never so hasty as to overlook proper safety regulations – he dumped himself back into the pilot's couch. At the same time as he was beginning to unclip himself, Wytskarn had finished misfolding the map and was stuffing it under his seat. He stood up, making the under-powered craft wobble perilously from side to side, and leant over Brynt's side to root about in the stowage pockets.

Brynt swatted at his arm. 'Get back over before we capsize.'

'Where's *The Book*?'

'Sit down. This is enough your fault as it is.'

'Tromm!' Wytskarn sat back down, but did so with a small pocket ledger that he had drawn from the seat's back sleeve. He muttered to himself as he flicked through its brass-edged pages.

The Book, as it was approvingly called by the Grundpilots who relied upon it, was a detailed log of weather anomalies, navigational charts and other assorted curios and hazards describing every known and half-known sky-path within a given region of the Mortal Realms. This was the fourteenth printing of the Nav-League's Ulguanite edition. Volume Forty-Six. Nakarth and Misthåvn.

'Give it up,' said Brynt. 'There are no markers to be found. If the admiral couldn't guide his own flagship through the shadow-paths then neither can you.'

Wytskarn raised a finger from the page and, with his eyes still on the tabulated pages of *The Book*, indicated an unprepossessing patch of gloomy cloud to starboard. 'I think we should go that way.'

'Why that way?'

The older Kharadron shrugged and closed *The Book*. 'A feeling. An instinct. Call it duardin intuition.'

'I'd rather stake my life and ship on duardin science.'

'Would crashing over some other patch of Nakarth be so awful? Are you looking forward to crashing onto this bit for some reason I ought to know about?'

Brynt muttered under his breath but his gunner had a point. They'd get nowhere by staying put.

'When we get back to the *Han-Gorak*, Hikkram and I are having stern words about the proper spirit of the Code.'

Wytskarn chuckled and strapped himself back in.

'Thirty minutes, mind,' said Brynt. 'Thirty minutes and then

I'm setting us down. While we still have fuel to do it and end up in one piece. After that, we'll just have to try and make it to the Realmgate ourselves on foot.'

'Might take a while.'

Brynt decided not to answer. It would probably take forever.

Sistromm rattled through sky as black as smoke. Strands of storm-dark cirrus buffeted and snaked across her cockpit and the two Kharadron sat brooding and silent in their respective seats. To Brynt's instruments they looked like nothing at all, except for everything they could not possibly be. There were times when he would look up and see what appeared to be a flotilla of sky-ships or an angry harkraken, or even a bearded face emerging from a cloud bank. One time he even imagined seeing Barak-Zilfin itself, its gun-turrets and endrin towers perfectly described in cloud and shadow up to the moment that he turned his head towards it. He gave it no mind. Or told himself that he did not. Ulgu was a place of obfuscation, not revelation. They all knew it. He trusted his instruments more than he did his own eyes and instincts, and his instruments told him there was nothing there.

Wytskarn hummed a few bars of a sky-shanty under his breath. It was not one that Brynt recognised, and he had sailed under every sky in the eight realms. He was tempted to reach up to the gunner's cupola and throttle him. The Code was very strict on corporal punishment, requiring a signed affidavit from a direct superior, but Brynt was prepared to overlook the stipulation just then. It would probably be worth it. The prospect of a court martial seemed unlikely.

'Just a little bit more,' Wytskarn muttered.

'It's been thirty minutes.'

'Twenty-eight by my count.'

'This is what got us into this mess to begin with.'

'Two minutes more,' Wytskarn growled back, a tone that Brynt had not heard the affable Kharadron take before. 'Thirty is what was agreed to. Are you a Kharadron that keeps to the letter of his bargains or aren't you?'

Brynt was stung into silence. He turned away, chastened and strangely ashamed, and caught what appeared to be a faint flicker of light as his lenses moved across its path. When the source then disappeared, he dismissed it as another illusion. But then it winked again, in exactly the same spot as before. He sat up, still half of a mind to let it go unremarked until–

'What's that?' said Wytskarn.

'You see it too?' Brynt was relieved. 'I thought I was imagining things.'

The light blinked out again, regular as duardin-built clockwork.

'It's the lighthouse,' Wytskarn cried, thumping the metal fuselage in triumph. 'It's got to be.'

'How in Grungni's sooty beard did you ever find it?'

'All in the charts, lad.'

'Are you saying the admiral can't read a map?'

'That's speculation above my contractual level.'

'We could plot our own route to the Realmgate from here,' Brynt said, thinking quickly. 'There should be spare fuel and some basic tools aboard the lighthouse. Assuming the lighthouse master is abiding by Company regulations.'

'Is that what you want to do now? Go home?'

'You still want to try and find the fleet?'

'You don't?'

'It's impossible!'

'You thought this was impossible.'

'And it is! A miracle is what this is. And now you want another one. I'm not a religious duardin, so I'm not sure exactly how it works, but I'm pretty sure that's pushing it.'

'It's what the admiral's paying us for.'

'As *Sistromm*'s captain I'm invoking *ungraz throlt*. The admiral's led us to a lost cause and our contract with him is hereby nullified.'

'You think that'll hold water with the codewrights of the Sky-Fleets Guild in Barak-Zilfin?'

'If ours is the only story they ever hear of it, it will.'

A sharp intake of breath rasped through the other Kharadron's filters. *'Kazar valrhank.'*

'Don't you go quoting the Company motto at me.'

For a long minute more, the two stared at one another from either side of the big carbine barrel. Brynt gave in first.

'Do you really think you can find them again?'

'I've no great wish to be shipwrecked without profit either, believe it or not.'

Brynt scowled and turned to the controls. He gripped the stick as though tempted to snap it from the box and toss it overboard. To his surprise, he found himself trusting his gunner's better judgement.

'If we don't find them then we won't have fuel enough to land.'

'I wouldn't have wanted to land here anyway,' said Wytskarn. 'There's naught down there but aelves. And cruel, bitter aelves at that.'

A string of lights climbed out of the dark sky in constellations, the familiar and welcome outlines of a Kharadron sky-fleet in the line of battle. His elation was brief. Aethershot traces and air supremacy mines punctuated the darkness with pulsing lines and brilliant waves. Dragonfire swabbed the duardin vessels' iron decks like something illuminated from a retired arkanaut's nightmare.

'We found it,' he breathed.

'What's left of it,' said Wytskarn.

The *Klinkharn* was gone. And the *Grimnyn Az*. They were short a gunhauler.

Black dragons and their lordly aelven riders swooped and harried the embattled vessels, a dozen strong, and flocked by daemon-winged aelf women like gunship carriers scaled in black. Even while Brynt watched, a host of the winged aelves descended on the *Stukker*, and while the frigate's arkanaut crew and Grundcorps left her guns silent to fight the harpies off, a black dragon spewed noxious black fumes across her deck. Even from such a distance and surrounded by thunder Brynt could hear the screams. While the crew burned, the dragon tore the ship apart. A handful of Kharadron got themselves to sky-rigs and jumped. But not many. Brynt watched the *Stukker* disintegrate, finally losing its grip on its endrin and dropping like a thing overlooked by the gods of the realms until that moment.

Brynt swore, and meant it in a way he never had before.

'Khinerai Lifetakers,' said Wytskarn. 'Daughters of Khaine. And, if I'm not mistaken, their brethren of old from the Orders Serpentis. These were their lands, you know. Long ago. Before Chaos drove them from the Thirteen Dominions and into the welcoming arms of Sigmaron. They were noble creatures once. Ungrateful *thaggi*.' The Grundpilot's ancestor mask issued a grumbling sound. 'Long is the list of Grudges owed to these particular lineages of aelf-kind. Longer than my beard and yours tied together.'

'You know more about it than I do.'

'Mayhap. Mayhap I do know a little.'

'What do the Daughters of Khaine want with the admiral's treasure?'

'Maybe they're under the impression that it's not the admiral's?'

Brynt glanced at the dashboard. 'The tanks are as good as empty. We'll be no good to anyone in the air. We need to put down.'

'Then take us in, lad. Nice and slow.' Wytskarn pointed. 'There's the flagship!'

The *Han-Gorak* had never looked more imposing or more

ponderous than she did then, surrounded by enemies, her escorts crippled and aflame. Her long deck crackled like a string of fire crackers in the Ulguanite night, decksweepers and fumigators just barely keeping the huge capital ship free of glaive-wielding she-aelves.

Brynt took *Sistromm* in, gritting his teeth as she rattled her way through a wide grimace of a turn around the battlefield and through.

A Khinerai aelf swooped onto them with a gut-twisting shriek. She dropped from starboard, outside the arc of *Sistromm*'s main gun, and far too small and agile to be brought to bear in any event. Brynt ducked his head as her thrusting spear scraped across the undamaged side of the endrin stanchion, drawing sparks. The Khinerai flapped back like a bat that had just struck a glass screen. Wytskarn drew his handgun and let off a pair of quick shots that both missed. The Khinerai wheeled and looped back. There were two more coming with her.

They were practically on top of the flagship now. The battle was all around them. Bigger ships and richer targets were everywhere, but *Sistromm* was starting to draw notice all the same.

'Can you keep them off us for just a minute?'

'No.'

'Not even one?

'Not even.'

Brynt glanced up the gunner's cupola and snorted. He was not even sure what was so funny. 'Well, do what you can.'

'Aye.'

The endrin gave a splutter. The gunhauler dropped a dozen beard-lengths before recovering about half of the lost altitude and levelling out.

'*Skarrengit*,' Brynt swore.

'Was that what I think it was?'

Brynt checked the fuel gauge. The gunhauler chugged determinedly on, but with an increasingly thirsty sound and a precipitous loss of speed. They were also, though it was not as immediately obvious, already losing height. 'Aye. It probably was.'

'Are we going to make it?'

Brynt peered out over the fuselage, over its golden trim and to the sky below it. The *Han-Gorak*'s running lamps had grown paradoxically dimmer as closeness spread them further and further apart. Her deck had become correspondingly huge, like a mountain laid flat on its side and attached to an endrin. Racing towards them.

Impossible to miss.

'Aye!'

Wytskarn screamed back. 'Why am I not reassured by your tone?'

Brynt ducked his forehead to the dashboard, closed his eyes, and covered his head with both hands.

The ancestor mask was a hot iron against his cheek. One of his lenses was broken. The broken glass caught the mad dance and flicker of flames and reflected it a hundred ways. It made his head hurt. His eyes were gummy, his head pounding. He could taste metal in his mouth, suggesting that his skysuit's filters were clogged, but the reasoning was a while in coming. For some time beforehand he just lay there, slowly baking inside his Grundstok armour, drawing hot, acidic water through a drip straw as he came to. He was face down on the dashboard.

He sat up stiffly and looked around, confused. Then he remembered.

With a start, he began fighting with the seat straps and buckles to get free. He remembered the landing: the impact, a few seconds of screeching and skating, flipping over and then... blackness. The buckles resisted, refusing to come undone. He pulled off a gauntlet and threw it away, then tried again with bare fingers. The hot metal scalded his fingertips. He cursed, tears springing from his eyes. He shook his hand out, gritted his teeth, and went in for it again. He howled, sweet smoke rising from his fingers. But the buckle snapped loose and he was out.

He struggled free of the cockpit. Easier planned than done. The fuselage had been warped by the crash landing, folding the gun housing over the roof of the cockpit and pinching it shut. He wriggled, squirming, clutching his burnt hand to his chest, and somehow managed to work a leg loose. He went sliding backwards down the body of his craft, landing on the ploughed-up metal of the *Han-Gorak*'s deck in a clatter of Grundstok gear.

On hands and knees, he reached up around the back of his neck and fumbled with the helmet clasps. He gasped as it came free of his head. The air was thin and poisonous with Ulguanite magic, hazardous to breathe without proper apparatus, and smelled of recent murder. But it was better than struggling on with a blocked filter and a broken lens, his head sealed in an oven.

He looked up at his stricken gunhauler. There was barely enough of her left to be salvaged for scrap. The endrin was gone. Projected above the fuselage as it was, and already severely stressed, it would have been the first thing to go. Bits of it accounted for the long glittering trail of metal slag that extended out from it along the deck. A fire burned in her nose cone, and in the weapon magazine. Brynt was fortunate that there had been so little aether-gold left in her tanks. Otherwise, he might never have woken up. Unless one believed in the promises of the gods.

He pulled himself to his feet, swayed a moment while he recovered his balance and adjusted to the capital ship's yaw, then staggered determinedly from the crash site. Empty tanks or not, he was thinking clearly enough to want as much distance between himself and the slow-burning wreck as possible.

Small fires pockmarked the deck. The screams, bangs and shouted oaths of battle rang out from everywhere, but in the strange gloom of the realm it always seemed to be coming from a place just beyond his sight. Brynt could make out little of the ongoing battle but for the occasional Khinerai that swooped overhead with terrible screams.

Like a dreamwalker he stumbled towards the sound of fighting.

Wytskarn appeared out of the flames, but in some strange and uncanny way it was no longer Wytskarn.

The other Kharadron, like Brynt, had removed his helmet, but his real face was so similar to his ancestor mask that to see it uncovered was disarming. His beard was huge and glorious, albeit of an entirely impractical length, managed with a hundred golden braids and spreading outwards into his thick mane of white hair. The primitive duardin axe that Brynt had thought so little of at their first encounter dazzled now, its runic blade arresting the attention that would otherwise have been captivated solely by the beauteous nightmare coiled across the burning deck before him.

Brynt stumbled to a halt. He stared, slack-jawed, at the horror of the aelven queen.

Her voluptuous beauty was the equal in every way to her serpentine monstrosity, such that both could co-exist in a single thought and neither contradict the other. Vast wings of black shadow and a crown of snakes formed a living halo for her proud form, her viperous lower section slithering and coiling as she pressed her Kharadron foe with a darting spear and long envenomed talons. Wytskarn, for his part, did not act with any drastic haste to counter. He was a duardin. Slow and steady was his way. But nevertheless there was a blurring to his movements, as of many hundreds of moving parts all coming together in unison to culminate in his axe, time and again, turning aside the aelf queen's spear.

Brynt felt himself go weak at the knees. He knew who this was. There was no Kharadron currently plying their trades in Ulguanite skies who would not have recognised her instantly.

Morathi. Mother of Malerion. Oracle of Khaine. Demi-Goddess of Shadow.

The sky-fleet was surely doomed.

'Wytskarn…?'

Although the effort of matching the aelf queen – and match her he surely was – was clear, Wytskarn looked across and managed half a grin.

'Can't talk now. Busy.'

'How… What…?'

'It's all right, lad. I've got this. As a matter of fact I've been looking forward to it for many a long, hard year.'

'You will pay in blood for every moment you defy me, bearded one,' the aelf queen snarled, her serpent crown appending a trailing *hsssss* to her words. 'Give me the shard and I promise you your ending shall be swift, if not painless.'

All the while they spoke the aelf queen appeared to diminish in Brynt's eyes and the Kharadron to grow, until the pair fought one another almost as equals, in stature as well as in physical potency. With a noise that was part roar and part grim, humourless laugh, the Kharadron slowly beat the aelf queen back.

Morathi shrieked in frustration, her perfect alabaster features transforming into something monstrous.

'By my ancestors, you've aged poorly,' Wytskarn muttered.

Brynt could not believe what he was witnessing.

'Away with you!' Wytskarn turned his way and yelled. 'Even I cannot hold her off forever.'

'Even you…' Brynt murmured, dazed. 'Who *are* you?'

Wytskarn ignored the question. 'Steer the admiral from these dangerous skies and see him right onto his course for Chamon.

His trinket will be worth a share or fifty in the years to come if I'm any judge.'

The aelf queen issued a scream of rage and, just for one moment it seemed to Brynt, of recognition, as the Grundpilot battled her into a retreat.

He had cleared Brynt a path. Taking his chance before the Shadow Queen could find a way to disarm him again, he did as he was told. He fled.

Most Kharadron would scoff at superstitious talk of 'duardin intuition' but it was true that most had a solid sense of where they were, relative to where they meant themselves to be. The Khinerai and their dragon allies had wrought immense damage on the *Han-Gorak*, its familiar layout warped by fires, gouge craters and steel wreckage and turned into a labyrinth by the magicks of Ulgu, but Brynt found his way unerringly through it. A few minutes later he found himself looking up at the aftcastle where the great tanker's helm was housed. He clattered up iron steps, into the stout keep of riveted sheet metal that Admiral Brokkenthrom had welded on to shelter his steersman from the hostile elements, and from enemy attack. He could only hope it still held. The door was unbarred. He burst inside.

It was deserted, but there was no sign of battle that Brynt could see. The steersman had presumably been drawn off by the battle elsewhere and was either yet to return or had been slain. A lock had been slid through the enormous wheel to hold them steady. Too much in haste to fuss over the locking bar, Brynt kicked it in until it bent and then slid out from around its axle. He took the big handles of the wheel, wincing as his blistered palm wrapped around the cool metal, but held firmly on regardless. He hauled it to port, the signal beacon of the lighthouse still bright in his mind despite the manifold obfuscations of the shadow-paths. He did not question it. He just knew that it was so. Sweating with effort, he fought to keep the dreadnought off its old heading. The *Han-Gorak* was a thousand times the tonnage of *Sistromm* and with a mind of her own, but gracelessly, arduously, Brynt felt himself getting the better of her. Her monster prow dragged slowly to port.

'What are you doing?'

Admiral Trem Brokkenthrom and his wealthiest arkanauts, a heavily armed troop kitted out with the finest skyhooks and volleyguns aether-gold could buy, came pounding up the aftcastle steps and onto the helm. Their armour was practical and unshowy, but very fine in the Kharadron's understated way.

'I'm getting us out of here,' said Brynt, straining his muscles against the reluctant wheel. 'Hopefully before it's too late.'

The admiral held up a gauntleted fist and the arkanauts lowered their guns. 'It doesn't look or sound like an aelf to me. Don't shoot him yet, lads. Until I tell you to.' His eyes narrowed. He still wasn't wearing a helmet. 'Gambsson, isn't it? The Grund-Commander's second?'

Brynt nodded, teeth clenched with the effort of manhandling the *Han-Gorak* to her new course single-handedly.

'I thought you were lost.'

'So... did I.'

Trem grunted, and with a jerk of his head sent a pair of arkanauts to aid Brynt at the wheel. Brynt gasped as they took their share of the burden. He had always thought himself sturdily built and strong. He knew now that he had been mistaken.

'The rest of you,' he panted, pointing weakly towards the forward portholes and the open-door hatch. 'Turn your guns that way.'

'Do as he says,' said the admiral irritably.

'Where is the aelf treasure?' Brynt asked him.

'Safe below,' the admiral grunted. 'Locked and locked again, and hidden for good measure. Not that it's any business of yours, the way I see it.'

'I just passed *Morathi* on my way in here, and she wants it, so as of this moment I'm making it my business. And you'd best not complain about it if you want to make it back to Barak-Zilfin in one good-sized piece.'

The admiral blanched. 'The Shadow Queen is here? On my ship?'

'My gunner is keeping her busy.'

'Hikkram?'

'No. Wytskarn.'

'Who's Wytskarn?'

'From old Jonti's boat. You know old Jonti.'

Clutching the sore muscle of his shoulder in his burnt hand, he limped to the nearest porthole and peered out from the side of the aftcastle keep. On the decks below, besieged groups of Grundcorps and arkanauts held the Khinerai at bay with crackling bursts of firepower, while above them capital ships duelled with dragons and, somewhere further below, a goddess and a thing he did not know how to name waged war. The Kharadron mustered under the aftcastle's metal roof with their guns were silent a long time, watching, listening, feeling as the tanker settled onto her new bearing. Brynt could almost see the wink of light in the distant shadows.

He could only hope that the *Han-Gorak* would make it to the Realmgate in time, while they still had a ship and enough of a fleet left to make a fist of it should Morathi decide to pursue them all the way to Chamon. In a way, it didn't matter to Brynt what happened next. He had done his part in all this. All that his contract demanded of him.

And even a little bit more.

At length, the admiral broke the silence. He turned to Brynt.

'Who's old Jonti?'

GRAVEYARD
OF LEGENDS

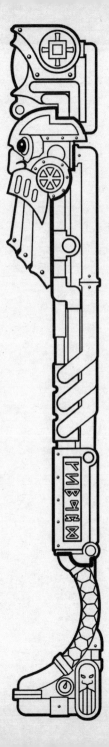

'Amongst the many sagas and tales of the duardin there have been legends beyond number. Many of them walk amongst their descendants still. And some are more legendary than others...'

After six weeks in the desert with a Khainite aelf and a Fyreslayer, Dethyn Marwdwyd was ready to concede that he had made some bad choices. He scrunched his eyes tight and backed away from the bladegheist drifting slowly towards him, trying to shut out the clamour of the battle and think. *Think*. He was not accustomed to working under this kind of pressure. It was really not a fair test of his abilities at all.

'Etcannan a Morr...' he tried, eyes still closed, hand weaving semi-consciously across his breast.

Nothing happened.

Think, Dethyn!

It was absurd. He had spent so many hours in the libraries of the Whitefire Court studying the pages of the *Liber Spuria* that he could practically read the words off the inside of his eyelids.

He took another quick step back and repeated the gesture, and with the confidence of a magus of the illustrious Hallowheart Colleges, declared, '*Et*cannan a Morr.'

Still nothing.

'Damn it.'

He opened his eyes and cried out. The revenant had drawn much closer than he had been expecting. Yards away. The gleam in its hollow eyes chilled his heart and froze his limbs fast. Its slack features leered, a straggly beard misting out into the amethyst corposant upon which the spirit seemed to fly.

'Et*can*nan a Morr. Etcan*nan* a Morr. Etcannan *a* Morr.'

He felt something. A tug on his fingers. *Yes. That was it.*

Retreating until his back was up against the Ahramentian waystone, he cleared his throat, flexed his fingers and went again. His young voice boomed.

'Etcannan *a* Morr. Tashtara enthral!'

The chill of the endless beyond swept through him. His outstretched arm became transparent, and infused with the same purplish light as the spirit that stalked him. The pull of the Nadir tugged on it, so strong even from across the aetheric void and the barriers of the realms that he almost fell forward onto his face. He clapped his other hand to the shoulder to keep himself from pitching forward onto the wraith's axe.

'Enethral elestrae!'

The amethyst bolt leapt from his hand and ripped through the advancing spectre. The nighthaunt dispersed like pipe smoke through an open window. Only the very real, rusted metal axe it had been carrying remained behind, clattering to the ground at Dethyn's feet. He stared at it. He couldn't believe it. What started as a relieved gasp became a giddy laugh.

I did it – I used real *magic to banish an* actual *nighthaunt.*

His colleagues at the Whitefire Court would be so jealous.

'Very good,' Maleneth shouted, the aelf shadowblade drawing her leg out from under a spirit's axe-stroke, twisting her slender body and then back-flipping over the thrust shield of another.

'If you could just do the same thing about, oh, forty times more, that would be wonderful.'

Dethyn lowered his still-numb hand and gawped at his bought companion. The aelf jinked, darted and rolled through the arid sands like something between a street contortionist and an acrobat. She wore very little: a number of leather straps that appeared to function more as sleeves for blades and poisons than as actual clothing, and a few carefully positioned armour panels that did nothing to hinder her dexterity. While he watched, the aelf reversed the knife in her right hand to block an axe-blow to her neck. She allowed the impact to freely spin her, the eerie blood gem she wore at her collar flying wide on its chain, and delivered a scissor kick to the side of the wraith's helm, which passed right through its bearded face.

'Necromancer!' she screamed, as the weight of insubstantial foes pushed her further towards the crest of the dune and the long drop to the desert floor below.

Dethyn shook his head. His mouth felt very dry all of a sudden, and he did not think it had anything to do with the heat of Aqshy.

'Etcannan *a* Morr!' he yelled. His hand, already semi-aethereal from his last casting, drew even more easily on the winds from Shyish this time around. 'Enethral elestrae!' He vaporised a second spectre. 'Elestrae!'

Purple flames wreathed his arm up to the elbow and leapt to engulf a third foe, rendering it down to glowing, ectoplasmic gloop. The dry voice of Shyish whispered in his ear, as though the spell took on a life of its own even as it emerged from his lips and fingers. Unthinking, he repeated its words aloud.

'Tavishan eska ga!' Spectral flames ribboned from his hand in a torrent, frigid to the touch, and turned a dozen nighthaunts instantly to purple smoke. With a pained grunt, he gripped the arm by the bicep and pulled it forcibly from the Realm of Death.

'Better!' Maleneth yelled. 'Definitely better!'

Dethyn felt a prickling warmth of pride, everywhere except for his ghostly hand.

Turning his back on the fighting, he crouched down to check on the arcanoscope, kronuscounter, brightfield and the rest of the arcane apparatus he had set up at the foot of the waystones before the nighthaunts' attack.

He breathed out a sigh of relief. The instruments were undamaged. He brushed the frost of death from the crystal dial covers with his robed sleeve.

'What in the bloody hells of Khaine are you doing now?'

'I...' His voice hitched. The aelf, frankly, terrified him. 'I still need to take a reading of the levels of death magic in this location.'

'I am guessing it will be *high*.'

'The Whitefire Court want to map the aftershocks of the death quake in Ahramentia. I can't just make numbers up – the high magister would kill me.'

'Would he really?'

'He really would.'

'What a charming coincidence. So will I if you don't keep fighting!'

Fiddling with the widgets and sliders on the side of the kronuscounter, Dethyn watched the dials wobble, waiting for the needles to settle. They stilled. He held his breath lest the tiny amount of extant magic in a wizard's mouth upset the reading and counted silently to five.

They held steady. *There it is.* He quickly carried out the mental arithmetic involved in cross-referencing the various aetheric indicators into a single figure and absently drew a monogrammed pocket book from its carry case. Opening it to the proper page, he went to the bottom, drew a pencil from the ring-slot along the ledger's spine, and neatly filled in the latest reading.

'Is my fighting for my life distracting you?'

'No. It's quite all right.'

'I am so glad.'

Dethyn closed the pocket book. 'We may now leave. Just give me half an hour to pack everything away.'

The aelf screamed a word that Dethyn was very glad he did not understand.

He reached out to close the outer doors over the kronuscounter when the needles started to beat like glitterfin tails and then, all of a sudden, each one dropped hard to the left. *Zero*. The air grew hot and still. The taste in his mouth became sulphurous and his eyes stung. He began to sweat.

He had travelled to mystic sites all over Ahramentia and never seen a zero reading. It was theoretically impossible. It was philosophically unthinkable. It was as though, in that one place, the primacy of death had just been violently usurped.

'Die like a real dwarf, you wretched spectre!' Gotrek Gurnisson bellowed at the particularly stubborn wraith that swirled around him.

The gheist glittered like a candle flame with the weakening of the Shyish wind, but some stubborn will of its own kept it from fading completely. Gotrek snorted like a bad-tempered bull being unwisely goaded, and flailed about him with his axe, dousing himself in flame with each swing. He was thigh-deep in the dune but did not seem to mind, so long as the dead continued to oblige his axe by meeting its edge. The weapon's boiling fury lit a haggard scowl. Sweat poured down Gotrek's craggy features, pooling between gargantuan muscles and steaming off as the golden rune of power embedded in his chest throbbed. Faster. Brighter. Its brilliance fractured through the wraith's sullen armour like firelight glimpsed through thick ice.

'Join your ancestors at peace, spirit, and tell them that Gotrek son of Gurni sent you there.'

The strobing of the rune grew in power, the blinks coming so shortly apart that Dethyn could no longer discern the dips in brightness except on an intuitive gut level.

'Rest! Or I will hold you face down until whatever dark force animates your dead limbs stops them from twitching!'

Dethyn raised a hand to shield his eyes from the golden glare. 'Remarkable,' he muttered, just as the Fyreslayer exploded.

Maleneth flew at Dethyn, tackling him at chest height and knocking him to the ground before the first wave of bright magic hit. The aelf's jewellery sizzled against her bare skin. She gritted her teeth and cried out but did not thrash or flinch, and so did not return to the aether in puffs of purple smoke like the gheists who hovered over them both. Even Dethyn's apprentice robes, tailored for him from aqshram wool and designed for the Realm of Fire's worst extremes, smouldered in the outpouring of the Fyreslayer's heat. Around them, stricken nighthaunts shrieked and burned like flies caught in a bright mage's fireball.

The aelf cautiously straightened, glass crunching as the vitrified sand she had been lying over snapped in the absence of her weight.

'That duardin will be the death of me, long before the knife of any hag finds my back.'

Dethyn silently worked his mouth. He could not tell if the sudden event of being pinned under the aelf assassin was a pleasurable one or not.

'What… what just happened?'

'*Gotrek* just happened. I would like to say that you get used to it.'

'Gotrek…' Dethyn sat up and turned to where the Fyreslayer had last been.

Impossible, he thought. *Impossible*.

Gotrek's broad shoulders were slumped as if the burden of the greataxe in his hands had suddenly become too great. His tattooed chest heaved, the rune that had been beaten into the muscle there dull and flat as regular gold. Even his great crest of hair looked somehow diminished, the golden streaks assuming a more silvery hue.

The wraith lord before him remained defiantly upright. Its spectral outline flickered as though somehow, in some long ago place, its body burned in fire. It raised a shield embossed with the runes of ancient royalty. Strands of hair and beard glimmered in winds unfelt, splitting and fraying into smoke and aether. Gotrek bared his teeth and spat.

'You think me impressed?' he growled, tottering forward a step before collapsing to one knee.

The wraith lord brought the butt of his axe to his brow in salute.

Dethyn quickly stood and rolled up his sleeves, wracking his brain for the most powerful spell of banishment or unbinding he could think of. Though what he could accomplish that the Fyreslayer himself could not, he did not know.

Maleneth lowered his hand with hers. 'Do you not have some equipment to pack?'

'The wraith will kill him!'

It seemed to Dethyn that the aelf was smiling, but that was surely his misreading of her inhuman nature. 'How very sad that would be.'

The wraith lord swept up his axe. Gotrek struggled to lift his own, and with his one good eye watched the other weapon rise. He almost seemed to be smiling too.

What is wrong with these two?

Before the blow could land there was a terrific *crack*, as of a rock being cleft in twain, and the wraith lord fumbled his blow and shrieked. Gotrek snarled, as though seeing the would-be deathblow slip wide of his forehead was a source of outrageous consternation, and brought his own axe sweeping up and through the spirit's chest. With a last fractured wail, the revenant boiled off and came apart, leaving Gotrek, kneeling and reduced, in the burnt sand of the dune. He huffed and sputtered, plastered in sand and steaming aether, nostrils flaring as he sought his abruptly vanished foe.

'What did you do?' he grumbled, addressing someone or something behind Dethyn's back.

The battlemage turned. His mouth dropped open as the Ahramentian waystone listed like a hewn tree and slowly, slowly, with a wearied *creak* crashed in a thud of sand. The duardin who stood over it brushed dust off his hands as though impressed by some particularly fine axe-work. A heavy cloak ruffled about him. He had a pipe in his mouth, a broad grin surrounding it.

'Saved your life again, by the looks of things,' he said.

'Are you expecting a thank you?' Gotrek carped back.

Dethyn looked up from the shattered column, to the stranger. 'What *did* you do?'

The duardin shifted his pipe in his mouth and frowned down at him from the lip of the dune. 'There an echo out here?'

'This stone has stood here for thousands of years. Six months of my work. Ruined!'

Gotrek glared at him. 'Is it pity you're after, manling?'

'But…' Dethyn began, remonstrating towards the newcomer, but some evil look in the Fyreslayer's solitary eye told him to stop talking if he valued his skin.

'Witromm,' said Maleneth, clapping her hands silently to the amulet she wore at her throat. 'I thought we had lost you in the Silver Tower.'

'Funny,' said Witromm. 'I thought I'd lost you.'

Dethyn turned to Maleneth, who smiled daggers.

'Better to wonder and not ask,' she said.

'The Mortal Realms are vast,' said Gotrek. 'Or so I'm forever being told. What bad luck brings you to the Parch to darken my beard again?'

'Ahh,' said Witromm, his good mood souring. 'That.'

Dethyn plucked a bent coil from the ground. The kronuscounter was quite ruined. Panelling was strewn all over the dune, alongside blackened ivory and smoked glass. The burnt, acrid smell of copper elements and solder hung in the hot air like a taunt. He stared miserably at the charred wire. *Well*, he thought, *that is that.* There was no way he was going to complete his mission now. Even if he could retrace his steps without his apparatus, and somehow repeat the last half year's work to account for the destruction of the waystone on the regional flows of magic. It would be less arduous by far if he were to just resign from the College now. He was probably far enough away to make a go of it, and the mad idea of taking up permanently with Gotrek and Maleneth and slipping off to Anvalor or Edassa carried a certain rugged glamour.

'You want me to take a look at it, manling?'

The muscular Fyreslayer glowered at him. Dethyn did not think he had done anything in particular to offend him. The realms, it seemed, offended him enough. What a berzerker like him thought to achieve with a complicated piece of Collegiate arcana in his hands, however, was beyond Dethyn's imagination.

'I'm afraid it is quite broken,' he said, endeavouring to sound polite.

Gotrek shrugged and continued to sharpen his axe, muscles rhythmically bulging and sinking to the movement of stone over blade. He seemed unperturbed by the flames tickling at the ends of his beard.

'It's some strange luck that brings you this far from anywhere,' said Dethyn to Witromm, 'given how and… and where you and my companions were last parted.'

'It is,' Witromm nodded. 'It is at that. But the spheres turn in strange ways, as they say, or once did somewhere, and mayhap it was meant to be.'

Dethyn cast away the useless bit of metal. 'You couldn't have come a little earlier? Before Gotrek destroyed my work.'

'You think you are the only one who now regrets this excursion?' asked Gotrek. 'It is too hot. The sun is too bright. It hurts my eye and gives me a headache. And where are the ruins of civilisation you swore I would see if I followed you into this gods-cursed desert, wizard? A great deal you promised to me, and I've seen naught of the Agloraxi but the odd lump of stone.'

'I am ruined!' countered Dethyn. 'Destitute! Can you get that into your head?'

The Fyreslayer thought a while, regarding him levelly the entire time. The whetstone slowed. 'I have a dire thirst.'

Dethyn threw his hands up in despair.

'I hope you were not looking for sympathy,' said Maleneth. 'Gotrek Gurnisson has none to spare for others.'

'I'll have you know, aelfling, that I've a caring disposition and a soft heart.' He sniffed, tinkling his nose chain. 'Except for when I'm thirsty. And hot.'

'I apologise for the inconvenience on your studies, young wizard,' said Witromm. 'But the only way to send yon wraith king back to his barrow was to break the spells that kept him from being banished.' He gestured to the sundered pillar.

Gotrek grunted something pointed, but was otherwise content to work at his already hellishly sharp blade.

'The waystones have stood over this part of Ahramentia for millennia,' said Dethyn. 'They helped to control the magic and channel it through the lands of the old magocracy. They have nothing to do with binding the dead.'

Witromm drew on his pipe, smoke puffing from the corners of his mouth. 'Well, I never did go to any school or suchlike. You're the expert in it, I'm sure.' He turned to Maleneth. 'The tomb of my ancestors lies in the desert hereabouts. Or is it my descendants?' His brow furrowed in thought. 'The years have come and gone and come again and I fear I've lost track. Whoever they were, it's been too many long years since a duardin passed to pay his proper respects. I might have left it longer yet, rather than sooner, young wizard, but the death quake had me anxious. Rightly so, as it seems to me now.'

'Then the shades that attacked us...' said Dethyn. 'They were... what? Honoured slaves? Artisans of the Agloraxi?'

'Is that all my kin are to you, manling?' said Gotrek, his voice low and rumbling and suddenly more dangerous by far than any of Maleneth's pointed threats. 'Smiths and builders and makers of pretty baubles for human kings? We who built empires before the ancestors of your Sigmar first picked up a sharpened flint? Is this what your man-god would have us be? Is this what he has made of Grungni and his apprentices, having already seen off the liar Grimnir in another age?'

Dethyn wilted before the fury of the Fyreslayer's one-eyed gaze.

'As it happens, the duardin entombed here *was* a builder,' said Witromm softly, with an eye on Gotrek, who grumbled but said nothing more. 'Many fine things he made for the Agloraxi mage lords before succumbing to old age. But a king he was too, and interred with great honour by the magocracy in the tomb he himself had built. Ringol Magemaker was his name, and he was a legend in his own time. That time, sadly, is long past now, and eternal rest was his life's reward.'

'The word of men and wizards is worth as much as it ever was, I see,' commented Gotrek.

'Don't be too harsh on the Agloraxi. Few even are the duardin who can see all futures.'

'The greater revelation to me is that duardin have souls,' said Maleneth.

To Dethyn's surprise, the Fyreslayer merely glared at her. 'You tease, aelfling, and unwisely, but this one time only will I let it pass unanswered. Many times before now have I confronted the shades of my own folk, and every time has it been a source of grief to me. There was the time I followed my father's footsteps to stand upon the cursed moors of Hel Fenn, and again as I ventured with my human companion into the lowest Deepings of the Karak Eight-Peaks, once the great jewel of the lost kingdom of the dwarfs, and not least in your own Realm of Death. There was a kinship there that yet bound them to me in friendship even from beyond the grave, and they yearned for the peace that I could grant them. Not at all like these *things* we just fought.'

'The Nadir pulls and distorts,' said Witromm. 'Even…' And here he gave a tired smile, 'Even those of us not yet in our grave who have lived too long past our time.'

The Fyreslayer scowled. 'My time has been duly past well before the Great Necromancer decided to turn his realm inside out.' He turned to Maleneth and bared a broken row of browned teeth in what, on a face less horrifyingly savage, might have been a grin. 'See, aelfling? I know what the death quake is.'

'Lunatics,' Dethyn muttered. 'I've surrounded myself with lunatics.'

'What was that, wizard?' said Gotrek.

'Err… nothing.'

'There's an evil here that needs putting properly back in its box,' said Witromm. 'An affront to the spirit of our children and fathers that needs answering. Since I've cost you a doom today I'll let you come along if you wish to.'

Gotrek frowned long in thought. Maleneth looked away so he would not see her thin smile.

'No,' said Dethyn.

'Who asked you?' Gotrek snapped.

'As your employer, I forbid it.'

'Didn't you just say you were destitute?'

'What about your advance?'

'What advance is this?' The Fyreslayer turned to Maleneth who was making no further effort to conceal her mirth.

'I believe that Gotrek is unfamiliar with the concept of Aqua Ghyranis as a universal currency.'

The Fyreslayer looked appalled. 'You mean to tell me that *that* was my fee? *That* is what I slogged all the way into this blasted sandpit for?' Grumbling under his breath, he went roughly back to work on his axe. 'I already drank it.'

Ahramentia was all desert, bounded by the Flamescar Plateau and its great cities to the south-west, Anvilgard and the nation of Golvaria to the north, and the green lands of Hallowheart to the east. It was where hermits went to escape from civilisation and where antiquarians went to seek it. It was where rogue spells and lost armies alike could vanish without trace. It was a grave-yard of legends.

It had not always been so.

In the Age of Myth it had been one of the wonders of Aqshy, the winged capital of the Agloraxi Empire casting its benevolent shadow over a verdant domain. Those who studied such times, even mages of the Whitefire Court, felt it wisest to shake their heads at the magocracy's excesses, to mutter the expected pieties, but Dethyn could not avoid a sneaking regret at their fall. Their magic, so went the legend, had scoured the Great Parch of Chaos until Khorne himself had risen from his Throne of Skulls to shatter Ahramentia in his rage.

A land did not quickly recover from such blows. If ever. Many things, however, had found a way to live in the rubble of the magocracy's fall.

Mordants dwelt in old complexes buried beneath the sands, fas-cinating in their own right for the ancient customs they kept, but challenging subjects of study to say the least. Beastmen, warped by the terrible magicks unleashed by the city in its last great gambit to lay low the God of Blood and Battles, roamed the desolation in hungering packs. Many wore scraps of clothing and the time-forgotten emblems of royal houses, but what they meant no wizard now lecturing at the Amethyst College could say.

And then there were the colossi. The slave-titans of the Agloraxi themselves.

They appeared frequently in the sands, never near, the mirages of giants glimpsed briefly in a sandstorm or a lance of sunlight across the eyes, and all the more terrifying and wondrous for being untouchable. Hundreds set out each year from Hallowheart alone in search of the fabled colossi, for the secret of their manufacture or for the lost treasures to which they might lead if followed. They had not proven terribly difficult to find.

It made him wonder what happened, exactly, to those who sought deliberately to approach them more closely.

Gotrek had watched them keenly from afar, a strange mix of avarice and longing in his one eye, but had thus far shown no inclination to seek them out: not while his word to Dethyn and now Witromm still bound him.

Most of the desert's feral denizens had learnt by then to avoid the foul-tempered duardin and his fyresteel axe, and so their journey, those first few weeks excluded, had been unexpectedly peaceful. In that at least, he had proved worthy of his keep. The attack by Ringol Magemaker and his nighthaunts had been the exception. In its aftermath, their journey into the deeper desert once again became marked by an absence of trouble. Whether that had as much to do with their new companion, Witromm, as it did to Gotrek, Dethyn did not know.

All he knew was that they were both equally intent on finding where trouble had gone.

* * *

The heat dropped by degrees.

It was little more than a breeze at first, faint and bone dry, a ghost touch that parched skin barely noted at all, but after a few hours of it Dethyn was shivering. His skin, even under his bright Aqshian robes, was goosebumped. The hairs on the backs of his hands stood on end and quivered. The recording apparatus he had brought with him may have been ruined beyond repair, but no battlemage of any training at all would have needed a kronus-counter to sense the saturation of death magic that was building in the air and in the sand.

He could feel it. Quite literally in his bones. His skin was becoming paper, his joints calcifying, every forward step becoming associated with an arthritic twinge and a deeper chill. Before too long he was hunched and hobbling like an old man going bare-foot through the ash. *I can turn around any time I like*, he thought. Then he thought about the vast amount of desert between himself and Hallowheart. Or the even vaster distance were he to journey instead to Anvalor or Edassa. He thought of doing it without Gotrek and Maleneth.

He trudged glumly on.

Maleneth did not seem to suffer it at all. Whether it was the rumoured near-immortality of the pure aelven bloodlines or some favour of her Murder God that protected her, he could not say. He conceded it also possible that a trained shadowblade was simply better at not showing her pain than he was. Her skin became pro-gressively paler and bluer as the chill became biting, but she did not once shiver nor show any sign of discomfort, even as Dethyn felt certain his fingers would crack and grey hairs fall from his head. Witromm stomped along beside them like an old comrade, a proud mentor or a commander-turned-friend from some other life, supping stoically on his pipe. On those rare occasions that he did seem to look up and notice the growing chill, he would draw in his cloak a little and smile faintly, as though just stepping out from his favourite tavern.

Gotrek, meanwhile, strode several long paces ahead, determinedly in the lead and determinedly alone. The Fyreslayer already looked as old as it was possible for a living being to look. Even with Witromm just a short way behind him, white-haired and long-bearded, Gotrek somehow looked the elder of the two. The bags under his eyes were heavier, the crags in his face went deeper. Some great weight bore down on his shoulders and on his soul. It was as though Shyish had done its worst to Gotrek already and had no purchase on him now.

Heat, both physical and arcane, hazed off the Fyreslayer so that he appeared to wobble, the brazier at the heart of his greataxe fuming. Dethyn briefly considered running up ahead to walk alongside him and share in some of that warmth. This was still *his* expedition after all. Rather quickly he thought better of it.

Stiff joints, he told himself, not entirely convincingly.

Something funny happened to sand when it was cold. Dethyn had never known that. It became clumpier, almost like a heavy soil. In one sense it was easier to walk over, with none of the sucking and dragging that he had come to expect from the dunes, but it was also deceptively loud, the whisper of hissing grains replaced by the clump of boots. Maleneth would have moved soundlessly over broken glass, while Witromm instinctively lightened his stride. Dethyn did the same without realising it, the death in the air taking twenty years from his life and twenty pounds from his step, or so it seemed to him.

Gotrek, of course, seemed determined to raise as much noise from it as it was mortally possible to make.

'Do you mind?' Dethyn hissed, after it had all become a bit much.

The Fyreslayer turned to glare at him. The mad look in his one eye cowed the battlemage more completely than any raised voice or threat of violence. 'A dwarf can tread as softly as any aelf when he chooses to. As any greenskin who's ever had his throat slit by a dwarf ranger will tell you, if you were to go far enough into the right underworld in Shyish to ask. I choose not to. Shall I tell you why?'

Dethyn nodded dumbly.

'Because if you think a foe without bones or body hears as you or I do then you are more of a fool than I thought you were.' Muttering something disparaging about the state of education in Hallowheart's colleges of magic, Gotrek continued on his way, stomping even more heavily than he had before.

'I see something,' said Maleneth, and though Gotrek was by that point a crested blur in the dust ahead, even he did not gainsay her or argue that his one eye saw better.

An hour of mindless trudging and rising aches later, and Dethyn saw what the aelf had.

Reddish grains blustered through a shallow bowl, revenants of dust and sand conjured by the cold wind and sent swirling across the wide plain. Two square-sided stone pillars, identical to the others that Dethyn had visited in the desert, with the exception that here they came as a pair, flanked a sandy causeway. Runes showed dimly golden in their basaltic faces, their hard edges gnawed by sand and time. The causeway followed a gently rising floor towards a doorway of basalt and gold. Runes that he recognised as Agloraxi engraved both uprights, and the horizontal. There was no physical door to bar passage. The gateway was open. But the sheer potency of death magic emanating from that tomb, for a tomb it surely was, was so great that Dethyn could barely take a willing step towards it, never mind defile its sanctity.

'Smell that?' Witromm withdrew his pipe. 'It's worse than I'd feared. I should have come sooner.'

As Dethyn attempted to read the weathered runes upon the

entranceway, a void through which no sand blew drew his eye towards the causeway. It was squat, broad as a barrel, and slowly, to Dethyn's rising horror, the winged outline of a helm and the wide circumference of a shield showed through the dust.

'Go back,' Ringol the wraith king hissed, his voice the drag of quicksand. 'Leave us to our rest. Trespass no longer on the lands that were given us.'

'We knew not that these lands were yours,' Gotrek shouted in reply. 'You are dead and left behind no kin. Your claim on this desert expired with you.'

'Go back,' the spectre warned again. 'Leave us to our rest.'

'You are not at rest.' Witromm raised his hands, his lit pipe still in one of them. 'The Doomseeker speaks falsely, for we are kin, you and I. Let us enter, to pay our proper respects and renew the wards upon your door.'

Gotrek muttered under his breath, loud enough for the orb of Ulgu to hear. 'I'll save you the time and tell you now what I think of this house's wards.'

Witromm prepared to take a step forwards.

A cold breeze rose up, disturbing the hackles at the nape of Dethyn's neck and stinging tears from his eyes.

'Wait!' he cried, but too late.

The duardin's boot pressed into the sand.

A quiet moan rang from the dunes. Dethyn raised his eyes as rank after rank of ghostly warriors emerged from the aether, drawn out, it seemed, by the blowing wind. Their beards blustered as though in a gale from Shyish rather than a breeze, long coats of splinted mail rattling like a chainghast's bonds. They carried handaxes of notched steel, and broken shields. The emblems of the Agloraxi and the Ahramentian duardin tore from tattered banners above their helms. The ghost of Ringol Magemaker surveyed their ranks from his vantage and was pleased.

'*Go back. Leave us to our rest.*'

Witromm stowed his pipe into a pocket in his cloak. 'I can't do that.'

Dethyn was not sure that he even saw the duardin draw his axe, but all of a sudden there it was in his hand and he was charging across the desert floor towards the causeway. Gotrek, it seemed, was as surprised as he was, for the Fyreslayer gave a furious bellow at being second to the fray and barrelled after him.

Maleneth put a restraining hand on Dethyn's shoulder. 'And so it begins,' she sighed.

The dead swirled down the slope of the dune. Not as an army, but like a floodwater that had been held in check for too long and had now been released. They rushed the two duardin, bearded faces snarling in a foam of ghastly green, and Dethyn fully expected to see Witromm and Gotrek swept away by it, the flood of spirits racing very soon thereafter towards Maleneth and himself.

The wave did indeed crash over Witromm, and Dethyn flinched, barely able to watch as tattered aether sprayed into the air. Then he saw the duardin's horned helmet, his runic axe flashing, night-haunts perishing by the score with every furious swing.

And then there was Gotrek.

The Fyreslayer hit the undead like something hurled from Azyr.

'You have cheated me out of one worthy scrap already,' he roared, jostling with the other duardin for a footing on the causeway. 'Do you think I would let you get away with another?'

Witromm shoved back against Gotrek's shoulder with his own, the two duardin establishing a sort of equilibrium whereby Gotrek hacked left and Witromm right, both striving against the other and in so doing driving themselves in lockstep up the causeway. It might technically have been described as fighting side by side, but not by anyone who had ever seen it. The two were matched in almost every way. To see them in battle together was astounding.

Like being at the Battle of Burning Skies, watching Sigmar and Teclis and Gorkamorka unite to do battle with the Everchosen.

They might almost have been brothers.

Witromm swung his axe and sundered a wooden shield. 'Is it their rest you seek, Gurnisson? Or your own?'

'Are you my mother, longbeard?'

The wraith king blew a direful note on a horn of brass and bone, and a new contingent of dead charged out of thin air to reinforce the rear ranks of those fighting to stymie the champions' ascent. Though lacking in any substance beyond the ancestral wargear they bore, their weight of numbers ground the two duardin to a halt. Denied the room to properly swing his greataxe, Gotrek headbutted a spirit's shield until it broke. A rusty axe blade struck the lion-headed plate he wore over his shoulder. The Fyreslayer simply roared with laughter.

Dethyn watched. He thought again about running away. *Anvalor is supposed to be lovely at this time of year*, he mused.

The wraith king's reinforcements were starting to lap around the two duardin. Unable to properly surround them on account of the twinned obelisks that they appeared unwilling to move through, they were flowing down the dune towards Dethyn.

His mouth dropped open. *Now, how did that spell go again?*

'Errrr...' he said, backing into the aelf.

'Witless fool,' Maleneth hissed as she rushed to intercept the coming warriors.

An axe rose from the insubstantial foam of the front rank, which she caught with her own flashing blade before turning on a coin and stabbing a second knife into the spirit's eye. There was something profoundly supernatural about the aelf's weapons. As with the Fyreslayer's rune, however, Maleneth had always actively discouraged his interest.

The spirit shrieked and perished in messy fashion, ectoplasm frothing from its eye socket as it turned to mist. Maleneth whirled away as the rest came at her, dancing with them almost, like a witch-aelf at the Khainite blood revels that he, like everyone in gods-fearing Hallowheart, had most certainly never attended.

He took another few paces back, just to be safe, and raised a hand. The joints in his fingers cracked and popped as he threw his spell into the host and sent another warrior flying apart. Maleneth parried another blow, her riposte leaving a knife stuck in a revenant's shield. Dethyn blasted it into oblivion. Then another. And another. His hand was painfully numb, but he was almost starting to enjoy the fight.

Maleneth had retreated all the way back to his side. Still they came. He worked his fingers through a new form. Faster than he could think.

'Tel'ethrin nigarath hala!'

The warriors of the spirit host looked confused. And then, very slowly, like someone who had woken from a bad dream and found themselves with a bloody knife, the nighthaunts put their weapons down.

Dethyn let out a giddy laugh and reached for Maleneth's arm. After that, he was feeling quite faint.

The shadowblade clapped her hands. 'Very good, necromancer. Can you make them do tricks as well? Sending them back against their king would be particularly good fun.'

'Of… of course,' Dethyn managed.

'*Go back!*' hissed the voice of the wraith king. '*Leave us to our rest.*' He brought the horn to his cold, green lips and blew.

The dazed spirits shook their heads and looked again to their weapons.

Dethyn chanted in a panic, but Maleneth interrupted the incantation mid-flow by grabbing him by the wrist and pulling.

'With me,' she said. 'Once again that mad hog of a duardin has himself in the right place at the right time. You cannot beat a host of the dead without eventually having to cut the head off its leader.'

They found Gotrek cackling merrily by the time that Maleneth had fought their way up the causeway through to the two duardin. The desperation of their situation had resulted in an inordinately positive effect on the duardin's temper.

'I thought you had run away or died, aelfling!'

'I considered both,' Maleneth replied.

'Consider your debt to me repaid in full, longbeard. This is as good a fight as the one you cost me, and a worthy cause to die in.'

'I'll not hear of it,' Witromm replied, struggling against a night-haunt's shield. 'Not when there's work still to be done.'

'The debt is honoured when I damn well say it's honoured.'

'It's my debt to honour, and I say not yet.'

Gotrek snarled as he beat his way through a wooden shield and incinerated the ghost that had been holding it. 'The cheek,' he muttered, then raised his gaze and attempted to wipe ecto-plasm from his brow. His brawny hand passed straight through it.

'*Let us rest,*' cried Ringol.

'Then lie down and rest,' said Gotrek, shaking his greataxe at him.

In answer, the wraith king hefted his axe and shield.

Gotrek grunted in what appeared to be understanding. 'Get me up there, necromancer.'

'I… What?'

'Can your foul wizardry transport me across this rabble to strike at their king, or can't it?'

Dethyn puffed himself up, appalled by the Fyreslayer's casual dismissal of his craft. Not to mention the total lack of contri-tion for months of research ruined. And the probable imminent death. And just who was paying whom for the privilege of all of this anyway?

'I *might* have once read a spell that–'

'Good! Get on with it then.'

'It's just that I–'

'I'll throw *you* up there to fight him before I ask you twice.'

Dethyn gritted his teeth. 'It might sting a little.'

Gotrek set himself as though for a blow in some barbarian head-butting contest. 'I'm r–'

Dethyn made a sharp gesture, and the air around Gotrek greyed and wavered. The Fyreslayer glanced over his shoulder, perhaps sensing the ice breath on his back, as a trio of cloaked wraiths emerged from the tear in the realms and took his shoulders in long-taloned hands. His one eye blazed with the fury of betrayal as the spirits dragged him back with them into their underworld domain. The rent in space healed with a pop and a swirl of returning colour.

'What did you do?' said Maleneth.

Good riddance, Dethyn thought, moments before the Fyreslayer was thrown back out from the oubliette dimension into which he had been briefly cast, looking several years older and a good deal angrier, further up the causeway. After a quick look around to re-establish his bearings, the Fyreslayer whipped his axe up high above his head and hurtled the last few yards towards the Magemaker.

His axe descended like wrath itself. The revenant blocked with his own humble blade and countered with his shield. Gotrek turned his shoulder into it and drove the spectre onto its heels. He roared, his axe already swinging. The wraith flickered, striking the axe to guide its flaming arc overhead and then followed through with a chopped slash through the muscle of Gotrek's chest. Blood trickled from the cooling wound. The Fyreslayer even bled stubbornly. The rune in his chest hissed and sputtered as though enraged, the gold clearly on the brink of some kind of ignition, but the duardin exerted his will and it fizzled down.

It had not been enough to vanquish the wraith king of Ahramentia last time. There was no reason to believe it would be now.

'Help me, lad,' Witromm shouted, straining single-handedly against several ranks of nighthaunts and a shield wall, but still somehow managing to grunt and gesture towards the waystones just out of reach ahead. 'Can you help me as far as yonder pillar? It's that that needs to be destroyed. Not Ringol Magemaker, may the ancestors forgive him.'

Had it been Gotrek who had asked it of him then he might have argued. He would certainly have questioned why. But coming from Witromm, this stern but companionable longbeard that he had met but days ago in the desert, he simply nodded and said: 'I'll try.'

He waved his hand and spoke a word of power and a row of shields clattered to the ground as the spirits holding them vanished into the aether. Witromm barrelled into the breach with a gruff-voiced roar. Maleneth vaulted after him, orbited by flashing knives.

Dethyn hurried after them both, keen not to be left behind.

Coming to the foot of the pillar, Witromm drew back his axe, like a woodsman sizing up a mighty trunk, and hewed at its base. Runic metal chipped away at runic stone. The spirits massing over the causeway halted in their attack and screamed. Dethyn too felt a similar wave of dizziness and nausea as the flows of magic, in particular the amethyst colour to which he was most sensitive, became erratic.

The waystones, he thought. *Of course.* So *that* was what they had been built to do. *That* was what had gone wrong in Ahramentia.

He turned to the second pillar, just out of reach over the other side of the causeway, while Witromm hacked furiously at the first and Maleneth resumed her efforts in holding back the enraged spirit hosts. For all her qualities, however, the aelf was no Gotrek

Gurnisson, and the front line of a melee was not the place to make best use of her skills.

Putting her increasingly curse-laden appeals for aid from his mind he focused on that second pillar, concentrating on the magic that now blew in fits, like a storm about to break. He drew it to him, extinguishing a dozen wraiths in his vicinity and drawing a shrill cry from the faraway figure of Ringol Magemaker. A broiling cloud of amethyst, visible only to his witch-sight, swirled around the foot of the obelisk, stricken by uncanny lightning.

Dethyn clenched his fist.

The pillar cracked. It began to topple. And then, with a crunch, it collided with the other column. Bits of rock exploded from its base, showering them all, and already weakened by Witromm's axe-work, it fell too.

The spirits wailed and, like tiny flames suddenly covered over by a jar, every one of them was snuffed out.

Gotrek lifted a hunk of masonry that three strong men together would have struggled to move. As he examined it, the glittering fires of his golden rune brought to life the stone's fragmentary inscriptions, but his own expression was inhuman, unreadable.

'This is dwarf work, right enough. In any world would I know it. Its protections should have outlasted the age.'

'In a way they did,' said Witromm, looking down his large nose from over the Fyreslayer's shoulder. 'What happened here was naught to do with those whose hands helped make them.'

'Then why destroy what they built?'

Witromm stroked his beard as he thought. 'You were an engineer, I'm told.'

'Once,' said Gotrek. 'Long ago. Though hardly for any time at all in the scheme that my life has become.'

'Well, think of these waystones as irrigation. As drains, of a sort.'

Dethyn gave an unconscious snort. It was a little more compli-cated than that. But Witromm continued as though he had heard no interruption.

'When the winds of magic drop away and blow gently they are naught but pretty monuments, but when the winds blow hard they allow it to be siphoned away, keeping the lands here sane and stable. At least in comparison to Golvaria or the Flamescar Plateau. It suited the duardin, and I daresay it suited the Aglor-axi too.'

Gotrek nodded, understanding tempering the hostility in his eye. 'I see. The necroquake.' He glanced at Maleneth. 'Is that what we're calling it?'

The aelf smiled thinly and dipped her head. He turned back to the huge stone in his massive hands.

'I see,' he said again.

'They were never designed for a storm like that one,' said Witromm. 'The sluices are flooded and there's nowhere for all that death magic to go. It's backed up, spilling over. The waystones are keeping Ahra-mentia steady, just about, but at the cost of the stones and those who built them. Or...' He coughed, waved his hand vaguely about as though dismissing a strange odour. 'Or something like that.'

Gotrek growled, muttering something flinty under his breath.

'Why do you hate the dead so much?' Dethyn asked, as gently as he could.

'Because it's unnatural,' Gotrek replied.

'They're just... dead.'

Gotrek scowled at the rock in his hands for a moment. Then he let out a rugged sigh. His shoulders seemed to sink an inch. 'I don't hate them, wizard. I pity them. And I envy them.'

'Envy?'

'Aye. Is that so odd? I envy them. They have all I ever craved in life and still they come back.'

'It's hardly their own doing.'

'We'll see. One day, we'll see.' Gotrek let the lump fall from his hands. It landed in the cold sand with a *thud*. He looked very tired, more tired even than he had been after his first battle with Ringol Magemaker and the expenditure of his rune's strength. 'Are we done here, longbeard?'

'Not quite,' said Witromm. 'There's one last thing the duardin of Ahramentia need us to do.'

Gotrek was the first into the tomb. The first probably in a thousand years. His axe and his rune and the golden strands of his tall crest crackled like a lit brazier in the darkness, illuminating the runic scripts and reliefs of a low, sloping passage down. Witromm followed, and one could be forgiven for wondering if he, perhaps, had a certain glow as well. It was difficult to be sure, with Gotrek there beside him, the way the constellations of Azyr came out only when the orb of Hysh had passed, but there was a shimmer of power there, well buried, but which a wizard's eye could discern. Maleneth took up the rear. And as confident as Dethyn might have felt about broaching an ancient tomb with duardin of such prowess in front of him, having the shadowblade behind him brought him quite effectively to his proper senses.

Dethyn expected the corridor to descend forever. It was what the imagination demanded when considering the burial complex of the Agloraxi builders. But the walk took less than a minute before opening out into a larger chamber. The reach of Gotrek's firelight extended for a hundred yards or more until it glanced off the metal insets of sarcophagus lids and the gemstones of murals. Dethyn stared about him, dumbstruck. Metals and jewels were not prized as currency in Hallowheart, nor possessed of any inherent value, but beauty was beauty, and the tomb of Ringol Magemaker boasted it in abundance.

The Whitefire Court had no idea that this place existed, a physical link back to the magocracy of old. Perhaps this, and Witromm's testimony, would placate them enough to overlook the loss of their equipment and Dethyn's failure.

'What are you still doing here?' asked Gotrek.

Dethyn looked up, assuming the Fyreslayer had read his thoughts and had been addressing him, and received a cold start when he saw the shade of King Ringol hovering an inch off the ground before a particularly ornate tomb. The spirit's appearance looked torn, like a banner hacked by many blades, as though a powerful wind blew on it from some quarter Dethyn could not quite make out. The battlemage looked around, his heart suddenly high in his mouth, and saw hundreds of faded, tattered shapes watching from the murals and icons of the far walls.

'*We were promised rest,*' said Ringol, in answer. '*I was promised.*'

'I was promised things too,' said Gotrek. 'I'd say we're both of us made to look like fools.'

'There is no rest for you here.' Witromm took a step towards the tomb.

Dethyn was not sure if it was possible for a spirit to tense, but that was what Ringol appeared to do, raising axe and shield and drifting to block the duardin's approach.

'*My rest…*'

Gotrek growled, tightening his grip on his greataxe, but before the Fyreslayer could move or speak Witromm had taken another step forward, his arms spread as though he meant to embrace the wraith king. His kin. Or so he claimed.

'This is not rest,' he said. 'It is time for you to move on.'

'Aye,' Gotrek added. 'Away with you, and leave this realm for the living.'

Ringol paused for an age of thought and then nodded once. A sigh swept through the buried hall and the wraith king swept back, clearing a path which Gotrek stepped into, swinging his axe up like a woodsman set about splitting a log. There was a resounding *crack* that echoed in the deep hall as Gotrek's axe staved in the sculpted effigy of the Magemaker on the tomb's lid, and when Dethyn raised his eyes from the desecration the wraith king was no longer there.

He looked around. There was no sign at all of the Magemaker's kin and subjects. The tomb was as silent and dead as the other monuments of lost Ahramentia, although it occurred to Dethyn that with several of the waystones toppled they may no longer be quite so dead. He wondered if it was a good thing that they had done here, although something about Witromm's contented demeanour made it difficult to believe otherwise.

The old duardin had already drawn a pipe from his breast pocket and was tamping dried leaf into the bowl with a little finger. He leant towards Gotrek, one bushy eyebrow raised in question, and the Fyreslayer grunted and lowered his greataxe in response. Witromm smiled as though the stars had aligned and the realms, after an eternity of waiting, put themselves to rights, and lit up using the sacred forgeflame burning at the axe's head.

Maleneth looked at them both in amazement. She was not the only one.

'Where exactly did they all go?' said Dethyn.

Witromm shrugged, puffing contentedly. 'A better place, I'll warrant. A much better place.'

THE
WHITE-BEARDED
ANCESTOR

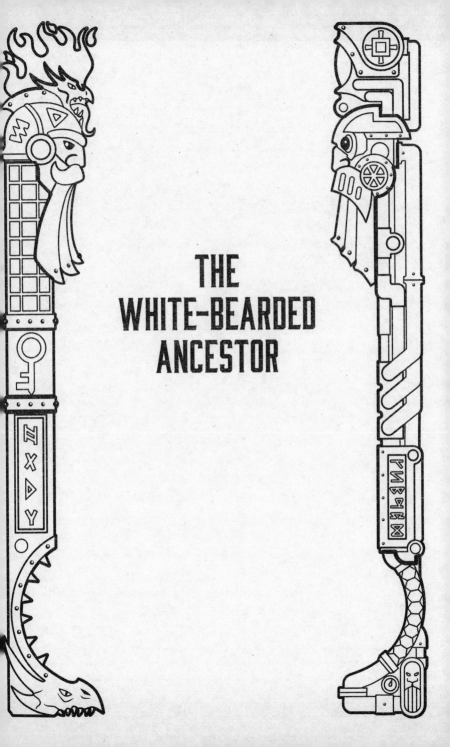

'For the God-King of Highheim I did capture the Winds Celestial, and forge them thus into bolts of thunder that he might wield in wrath. For Sigmar too did I mine the Broken World, construct the Apotheosis Anvil ere its lighting with Dracothion's flame, and lend thereafter the skills of the Six Smiths and the knowledge of working sigmarite. I did these things, for my debt to him is beyond repaying, and beyond speaking. I would have given more had he asked, but ask he did not, for Sigmar is wiser now than once he was, and unsubtle in his wisdom. In metal and thunder did he wish his warriors clad, that they might be the blunt face of the weapon with which Chaos is struck from the Mortal Realms. I gave these things gladly. My oaths did demand it. And such baubles were easy for me to part with.

'My own people, I know, are made of sterner stuff…'

The Maker breathed light into the cold furnace. Golden dust sprinkled over the old coals, catching in the kindling and lighting. He raised his hands to them, warming his calloused palms, and smiled, taking a fire iron to spread the heat and working a hand bellows to feed the flames. It felt good to be at work again. Since the fall of Elixia he had wandered long and far, but here he would build himself a new forge.

For the moment he worked alone. His apprentices had been bequeathed to the Forge Eternal in service of a debt that would never be repaid. The furnaces would remain unlit, with the exception of one.

For now.

The Maker took up his tools. Some of them would have been recognisable to any mortal smith. Hammers. Fullers. Reamers. Tongs. Others would have had them dumb with wonder and struggling to understand their purpose. The Maker had designed them himself, and had not made them for the working of metal.

Employing a set of tongs, he picked up a fuzzy ingot of potential. At the core of his creation's shape would be his own remembrance. A king of the duardin when they were still a united race. A teacher of men and a friend of aelves. The bane of Chaos. Works unfinished and grudges unsettled.

'Vengeance will be yours,' he muttered. 'When our foes are great, I will return to my people. When the foul creatures of this world bay at the doors, you will take up your axe once more and your ire will rock the mountains.'

He held the mote to the anvil, and began.

> 'Who is this white-bearded wanderer? From whence
> does he come, that all duardin peoples recognise and
> know him? And where does he go when his act of
> charity is done…?'

Blood ran down the Skarn Karak in a pair of oozing rivers. Swifter than the magma that had once followed those courses it ran, and no less hot, for it was by no earthly bidding that it was liquid, nor any living warmth that bade it flow. No stone would this lava make when it cooled. No continent would it forge where it emptied into the Vitriol Sea. No. Follow these courses to their unnatural springs and one would find oneself broken and weary upon a vast plain of fresh-hewn bodies and broken shields, feet sinking into ground softened by spilled offal and gore, lungs labouring on air that was near-unbreathable for its thick, iron reek. To those warriors who were even then fighting, bleeding and dying on Skarn Karak to keep those mighty rivers running full, no such distinction between the Realm of Fire and the Blood God's own ruinous dominion existed.

The Maker, observing the battle from its adjoining peak, could forgive such foolish misconceptions.

But he knew better.

He had followed those rivers, had stood upon that plain, had gazed upon the seat of the Blood God himself and turned his boundless craft to the unmaking of his fortress of brass. And he had failed. Only the second time in his long, *long* memory that any metal had defied his will. He shook his head. Of all the regrets he had accumulated over his many centuries, that one remained perpetually keen.

Limping to the ridgeline, the Maker drew his heavy cloak about himself and looked out. Hordes of Khorne's Bloodbound heaved against the mountain, as if to take it by its magmic hair and bring it low. Across the distance that separated mountains, the Fyreslayers of the Skarravorn lodge were almost indistinguishable from their foes. Both sets of warriors were equally robust and muscular, the duardin as ferocious in defence as the Bloodbound were in attack, their thick arms and torsos clapped in blood-red and gold, the ranks of both intermingling with a similarly violent, almost joyful abandon. Only the blue glint of spinel and sapphire – rare stones in that part of Aqshy but mined in abundance from the Skarn Karak – definitively gave away the presence of a Fyreslayer. Their hair, fed into extravagant red crests through tall helms, wobbled like a spreading inferno above the mountain-spanning melee.

The Maker sighed, feeling a familiar pang of old hurt. It was as though he looked down off that ridge and saw his brother.

In a way, he supposed, he did exactly that, and that was some comfort. He liked to believe that this was as his brother would have wanted it, if not exactly as he would have planned, for his brother never did *plan* much of anything. But the mind of a god was never an easy thing to unpick. And the faiths that grew out from them rarely behaved according to their intention.

He observed the battle for a time, chewing his beard in thought. Fury met fury. Frenzy met resolve.

The Bloodbound had the numbers. By older gods of forgotten names did they have the numbers. But the Fyreslayers had good ground, fortified lines carving up the higher terrain, and the determination to hold on to every fire-blackened square inch of it. There was no shifting a duardin once he had it inside his skull that a particular fluke of geology was his own. That was as true for the Fyreslayers as it was for every other distant off-shoot of their ancient kin, and would remain so, long into the Maker's dim and uncertain view of his descendants' future.

A deathbringer managed to make her howl heard above the tumult, sanctifying her kills to Khorne as her whirling axe took heads and arms, before the battle's swells swallowed her again. A magmadroth reared onto pillar-like hind legs, lifting the runesmiter on its war-throne high over the melee. With a gesture, he turned the earth molten beneath the Bloodbound's feet. Bodies hissed and reddened as they made a bridge across the cooling rock, howling blood warriors soon overrunning even the great spawn of Vulcatrix once more.

At the nearby rattling of scree, the Maker turned from the battle and looked down. A band of Bloodbound scrambled up the ridgeline not far from where he stood, no doubt looking to exploit the vantage for similar purposes to his own and attack the Skarravorn from the flank. A bloodstoker led them. He was a giant in dripping armour, his face a brutalised thing encased in a helm that appeared to have been made and fitted by the simple expediency of emptying a crucible of molten brass over the warrior's head.

That alone was enough to earn the Maker's pity. These berzerkers had all been human once. No worse or better than others. A craftsman did not blame the wood that had been left outside to rot, nor the metal that had gone into an Azghorite forge. But shoddy work was unforgiveable. He'd not spent all those centuries sharing the secrets of smithing and stoneworking with the

Mortal Realms to be mocked with such deliberately careless craft on his own doorstep.

It might have been his ire that allowed his presence on the overlook to be felt, or perhaps the bloodstoker was simply unusually perceptive for a follower of Khorne. The warrior lowered his whip and turned to look over his hugely muscled shoulder.

The Maker reached for no weapon, though he carried plenty. Nor did he make any attempt to restore the clever array of glamours that the bloodstoker had somehow managed to look through. He nodded once, casually as though in greeting, as if to confirm the startled recognition he saw in the sudden recoil of the warrior's muscular shoulders. The bloodstoker issued a yell to curdle the blood, then turned in a spray of grit and fled back down the mountainside.

Unnerved by their leader's behaviour, the saner elements of his warband quickly withdrew. The rest, unled, understrength, completely unrestrained, were gleefully torn apart by the Skarravorn.

Not one of them felt a hint of the Maker's presence at their backs.

'You could break this siege in an hour.'

The words came on a distant wind, and with them came an electricity that filled the Maker's beard. He glanced over his shoulder, and grunted. The ill-defined human shape of a lightning zephyr crackled alongside him.

'If you would but show your hand.'

'That's especially rich,' said the Maker. 'Coming from you.'

The mote fizzled in silence. Accepting the charge, as well it might.

'I cannot fight every battle.'

'No,' the Maker agreed.

A deep sigh fizzed through the thick, bloodied air. For a moment afterwards it felt almost fit to breathe. But only for that one short moment.

'*Would that your brother was here beside us still.*'

'Look around you.' The Maker gestured to the battle. 'He fights yet.' His eyes narrowed as he turned to look directly at the apparition of Azyr. 'Harder than you or I, I might say. If I were feeling harsh.'

'*If I could have commanded his axe to the Burning Skies...*'

'We all make our own beds. Even you.'

'*Do you still blame me, old friend?*'

The duardin smiled grimly. There was humour in it, but this was an Age inimical to laughter. 'He was always doomed, that one, since before you found us both shackled to that mountain. He would have had it no other way.'

'*What is lost shall be remade.*'

The Maker nodded, turning back to the battle. 'There's nothing that can't be remade.'

'*Then join me now. Gather what remains of your people and lead them to the safety of Azyr while there are Realmgates still open to take them.*'

While the Maker looked on from afar, the screaming horde of Bloodbound forced the Vulkite fyrds slowly upslope towards prepared positions in the heights. A single youngflame caught out by the retreat battled the blood warriors mobbing him from all sides while the kin of his fyrd called out in impotent wrath. The Maker's heart quickened, just for a spell, as it recalled what it was to fear for living kin. The Vulkites roared and pushed back against their slingshields, but there was no reaching the boy through such a berzerker press.

'*Let me take them,*' said the voice.

The Maker said nothing, still watching as a white-haired old hearthkarl raised his axe up high above the crowd, hacked down a bloodreaver, and then took his place. Then he cut down another. And another. Advancing with every stroke until somehow there he was in the midst of the melee, fighting side-by-side with the lost lad. Under the cover of the elder's glittering axe, the pair withdrew to the fyrd, there to be welcomed by the songs and the acclaim of the youngflame's kin.

He nodded to himself. Sometimes there was no way forward. Until that way was found.

Pulling his hood up over his grey head, he turned to walk away. The lightning zephyr sputtered and faded as he walked through it and away from Skarn Karak. The future was not the Maker's to see, only to shape, but he knew that the strength of the Skarravorn would be equal to this test. Others would falter. It was true.

But there was nothing that could not be remade.

This time, it would not be remade by him.

'Masters of stone and metal and the makers of intricate machines are they...'

The Maker huffed his way up the Syari mountain. He scowled to himself as he dragged his game leg up the harsh slope, his steel-capped walking cane skidding in the neglected road's grit.

Why does it always have to be mountains?

He had only himself to blame for it, he supposed. No one had forced him to teach their forefathers how to dig, and how to work the metals they brought to light. At least he did not think that anyone had. The memories were faded, like runes on an ancient's tomb, and he could not wholly recall them now. It might equally have been a good story he had once heard. Stories, particularly the good ones, had a power that way that even the gods might envy.

The last time the Maker had made this particular ascent it had been in the comfortable back seat of a steam wagon, bound for the newly opened gem fields with a bawdy company of miners from the gates of Xintil. The road then had been wide and paved with white marble, the slopes dotted with forts and ale-rests and little villages. Traffic in both directions had been heavy with workers and trade. Now, the marble slabs looked as though they had been pulled up one by one by gargants taught to wield picks. The homes of the duardin were rubble. And there was no traffic. Just the steady, hurried trickle of duardin running the other way, their kingdoms reduced to the packs on their back.

Even had the Maker not come cloaked in his usual guise of anonymity, he doubted whether any of those refugees would have looked up from the ground long enough, or cared enough, to notice him. They would likely not have had kind words for him if they did.

The Maker had seen every type of woe that had been levelled against his people. Grief and hardship were no strange sights to him now, if they had ever been. But there were no obvious signs of battle here. No armies had fought over this mountain.

The realm itself rejected them.

Leaving the path for a spell, the Maker limped up a loose incline to a rugged shelf where the view was better and sighed at what he saw.

The neighbouring peaks across the vale were crumbling. The entire vista seemed caught in a state of deconstruction as the magic that had ordered them so perfectly now turned dark and wild. One mountain had cracked like a clay gourd, the white light of Hysh blazing out along the fissure lines. Another hung in mid-air, millions of tons of blasted rock drifting very slowly apart. The peak which he now climbed had weathered the worst of the Spirefall – the Lumineth displaying characteristic egocentrism and élan even in naming the implosion of their civilisation – but this was a calamity beyond even the tenacity of stubborn folk to endure.

He cast a last, sorrowful look across the vale. There had been beauty here once. An order and a symmetry that had both baffled and delighted him. And oh, how his aelven host and counterpart had delighted in his stubborn attempts to unpick this one landscape's hidden meaning.

With a sigh, he returned to what was left of the road. Where his feet fell, broken slabs became whole again. At least for as long as it took him to move on. As the old saying went, there was no point setting the flags before the walls were up. He could not fix the mountain. Or more to the point, he could, but he did not see the point in doing so.

The Lumineth were not nearly done with destroying themselves just yet.

His journey to the upper reaches of Skarrabryn, as the mountain was known, took four days from start to end, but the Maker took no reckoning of the passing time. He knew where he wanted to be and when, and so tended to be in the right place at the time he meant.

The gates of Brynt-a-Bryn, light of lights, the seat of the duardin kings in Syar, were sixty feet tall and supremely defensible, set hard into the mountain. The scarp before it had a wild and rocky beauty of its own, a naturally cut ladder of outcroppings and ledges connected by stone bridges and the winding of the road. Duardin families thronged every available scrap of level ground. Pitching tents. Herding beardlings. Loading wagons. Even more streaming through the open gates despite the muscular efforts of duardin Ironbreakers and aelven warriors in sun-yellow robes and gleaming mail to marshal the flow.

Wandering over the final crumbling arch bridge brought him to a craggy berm crammed with idling steam wagons. The lead engine was fetched up across the bridge with the rest bottled in behind. The small rear compartment behind the riveted iron dome of the boiler was laden with loose goods and overfull chests. A

DAVID GUYMER

pair of hard-worn boots stuck out from the engine's undercarriage, a few silver-grey wisps of magnificently long beard poking out with them.

A meaty fist emerged from behind the front wheel, and waggled some kind of spring-loaded adjustable spanner in the Maker's direction.

'Hand me a *fut*-grade socket wrench, would you?'

The Maker's eyebrow lifted in surprise. He turned to look behind him, but there was no other helper or apprentice that the duardin might have been speaking to. Everyone else nearby was either hurrying off down the hill on foot or busy with their own vehicles. He looked down. A pack full of tools lay unfurled over the pitted stretch of road parallel to the wagon's running board. The Maker nodded.

A good set of tools. Well kept.

The hand snapped its fingers. 'Come on, come on.'

The Maker picked out the *fut* from the selection of socket wrenches and passed it down. The hand took it.

'Thank you kindly.'

The chassis rang to the sound of clanks and bangs. There was a liquid gurgling, followed by a muffled shout of triumph. The hand reached out with the newly greasy tool and banged on the wagon's side.

'Done! Off with you now, but go easy if you mean her to hold out until Xintil!'

The engineer slid himself out. His overalls were smeared from collar to ankles in oil. His face was black and shiny, just a few white strands of a fulsome beard and scruffy mane of hair showing through. Behind him the wagon juddered, the steam boiler whistling as pistons and cylinders began to chug. The carriage rocked from side to side, but that, the Maker reckoned, had as much to do with the excitement in the front cabin than any action of the duardin engine. The engineer glowed with satisfaction, smearing filthy hands on a slightly less filthy bit of rag, and looked up. His eyes, bright circles of white in his dark face, glazed slightly as they passed across the Maker.

'Thank you kindly,' he muttered again, tugging once on his beard before bending to wrap up his tools.

The Maker nodded towards the wagon. 'They're about to leave without you.'

'It's not my wagon,' the duardin said. He nodded his gratitude once more as he gathered up his large bundle and started off down the line to where another vehicle appeared to be suffering from boiler trouble. He traded shouts with the elderly matron on the front bench as he clambered up onto the back to inspect the valves.

The Maker was surprised to find that he was smiling.

An uncomfortable prickling sensation grew across the back of his head, a feeling he had grown so unaccustomed to he did not recognise it at first.

Being watched.

He turned, and his eye caught that of an aelf guard. The warrior was clad in bright sunmetal and silver, a surplice of dazzling white flapping in the mountain breeze, and a tall helm with a shining plume. The aelf's slender form conveyed elegance and grace, but at the same time a tremendous sense of power that even the Maker, perhaps especially the Maker, could not overlook.

A moment passed as the two figures regarded one another across the busy berm. The smile returned to the Maker's face and grew. The aelf dipped his silver helm.

The Maker limped through the crowds to join him at the gate. 'I almost didn't recognise you under that getup. We've not spoken since that business with your brother and your distant cousins took you from Highheim.' He looked up at the tall aelf. 'You've changed.'

'We all have,' said the aelf, his voice light, but rich. Like a precious metal. 'I hear that even you have forsaken Mount Celestian.'

'Forsaken is a stronger word than I'd use. But aye, the white halls were feeling somewhat empty these days.'

The aelf looked over the crowds, his vantage taking in the entire sea of heads and the jagged peaks of the mountainous vista beyond the precipice. His helm swayed lightly, side to side, like a blind man trying to fix something in his mind.

'Your people will be missed.'

'Is that praise for my folk I hear?'

The aelf glanced at him sharply.

The Maker laughed. 'Go on, say it. Say it and whatever boon you have come here to ask of me will be yours.'

The aelf looked away. 'What makes you believe that I wish a boon?'

The laughter faded. The Maker's expression became stern. 'Why else does anyone ever seek out the duardin? There were duardin in the mountains of Syar long before there were aelves, you know. But there was room enough for all, and so the kings of Brynt-a-Bryn welcomed the coming of the Lumineth as partners and friends.'

'This is our realm,' said the aelf, but softly. 'It was not in your power to have denied us.'

The Maker shrugged off the argument. 'And then along you come and wreck it all.'

'If this was a disaster that could be averted with a blade alone then I would gladly offer you mine. For aelf and for duardin. The legions of the Prince of Lust cover nine of the Ten Paradises, all except the innerlands of Xintil where the fortress-cities of the God-King still hold. These I can fight, and will, but the realm...' The silver helm turned back to the Maker. Sightless eyes regarded the duardin levelly. 'The realm I cannot mend. But you could.'

'Maybe I could. What became of the supposed skill of the aelves?'

'My brother might have been capable,' said the aelf. 'But he has withdrawn. He blames himself and meditates on the true moon and will do nothing to save his children.'

The Maker shook his head. 'How many children will that one create and then cast aside?'

'My brother sees too keenly,' said the aelf. 'He perceives every flaw in everything and is incapable of overlooking it once found. He was made to see the wisdom of mercy before and will again, but not before considering every alternative first. I hoped that you would see it sooner. Stay. Present yourself to your people and convince them to remain. If you will mend this realm then I will hold this Paradise.'

The Maker frowned, giving the offer its serious due.

He watched as the old engineer he had aided earlier clambered finally into the front bench of his own cart, a pair of younger apprentices still loading guns and equipment and gold-bound ledgers of lore into the rear. Other duardin, driven and on foot, waved and shouted their thanks. No profession was more respected amongst the duardin, even in its more warlike Aqshian offshoots, than that of the maker. Standing on the front board, the whitebeard turned to the gate and raised a fist in greeting and farewell.

The Maker nodded in return. 'Best of fortune on your journey,' he said.

'Perhaps I will see you again in Azyrheim,' the duardin called. 'I'm thinking of founding an engineering school, and I'm sure I'll have need of a duardin who knows his *fut* from his *odro*.'

The Maker waved him off. 'Away. It's a long way from here to the Azyr gates of Xintil.'

The Maker watched the steam wagon puff across the bridge, part of a long train of steam and iron snaking its way down the dying scarp.

'So much will be destroyed,' said the aelf, watching too. 'So much that will never see the light of Hysh again.'

'Aye,' said the Maker, but beneath his great beard and the depths of his hood he was smiling again. 'You're not wrong.'

> 'Under the stewardship of their ancestors will they prosper...'

He prodded the cold ash with the steel tip of his cane. Digging. As he had once taught mortals to dig. He muttered an old ditty as he worked, words that came from the innermost depths of his own mortal youth and which even he did not recall the meaning of now. He grunted as his efforts exposed the dark wooden curve of a barrel. He crouched beside it stiffly. An immortal wasn't immune to his body's cares. He simply suffered them for a little longer.

On his knees, he took the rim of the unearthed keg and heaved. It came up with a gush of soot. The Maker coughed. Something sloshed inside. The sturdy wood had not been breached, but the heat would undoubtedly have ruined its contents. There was something written on the barrel. A sigh escaped his lips as he cleared away the grime with his thumb. Half a dozen bold Xs were all that the fire had left.

This had been a cask of the good stuff.

Above him, the wooden skeleton of the Bearded Dragon inn and brewery sagged against the dreary grey of the hill. Between the beams of rib and spine, the silver-plated moon of Ayadah hid itself from the shameful sight behind fleeting scraps of cloud. The humpbacked mounds of the neighbour hills rang with discordant laughter and the occasional piercing screech as the colourful armies of the Changer pursued the last of the Edrundour duardin into the Copperback Hills. But even that sound was muted. As though the country had turned its back on their suffering as their god had, and cared to hear it no longer.

The Maker ran his hand over the burned lettering on the barrel. There was a murmur of power, the faint and distant note of hammers striking metal or chisels working wood, and where his hand passed, the runic symbols shone clear and golden.

'Duardin will drink here again some other day,' he muttered, not intending it for a promise, but his kind could speak in no other way. 'When your roof is mended and your cellar stocked with ales this good I will stop here and sup again.'

'You come too late, Maker.'

Ash and gravel crunched under his knee as he shifted. He looked over his shoulder. The burnt remains of a duardin lay near to where the bar must have been. The corpse was fresh, as judged by the age of the wreckage he lay under, but the fire had already made him a skeleton. An axe lay on the ground beside him. In a rare moment of generosity towards bad work he made approving note of the more recent notches on its blade.

The old brewer had not burned alone.

'They are with me now.'

The voice came from the corpse. A faint amethyst wisp-light illuminated the black sockets of his eyes. A small portion of that light trickled from his gaping mouth, dimming and brightening with his whispered words.

With a wince, the Maker rose.

'You are growing old.'

The Maker nodded. 'That's the way of it. I wasn't expecting to hear your voice out here, old spectre. I heard you'd pulled back to Shyish and shut the gates.'

'Death is everywhere, never more so, and I am Death.'

'Even the aelf-god and the Great Green stood by Sigmar at the last.'

'And where were you? His closest ally?' The skull twisted slowly around to face him. Burnt flesh creaked and dry bones popped.

'No, no, none of that.' The Maker planted the foot of his cane on the corpse's cheekbone and held it in place. 'Have you no respect for the dead?'

'The dead are mine to possess. Mine to do with as I will. That was the concession that all the Pantheon made to me. Long before the barbarian king ever raised his grand folly above Mount Celestian.'

'I keep my promises, old bones. I thought you knew me better than that.'

'I am not ignorant of what Sigmar builds in secret.'

'Not much of a secret then, is it?'

Amethyst fire glared coolly from the corpse's eye sockets. *'He cheats me. They all cheat me. You mask your guile with jests and vulgarity, but you cheat me too. I know it. And all will know the fullness of it in time. Or am I to believe it coincidence that he plunders the souls of the dead and near-dead for his great work while leaving the duardin underworlds unmolested?'*

The Maker shrugged. He made to leave. Released from under his cane, the skull pivoted towards him.

'I respected you, Maker. You, alone amongst all the others, I thought would understand. You, who would address the impermanence of mortality with stone and iron, shackle your wayward impulses with the hidden gears of your own industry. You, alone, I respected. Even as you cheat me of my due.' The lights in the skull's deep, fire-blackened sockets flickered hungrily. *'Do you even know how many duardin have joined me in my realm since the last of the gates to Azyr were sealed?'*

The Maker's expression became stern. He knew the exact number.

'I know that Sigmar offered sanctuary to them all and you declined. I know also that the Luminous God offered the same.'

'A bunch of gossips is what you all are,' the Maker growled. 'And yet you wonder why I left Highheim.'

'Why? Why send them to me instead?'

'I've nothing to say. I ask you to please begone from my fallen kin and leave me to grieve the ruination of my realm in peace.'

'*Aid me as you aided him,*' the voice hissed. The wisp-light deepened with the sudden intensity of its words. '*Give me the keys to the duardin underworlds, and with such tools will we remake Shyish into a fortress of Order as will endure unto the end of things.*'

'No.'

'*I will find them if I must. I will break them, and devour their guardian spirits and false-gods as I have all others.*'

'No you won't, or you wouldn't have bothered to ask. Because though you clearly don't know me nearly half as well as I thought you did, I do still know you. Now...' Shuffling about, he rested the foot of his cane back on the mail vest draped over the duardin skeleton's ribcage. 'I asked you to get out of my kinsman's body and leave me in peace. I even said please.'

'*All things that are dead belong to me. Whether they come to me singly or in their trillions, they are mine, and I know when one is absent. You hope to hide something from me. I see through you.*'

'I'm not asking nicely now.'

The Maker's power was not greater than that of the Undying King, and most certainly not where it pertained to the spheres of Death. Theirs was a rivalry for a new and untested Age. Its limits had yet to be measured.

But the Maker was here.

Nagash was not.

The arcane metallurgy of his cane blazed as it became a conductor of godly power. The skull screamed, its jaw falling open and fusing stiff as the wisp-light fought, flickered, and then was snuffed out.

The Maker coughed again, withdrew his cane, and then leant on it. A shuddering out-breath of what later generations would call aether-gold glittered in the air in front of his face.

The brewer's bones gleamed. They had been turned to solid lead. 'Rest in peace,' the Maker muttered, and left.

'He will remind them of the old ways...'

The sky turned red, the final sunset at the end of days. Blood dripped down the delicate spires of the Ahramentian mage-lords, windows of reflective glass rattling in silver fixtures, and steam bubbling up from ornamental lakes and swimming baths. Thick clouds rolled in from across the vast savannah, stacking over the great airborne city into the shape of a colossal brass axe. And beyond that hard edge of blood-red cloud, through the thinning skies and the warping optics of Chaos, there lay the hint of something even more terrible.

A sharp red face. Horns. Yellow eyes ablaze with unspeakable hatred.

The deity looked down on the Ahramentian capital from its high place above the Realm of Fire, reached out across the cold cosmic void, and pronounced its end.

From a hundred miles away, the Maker heard the city scream. The cries were not of horror. That would have been explicable and a thousand times less awful. Rather, every voice in the city from its lowliest slave to its mightiest mage-lord looked up into the harsh face of that god of gods and screamed their rage. Even the Maker himself, insulated by divinity and distance, felt the same inconsolable urge to take up arms and bloody himself in pointless battle against that thing. Indeed, he may even have suffered it worse. He, after all, alone in that place, had some power to avert what was coming. Or at least to draw the butcher's ire for a moment or two.

Lightning bolts and fireballs and beams of light jagged upwards from the city's mage towers and splashed across the Blood God's brass vambraces and blood-hardened skin. The sky shuddered with the terrible wrath of gods.

The axe descended.

Ahramentia fell.

The Maker swept up his cloak as the shockwave from the act of city-murder rolled out from its epicentre. Grasses burst into flame, trees were torn up by their roots, the dust of a screaming wasteland, newly born and wrathful, hurling itself at whatever it could hurt. In a matter of seconds it reached the Maker. The wave hit like the fist of Drakatoa, the living avalanche, dust and debris smashing against an invisible golden shield.

Though the onslaught had come on quickly, it took an age to stop, falling away gradually until the Maker felt it safe enough to lower his cloak. Red sand slid off. A small hill of it had heaped up around his boots.

The clouds split and thundered, and a blood rain started to splatter over the youngest, angriest desert in the Realm of Fire. The Maker drew up his hood. A hundred miles away, the sundered halves of Ahramentia crashed to the ground. Its final death came in near silence, cushioned by deadening sand.

The Maker felt its tremors through his boots. He was, he realised, standing on the last intact piece of Ahramentia: a single, immaculately preserved paving slab, shielded by the making power of his feet.

There was a whimper from behind and he turned.

A mother in a scarlet shawl was crouched over two young beardlings. Behind her, an old longbeard in a splinted mail vest stood with a stout axe over his shoulder, too proud or too stiff-kneed to cower. His white hair was singed and still smouldering, a pair of scorched red rings making his eyes unnaturally wide. He was staring upwards, swaying like a statue that had been prodded with an axe.

'Blessed Grungni,' the mother whispered in the youngsters' ears.

The Maker winced. 'Go on,' he offered gently. 'There are parts of Golvaria and Callidium that haven't fallen yet. Maybe you'll find one of the lodges around Vostargi Mont willing to take you in.'

'The Fyreslayers?'

The Maker shrugged. 'Why not? They are duardin, are they not?'

The mother opened her mouth to answer, but found she had none.

'We were going south,' the longbeard managed to croak.

'The Blood God has just ended your empire, friend. Plans can change.'

'South,' he said again, firmer this time. 'I'll run, aye, in good time. Only after I've seen to the wards on Ringol Magemaker's tomb and am sure that my grandfather sleeps through his doom as was promised him.'

The Maker had walked far these last decades and had seen much, but he found himself touched by the old longbeard's stubbornness nonetheless. He adjusted his hood, and for a brief moment permitted the four duardin a true glimpse of what lay beneath it.

The longbeard staggered, but still did not kneel. The beardlings stared up with open mouths. They would forever remember this moment, the time their grandfather had stood before the Maker himself and received his blessing. It was a story they would retell and lend power to, long after every account of Ahramentia's fall had faded.

'You could have saved them all,' the longbeard muttered.

'This time,' the Maker conceded, resetting his hood. 'What of next time, and the time after?'

The longbeard had no answer for him.

The Maker tugged lightly on his beard, and bade them all farewell.

* * *

'*...and he will guide them towards the new.*'

Karak-a-Zaruk, last and mightiest of the old duardin strongholds in the empire's Chamonic heartlands, had left its final gambit a shade late.

Warriors in iridescent armour galloped down its wide-paved roads under banners that changed from moment to moment. Mutated dragons with multicoloured scales, a terrible wisdom in their eyes, descended from on high to deposit Kairic acolytes into the highest and most inaccessible tiers, laying fortresses low with mild swipes of their claws or the changing fires of their breath. Even from the sewers, the city's former pride, iron grates that had prevented skaven and Moonclan invasions for centuries flowed with a kaleidoscopic slurry. Where that weird ectoplasm oozed onto the street, it lifted itself up and ran, becoming a giggling legion of long-armed, crook-legged horrors, capering into the doomed city and spraying it at random with pink fire.

In those arcane fires even the hardest granite and most patiently forged duardin steel shimmered and turned liquid. And once the stout dwelling or proud icon was naught but a reflective pool of uncannily twitching metals, some new horror would pull itself out, as if from a hot bath, shake its overlong fingers, and run shrieking after its daemonic brethren.

The Maker saw it all.

He saw it and he did nothing.

Between the third and second tiers, the gates were crowned by a triumphal arch that lionised Karak-a-Zaruk's final victory over the Dyrwood Ironjawz and the civilising of Odrenn. It was already failing as the Maker passed under it. No sooner was he through than it finally gave. The commemorative stonework of the right-hand pier burst with a sound like a discharging rifle. Marble sprayed across the victory courtyard as the keystone, carved into a heroically bearded bust, parted company from its haunches and toppled.

It fell straight towards him.

'A little obvious, aren't we,' he muttered, extending a measure of his power and nudging the giant stone aside.

The column listed as it fell, as if of its own natural accord rather than his, passing a beard's-length to his left and crashing into the roof of a meat vendor's outdoor terrace that just happened to be sheltering a large group of duardin. The Maker cursed as broken tiles and powdered red clay showered the doomed duardin.

But when the stoutest amongst them looked up they saw to their amazement that the roof above their heads was miraculously undamaged. The formerly triumphant arch lay in a thousand pieces over the thoroughly obliterated remains of everything else in their street. But by a tremendous fluke of luck, the destruction ended right at the terrace's brushed steel gate.

Without lingering to count their good fortune, warriors in red cloaks with bone-white wooden shields shepherded their charges off the strangely preserved terrace and onto the devastated street. From there, they fled uphill as fast as duardin legs could bear them, towards the assumed if dubious safety of the fourth tier.

'*I see you.*'

The words came less as a voice and more as a feeling. It was everything and it was everywhere. It made every grain of debris in the courtyard tremble.

And not just the debris.

'*See me.*'

The words bounced off every weakened cornice and defiled capital, each echo subtly twisting their message until they meant the opposite of what had originally been inferred, or perhaps nothing at all.

'Here we are.'

Revealing himself here, after all these years of wandering, might have been a mistake. But then what exactly was the point of being a god if you could not bend your own rules from time to time? Karak-a-Zaruk was one of the last duardin cities still free. It was certainly the largest.

There were things, despite those same wanderings, that he still wanted, hoped, *needed* to see.

An avian shriek came from what was left of the archway, and a burst of crawling magicks cleared the rubble barring passage from the second tier. An enormous winged creature swathed in a silken shroud and holding a wizard's staff stepped through the wreckage. Standing twenty feet high where its stooped neck met its hunched shoulders, the Lord of Change towered over the Maker.

Until the Maker decided that it ought to be otherwise.

The daemon sorcerer cringed back, but did not flee.

'I'll not insult us both by asking if you know who I am,' said the Maker, unfurling his cloak and drawing a weapon. It would have been indescribable to mortal eyes. It was a great-mace and a blunderbuss and every weapon in between, none of the above and a little bit of all.

The greater daemon, of course, saw it for what it really was. Its screams cut abruptly short as its head and shoulders exploded like a jellyfish crushed under a rock, but there was something equally satisfying about watching its chest gout ichor before crumbling back into aether.

He lowered the weapon.

A rumble of mirth, or wrath, or perhaps both, passed through the groaning stonework. Tiles slid away from broken roofs with a clatter like rain drumming on a metal shed. Paving slabs worked themselves loose and rose to wobble a foot above the road.

'This isn't a fight you want,' said the Maker, raising his weapon defensively. 'It's not your war. Leave me to my business and I'll not interfere in yours.'

A small group of duardin still sheltering in the shop behind the terrace screamed as the building began to quake.

'Get on!' the Maker yelled at them, waving the stubborn fools after the clan warriors and their kin. 'Get out!'

At his urging they upped and ran, and not a moment before time. The last one out was an old longbeard with a padded jack and a crossbow cradled in his arms, shouting directions to the others as the streets ahead of them morphed and changed. The door lunged out to bite him as he fled. It missed by inches and he did not look back. Probably wise.

Some things could never be unseen.

The house was rippling with change, colours shimmering as it transformed into a jellied mass, windows running together into a singular iridescent mass of eyeballs. The floor heaved and shuddered as its foundations tore up out of the ground as squirming tentacles. The Maker blasted one that rippled too near for his comfort, but another just as quickly tore loose of the ground. The entire structure rose up as it mutated to best resemble the impossible creature that had chosen to inhabit it with this morsel of its being, and which now looked out from behind those clustered eyes. It grew. And then it grew. Until that eye was all the realms, and the Maker was forced to step back from it and lift his gaze higher to keep it all in view.

There was nothing he could have seen in the sky behind it that should have been able to make him grin.

Yet grin he did.

From the summit of the ninth and uppermost tier, a thing never before seen in the Mortal Realms was taking off. A fleet of crude but ingeniously fashioned vessels rose from the spider-web of steel bars that festooned the city's inner walls. They were airships, but these craft harnessed neither lighter-than-air gases nor the power of steam to drive their flight. They used endrins, burning the by-waste of the Maker's own forge to produce lift and power and, in so doing, they had achieved a feat of science that had not been taught to them by the Maker. They had risen, literally, to the challenges of the era. They had outgrown their infancy and surpassed him.

As he had known, *hoped*, they would.

The godling did not turn to look. It did not need to.

'What do you think you see?' said the wordless voice.

'I see nothing. Only hope. But maybe in this my eyes see further than yours.'

The Maker lowered his weapon. One day, perhaps, there would come a time to use it. But not today.

He limped backwards, leaving Karak-a-Zaruk to burn and its conqueror to plot and rage while its people fled to the skies.

The duardin would fight another day.

> *'History is recorded by the victors. This much is true*
> *and has always been known. But who are the victors?*
> *The victors are those who endure the longest.'*

The Maker swung his hammer, the sound of it hitting the anvil ringing out through the deep underhalls of the Iron Karak. The hammer swung, and swung again, the echoing *bangs* telling a story of their own, one that grew with each retelling as it echoed through the steel vaults. The air became hazed with his exertion, aether-gold enough to lift every sky-port in the Mortal Realms and keep them aloft for fifty years drifting like shining dust.

How long he had laboured there he could not say. Centuries, almost certainly, but it did not matter. It took as long as it took. As any good smith knew.

The substance he hammered against his anvil was formless and ephemeral, and yet was harder in its own way than sigmarite or celestite. It was the Legend of the White-Bearded Ancestor, the accumulated stories and lore of all the duardin peoples. It resisted shaping, but he was Grungni the Maker. He could work any material, if given enough centuries to work at it in peace.

He nodded finally, breathless and weary from his labours, and set down his hammer and tongs. He reached out to his creation.

Its hand grasped his.

The reforged duardin stepped out from the anvil and, for the first time since the departure of the Six Smiths to Sigmaron, the Maker welcomed a near-equal to his forge. The duardin, still white-hot from the heat of his making, dipped his head in greeting. The Maker returned the welcome in kind.

'Father,' the duardin grunted.

'You remember...?' said the Maker.

'Everything.'

'Then I fear you've the advantage on me. The ages have taken so much.'

The duardin looked down at his hands, staring at them not in wonder so much as in fascination at another master's work.

'I'm not sure what to call you, now you're here,' said the Maker. 'You've worn so many names. Not least the one by which I once named you.'

The shining duardin looked up.

A fierce aura blazed off him, a brilliant halo of silver-white that burned through his long white beard and wild mane of hair. He would cool in time, but always would he be greater than the mere sum of his forms. To the Maker he was potential, vivid and pure, all things to all duardin.

'You know my name.'

The Maker smiled. 'Aye. I suppose I do. And so do they.' He

gestured to the great door of his forge. It was locked, even though he was alone in this fastness, far from friend and foe alike. Habits died hard. 'The duardin have become strong through their trials. As I had always trusted that they would. But they have also become divided. It's time for them to feel my hand again, to remake that which was once whole. But we duardin aren't so quick to forgive a wrong done to us, and the wrong I did to them was great indeed. The centuries that have passed since the Age of Myth have been too long and bloody for them to follow me again, and Grimnir is not yet ready to return. There's only one thing they all share in common, one duardin who can unite them all.'

Grombrindal sighed and picked up his axe. 'Best make a start then, hadn't I?'

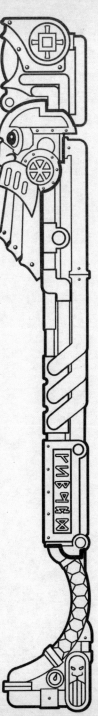

LORDS OF STONE,
FIRE AND SKY

'What are a people but the sum of all their stories? It is how a culture is made, the mortar with which each individual is set in its place. This is true of all peoples in the Mortal Realms, even those that many of my peers and kin would hesitate before calling people at all. But do the orruks not have their own myths to give them purpose? Did Teclis, in his supposed enlightenment, not teach the aelves of the former glories from which they have descended? Do the pawns of the Dark Gods not justify their depravities with grievances as old as the hatred of one thinking being for another?

'But stories are not immutable. They change with time and with telling to fit the need of a people, and the duardin have as many stories as they have kingdoms throughout the Mortal Realms. Amongst them though, there are stories that all duardin share, and that have changed but little with time and geography. Because, deep down, underneath the armour and the runes and however they have adapted themselves to the challenges of the age, there is a part of them all that has changed but little as well...'

CHAPTER ONE

Strahl Aelsson leant and tapped the glass front of the large aethermatic clock facing him from his bedstand. The device gave accurate time for all eight of the Mortal Realms. Seven lesser faces, in metals corresponding to the realms' signature hues, surrounded the great bronze primary of Chamon, the source of the great windstream, the *strahlstrom*, and the central cog in the great machinery of the Cosmos Arcane. To his annoyance – although not, it had to be said, entirely to his surprise – none of the displayed times or their rates of change were altered in any way. The skeletal hand of Shyish continued on its methodical crawl around the circumference of its sphere. The golden arrow of Aqshy whirred with such haste through its rotation that it made Strahl's eyes water to follow it.

It was hypnotic, and he hadn't the faintest idea how it worked.

His mother had brought in tutors from all the great sky-ports, to instruct him in aethermancy, astrolocution and forecastination, and Strahl had tried to learn, as he always tried, but none of it had taken and he had reluctantly conceded that the cosmic sciences were not for him. Cutting her losses rather than persist with a failing venture, a knack that had helped make her rich, Ael Dunrs-dottir had summarily dismissed the tutors and hired new ones. Masters in khemistry, endrineering and navigation had made the long journey to Karag Dawrkhaz in their place. Strahl supposed that he ought to be grateful. Most mothers would have given up by now, surrendered the likelihood of ever finding something at which her son might excel, but Ael Dunrsdottir, master code-wright of Barak-Nar's Guild of Codewrights and magnate of Karag Dawrkhaz, had not become the duardin she was by accepting a negative return on an investment.

Strahl watched the time partition itself unfairly across the Mortal Realms for a while longer. He was, he decided with immense gravity, very late indeed.

With that determination made, he slid his feet into his boots, tugged his gun belt down from the bedpost at the foot of the bed and buckled it around a waist that was growing into a full and stately duardin's girth. Out of habit, he checked the draw on the brace of volley pistols, and checked them again, then that his aether-charge knife was where it ought to be. He was safe enough in the port, but diligence didn't cost anything, particularly out here on the frontier.

With the belt sitting tightly, and his weapons within easy reach, he looked over his shoulder and allowed himself to feel some-thing close to contentment.

Brigg sat at the writing bureau, using the polished copper plate that functioned as a mirror to dress her hair. As was the way of her people she wore very little that a Kharadron would consider clothing, but for a hefty-looking belt that took the severe form of an ancestor-face in thick gold plates and a short skirt of leather scales and fyresteel rings. Strahl could get himself serviceable in the time it took to slide on a pair of boots, but for Brigg it was an involved and awe-inspiring process that, according to aethermatic timekeeping and the progression of light across the wall, was the work of about forty-five minutes. The hair that seemed to occupy the majority of her attention and time was a rich, golden red, drawn up through the funnel of an ornate helm and then out through an open roof resembling the open jaws of a hair-spewing magmadroth.

Strahl could have watched her all morning but, urged on by the ticking of the timepiece, he forced himself to speak up. 'Are you done with the mirror? If I'm any later to *trommraad* then Ael will rouse the Grundstok to search for me.'

Her eyes were a magmic red, the bridge of her wide nose and her cheekbones freckled in various shades by old burns and heat blisters. There was a smile in that face, somewhere, in the same way that a river of lava might have gold in it, and a duardin would be equally well advised against spending too long looking for it. With a few final adjustments, she rose from the stool and crossed to the window. Strahl was up from the bed before she was fully out of the seat, and sliding into her place at the bureau. He picked up a beard comb and peered into the mirror. He could be presentable in two minutes, but if he could impress his mother with a little extra effort then he would, particularly as he was late already.

With an enigmatic shake of the head, Brigg looked out over the busy sprawl of piers and walkways that projected from the virgin summit of Karag Dawrkhaz. Windlasses and cranes filled the thin air with a constant mechanical chuntering, feeding the vigorous young outpost's hunger for raw materials and expanded frontiers. Brigg loved the view. It was one of the reasons they met for their all-too-infrequent trysts here. The ruins of former hill farms and ranger cabins, left desolate with the departure of the old kings and never resettled, dotted the mountain's lower slopes.

The lines of distant sleet made them grey, like an ancestor's sorrow. The monolithic entrance vault to the Great Hall of the Dunra-kul, the Gate of Throngs, and its fortresses was just about visible too, if one held onto the top of the frame and leant out a little, as Brigg was occasionally wont to do. It was as tall as an admiral's flagship from endrin rig to tail shaft, made of grey marble and emblazoned with runes that few but the followers of the old ways could now read in verdigrised bronze.

The view from Strahl's own room was even better, but the corridors in that section of the city-port were too heavily guarded by his mother's Thunderers. For all Ael's declarations of neutrality over the skirmishes that went on in the deeps, she still laid claim to this mountain, and trespassers were liable to be shot. One couldn't be too careful, although there were times when he suspected that Brigg actually enjoyed the danger.

Another reason they always met here. A compromise of a sort.

'And if your mother's Thunderers were to kick down this door and find us together...'

Brigg turned from the window, framed by the lofty view, a few flecks of snow settling in her shiny red hair. Strahl hadn't been long in Ael's new holding, but snow seemed out of keeping with the climate and the season. And the summit of a volcano. Brigg had all his attention however and he didn't consider the weather further.

'What would you say?'

Strahl set down the beard comb while he thought. The delay was answer enough for Brigg. She turned back to the window.

'I should go,' she said. 'You're late.'

'I'm going to ask her,' he said quietly, looking not at her but into the brass-tinted eyes of his own reflection, as though he was the one who needed to be convinced. 'Today. Now.'

'I'm not waiting for you to ask her. I want you to *tell* her.'

'Like you've told your father?'

Strahl immediately regretted his words. One didn't lightly challenge a Fyreslayer.

'I'll tell him,' she said. 'And you know I'll tell him. But I'll not walk through that particular fire if you lack the courage to go with me.' She glared at him from the window, so unlike his mother and yet so very much the same, just *waiting* for him to do or say something that would prove himself worthy of her time and gold.

With a sigh, he shuffled his stool back along the metal floor and pulled out one of the drawers of the bureau.

He resented her then, for forcing him into something he had put a tremendous amount of thought into presenting properly. He was tempted to just let her walk, if that was what she wanted, but forced himself to be the cooler head. The Fyreslayers were quick to wrath, but they didn't hold a grudge like some other duardin might. If he were to let her storm out now then she'd have forgotten about it before she was out of the corridor while he'd be the one left seething for the weeks until they were next able to meet.

Drawing the thick sheaf of crisp white papers from the drawer, he set them on the desk. He brushed the top sheet lovingly. Each page was dense with neat runic script, professionally typeset and printed by a codewright specialising in the spousal artycles. Karag Dawrkhaz was a small frontier settlement at the very edge of the Spiral Crux, but wherever two Kharadron gathered there were shares to be made by those who knew how to properly interpret the Code.

'You and your paper collections,' said Brigg teasingly.

'It's not a…' He lowered his voice, and looked nervously around. This was a little-used part of the port but, even so, there were things a duardin did not discuss aloud. It had been hard enough overcoming the embarrassment to commission the codewright. 'It's a spousal contract.'

'A spousal–?'

'Shhh! Do you want the whole mountain to hear?'

Brigg walked across from the window, leaning over his shoulder, her closeness a warm pain against his skin, as she flicked through the stack of pages. Her eyes glazed over the unfamiliar written form of the tongue they both shared. Even if she'd been able to decipher the Kharadron runes, she would probably have been flummoxed by the dense legalese.

'How could it need so many pages?'

'It's only ninety-seven. Why? How many will you need?'

Brigg did not look quite as impressed as he had expected her to be. 'None!'

'It's only the standard artycles. Footnotes cost extra, of course.' Strahl was getting the powerful impression, however, that a line-by-line walkthrough of the contractual terms could wait for another time. 'It lays out my net worth, prospects, guarantors. Sets a legally binding estimate for the growth of my assets and your rights to legal redress should my promises fall short over the stipulated period.'

'How… passionate.'

Strahl breathed a sigh of relief that she understood. 'You've *no* idea how expensive codewrights are, and particularly those specialising in the spousal artycles.'

She smiled then, truly, a glimpse of her heart so rare it was like seeing the clouds opening and gold raining from a full conjunction of the realmspheres.

'Then you'd better get to your mother's council, before she's in too foul a mood at your lateness to sign it.' Picking up the beard comb that Strahl had left on the desk, she put it away in the open drawer and then closed it. Before Strahl could protest, she gripped his beard so tight that it hurt and then leant down to kiss him fiercely on the lips. It tasted like dragon's breath. 'Sometimes, I think you Kharadron trim your beards so close to your chins that it shortens your memories. That's why you need to write everything down.' Without gentleness, she let go of his beard. 'Be sure she signs it. If you forget it'll go badly for you.'

Massaging his aching chin, he scooped up the ninety-seven pages of the contract. Getting Ael's signature on the contract was not actually what worried him. He expected her to be appalled. A dirt-shoveller. *A Fyreslayer*. He expected yelling and threats of disinheritance. But he had disappointed her before and was fully resigned to the likelihood of disappointing her many times more in the future, and Ael was, almost to a fault, open to being reasonable if a case could be argued in the proper terms, with all its particulars neatly laid out in writing.

No. It was getting the counter-signature from Braegnar-Grimnir, Auric Runefather of the Dunr Lodge, that was putting the terror in his heart.

CHAPTER TWO

Kolram Dunrakul, Dispossessed lord of the Dunrakul Clan and king of Karag Dawrkhaz, frowned across the mile or so of subterranean hall that separated the two armies. His beard guard crunched into its new shape, the shimmering pattern of silver and bronze rings adopting their more wrathful expression.

The Dunrow Deeping – as the old maps marked the halls – had been infested by grots of the Kneebite, Deffstinger and Yellowstripe Spiderfang since before the final departure of the Last King to Azyr, and the evidence of their occupation was in the shame of every stone. Webbing strung from column to column, the faces of Kolram's ancestors cocooned in black silk, rendering whole swathes of floor impassable and glistening from the furthest walls like spit. Most of the glimstone sconces were empty. Those that had escaped the grots' inquisitive fingers guttered evilly, corrupted by the long hand of Chaos during the Dunrakul's years of exile. The occasional scrawny limb or spider-leg poked out of a pile of detritus, but otherwise it appeared as though the Spiderfang had given up the Deeping before the Dunrakul had fallen out of marching order and formed into battle lines.

Clan warriors in royal bronze and knee-length mail locked shields and made a wall. Stern blocks of heavily armoured Ironbreakers refused both flanks. Quarrellers and handgun-armed Thunderers followed them into position. Engineers pushed organ guns and cannon up onto hills of rubble, hammering wedges under their wheels so that they would not roll down again the first time they were fired. A quartet of sturdily built Hammerers set down the royal litter while two more, hand-chosen as the strongest in the clan, hurled the Dunrakul oathstone as far ahead of the battle line as they could. To a smattering of restrained cheers, and the grumbling of a few longbeards who recalled his father, the late King Kurun Dunrakul, having once mounted a stone better, Kolram stepped down from his litter and climbed gruffly up onto the oathstone.

With an expression that, had it been cast in bronze instead of aged flesh, could have been mistaken for a clan icon and installed upon a shield, he studied his enemy's lines.

'They look so... gaudy.'

The longbeards of his inner council and the Hammerers of his bodyguard nodded sagely.

'It has always been the Fyreslayers' way,' said Braztom.

The lorekeeper was an elderly duardin with a frosted monocle wedged into one eye against the side of a bulb nose. He leant against the handles of a gilt-banded trolley, his white-blond beard wisping across the cushioned interior that held the bronze-plated pages of the *Dunrakul Kron*. The ancient tome was a detailed history of every wrong done to the clan over the three-and-a-half millennia since their first establishment in Karag Dawrkhaz, continuing through their lengthy exile in Azyr, and picking up without pause following their return. In rare moments of solitude, Kolram would sit in the throne of his distant fathers, flick through the great *Kron*'s yellowed pages, and reflect on how much work there was still to do if every wrong was to be made right and all that was new remade as it had once been.

Kolram was appalled, but morbid fascination wouldn't let him tear his gaze away. 'Gold is meant to be put away in a box and buried, to be brought out and counted on special occasions, not waved about as though it grows on trees.'

'There's a school of thought that it's also for spending.'

Standing at the foot of the Dunrakul oathstone was a duardin of long years and obvious importance. His beard was at least as lengthy as Braztom's, but fuller, and far prouder, its thickness dressed in heavy rings and drawn into braids that wound many times around his ample waist. His red cloak was dirty, as if from many years spent wandering beyond the halls of his ancestors, but trimmed with gold that signified wealth in spite of the age's current travails. Silver mail and the occasional jewel twinkled beneath the folds of his cloak. The axe in his hands, its shaft resting on the floor while the duardin leant across the head, was one of the finest that Kolram had ever seen. Runes of the old empire decorated both blades, glowing with an unsubtle power that filled Kolram's eyes with tears at all that had been lost, and his heart with avarice at what might yet be regained.

Kolram felt his eyes slowly cross as he tried to recall who the longbeard was.

'Gromrhun, your majesty.' The duardin took the long-stemmed pipe from his mouth and tugged respectfully on his beard. 'At your service, and your fathers'.'

'Of course. Of course.'

'What's that *chuf* they're wearing?' said Hangrark, warden of Kolram's Hammerers, oblivious to his liege's exchange.

'That'll be gold again,' said Gromrhun.

Braztom adjusted his monocle and nodded that this was so.

'Ridiculous,' Hangrark muttered.

Looking away, Kolram glanced down his own line. From his high vantage atop the oathstone, he could see the two blocks of longbeards where his grown sons were being chivvied to stand up straight, tuck their beards in, and advised, with much demonstration, on the proper technique for holding an axe. For centuries, the children of the Dunrakul Clan had been schooled in Azyr and Kolram saw no reason to break with that tradition in spite of the clan's return to the halls of their ancestors. After thirty years in the academies of Azyrheim and Sigmaron they had returned with all manner of new-fangled ideas and ways of doing things, and the longbeards clearly had their work cut out.

Raising a gauntlet, each finger joint and knuckle picked out with a pale cabochon stone, Kolram beckoned for his horn-blower and heralds.

'Lorekeeper,' he said, choosing to ignore the frustrated raspberry that Gromrhun happened to blow at that exact moment. 'Announce my claim.'

Braegnar-Grimnir, runefather of the Dunr Lodge and king of Karag Dawrkhaz, wedged his thumbs under his golden belt, stuck his tongue through the ring that pierced his upper lip and tried to hear what was being shouted at him over the fyrd's jeering.

'What's the grey *ufdi* barking on about now?' he yelled at whoever was listening.

Battlesmith Dremm answered him with a voluble sigh.

Braegnar-Grimnir clapped him on the back and laughed. 'Master of blade, forge and song indeed – age has not dimmed your eloquence yet.'

'He says that he claims this hall by right of ancestry.' A warrior karl with a vibrant shock of white spilling from the throat of his golden helmet and a beard that resembled a wall of flame across his well-muscled chest stood with crossed arms amidst the mass of Hearthguard. The ur-gold runes that embossed his forearms were numerous and of peculiar design. 'He says that he's the son of Kurun, who's son of Kordrekk, who's son of Krand, who's son of Korn, who's son of Korgrun Dunrakul, the Last King of Karag Dawrkhaz, and invites you to acknowledge his rightful claim to these halls and withdraw to the lower deeps.'

'I invite him to acknowledge my fist up his *grung*.'

The old karl rolled his eyes. Dremm gave an indulgent smile, while the rest of the Auric Hearthguard making up the central mass of the royal fyrd laughed uproariously at their runefather white-hot wit.

'This is my hall,' Braegnar-Grimnir went on. 'As it'll one day be my daughter's. When Korgrun Dunrakul, the so-called Last King, abandoned the Gate of Throngs to our foes and fled to Azyr, was it not his true descendants, those who found strength in Grimnir, who held Karag Dawrkhaz for the duardin?' He beat his brawny fists against his chest. The ur-gold embedded in the former clinked against the runes standing proud of the latter. 'And over the centuries that the Dunrakul spent cowering behind the grey beard of the God-King, was it not the Dunr Lodge who held the magma-vault and its treasures from the grot kings and the Beastlords and the ghouls and the princelings of Change that coveted it? Was it not the Dunr Lodge, too, who bled for every hall of the upper deeps that was lost? Well, was it?'

The Fyreslayers roared. Every warrior was a hero clad in gold and decorated with a dead god's power. Their hair was swept into crests through snarling helmets, their beards splayed outwards across the breadth of their chests like beasts performing an intimidatory dance. They had no artillery, carried no missile weapons. They didn't need these things, didn't want these things, but slingshields, magmapikes and fyresteel axes were just as deadly, and often came as a surprise to those expecting nothing more from the Dunr than a berzerker charge and a fiery death.

Braegnar-Grimnir had lost count of the mordant kings and slaves of Chaos he'd cut down from afar with expressions of shock still on their faces.

'Duardin fighting duardin,' the white-bearded mercenary muttered with a shake of the head. 'A sorry day.'

'No different to yesterday,' said Dremm.

'Or the day before.' Braegnar-Grimnir's eye narrowed as he tried to place the old karl from amongst the countless wandering and itinerant fighters that occasionally lent his fyrds their axes. 'I don't know you,' he said bluntly.

'Azkaharr is my name.' The Fyreslayer dipped his crest. 'From across the Sea of Sages and beyond the Spiral Crux.'

'Are the lands outside the Spiral Crux and beyond the Sea of Sages so uncanny that the duardin there no longer slay their foes, or hoard their treasures from those who'd take them?'

The old karl pursed his lips in thought, then shrugged. 'In my experience, runefather, duardin are much the same wherever you go.'

Braegnar-Grimnir hesitated a moment before beckoning to Dremm and waving his battlesmiths over. The warrior-skalds pushed through the fyrd to his side, clad in golden kilts and jewelled tokens, with story-beads telling the ancient sagas dangling from their belts. Each bore aloft an icon displaying one of the many, near-identical, aspects of Grimnir. The Wanderer. The Slayer. The Honourable. The Doomed. Only the battlesmiths knew how to render every aspect and tell them all apart.

With one muscular, massively beringed hand, the runefather waved towards the opposing battle line. 'Tell him everything I just said, right back to the bit about my fist and his grung.'

* * *

'How *dare* he?' Kolram's whiskers bristled, hidden under several overlapping curtains of mail. 'Hear how he would slight the honour of my forebears in justifying his specious claims to my hall. Hark, Kothi. Hark, Kurrindorm.' He gestured towards his sons. 'See how we do the Fyreslayers and their kin a service by teaching Braegnar-Grimnir a lesson in propriety.'

'I see it, father,' Kothi called back.

Kurrindorm brandished his axe as though to show willing.

'Ach. You know how the Fyreslayers can be.' Gromrhun's tone was at once dismissive and tolerating of no nonsense. 'They speak before they think, and the words they choose often say more than they mean.'

'Then they should learn to keep their mouths closed, like proper duardin.'

Gromrhun shook his head. 'Or perhaps it's we who could do with taking a lesson from the sons of Grimnir. If we could only say as we mean from time to time, then perhaps we'd not have the enemies we do. There are grots and ghouls aplenty within these halls to keep all our axes busy.' He muttered darkly. 'And who knows what without our walls.'

'There's naught worth knowing without our walls.'

The longbeard grumbled, and clearly disagreed, but saw further argument as pointless. 'They're cousins are they not?'

'Oafish, rowdy, indolent cousins,' Kolram scowled. 'Cousins slapping barefoot and half-naked around my hall whilst insulting our ancestors.' He filled out his chest. Outrage alone lifted his beard an inch above his ribs. 'Open the *Kron*!'

A scandalised murmur passed through the Dunrakul shield wall as Lorekeeper Braztom cracked open the metal frontis, the *Kron* falling open at the middle, then licked his finger and leafed through to the next blank page. He muttered as he commenced the equally lengthy, equally worthy, ceremony of preparing ink and sharpening a new quill.

'Put that blasted book away,' said Gromrhun.

The assembled longbeards gasped.

'You dare insult the *Kron*...' Warden Hangrark muttered.

A change came over Gromrhun at the warden's accusation. His earlier affability sank, the bones of his face becoming somehow more prominent, his eyes deepening in hue, his expression growing haggard but, at the same time, stern. For a fleeting moment Kolram had the uncanny sense that it was him, and not Gromrhun, who had misspoken before a king. He coughed, perplexed by the sudden discomfort, and to the surprise of all, including himself, he waved for Braztom to reseal the *Dunrakul Kron* which, with great and unhurried ceremony, he reluctantly did.

Gromrhun nodded, a faint smile returning to his face as though a wilful young beardling had just surprised and pleased him. 'This is folly, your majesty. And believe me, that on the history and nature of duardin folly I'm *deeply* learned. Did you return from Azyr with your father, may he be forever remembered, to reclaim Karag Dawrkhaz? Or are you content to dwell forever in the wrongs done to your forebears in distant times?'

Warden Hangrark looked perplexed. 'I don't follow you.'

'We can do both, Gromrhun,' said Kolram. 'We'll spare these *bozdok* the ignominy of having their disrespect recorded in the *Kron* this time, but nor will past misdeeds be forgiven.' His heavy beard and its mail guard bunched up against his pauldron as he turned to glance over his shoulder. 'Thunderers!'

'Folly, I say,' Gromrhun complained, over the stiff clatter of duardin marksmen loading weapons, cocking them, and bringing them up to aim. 'The Fyreslayers make their stand for honour's sake, as we do. I urge you, majesty. In the name of all your ancestors who were both wise and proud, don't let a simple show of force turn into one more reason for Kothi and Kurrindorm and young Brigg to be at war when you are gone.'

Kolram made a slight gesture towards the Fyreslayer lines, one finger in his mailed gauntlet curling in, as though calling over the beer-matron in a crowded hall. The handguns were about a mile out of range anyway.

If this descended into violence it would not be of his making.

'Give them a warning volley.'

Gunfire crackled along the Dunrakul's long, thin line. The sound reminded Braegnar-Grimnir of a wing being twisted off a roasted ghyrlac at a pre-battle feast, or of something pyroclastic but harmless being tossed into one of his brothers' forgeflames. He cracked a broken-toothed smile. Both memories were joyous ones. The dispirited echoes passed between the chipped and crumbling pillars of the dilapidated old Deeping, brushing past spiderwebs that shivered for a time thereafter. A dreary blanket of powder-black smoke rolled over the distant duardin's heads and briefly stole the army from the Fyreslayers' view. Braegnar-Grimnir made a show of looking up and down the leading rank of his fyrd.

A few of his more boisterous fighters laughed.

'Are the *griki* shooting at us? Their aim is as weak as their beer.'

'A warning salvo,' Azkaharr grunted. He had his arms wrapped in a self-righteous huff over his huge beard. 'They're just letting you know they're here.'

'By shooting at us.'

Azkaharr let out a sigh so caustic it caused the whiskers of his moustache to smoulder. 'If they wanted to shoot us, they'd have opened with their cannons.'

Braegnar-Grimnir turned to Dremm, who nodded.

'We've made our point,' said Azkaharr. 'They've made theirs. Now let's talk to them and end this before duardin and duardin start killing each other for the amusement of the Yellowstripe grots lurking in yonder vaults.'

'Oh, we're going to go talk to them.'

The karl raised an eyebrow. 'Really?'

'In the only language those hairless *kruti* understand.'

The berzerkers in his immediate vicinity roared their approval.

Azkaharr sighed, setting his upraised eyebrow back down like a duardin with a heavy load. 'That's what I thought.'

Gripping his latchkey grandaxe in one large fist, Braegnar-Grimnir pumped the other over his tall crest. Vulkite Berzerkers shook their axes. Battlesmiths stamped their icons. Sensitive to the changing mood, the runesmiters lifted their forge keys and, seemingly in tune to the rhythm set for them by the battlesmiths, began to strike them with small ceremonial hammers. The golden note they made when struck lifted the fyrds into a frothing madness as the runes in their bodies began to burn. Braegnar-Grimnir, more richly appointed than any other warrior, burned like a pyre for the vengeful dead. He was unsure if the tempo set by the battlesmiths was a deliberate match for the beating of his heart, or if they and the runesmiters conspired somehow to goad it into beating faster.

Azkaharr alone seemed unaffected by it. It was as though his runes were not truly ur-gold at all, either immaculate forgeries of Grimnir's remains, or responding to an entirely different level of summons, one that the Dunr priesthood could not reach.

Braegnar-Grimnir fought to ignore the pounding of a dead god's golden fists on the backs of his eyes and *look* at the old karl.

The thought turned to smoke before it could be realised. Burnt to cinders by Grimnir's wrath.

'Sometimes, I'm sure that I'm wasting my breath,' Azkaharr was saying, although Braegnar-Grimnir barely heard. If he had, then he might have recognised that there was something strange in the oldflame's words, over and above the usual grumblings of a fading elder. 'Given the choice between rebuilding the civilisations of Myth and saving you bloody-minded fools from yourselves, I know the task I'd rather take on, but, alas for me, the charge of simply defeating all Chaos had already been claimed by another. And yet here I am, burdened with the duardin's twin curses of pessimism and stubbornness.'

Azkaharr sank into the great, swelling flood of the Dunr fyrd, and disappeared.

An outraged grumble ran through the Dunrakul shield wall, carrying through to the missile units and artillerists behind them.

They were charging. The bloody savages were charging.

The Fyreslayers surged down the Deeping Hall at surprising speed for duardin, flowing into every passable bit of floorspace like a river of fire. There were no ranks at all, no formation to speak of. If there was any discipline at play it was of a kind so foreign to the Dunrakul that Kolram couldn't recognise it. The Dunr weren't a horde of the kind the Dunrakul were used to opposing in the deeps, their numbers were too few, but in truth they were little better than the Kairic marauders who'd once sought to usurp the first deep. In fact, they were worse. They were duardin, blessed by Grungni with the same craft and skill he'd bestowed upon the Dunrakul, and yet barbarism had been their choice.

'We should retreat.' Gromrhun made a sour face as he emptied the bowl of his pipe by tapping it out against the broad cheek of his axe. 'Sound the horns, draw the shield wall back to the guns, and cede a yard or hundred.'

Kolram was appalled. 'Cede?'

'Let the Dunr run themselves out. Give cooler heads and whiter beards the chance to win out this day, and save the ink in your *Kron* for the grots.'

Kolram took a deep breath, his shoulders square to the oncoming horde. He looked down at the horned, highly decorative helm of the longbeard below him. 'Look at me, elder.'

Gromrhun turned his face towards him. The flickering of the clan warriors' torches distorted his features: his beard became fuller and lengthier, until it almost seemed to cover the entire floor and fill the hall, while the bags under his eyes weighed ever more heavily on his frown.

'Do I, or do I not, stand upon the Dunrakul oathstone?'

The longbeard looked decidedly unimpressed. 'Aye. And a right kingly *wazzok* you look up there too.'

Kolram bridled. 'And is it not here written,' he hissed, 'in the unbreakable runescript of the ancients, that wheresoever this stone falls is the point from which no duardin of good name shall retreat?'

Gromrhun sighed. He slid his empty pipe into the inside pocket of his red cloak and looked away. 'Aye. It surely is.'

With the longbeard reminded of his place, Kolram returned his attention to the Fyreslayers. They were halfway across the hall now, limbs blurring like objects viewed through a haze of heat as they covered the intervening ground and its obstacles, generating an ungodly howl as they came, each warrior a golden piston in a steam-powered contraption of terrible power.

'They push us!' he cried, his voice deep and unafraid. 'They test our resolve. When they see that it is harder than the stone for which we fight they will break, and trickle back to the Under-deeps from which they sprang.'

Braegnar-Grimnir, a berzerker in thrall to the cause of a right-eous doom though he was, would not test his bare-skinned rabble against a disciplined line of armoured warriors. Barbarian hordes had overwhelmed the duardin armies before, of course, many times. If they hadn't then the Dispossessed wouldn't now be the diminished power in the realms they now were, dependent on the charity of Azyr, and the *Dunrakul Kron* would have been light enough that even old Braztom would've been able to carry it without its trolley. But no horde in history, however numerous, bloodthirsty, or convinced of its own infernal cause, had ever broken a well-drilled duardin battle line. Not in pitched battle.

They'll break, he told himself. *They'll break.*

Raising his jewelled gauntlet, he called out for Thunderers and Quarrellers to take aim, artillery crews to lower their elevations and shorten their fuses, clan warriors and longbeards to brace shields and stand ready. In his next breath, he commanded the Ironbreakers to await his signal before hinging inwards from the flanks and annihilating the berzerkers between their gromril beard guards and the wooden shields of their kith. As they had practised a hundred times over against the armies of grots, ghouls, orruks and the manifold variegations of Chaos.

But it wouldn't come to that.

The Fyreslayers were going to break.

Kolram glanced down from his oathstone, a brief flick of the eyes, and found that despite the close-packed ranks of Hangrark's Hammerers, Gromrhun seemed to have vanished from the front rank, nothing in his place but the lingering hint of disappointment and shame.

Kolram felt his hand waver.

With the stubbornness of kings, he held the order to open fire. The scent of brimstone and melted gold from the onrushing horde prickled the hairs of his nostrils. The shouts of the Dunr grew louder in his ears. And still he held the order.

He'd not be the first to draw duardin blood. But nor would he surrender an inch, never mind a full yard, of his rightful claim.

The Fyreslayers were going to break.

Or, by the mailed fist of Grungni, he'd make them break.

CHAPTER THREE

Ael Dunrsdottir took a long draught of hot, spiced ale and then set the tankard down on the chart table, clamping one unruly corner of the large map under its magnetic base. The wind, nevertheless, did its utmost to burrow beneath, rifling under the paper like invisible mice until old Wyram got up with a sigh and winched down the storm shutters. He was blowing into his hands and throwing snow from his beard as he stomped back to the table. *'Just a little unseasonal weather,'* the sky-captains said, eager to avoid missing out on lucrative trades with a lockdown of the port, but there was a difference between *unseasonal* and *unprecedented*. Ael had spent months in the public libraries of the Barak-Nar Nav-League, studying the wind patterns of the outer arms of the Spiral Crux before committing her shares to this venture. She'd never seen the like.

Muttering in thought, she brought a pair of reading glasses to her cloudy blue eyes and leant in over the chart. The navigators and forecastinators had updated it just that morning with the latest soundings, filling it with meteorological symbols and shorthand.

'So...' She straightened, the slight twinge in her lower back eased by the support of her arkanaut gear. The glasses went down like a counterweight. 'This is what's behind the bad weather that's left several thousand shares worth of trade goods languishing in dry dock and had the *Bokram* petitioning for safe harbour.'

'It's more than a little bad weather, mistress,' said the forecastinator-captain, a broad-shouldered duardin named Zorek with a short beard, shrewd eyes, and a vulcanised suit of sky armour bearing his guild's particulars.

Zorek set the index finger of his rubber gauntlet down in an area of particularly dense notation. He sucked in through his teeth, shaking his head gravely.

'There's a region of deep barometric pressure that's been building to the south and west of Karag Dawrkhaz over the past week or so. Very deep. I've consulted the oldest charts we were able to copy out and bring with us, right the way back to King Korgrun, and I've found nothing that compares.'

'And you're sure it's coming this way?'

'Aye. As slowly as it's moving, it's not deviated so much as a degree. It's uncanny. However the windstream pushes and blows, this storm seems intent on landing here.'

Ael rubbed her whiskered chin. 'How bad's it going to be when it does?'

Zorek gave her a baffled look.

A glance around the chart table brought only more of the same: shaken heads, concerned faces, or the stony looks of those who recognised that this was the Forecastinator Guild's call, and on their heads be it.

'Then I suppose there's naught else for it but to batten down the hatches.'

The master of Karag Dawrkhaz's Guild of Usurers, a duardin named Threngthorm, pursed his lips. 'At the very least we can bill the Barak-Zon Admiralty for the *Bokram*'s mooring and make a little currency from her stay.'

He was dressed somewhat more ostentatiously than the miserly image his organisation preferred to put across, with some modest filigree in his beard and a signet ring on one thick finger. He, alone amongst the elders of the trommraad, was not entirely grim-faced by the prospect of bankruptcy. The usurers always did well out of a new enterprise like this one, financing new trade routes and filling the skies with the ambitious and the hopeful, and paying themselves a handsome rate of interest for the service. Ael didn't expect Threngthorm to shed any tears over his bulging ledger if he were obliged to repossess the port-city on behalf of the guild.

Bringing the lenses back up to her eyes, Ael pointed towards a set of numerals, written in plain runic alongside the shorthand, in a front ahead of the storm. 'And these numbers here. How accurate are they?'

Zorek huffed, offended by the implied allegation that they might be anything less than completely accurate.

Ael licked her lips, looked around the table. 'How much aether-gold are we talking about?'

The forecastinator-captain reached across the table, drawing his hand slowly across the chart in line with the directional symbols, mimicking the projected movement of the storm towards Karag Dawrkhaz. 'The deep-pressure front's pulling in cloud-deposits from all over the outer arm and pushing them ahead of it. Conservatively...' He paused. 'There's a million shares coming towards us. At least.'

Covetous mumbles and a handful of low whistles passed around the table. Ael felt her fingertips tingling, and not with the cold.

'Enough to keep Barak-Nar aloft for half a year,' Threngthorm mumbled.

The effort of maintaining a decorous expression and not giggling in delight at such wealth, trailed by a once-in-a-millennium snow-storm or not, sent a shiver through her spine.

A million shares. Conservatively.

At least.

It exceeded the personal fortune she'd sunk into this venture by about a hundredfold. She turned around and threw a glance towards her office, a glorious title for a corner table and alloy chair at the back end of the wardroom. On it, in brass picture frames, was her certificate of nobiliary and the title deeds to Karag Dawr-khaz, both of them airtight in their veracity as confirmed in a court of the Code, and acknowledging Ael Dunrsdottir as the heir to King Korgrun Dunrakul. After a thousand years, there were legal heirs to the so-called Last King everywhere, but few with her knowledge of the Code or credit lines with the Banking Unions.

'What do you want with a mountain anyway?' her friends and detractors had asked, but every sky-ship needed a dock, and the frontiers of the outer arms were ripe for expansion. The small frontier post she had constructed near the summit had moor-ings for two dozen vessels and she already had advanced plans for expansion: the Architectural Guild were currently drawing up blueprints for two, significantly larger, docking tines capable of receiving the gigantic krontankers and their escort fleets, which, as everyone knew, was how the real wealth was transported. Karag Dawrkhaz was near enough to the great sky-ports of Barak-Zon to the west and Barak-Mhornar to the south to draw in ready trade. And yes, there'd been some duardin here already with contest-ing claims, but nothing that would stand up before an Arbiter of the Code.

'A million shares...' she repeated dreamily, patting her pockets in thought.

'It'd have to be a damn good ship.'

Everyone turned to Vice-Admiral Anfrik Drakksson.

The admiral had left the skyfleet of Barak-Zon to pursue the eccentric wheeze of spending retirement with solid rock under his boots. Where most of the trommraad were wearing altitude suits and light breathing apparatus, Drakksson was clad in bulky, sunset-red arkanaut armour. He looked like a belligerent ironclad attended by tenders and frigates. The suit was old, with annealed plates and patched hoses, maintained not simply for ages' sake, as some duardin might, but because no Kharadron ever got wealthy and stayed wealthy by throwing something that was still perfectly serviceable away.

Ael liked the admiral. He made a refreshing change from the bankers and khemists.

'A damn good ship,' he said again. 'Not just to ride out the storm and endure the cold, though she'll need some iron in her bones for that too, but to carry that much aether-gold in her tanks.'

'Don't we have the ships?'

'Not of the tonnage you'll need. Nor the power.'

Ael scowled, thwarted by basic arithmetic.

While she thought on it, old Wyram, sitting on a stool across from her, suddenly put his head in one rubber-gauntleted hand and groaned. The other greybeards looked at him uncertainly. None of them, now they were presented with the fact of him, were quite sure how long Wyram had been there and whose interest he represented, but he had all the right accreditations and came with glowing references.

At least… Ael was almost certain that he did.

'Too much mulling spice in your ale, Wyram?'

'It's the deep pressure,' Zorek said, his voice rising to near-hysterical pitch. 'My apprentice, too, was complaining of a nose-bleed before this council. We'll all be kitted out like the admiral in full Xenithal environment gear before this passes, mark my words.'

Wyram pinched the bridge of his nose and shook his head. 'It's nothing. Our brethren below engaged in more of their usual tom-foolery. That's all.'

'When are they ever not?' said Threngthorm.

'The wastefulness weighs heavy on my heart nevertheless.' Wyram took a fortifying sup of mulled beer. 'Rest assured, mis-tress, we'll discuss it later.' He waved apologetically towards the admiral. 'You were saying something about ships.'

'What about the *Bokram*?' said Ael. 'Unless I'm mistaken, she's a Gromthi-class ironclad.'

'You're not mistaken,' said Drakksson, impressed by her mas-tery of the port-city's paperwork. 'A fine class of ship too. An older design, to be sure, but in my book none finer ever sailed free of the shipyards of Barak-Zon.'

'Could she do it?'

'Bring home a million-share? Not in three round trips. But she's got the deepest hold of any ship in your dock, and she's tough enough.'

'*Will* she do it?' asked Threngthorm.

Before anyone could answer the usurer's question, the Grund-stok Thunderers standing guard by the door drew everyone's attention by moving to open them. Ael's heart sank as she saw who came hurrying inside. She'd been hoping he had simply overslept or forgotten. Her adopted son half ran into the ward-room, bypassing the saluting Thunderers, clutching a modest stack of papers underarm. Trying to look as though he wasn't absurdly late, he walked to the chart desk, avoiding eye contact with everyone until he could no longer avoid acknowledging the presence of his mother. He bowed, saluted, then cleared his throat, looked away, and proffered the papers as though they excused everything, starting with the last ten years.

'I'm sorry I'm late, mother, I–'

Ael waved the papers, and the boy attached to them, away. If she'd ever had the time or the inclination to find herself a husband of reasonable means and produce an heir of her own then she'd be sorely tempted to go ahead and do so, and return Strahl Aelsson to the conservatory with a suit for breach of contract.

'You may not have noticed, just arriving and all, but we're in the middle of something important.'

'I only need a–'

Ael raised her glasses to her face and glowered at the boy through them. 'Is it Brynruf?'

'I...' Strahl looked around, hoping for support amongst a group of greybeards looking studiously elsewhere. Only Wyram managed to afford him a sympathetic smile. 'No, mother. It's Angruf. Brynruf is the day after tomorrow.'

'And is Angruf the day for signing new contracts?'

'No, mother, but this is–'

'Do you know what would happen if I started signing contracts whenever they happened to fall on my desk?'

'Can I just–'

'Chaos!' Ael threw her hands in the air. 'Anarchy! Gunhaulers flying backwards!' She tapped her finger on the table, inviting Strahl to deposit his papers there, which, though fighting down an obvious desire to protest, he eventually did. With the interruption dealt with to everyone's satisfaction, she cleared her throat apologetically and gave her attention back to Admiral Drakksson. 'Forgive me, admiral.'

'Quite all right, mistress. We were all young once.'

'I know, but contracts on Angruf...' She shook her head at the rebelliousness of youth. Strahl looked set to combust with whatever it was he wanted to say, but in the end looked down at the floor and said nothing. 'Where were we?'

'The *Bokram*, mistress.'

'Then it's decided,' said Ael. 'We'll make them the offer, the standard percentage on a million-share and a waiver on mooring fees already accrued. And any other ship that's willing to take on the risk and open up their holds for as much aether-gold as they can carry is welcome to sail under the *Bokram*'s flag.'

'We should put one of our own people in charge of the *Bokram*,' said Threngthorm. 'Along with the Grund-commander and a squad of Thunderers. In case having a hold-full of aether-gold should go to the captain's head.'

The elders nodded sombrely. Honourable duardin though they all were, who amongst them could say they'd not *bend* the Code just a little for their part of a million-share?

Anfrik Drakksson seemed the most logical duardin to send. He had more experience of skyfaring than anyone else around the chart table, probably everyone around the chart table combined, and he hailed from Barak-Zon – which might count for something with the crew of the *Bokram*, who were bound to resent the imposition of whomever Ael chose. More importantly, he didn't need the shares. But he was retired, and with good reason, and Ael wasn't sure he had the sky-legs to manage the storm that was about to hit.

She looked around the table. Zorek. Threngthorm. Wyram. The elders of the Nav-League, Aether-Khemists Guild, Endrineers, Cloudminers Consortium, Dockworkers Guild, and sundry minor groupings of the Karag Dawrkhaz outpost's Kharadron.

It occurred to her that there was only one person here she could fully trust and yet easily spare, should the worst come to the worst and everything fall groundward.

A Kharadron always prepared her finances for the worst.

She gave the order, and adjourned the trommraad for another week.

CHAPTER FOUR

Sjarpa Longtooth and the beastriders of the Thunder Hand were late to the feast. He wasn't surprised to find that the rest of the Alfrostun and their allies had tucked in without him. Frostlord Sturmur Rockbelly had always been impatient, and he led the ogors of the Fighting Hand and Eating Hand in pushing through the town's outer defences. They were pale blobs of muscle and blubber, cloaked in pale blue and white and barely distinguishable from the blizzard. The skalgs on their stonehorns were large enough to pick out, though – and to hear, barking out Sturmur's simple orders and delivering harsh blasts on their horns whenever a pack wandered too far from its huskard.

The town itself was small and made of stone, wedged in a valley between flat-topped peaks. Like a fingernail stuck in an ogor's teeth. Frozen mosses grew up the stone walls of farm buildings and houses. Snow lay heavily over collapsed roofs. Walls surrounded the town. Others parcelled up the hillsides, but the neat squares had been buried under the snow or demolished by stonehorn beastriders.

Sjarpa had eaten here before, though it looked different now. His had been a long Mawpath, but it was coming to its end.

Though the Everwinter was close enough to gnaw through the thick furs that cloaked his back, Sjarpa reined in at the escarpment overlooking the town. A horde of monsters crunched to a halt behind him.

Sjarpa turned in the saddle as the beastriders of the Thunder Hand followed him out of the blizzard. Their flesh was blue. Their lips were chapped. Snow stippled their eyelashes and their beards. The monstrous beasts they rode came in every hue of the Everwinter, standing seventy hands high at their hump shoulder and swathed in fur so shaggy that a man-sized creature couldn't even stab through it with a blade. Snow lay across the length of their tusks, and over the broad cliff of bone that shielded their dullard eyes. Their bones were ice. Their blood ran blue... Sort of. Their bodies were so cold that their blood didn't really run like a liquid at all.

Sjarpa threw his fighters all the usual gestures of greeting, miming the tearing and sharing of meat.

The first that came was Brogg Threeteeth, followed by Skag Vulture-Keeper and then Ulf the Strange. Njal Icebreaker, biggest and fattest of the Thunder Hand after Sjarpa himself, rode up and belched in welcome. Reminded that he was hungry, the ogor reached into his paunch-sack for a snack, which waved its arms and screamed, until Njal stuffed it in his mouth and started to chew.

The others looked at him hungrily. Most hadn't eaten in several hours. Even Brogg, who'd taken nothing but stew since a Stormcast Eternal had smacked him in the mouth with a thundermace at Greenfire, dribbled until his beard froze into greasy spikes.

'We're late,' Njal mumbled around the ground-up meat in his mouth.

'We'll eat more later because of it,' said Sjarpa.

'I want to eat more *now*.'

'The feast's almost over,' Ulf added.

'No.' Sjarpa looked over the decrepit town with narrowed eyes. The place looked abandoned and that didn't sit right in his belly. This was a duardin town, and once a place had duardin in it, it would never be rid of them. 'No, this feast is only starting.'

'Not much of a feast,' said Skag.

A pair of duardin with good-eating on their arms came sprinting up the slope from the town, axes raised up high and yelling as though they meant to take the entire Thunder Hand on their own. It should've been impossible for creatures that small to move so fast, but their bodies seemed to be making a heat that melted them a path through the snow.

Sjarpa drooled.

'Spicy,' said Njal, stuffing the limp, half-finished snack back into his bag.

'Not enough to go round,' Skag complained.

'There'll be more later,' said Sjarpa, and yanked hard on the reins, bringing his mount's heavy tusks swinging across the duardin's path.

The nearest morsel ducked its head as the thundertusk ripped through its tall crest of hair. It gave a bark of derision, before Sjarpa slapped the thundertusk's pinhole ear and encouraged the monster to stamp on the angry duardin's head. There was a crunch. Blood sprayed out from under the monster's splayed toes. Sjarpa's belly gurgled.

Duardin could be tough even for an ogor. They needed to be well softened.

Squelching its foot from the duardin's remains, the thundertusk ploughed on, its horns swaying in time with its gait, idly bringing down several belly-widths of crumbling drystone.

With a ululating cry, the second duardin leapt and smacked its axe into the haunch of Brogg Threeteeth's beast. The thundertusk only dimly noticed, leaving the duardin to cling grimly on by the axe as the monster turned a slow circle whilst trying to scrape the duardin off with its horns. With the duardin so totally outnumbered, the rest of the Thunder Hand forgot about the feast for a moment and enjoyed the slapstick.

The duardin, however, hadn't been idle. Wiggling its axe free in a steaming hiss of blueish thundertusk blood-slush, it dropped twice its own height and landed on its back in the snow.

The Thunder Hand roared in approval as the snow went up in a plume of steam. The fog swallowed the duardin whole. He could've escaped and probably should've, but instead hewed frenziedly at the thundertusk's fetlocks. Somehow managing to forget the duardin butchering his indifferent mount, Brogg cursed the other beastriders for their laughter.

With a world-weary grunt, Sjarpa took a firm handhold on his paunch and hauled it to one side of the saddle. Its weight pulled the other leg after it, and allowed him to slide down the thundertusk's icy flank. He thumped into the snow and winced. His knees were the only part of him that felt however old he was.

Yanking an iron harpoon from its saddle quiver, he waved his hand through the steam and stomped towards Brogg's thundertusk.

The ruddy-haired duardin came roaring out. Strength blazed from every rune beaten into its bulging arms as its axe came down. Sjarpa thrust out his belly, thumping the wrought iron gut-plate into the duardin's face, catching its fiery axe side-on and slamming into its face. The duardin went sprawling in the snow. Anything else would've been knocked cold. But duardin had thick heads. It started to get up. Sjarpa kicked its jaw. The *snap* of its neck as its head twisted all the way round made his mouth water. He stepped on the Fyreslayer's axe and put the flames out with the cold emanating from his bones. Then he stabbed his harpoon into the shoulder to pin it in place and, with a sharp twist and pull, wrenched off the opposite arm.

Sjarpa stuffed it into his mouth. His eyes flickered closed in pleasure as his flat teeth ground up the tough duardin meat. He spat out the golden runes like pips.

Though his stomach growled in protest at giving up meat, Sjarpa stepped back from the red snow and gestured for the others to come and take their share. Brogg and Ulf practically fell out of the saddle to claim a limb while, behind him, Njal was already fighting off half a dozen hungry beastriders for the duardin Sjarpa had flattened under his thundertusk.

Sjarpa's gut knotted at the sight: a prophesy of leaner times ahead.

Licking the last of the duardin's juices from his beard, he turned back towards the town. Behind the Fighting Hand and the Eating Hand of the Alfrostun came the rest. Those that the Everwinter – the deep cold that followed the descendants of the Beastclaw tribe like a curse – had driven into Sturmur Rockbelly's Mawpath and forced into becoming either his allies or his meal. Huge carts drawn by shivering rhinoxen. Gutbuster ogors with snot icicles tinkling from their noses. Butchers warming frostbitten fingers over portable stoves, beating off the hungry with the flats of heavy ladles. There were orruks too. Bonesplitterz on grizzly white boars. Ironjawz in a riot of sharp colours and hard edges. Kruleboyz on hairless gnashtoofs, leggy and vicious enough to keep up with the Alfrostuns, but not nearly so well made for the cold.

Not since Borja Kragnfryr, the grandson of the great Frost King Baergut Vosjarl and the last ogor of the Winterbite to remember the time before the Everwinter, had a horde like it gathered under one leader.

If only Sturmur Rockbelly knew what to do with it.

Watching them squabble over the slimmest pickings, Sjarpa wondered what Borja would have done differently.

'What future do you see in the snow?' Njal asked.

Sjarpa furrowed his brow: Njal would never understand the sorts of questions that genuinely bothered his thoughts. 'These duardin were Doomseekers of the Fire Crown. It's rare to see so many in one place.'

'Do they wait for us?'

'Sheltering from the coming Everwinter, most likely.'

Njal laughed at that, as he should. There was no hiding from the Everwinter.

Shielding his eyes against the thickening blizzard, Sjarpa turned to look back the way he'd ridden. Thundertusk beastriders were still arriving. In amongst them, driven ahead by herd instinct and by the snapping jaws of the Everwinter at their hindquarters, came half a dozen unridden. From the cantle of each empty saddle, a huge chain flexed out into the cold, periodically pulling taut as the team of monsters hauled what appeared to be a vast block of ice out of the snow.

There was no hiding from the Everwinter, it was true. But sometimes, the Everwinter could be made to give something up.

Sjarpa pointed towards the town. 'Ride there, and make a fire.' With a glance over the shoulder, he gestured to the ice block being dragged behind them. 'A big one.'

CHAPTER FIVE

The name *Dawrkhaz*, in the old tongue, literally meant Good Hall. Perhaps once, before the coming of Chaos and the sundering of the duardin, it had been. Some still strove to make it that way again. The word *karag* referred to the volcano from which the stronghold had been carved in the years of old, and it burned as hot as it ever had.

The magma-vault of the Dunr Lodge had been constructed as a vast bowl in the mountain's deepest core, englobing fully the magma chamber that bubbled and churned beneath the depths of the ancient hold. As a work of devotion to a fallen god, it was awesome in its scale. Their home was a fresco, a glittering collage of ancestor masks hundreds of feet high, gold panelling, runic scripture and angular knotwork writ large and glowing red in the face of the volcano's heat. At balconies overlooking the magma, chorales of apprentice battlesmiths and priests of the Zharrgrim chanted prayers of swift heat and eternal burning. The particularly zealous did so from baskets, dangling over the molten ocean by fyresteel chains.

A realmgate to the Salamander's Spine in Aqshy, near to the

Vostargi Mont where Grimnir and Vulcatrix had slain one another in their epochal contest and where the hottest fires in the realms still burned, was rumoured to be submerged there. If it was anything other than myth then it was surely impassable, but it did as much as all the Fyreslayers' prayers to keep the memory of the Realm of Fire burning within the volcano's heart.

The string of igneous isles were almost invisible within the haze. Each rocky bar was interconnected, and tethered to the chamber's walls by fyresteel bridgework of peerless quality. Each successive islet harboured a magmic battleforge of rarer genius than the one before, a chain of fire-riven godheads glowering eternally on the precipice of final annihilation and vibrant creation.

The lava sea and its many isles were collectively known as Grimnir's Forge. With the loss of Grungni's Hidden City and the banishment of the Silver Wyrm, Argentine, from its lair beneath Mercurial Gate, it was claimed by many to be the hottest forge in Chamon. Any metal could be worked there. Even common ores assumed uncanny properties when subjected to its fires and handled with duardin skill.

Despite being claimed by the Dunr Lodge as the burning heart of their magma-vault, its position at the very centre of the volcano and directly under the main vent to the summit ensured that there was no single way in or out, and that whoever wished to could have access. Some said Grimnir had built his Forge with that purpose, although the priests of the Dunr dismissed that as sappy Azyrite nonsense. Secondary and tertiary vents branched off, furthermore, from the main vent, carrying geothermal heat and power to every level of the stricken hold. And in return, those same vents brought eager throngs of Dunrakul blacksmiths, and duardin from even further afield, back to the Forge.

Even the Kharadron, though they scoffed at fables of the Forge's mythical properties, had constructed an aether-powered funicular to ferry endrineers, and visiting scholars who'd paid well for the privilege, down the main vent from their outpost above the crater.

It was by this route that Brigg returned home, steaming towards the ocean of lava in a rattling cage of admiralty brass.

She shared her descent with a group of Kharadron. The car was more crowded than it would ordinarily have been, and with more than the usual sort. From their talk, Brigg gathered there was a storm coming, driving those that could to seek the shelter of the mountain. There was no evidence of any storm here. She eavesdropped on the endrineers' chatter for a while, picking out a word in twenty from the technical jargon, allowing herself a smile at their enthusiasm before recalling why she was angry.

She'd lingered in the Kharadron port for as long as she'd cared to, waiting for word from Strahl on his success or failure in winning his mother's permission. In the markets that dwelt alongside the outpost's sky-docks, duardin from the rival settlements and from abroad could still, as they did in Grimnir's Forge, mingle in relative security. But it wasn't a comfortable place for a Fyreslayer to wander alone. And that Strahl had sent no word, let alone sought her out, told her all she needed to know.

With a draconic hiss of hydraulic breaks, the funicular wheezed into its final descent, sliding into its docking tines with the rattling familiarity of an old Hearthguard backing through a privy door. Brigg's stomach lurched as mechanical clamps gripped onto the car and held it fast. Her fellow passengers didn't even break up their conversations as the car was drawn to a halt and the doors hauled open.

It occurred to her that the Fyreslayers and the Kharadron weren't so very different. They both carried the same fearlessness in their blood.

She thought of Strahl and scowled. They just showed it in different ways.

Brigg lingered in the car as the endrineers piled out, adding to the fire and bustle on the platform. A pair of burly, bored-looking Fyreslayers checked passes. One of them threw a wave to the arkanaut sharpshooter who rode in a cupola on top of the car. He carried a long-barrelled, gem-scoped aethershot rifle, in case of spiders. He waved back.

Brigg wondered, sometimes, what she saw in Strahl.

Her father would've seen her betrothed to a warrior, like Dremm the battlesmith, or her half-cousin, Rognar-Grimnir, from their sister lodge across the sea, and Strahl Aelsson was certainly not in that mould. He could fight, of course, a bit, although she knew he'd sooner not if he could avoid it. He'd certainly not last ten heartbeats in the Underdeeps of the karag in a Dunr hunting fyrd. The thought of her chosen being immolated by an enraged mother-magmadroth while complaining of dry heat and the unfairness briefly restored her smile.

By the time she disembarked the funicular, most of the endrineers had already dispersed. Their outlines wobbled apart from one another in the furious heat of the Forge.

The platform remained crowded. Kharadron workers wrapped in heat-reflecting foil suits operated the funicular controls from a pedestal, while maintenance crews performed routine checks on the car. Fyreslayers came and went freely. Occasionally, they were joined by Dispossessed engineers, or visiting cogsmiths from the free cities, conversing in a pidgin dialect cobbled together from various strains of the old root language and the technical terminology shared by all.

She watched as the disparate hosts converged at the lava sea, funnelled towards the nearest bridge, its suspender cables sticking up through the heat haze like a lizard's spines. It was impossible to believe that they were supposed to be at war right then.

'Kolram and Ael and Braegnar-Grimnir are at war. But this lot aren't.'

A Fyreslayer karl with a white crest pluming from his helmet and a knee-length beard of the same bright hue stood waiting for her within the bustle of the platform. The crowds seemed to flow around him, as though fearful of entering this oldflame's space. His face appeared ancient and set, like cooled lava, but his expression was one that looked as though it might crack at a moment's notice and smother all wrath it encountered with joy. He reminded her of a great-uncle who'd visited her hearth-hold often when she'd been small and her parents away at war. She couldn't recall the relative's name, but his face was seared into her oldest memories with his tales of travels in faraway lands and visits with distant kin.

Brigg had never wondered what had become of that duardin. He went where all Fyreslayers went: to the stone sleep, to await the fires of the Doomgron and Grimnir's muster.

The karl winked at her, as though he saw every secret in her heart, and she felt her cheeks grow warm.

'Do I know you, oldflame?'

He dipped his head, tugging respectfully on his beard. 'Azkaharr, my lady. From across the Sea of Sages and beyond the Spiral Crux.'

Fascination waged a brief insurrection against her more natural state of anger.

Brigg had never travelled, except in the sagas of the battlesmiths, and as Braegnar-Grimnir's sole heir she knew she never would. Unless it was at the head of a fyrd to take the fire of the Zharr-grim to her enemies' cities and empty their vaults of their gold. This was one thing she and Strahl shared in common. Wanderlust. She could picture them boarding a sky-ship one day, telling no one, making their own home somewhere out there in the realms, as her father's brothers had been forced to do when he'd been named Runefather of the Dunr over them.

They could go anywhere. Perhaps even across the Sea of Sages, and beyond the Spiral Crux.

'He's a healthy-looking lad,' said Azkaharr.

'Who?'

'Aelsson, of course. Why, have you been hiding another?'

Brigg coloured further, balling her hands into fists. She'd told no one about Strahl, and with sound reason. A godless, half-beard, cloud-straddler. *A Kharadron.* If her father were to somehow find out before she was good and ready to break it to him then he'd explode.

'Good teeth,' Azkaharr went on, stroking his beard thoughtfully. 'Decent head of hair. Sturdy thighs. A royal daughter could do far worse.'

'Enough,' Brigg hissed.

She glanced towards the two Hearthguard stood nearby, their magmapikes barring visitors to the Forge from crossing the bridge to the magma-vault in error. Neither had remarked on the oldflame or appeared to have overheard his words. He grinned at her. The ur-gold in his arms and chest glowed warmly against the ferocity of the Forge.

'What do you want?' she asked.

'I've a favour to ask.'

Brigg bared her teeth. Clearly, his intent was to blackmail her.

Azkaharr raised his hands as though reading her mind again. 'I'm not here to warn you off, lass. Nor to disapprove. Good luck to you, I say. A duardin ought to peek beyond his walls, or her walls even, from time to time. How's she to know what she'll find there 'til she does? Your father'll see that too, and respect it. In his time.'

Brigg unclenched her fists and lowered them to her sides. There was something about this karl that made her discount her earlier thoughts of treachery and feel faintly ashamed at having ever held them.

'Then, what do you want?'

'There's a storm coming, lass. A big one. And I'm looking for someone with as much reason to want peace between the Dunr Lodge and Dunrsson's Kharadron as I've got.' He grinned. 'Know anyone like that?'

'You want me to talk to the runefather for you? About what?'

'I'm glad you asked me that, lass.'

With a smile, Azkaharr leant in close and whispered in her ear.

CHAPTER SIX

Strahl Aelsson leant against the gunwale rail of the Gromthi-class ironclad *Bokram*, and watched her crew make ready to sail. The arkanauts toiled in the snow, the gemstone lenses of their helmets gleaming fitfully even when the duardin themselves vanished in the flurries. It was coming in thick. Strahl couldn't even make out the sky. Snow piled up on the deck, ankle-deep, before swabbers could brush it overboard. It heaped up over Strahl's armoured shoulders but he was barely aware of it, protected as he was under the heavy-duty insulation and padding of his arkanaut gear. And in any case, it had nothing to compare to the chill he was generating from inside himself.

The sky-ship bobbed slightly, feeling the pressure of the wind currents against her keel even in dock, and Strahl's grip tightened around the rail. He looked up, seeking the reassurance of the endrin atop the main mast. An aether-furnace of incredible power and a marvel of Kharadron ingenuity, it burned like a sun in miniature, assailed from all quarters by fluffy, white-cloaked hordes.

Strahl could feel its pulse through the deck plates. Through the rail that ran across his elbows. It was, he hoped, the exact amount of power that it took to lift a Gromthi-class ironclad, its aethershot carbines, its grudgesettler bombs, fragmentation charges, detonation drills, aethershock torpedoes, aethermatic volley cannon, and its air supremacy mine, not to mention a full complement of crew, Grundstok Thunderers, cargo and passengers.

The vibrations made him feel queasy.

Taking a deep breath of freezing, triple-filtered air, he leant further over the railing and tried to focus on the buildings of the dock. He told himself that they were not moving, even if they appeared to be yawing side to side.

A skysick Kharadron. It was absurd. Like a claustrophobic clanrat or a Moonclan afraid of the dark. If it had been anyone else then Strahl would've been the first to laugh at them.

But then, he thought ruefully, he couldn't really be skysick, could he? They weren't actually in the sky yet.

Like most Kharadron, Strahl had been born in the air, but living on a great sky-port like Barak-Nar was an entirely different experience to being aboard a ship. The skyborne city, although buoyed by the same technologies that lifted the *Bokram* now, was sufficiently massive that one had to be highly sensitive to detect the effect of the wind currents against it. Even then, Strahl sometimes had. He'd learned early on, however, to never bring it up, to feign digestive ailments when the winds above the Strait of Fangs blew with unusual venom.

The union that operated the sky-port's orphanages had assumed he was too young to remember. The loss of both parents, they believed, was something a youngling could overcome through grit and character. He'd tried. It was expected. But he'd never forgotten.

He pushed the memories away now, but it was like wrestling a canvas sail.

The Endrineers Guild had, by way of liability for the endrin failure that had downed the *Grond's Bounty*, paid for his placement within the Union of Conservatories and Associated Compassionate Enterprises. Even so, he understood that both the guild and the union had turned a reasonable profit on his subsequent adoption by Ael. The Kharadron put little stock in heredity, but in a meritocratic society like that of Barak-Nar it took guts and drive to achieve the position of shipowner and captain, as his first mother had, and the ambitious wealthy like his adopted mother, Ael Dunrsdottir, were prepared to pay for that kind of blood inheritance.

It made him feel almost as sick as the rocking of the ship.

Ael had been good to him in her own way. She'd been fair, and Strahl wasn't going to disappoint her again if he could help it. He'd proven himself poorly suited to the sciences, or to Ael's beloved Code, but skyfaring was in his blood. As much as it terrified him, he'd prove himself his parents' son if it was what Ael needed him to be.

'Have you ever sailed an ironclad into a category seventeen iciclone, with naught but Grungni's dying breath in your endrin and gold-lust in your heart?'

Captain Borg Helmensson stood above the companionway behind him. He'd been there some time, watching his arkanauts traipse up and down the gangplank, lounging against the bulkhead in spite of the roll of the deck. His armour was the sunset-red of Barak-Zon with a golden mask and pipework. Several lines of unpretentious citations for mercantile fortune and high valour adorned the breast panel. Given the militant reputation of the *Bokram's* home port, Strahl was not surprised to see that more than half of the decorations were for actions in war.

Strahl sighed. 'No.'

'Hmm.'

Helmensson leant back and looked up, as though contemplating the snow hitting his lenses. 'Have you ever had to run from bow to stern across a deck frozen with ice, knowing that you're two minutes or one small slip from the ground's embrace? Or, if no, have you ever been abroad in wind so fierce it has teeth, that the only reasoned thought in your head is that there must be a horde of screaming harpies hidden just beyond sight?'

Strahl thought again of the *Grond's Bounty* and felt ill.

'Do you mean to say you've never brought in a million-share haul, leading a fractious flotilla of unskyworthy buckets into the jaws of penury with the elements themselves breathing down your neck?'

'Aye,' said Strahl.

The last group of arkanauts belonging to the *Bokram*, their crimson armour standing out against the snow, pounded up the gangplank from the dock. The crew were not anticipating battle. At least, no more so than was realistic. The weather front that Forecastinator-Captain Zorek had plotted to the north-east – Helmensson's category seventeen iciclone – was of an order that most right-thinking lumprey and megalofin in the area would've already got well ahead of it. Only Kharadron with aether-gold tickling their nose hairs were mad enough to sail in the opposite direction. Most of the crates being carried aboard, therefore, instead of the usual surplus ammunition and extra guns, would be cold-weather survival gear, blankets, alchemical heaters, deck-sweeping flamethrowers, and semaphore rigs intense enough to burn a light signal through a blizzard.

'No doubt you attended one of the prestigious Skyfleet colleges then,' Helmensson went on. 'You're some kind of prodigy, I'll warrant, on the fast-track to admiral.'

'The first time I left Barak-Nar was when Ael brought me here.' He turned to Helmensson. 'This'll be my second flight.'

'Forgive me if I'm struggling to locate the qualifications that back up your commandeering of my ship.'

'You owe my mother a lot of money.'

Helmensson was silent awhile, then issued a salute. 'An honour to sail under you, Strahl Aelsson. May your command be short and profitable.' With that, the captain turned away, head bowed to the in-blowing snow, to assist his crew.

A whistle sounded from the aftcastle. Another returned its hail from the aft deck. Kharadron called out to one another, their gruff voices heavily accented by the high-altitude breathing kit they all wore. The bow was already as good as invisible from the stern, and the crow's nest from the weather deck, but for endrin burn and running lights. The endrin started to pulse faster as the endrin-master pushed it to burn hotter, its output causing the entire hull to vibrate like a toasting fork against a pewter mug.

'Cast away!' he heard Helmensson yell, somewhere in the blizzard. 'All hands, prepare to be off.'

Strahl gripped the gunwale rail in sudden panic, his mind an absolute blank on where he should be or what he should be doing now. His stomach dropped as the *Bokram* pulled away from the dock. An inch. A yard. A beard-length. Two. Too far to jump for it now, even if he'd wanted to. With a noisy clattering that was audible even over the wind and the hum of the endrin, the gangplank was mechanically withdrawn, broken down into segments and rolled back into the deck. A pair of crimson-armoured arkanaut crew waded through snow-laden wind to secure it.

The *Bokram* began to turn. Into the wind.

Strahl could still make out Vice-Admiral Anfrik Drakksson standing on the dock in his brightly coloured dress armour, flanked by his mother's best-paid Thunderers and holding his salute to the very last. The snow between them flew in weird directions, driven up, down and sideways by the contrary forces of a dozen additional endrins at work, the running lights of smaller frigates, wayfarers, and Grundstok patrol craft shining like companion constellations in the starless white, preserving the illusion of proximity to the port for a few seconds more.

He held onto the view for as long as there was a view to hold onto, hoping, somehow, that another figure in gold might yet join the admiral to see him off, though how she would have known to come he didn't know.

A duardin had to hope.

The snow swept across in a flurry, and Admiral Drakksson was no more. Strahl could no longer even see the mountain. He told himself he'd see Brigg again when he returned with his part of a million-share and enough glory to impress even her, although just then he had a hard time believing that any of them would be coming back. He glanced up the deck, forward, to where another Kharadron was leaning incongruously over the gunwale. He was unhelmed, snowy-white hair billowing in the crosswinds. Noticing Strahl's regard, he drew his pipe from his mouth and raised it in salute.

And then the snow stole him from view as well, but Strahl was left feeling strangely heartened all the same.

A duardin had to hope.

CHAPTER SEVEN

The gnoblars bickered as they built up the fire. Their language was shrill and spoken so fast that even Sjarpa, who could ape the sounds of aelves, duardin and even the star-lizards of Greenfire, could never understand what the creatures gabbled to one another. Tiny greenskins draped in furs and with gold-foil crowns on their heads directed underlings to toss broken furniture onto the growing blaze. This the gnoblars did with some relish, capering round the fire and throwing scraggly shadows over the old stone of the duardin hall.

The elders of the Oldenguts Alfrostun had all squeezed themselves inside. None of them looked entirely comfortable to be sitting without a moving beast under them while the Everwinter raged outside. The tyrants and butchers of the more important Gutbuster Mawtribes were there too, as were the warlords, prophets, seers, and eccentric champions that represented the orruk bands. The greenskins were tough. They took the cold as well as the Beastclaw, better than some of the Gutbusters even, but kept to their own informal bit of the hall lest they get accidentally sat on and eaten.

The ice block that Sjarpa had hauled out of the Everwinter had been set on log rollers, its chains transferred from the thunder-tusks to twenty sweating ogors to be dragged the rest of the way into the hall. With gloved hands, Njal Icebreaker and Ulf the Strange shimmied it up to the fire. The two ogors together could have pulled down a castle. The ice barely moved at all.

The entire hall stared expectantly at it.

When nothing much happened, a portion of the hall turned to Sjarpa Longtooth instead. Even from the greenskins' corner, the biggest of the Ironjawz bosses weren't shy about asking what the big fuss was about.

This, Sjarpa thought ruefully, was what Frost King Borja had used to call The Way and that which Sturmur Rockbelly was determined to learn: all the tribes working together as one. His own disappointment masked by deep-set eyes and flabby cheeks, Sjarpa lowered himself to his knees and pulled the glove off of one hand. Careful to avoid touching the ice itself, he prodded the ground in front of it.

Bone dry. Not even warm.

Sjarpa gave a rumbling sigh. It was disappointing that the gnoblars' fire couldn't touch the ice of the Everwinter, but not surprising.

'Nothin's happenin'.' Frorgen Maetsgral, the huskard of the Fighting Hand, uncrossed his enormously fat legs and got up. He swayed a little as blood went to his head. Drool trickled off the cliff-edge of his chin, a metal eyepatch made from a cave grot's shield sitting aslant on his face as his expression shifted from boredom to anger.

Sjarpa glanced at Sturmur Rockbelly. The Frostlord sat in a circle of rubble. Rather than duck his head to fit under the duardin's ceiling, he'd simply butted a hole through until it accommodated his stature. Bits of it were caught up in his white cloak, and in the tangled grey mane that fell across his face and as far down as his chest. He wore a gut-plate of dented brass that looked a little bit like gold with knapped spikes of rock sticking out. Sturmur was so impressively huge even the Ironjawz treated him with respect. The Frostlord gave the slightest of nods, and Sjarpa turned back to the huskard.

'I brought you into this world, Frorgen.' Sjarpa rose stiffly, shifting from ancient Svoringar to the brutish ogorspeak that the Gutbusters spoke and that all the greenskins would be able to understand. 'I tore you bloody and yelling and already hungry from between your mother's legs and spat your first meat into your toothless mouth. You're Huskard Jorl because the Rockbelly says so. I am Blizzard Speaker, chosen by the Everwinter, and only the Everwinter can take it away.'

By way of an answer, Frorgen thumped his chest with both hands, sending ripples running through his flesh all the way to his stomach, and butted his gut-plate into Sjarpa's.

The challenge was given.

With a *munch* of rough iron on iron, Sjarpa stumbled back. He barely felt it. His heavy paunch cushioned him well. But the sound rang out like a dinner gong, ogors clamouring into a maw-circle around the fighting huskards. Even the orruks, though there was no way they could've seen a thing, barked and yelled from the back. Their excitement for the fight was a flutter deep in Sjarpa's stomach. A dim echo of the belly-cramps that spoke through him for the Everwinter.

He thrust back. Gut-plates clanged a second time.

Sjarpa got two full hands of upper-arm fat and pushed the Huskard Jorl back. Frorgen set his enormous feet and roared a challenge in Sjarpa's face.

The maw-circle drummed on their gut-plates. Some bellowed

'Frorgen!', others 'Sjarpa!' Most didn't care, simply enjoying the fight and anticipating the chance to eat the loser.

Frorgen headbutted Sjarpa's jaw. Sjarpa shook his head until his jowls clapped together, spraying blood and drool, and threw a punch. Frorgen slapped it away on the meat of his arm.

'You said you'd find answers in the Everwinter. It'd show us The Way, you said.' His hands closed around Sjarpa's neck, squeezing through thick rolls of fat to crush the throat beneath.

Traditionally, the role of Huskard Jorl went to the strongest and biggest fighter in the Alfrostun. Usually. Often, it went to the one most stupidly loyal to the Frostlord. Sjarpa was bigger.

'And it will,' Sjarpa growled, wrestling him back. 'We just need a hotter fire.'

'How do we make a hotter fire?'

'More wood?' Njal shouted from the maw-circle.

'The Sun-Eaters of Forgefire Fjord?' cried Brogg, catching on.

Frorgen headbutted him again, but came off the worse for it, and the two fighters staggered apart. 'You rode too far,' he gasped, breathing wetly through a squashed nose. 'You made Sturmur wait too long for you.' He gestured dismissively towards the ice block that the Thunder Hand had returned. 'The Everwinter is angry. It wants back what you stole. And all of us as well.'

Just then, Sjarpa's gut gave a thunderous rumble, so loud it made the ceiling quake. A trickle of dust and powdered snow rained over Sturmur's head. The Frostlord looked up, giving the ceiling a blank-eyed scowl. The others, knowing full well the prophetic gift of Sjarpa's belly, fell quiet. They backed fearfully out of the maw-circle as it kicked and trembled a second time.

Sjarpa put his hand to his shivering gut-plate. 'You'd put words into the Everwinter's mouth like they were meat, Maetsgral?'

The huskard shook his head as he withdrew. 'I'd never–'

'Let me tell you a story of the Everwinter...'

Obedient children all, Frorgen and the rest of the Beastclaw sat down. Uncertain what was going on, the Gutbusters did the same. The orruks shut up. The only sound left was the crackle of the gnoblars' fire, the creak of timber frames against the first touch of the Everwinter, and the slow mouth-breathing of the ogors. Even Sturmur drew his lank grey fringe from his face on the back of one brutish hand and waited expectantly.

It was their hunger that made ogors the beasts that the realms knew them as, but there was no ogor, of any tribe, that didn't secretly adore a good story. They were never more innocent, never closer to what they might've been before the Everwinter, as when Sjarpa Longtooth sat them down for one of his. Unlike most Maneater braggarts, he was older than most of the stories he could tell. Ancient enough to have walked the Mawpath with the handful of mythic figures who were even older.

'Some say that the Man-God, Sigmar, cursed Baergut Vosjarl for his gluttony. Others say it was Nagash who loosed the Everwinter on the first Frost King for eating the bones of his favourite dead. Borja himself once told me it had been Gorkamorka. But the Great Hunter isn't so subtle in his curses. If the Everwinter is his beast then I say he set it loose by accident.'

The ogors laughed until several passed wind. Sturmur Rockbelly bared yellowed teeth and grimaced, which was as close as the Frostlord got to actual enjoyment, and Sjarpa knew that the Oldenguts had been appeased for another day.

'Such are the mysterious movements of the gods,' he said, turning slowly so as to catch everyone who had been standing in the maw-circle by eye. 'Even when they break a people in two and send one half to eat their way across the Mortal Realms, we don't know for sure who did it or why.'

At the end of his circle, his Mawpath, he finished where he began. With Frorgen.

'The Everwinter remembers The Way. But when it speaks, it's not always clear what it says.' He turned away again, speaking to them all. 'Borja Kragnfryr was last of the Frost Kings who'd followed Baergut on Gorkamorka's Great Waaagh!' The orruks at the back set up a hooting and a clamouring at the naming of their boisterous god. 'He was the last Frost King who remembered the time before the Everwinter, who could lead Gutbusters and Maneaters and even Firebellies until the Everwinter caught him.'

The ogors mumbled their dismay, though they'd heard this part of the story several times. This was the fate all Beastclaw dreaded: an eternity in the ice, a living death beyond the reach of everything but the freezing cold and their own insatiable hunger.

'It is his wisdom and guidance that Sturmur Rockbelly must have.'

Here, Sturmur gave a bark of laughter. His voice was as deep as the whirlway at the bottom of a frozen sea, and as warm.

'Guidance that Sjarpa promised.' The Frostlord moved under his cloak of furs, like the muscles of a stonehorn under its heavy pelt, as he leant forwards. 'Answer the Huskard Jorl. Where will you find me a hotter fire?'

'I remember Borja's last Mawpath,' Sjarpa said. 'I remember the Age of Chaos, how hard the Everwinter chased us then, and how deep. I remember, too, where Borja led the Mawpath to escape it. He knew, as I know, the one fire in Chamon hot enough to hold back the Everwinter.'

Sturmur sat back with a wave of his hand. 'There's no such fire.'

'I was there,' Sjarpa insisted. 'I saw the Everwinter break and flee.'

'Where?' said Sturmur.

'It belongs to the fire god of the Khazalid Kings. It's where the Mawpath had been leading us for many rumblings, because the Everwinter follows hard again. As it did in Borja's time.' He gave his head a shake. A rhetorical trick he'd picked up from a Maneater storyteller long before. After the Death Belch, the Life Song, and then the great Trampling from Ghur, the Everwinter raged now as never before.

'And they will let us use their fire?' said Sturmur.

Sjarpa dipped his head. 'They might.'

'Before we eat them or after?'

'Before.'

The Mawtribes murmured at that.

With granite slowness, Sturmur leant forwards. 'If Borja Kragn-fryr was so wise, how did he end up caught by the Everwinter?'

Sjarpa's smile was a cheese-yellow wedge, sandwiched between two greasy slabs of meat and stubble. 'Another story,' he said. 'For another time.'

If there was one lesson from Borja's time that Sjarpa had never forgotten, then it was this: always keep an audience hungry.

CHAPTER EIGHT

Kolram Dunrakul bit down on the wooden dowel that the alms matron had set between his teeth, gripped the armrests of his throne, and grunted in pain as she pushed a needle through his thigh.

'I hope you didn't cry so loud when the Fyreslayer hit you.'

Kolram snarled around the dowel and cursed the woman with his eyes.

'Good. My honour shouldn't have abided it.' She pulled the thread out the other side. Kolram gripped the chair and gave a muffled scream. 'Only twenty-three to go,' said the alms matron, with feigned cheerfulness. 'On this leg.'

The Battle of the Dunrow Deeping had ended in a bloody stalemate. Kolram had slain four of the pretender's honourless mercenaries but had been thwarted of his chance to test his axe against Braegnar-Grimnir's. Both sides had ceded the hall with such honour as they could lay claim to, and sent in their reckoners to tally the dead. Before the Yellowstripe could move back in and claim them for their own.

He winced, brought harshly back to the present moment, as one of the younger alms maidens dabbed his gashed forehead with spirits. She wore a purple robe that fell past her ankles. A white wimple wrapped her head, but for a round face made prematurely old by care. The goddess whose icons she bore on a chain around her neck was reputed to be dead, and a long time dead, but the priestesses of the Dispossessed would need a better reason than that to change the robes they wore and the prayers they sang.

His wife sat beside him in a smaller, plainer chair. Queen Silveg was a pleasingly stout, demure woman who barely glanced up from her embroidery except, just once, with modest satisfaction, as Kolram suffered. Their two grown sons were set up at a drum table playing some kind of Azyrite game of high strategy that involved two players taking turns moving black and gold tokens around a puzzle board. At the far end of the long hall, meanwhile, under the engraved arch of the grand doorway, Lorekeeper Braztom was seated at an ornate mahogany writing desk, bent over the open pages of the *Dunrakul Kron*.

It eased Kolram's suffering greatly to know that the perfidy of the Dunr Lodge did not go unrecorded. His muscles would ache for weeks, but the line of Braegnar-Grimnir would be burdened by their ancestor's ignominious conduct for generations to come.

'I told you, you should've withdrawn.'

Kolram started to see Gromrhun, standing on the faded red carpet behind the alms matron's back. His horned helmet was in his hands, like a petitioner to the throne, but with a look on his face that warned that he was the only duardin with wisdom in his gift that day. Silveg looked up, then back down. His sons muttered animatedly to one another as another gold piece dispatched a black, while Braztom worked diligently over the pages of the *Kron*, undisturbed, and did not turn their way.

Kolram spat out the dowel, grunting in dull agony as the alms matron continued to stitch his thigh back together.

'How did you get in here?'

The longbeard shrugged, as though that wasn't the question that ought to be vexing him just then.

Kolram nodded to an empty chair. 'Sit down, at least, since you're here. Let Kothi or Kurrindorm fetch you an ale. The ceiling won't fall around you.'

An expression of appalling weariness crossed the longbeard's face, and Kolram felt ashamed at having spoken so flippantly. 'I'd give my left foot for the chance to sit, your majesty. One day, perhaps, I'll get the chance, but I fear it'll not be today.'

Braegnar-Grimnir lay on the heated marble slab with his hands clenched into a single muscular ball under his forehead, grimacing as Battlesmith Dremm pulled metal shrapnel and shards of the Dunrow Deeping from his back. This work, as he did all work, the battlesmith engaged with great aggression and a song. Dremm had a voice that could enthral a grand fyrd, but absent the backing fury of battle, it became broken and lost the apparent ability to hold a tune. Braegnar-Grimnir was tempted to draw his hands out from under his forehead and clamp them over his ears. Although not for that reason.

'Duardin killing duardin,' Azkaharr was muttering as he paced the royal hearth-chamber, his bare feet striking embers from the stone floor. 'What a sorry day this is.' Coming to the heat-shrunken head of the varghulf that Braegnar-Grimnir's father had proudly stuck up on a magmapike for display, he paused, slid his thumbs under his gold belt, and pursed his lips in thought.

Braegnar-Grimnir had been just forty years old when he'd slain the monster. When he saw that trophy he was reminded not only of his first war-party as a warrior alongside his brothers, but also of his father's pride. His father was dead now. His brothers were gone. Because that was what disinherited runesons did. They struck out to found lodges of their own, or died in some equally doomed venture far from home. Chances were, they were dead too. He wondered how much of that, if any, the oldflame perceived when he saw that relic.

He looked up, over his shoulder. Brigg stood at the carved entrance with her arms crossed and a face like lava. He smiled, regardless. He let her get away with too much, he knew, but so long as she brought gold and glory to the lodge and married well, he'd allow her anything.

'Your position was one of strength, your intentions untarnished by blood,' said Azkaharr. 'You could've spoken to Kolram and struck an agreement.'

Braegnar-Grimnir turned his head against the slab. The cooler flesh at the side of his face hissed soothingly as it was brought into contact with the hot stone. A piece of meat turned on a grill. Dremm grunted out the chorus of his war-song as he pulled on a particularly stubborn shard of stone. Some combination of heat, injury, and being hectored as though he was a flameling that'd dropped his axe caused the runes in his muscles to sputter.

Azkaharr folded his arms over his beard, unimpressed, massively emphasising the girth of his arms and the breadth of his shoulders.

It was the runefather who looked away first.

'I didn't start that battle.'

'No...' Gromrhun scowled. 'But you didn't exactly move mountain and sky to stop it either, did you? And from what I gather, you *did* start the war.'

Kolram bristled at the accusation. Gripping both arms of the throne, he made as if to rise until the alms matron, with a surprisingly sturdy hand for one so devoted to hearth and healing, pushed him back down.

'Who've you been speaking with?' Without sparing the long-beard from his gaze, he pointed to where his sons looked back in startlement from their game board. 'It was one of those two, wasn't it?'

Gromrhun shook his head, yielding no answer either way. 'It's a grave shame that King Kurun was infirm in body as well as in mind by the time you and he brought the Dunrakul home from their halls in exile. He would've slapped more sense into you, I'm sure.'

This time there was nothing the alms maidens could do to keep Kolram seated. He rose like black steam from the shuddering engine of a war machine.

'Speak that way of my father again, and by the silver that lines both our beards you'll feel the back of my hand.'

'About thirty years ago, give or take, you vanquished the beast-herds that had despoiled the mountainside, routed the Kneebite and the Deffstinger from the first deep, and broke the wards of concealment to reclaim this throne hall for your own.'

Kolram sat slowly down and nodded. This was so.

'And what was your first act as king of Karag Dawrkhaz?'

'I sent Braztom and Hangrark with a delegation to the Dunr Lodge, to invite Braegnar-Grimnir to attend me in my new hall and pay tribute to his king.' Kolram dismissed the attentions of the alms maiden with an impatient frown. 'And had he but done so there would've been no quarrel.' He delivered a curt gesture towards Braztom, at the far end of the hall. 'So is it written.'

'This is his mountain too,' said Gromrhun.

'I'm not denying his right to *live* in it.'

'He'd argue to having a fair claim of his own for the kingship.'

Kolram's fist slammed into the armrest. 'He's wrong!'

The vehemence of his shout startled even himself, but it had the power of oath behind it, and he could not back away from it now. Even Gromrhun looked unsure about continuing to argue against such a mighty claim.

'He's wrong,' Kolram said again, more sternly. 'There can be only one heir, descended from the living blood of the Last King, and I am he.'

'The battlesmiths claim we're kin, Kolram and I.' Braegnar-Grimnir let out a laugh and then scowled, as though the spiralling pattern of veins in the marble of his bed-slab would be so bold as to say as much to his face. 'Distant though we are. Separated by ten generations, and more spilled blood as would fill the Cynder Peaks.'

Over his back, Dremm grunted approval of the poetic turn of phrase.

'Suffice to say, I've seen nearer kin than that star-spoiled *unbaraki* take up their axes and swear *barazakdum* to go as Doomseekers into the mountains. Kolram had an army. A home in the stars. The sanctuary of the God-King's own city. What was I born to, Azkaharr? What was my birthright? Battle on every front. I had to peel the enemies off my chest just to see which one of them had their jaws around my throat. My father, and his father, and every father before him to Korgrun himself went to the stone sleep without ever realising the dream of retaking Karag Dawrkhaz. And Kolram would take even the dream from me and keep it from my daughter.'

His voice rose in vehemence until, at its most furious, he found it too dangerous to employ further for fear of the fire it would unleash. It looked, for a moment, as though Brigg would use the silence to speak for herself, but Azkaharr, sensing the wrath in him, bade for her to stay quiet. Dremm, too, set down his tongs, and no longer sang.

'He could've raised himself a grand hall in Azyrheim. With the resources of the God-King, and the alliances in his gift, he could've had his pick of conquests. He could've moved his hall to one of the free cities, or founded his own stronghold in less *grob*-plagued heights than mine. I would've gladly done so, had my father chosen one of my brothers instead of me, and with not a thousandth of Kolram's prospects. But instead he had to come here, to this hole in the bloody ground, and claim for himself what the blood of my forebears made mine, and to *shame* me with the doing of what I could not, putting the fire to the Kneebite and the Deffstinger and winning back the upper deeps.'

Azkaharr sighed. In the belligerence of his bearing, Braegnar-Grimnir sensed understanding of a sort.

'We duardin and our pride. You speak of *allies*, runefather, and with the bitterness of a thirsty duardin lamenting his neighbour's brewery. You need only look over the next door's wall. You've an ally there in Kolram Dunrakul.'

'Listen to him,' said Brigg. 'We have other enemies. Kolram could be a friend of the lodge. And Ael Dunrsdottir too.'

Braegnar-Grimnir scoffed at that.

Ael was supposedly a cousin as well, and even more distant, though he'd only the Kharadron's word for it, which was worth less to him than the piece of paper she claimed it to be written on. At least in Kolram there was a kindred spirit. Kolram had come to his hall with an axe in hand, ready to carve out the kingdom he claimed was his. Ael thought she could cite the names of Barak-Nar loremasters and have the Dunr fyrds and Dunrakul throngs stand aside, tug on their beards and let her come on in and take their mountain.

At least Kolram–

He paused the thought.

Azkaharr was smiling at him in that way he seemed to have of looking deeply and thoughtfully into a thing. It was the same gift that the priests of the Zharrgrim employed to look into the fires of the Zharrkhul and seek truth, but turned upon the hearts of his fellow duardin rather than Grimnir's sacred flame.

'You resent Kolram for claiming the upper deeps, and that's as well. Competition between brothers is what's always made the duardin thrive. But between you, he and Dunrsdottir, you've strength enough to retake the whole mountain and keep it. You've all got the same dream, runefather. All that's stopping you is your pride.'

Braegnar-Grimnir grunted and looked away. 'Is that all?'

'Well...' Gromrhun sniffed, looking down to examine the scuffs on his helmet. 'That's a crying shame.'

'What is?' said Kolram, intrigued despite himself.

Gromrhun shrugged, as though charged with something secret. 'It so happens that Braegnar-Grimnir has passed word to me through an intermediary. A duardin of strikingly fine beard and wisdom.' The longbeard looked up, beyond Kolram's throne, stroking his beard wistfully as his gaze became distant. 'An elder of rare dignity and probity in these unsettled times.'

'Go on, Gromrhun.'

'He proposes a meeting, or so I'm told, to discuss anew the terms of your claim.'

Sitting back, Kolram rubbed thoughtfully at his chin. He didn't smile often. Doing so was akin to making water flow uphill – not impossible, but requiring of a great input of energy, and some application of craft.

He must have bloodied the pretender more than he'd realised. Could it even be that he'd been needlessly hasty in allowing Kothi or Kurrindorm – he was still unsure which of them it'd been – to order the withdrawal from the Deeping? With one more effort, even with one good leg and blood in his eyes, he might've claimed the hall for the Dunrakul. But they were where they were, and the least he could do was acknowledge a humbled adversary's grudging concession to reason with his own.

'He's prepared to acknowledge my claim?'

'Aye.' Gromrhun looked away and coughed. 'In a manner of speaking.'

'So, he's ready to apologise for being a stubborn, uptight, self-righteous, *thaggi*-loving *klutz*, is he?'

Azkaharr cleared his throat. 'Not in those exact terms, no, so if you could avoid putting it exactly that way in his presence then I'm sure things'll go better. I do, however, have it on some authority, that Kolram recognises the pointlessness of further feuding and wants peace.'

'He's welcome to a piece of–'

'Oh, father,' said Brigg, and rolled her eyes. 'Just talk to him and have done.'

Braegnar-Grimnir felt his jaw unclench. He really did let her get away with far too much.

'All right. Where does the *rutzi* want to meet?'

'I'm not having that lout up here,' said Kolram. 'No. Never. He had his invitation and he spurned it.' He shook his head at the appalling thought that Gromrhun's suggestion had set there. 'Traipsing sweat and goodness knows what else that savage might pick up from the Underdeeps between his toes.' He gestured down to the long, tattered carpet that the longbeard was standing on. 'This carpet was the property of the Last King. His household servants gave their lives to ensure it was spared from destruction. Generations of their descendants have toiled to see that they could one day emerge from storage in Azyr and return home.'

From his small table, far away, Lorekeeper Braztom was nodding sagely.

'I'll not cast the work of centuries into the midden so that Braegnar-Grimnir can sully my upholstery.'

'I'm sure the runefather would welcome you to his hearth-chamber with open arms.'

'And greet me as some kind of a supplicant to his hall? Preposterous!'

Gromrhun sighed. He sank into the chair that Kolram had offered him, cursing the stubbornness of the duardin.

Ael Dunrsdottir sat alone in the wardroom. The shutters had been drawn in over the windows. Tough slats of alloy steel, overlapping like armour scale, rattled under the pummelling of the gale. It was full day, according to the clocks, but with the storm battering the port and the windows sealed, the aether-lamps in the wall sconces provided illumination in Hysh's stead. The light they emitted was pale, odourless and clean.

The face of her son, abroad in that storm, appeared in her thoughts.

Shaking her head to clear it of such needless clutter, she concentrated on her work, turning the top sheet of the stack in front of her and adding it neatly to the pile beside it. She took up her pen from its holder in the desk. At the bottom of the new page, she signed her name with a brisk flourish. She dabbed tentatively at the signature. Not so much as a drop of wastage. Truly, the duardin were living through a golden age of science.

At the sound of footsteps, she looked up. She had been so absorbed in her paperwork she hadn't even heard the doors opening.

Wyram approached the desk. In light of the worsening weather, and in line with the majority of the port's inhabitants and crew,

Wyram had taken to wearing arkanaut armour as a matter of sartorial routine. His, however, was of a model with an archaic look about it that Ael had never seen before. The colours were of no port that Ael knew. The emblems that emblazoned the flat panels looked like a cross between old Khazalid, Fyreslayer script, and more modern forms, more amenable to mass production with movable type, that the Kharadron employed. 'One of the older ports,' Wyram had said once, when asked, and offered no more. Even Ael, inquisitorial by leaning, saw the grief in his face at sharing even that much and let the question rest.

The elder clasped his hands behind his back and cleared his throat.

Ael sat back in her small, lightweight chair and directed Wyram's attention to the papers on her desk. 'A spousal contract, would you believe? The boy's actually gone and left me with a spousal contract.' It was her turn to be wistful. As though she had clouds streaming through her fingers, leaving her behind somehow, even though she'd always thought she was exactly where she wanted to be. 'I'd no idea he'd even proposed an informal statement of intent. Or made a tentative first approach.' She smiled, recalling her first speculative investments in that volatile but, apparently, quite lucrative market, and blinked away a tear. 'He's grown up so fast.'

'They do that, I'm told.'

'I've been so busy. I fear I've missed his golden years.'

'Founding a new venture isn't for the faint-hearted, mistress.'

'No.' Ael frowned at the document in front of her. She supposed it would all be for naught soon anyway. The lost trade. The damage done to the port. Forecastinator Zorek and Threngthorm had already started to relocate some of their businesses to securer holdings in the fastnesses below while they waited for the storm to blow out. Unless Strahl brought the *Bokram* back with a bursting hold, they would all be ruined. Her finger rested on the second, unsigned, box in the page's footer. 'Who's the lucky counter-signatory, I wonder.'

'I really couldn't say.'

Ael's eyes narrowed. It was a look that'd chilled many an arbitration panel in her day. 'An interesting, *careful* choice of words.'

Mirth danced around Wyram's deep-set and incredibly tired-looking eyes. 'You can take the codewright out of the court, eh, mistress?'

'So long as it's not that pretty young skyrigger from Barak-Urbaz. You know the one I mean. The one with all the toes. Or that aether-khemist who came in on the *Drubblang*.' Ael sighed, setting her pen back in its slot. 'If he's absolutely set on marrying, then it should be to someone who'll make something of herself, and someone who'll demand no less from him.'

The elder smiled at that. 'You've nothing to worry about on that front, I'm sure.'

Putting the half-read contract from her thoughts, Ael sat back in her chair and looked properly at Wyram. 'You know, I told the Grundcorps I wasn't to be disturbed until dog watch.'

Wyram shrugged. 'I must've just missed them.'

'Remind me to review their commission.'

'Go easy on them. I've an unusually light step for a duardin of my girth.' He patted his girdle plate. 'And besides, I've come with a proposition for you.'

Ael spread her hands. 'The port's bankrupt and we've no ships.'

'The opportunity's right here in Karag Dawrkhaz.'

'How much money will it make me?'

'It won't cost you any.'

Ael snorted. 'A start, I suppose.'

'I'm proposing a truce. Kolram, Braegnar-Grimnir, and you.'

'When?'

'No time like now, I've always said. And it's a saying that's only got truer as the world's got older around me.'

'War isn't always bad for business.'

'Not always.'

'It can be a cursed nuisance though.'

'Aye.'

Ael drummed her fingers on the desk as she thought it over. 'I suppose I *could* do with less of Kolram invading the Grund-hangars every other week.'

'The Dunrakul used to call them gyrobays, and I believe Kolram would very much like for the Grund-captain to return them. But that's something to be haggled over when he gets here.'

Ael raised an eyebrow.

'I have it on the word of esteemed elders in the halls of both Kolram and Braegnar-Grimnir, that the Dunr Lodge and the Dunrakul were already planning a meeting. I'd assumed you'd not care for being left out and pre-emptively suggested that the meeting take place here.' He bowed apologetically. 'Why not take the steering hand, eh?'

Ael considered the proposition, but could think of no practical reason to refuse. As the elder had already pointed out, it would cost her nothing, and as she had pointed out to him in return, it wasn't as though she was too busy with real business.

Perhaps she could bill the other delegations for room and board. She could charge by the head.

'All right.'

'You'll not regret it, mistress.'

Wyram dipped his head and made to leave. Just as he did, the shutters rattled under a gust powerful enough to push its way through. The freezing air blustered its way around the room like a vandal, picking up Ael's neatly stacked papers and scattering them. The aether-lamps buzzed and flickered, despite their sheaths of protective glass. As though there was something inimical to Kharadron science behind that wind. Ael shivered in it, choosing to blame it on the cold rather than admit to harbouring such superstitions in her head.

Wyram bent to pick up the strewn pages of Strahl's contract.

'I thought Brynruf was contracts day,' he said, a smile in his eyes as he returned them to their proper piles on Ael's desk.

Ael muttered to herself, and shuffled the papers back into neat stacks. 'Be off with you. Arrange your meeting. Before I change my mind and charge them double.'

CHAPTER NINE

Strahl threw open the cargo hatch. Almost immediately, he was straining against it as the wind strove to push it closed over his head. Snow streamed in through the opening, misting up his lenses before the suit could adjust to the sudden drop in temperature. His armour chugged, the aether-furnace in the backpack spitting out chromatic sparks. The arkanaut suit's primary function was protection: from cold, thin air; from rival skyfarers' swords; and from the magical phenomena that became dangerously commonplace the nearer one sailed to the zenith, but newer marks of suit came with power support as standard. And Ael Dunrsdottir was nothing if not a patron of the latest innovations.

The hatch flew from his hand and *clanged* into the deck.

As much as his suit's furnace was giving to his natural duardin strength, he suspected the hatch's abrupt surrender had less to do with his own efforts and more with an abrupt shift in the wind. It was as though a sympathetic gargant had come along and kicked it open.

It wasn't snowing any more. The world *was* snow.

The air was prickly and white, just the occasional stolen glimpse of brass and chrome, the bold, statement colours of Barak-Zon turned monochrome. Colour, the storm said, was a privilege. Had Strahl been anything other than a duardin in arkanaut gear, he would've been dead the moment he opened the hatch. If the cold hadn't killed him, if the wind hadn't flayed his bones and howled as it did, then trying to pull that freezing air into his lungs would have. Arkanauts in snow-stippled armour slipped and stumbled across the tilting deck. They yelled at one another, but the storm stripped their shouts of words, context, meaning until their helmets were projecting only helpless noise into the wind. Strahl envied them. They at least had a task to occupy their minds. He'd come this far, overcome this much of his fear, and he refused to spend another of his last moments holed up below.

Crouching by the hatch, he attempted to close and seal it so no stumbling arkanaut would accidentally fall in. He couldn't raise it an inch off the deck. The wind was too strong. The sympathetic gargant of his imagination had sat down on the open hatch, chortling in the grinding voice of deep winter.

Resigned, he got up and ran, head down, half-blind, until he hit the gunwale. He grabbed hold of it, breathing out relief the way his armour periodically vented off unstable aetheric by-products and heat. Running his gauntlets over the rails, he felt for their shape.

The skyfleets had to operate and turn a profit under any conditions. From the blinding lights of Hysh to the impenetrable gloom of Ulgu and the spectral hazards of the Shyish Nadir, if there were fortunes to be made then Kharadron vessels would sail their skies. Borg Helmensson had given the briefest of tours on their departure of Karag Dawrkhaz: just enough that Strahl wouldn't accidentally fall overboard or fumigate himself. He'd learned that the starboard rails were cylindrical in shape. Those on the port side were hexagonal prisms. He laughed aloud as he felt the angles under his gauntlets.

Port side. The sterncastle and wheelhouse were to his left.

'Seam ahoy!' Captain Helmensson's voice reverberated through the speaker pipes mounted up on masts along the deck. If Strahl had been below in his cabin where he was meant to be, then he'd still have heard it through the plumbing there. *'Open the forward scoops and charge the collectors. All hands brace and prepare to take on cargo.'*

Strahl felt the rising pulse of the endrin masts as ship and crew responded to the captain's commands. Muted flashes, like sheet lightning, struggled against the snowstorm as power was siphoned off towards the collectors.

Lessons in aether-khemistry came slinking out of his subconscious. The collectors were essentially fine sieves of base metals, but they needed to be pre-charged with activated aether in order to attract aether-gold to the wires, drawing it from the cloud-seam as the skyvessel passed through it.

He wondered where these lessons had been all this time.

Head down, right hand to the rail, he made for the sterncastle. He passed arkanauts busily throwing netting over the gunwales, pitting their armour-enhanced strength against the capstans to rack open the forward scoops. After a few-score beard lengths, he pushed himself gunwale rail to stair rail, leant fully into the wind and dragged himself onto the companionway.

The sterncastle was a raised section of deck behind the main endrin mast and above the transom, containing the sky-ship's conning instruments and captain's quarters within the high, castellated walls of the poop deck. There were four duardin present, but they were barely distinguishable from one another, like machinery buried by an overnight snow. Their joints were caked in ice, only the vents on their aether-furnaces and their helmet lenses visible.

The steersman stood at the large wheel, pushing every scrap of useable power from his harness into holding the ironclad steady. The duardin at the semaphore array, working stolidly in spite of the blinding improbability of getting a signal through the storm, had to be the *Bokram*'s signalman. Which left one of the remaining two to be Borg Helmensson.

The question of which answered itself when the captain stomped about and addressed him.

'You should be below,' he said.

'I want to help.'

'Your mother had me sign a subclause that indemnifies her if you should come to harm under my charge. If anything happens to you out here then it comes out of the *Bokram*'s share.'

Strahl hadn't realised she cared that much. 'You need all the hands you can get,' he yelled back.

'This isn't the sky for novices, lad.'

Strahl regretted giving Helmensson the precis to his life story back in Karag Dawrkhaz. It was a bad habit of his when he was feeling sorry for himself and it invariably returned to bite him. Before he could make an argument in his defence, however, the fourth duardin, who he'd not yet been able to identify, called Helmensson over. The two officers and the signalman conducted a screaming conference that Strahl didn't catch a word of but which concluded with the captain nodding reluctantly and turning back to Strahl.

'You want to be useful?'

'Yes!'

'Good.' Helmensson flapped an ice-encrusted gauntlet towards his crewmate. 'My navigator can't take a decent sounding of our position from here. There're no stars to be seen, and the magic driving the storm ahead of it's playing havoc with the windstream. He wants to take us down, get a fix on wherever we are, make

contact with the rest of the flotilla if we can, then restore buoyancy and come back up.'

'Isn't that dangerous?'

Helmensson snorted. He really didn't need to answer that.

'What do you need me to do?' Strahl shouted back.

'I need you to poke your head over the side as we go down.'

Sjarpa Longtooth bellowed for the ogors to work faster. The storm
took a few of his words, but added its own snarl to his voice.
The Everwinter itself loomed over his shoulder. The snow was
its paws. The wind was its teeth. The ogors could feel it circling.
Even the orruks sensed the predator in the storm and answered
in kind. Frorgen Maetsgral had to put down a scrap between
the Axe-Snappa Ironjawz and the Leadfoot Mawtribe. When the
Coldtoof Bonesplitterz started pushing up against the Oldenguts,
complaining of the wind shrieking in their heads, Sturmur himself had been moved to fall back and break it up. He'd eaten six
orruks and their boars and claimed to be hungry still.

Sjarpa's bowels gurgled at the thought. Given as there was
nothing in them but half a Fyreslayer and some rocks, he took
it as the warning growl of the Everwinter.

It was close.

'On!' He urged the Alfrostuns into the valley ahead with a sweep
of his paw. 'Go on if you want full bellies and warm fingers by
the duardin's fires!'

Stonehorns plunged like monstrous snowploughs into the
passes. Mournfang riders followed, widening the cleared passages
and tramping them down, dropping steaming heaps of dung that
would keep the snow from settling again for a short while at least.
Long enough for the Icebrow Rangers to see the horde through.
The mountainous route would've been impassable to most. It
was barely slowing the ogors down. Sjarpa saw the brightest of

the Gutbuster tyrants watching the Beastclaw work. Ogors were slow to think. Slower to change. They spoke in simple terms, and amused themselves with simple things, but they *weren't* simple. As the Maneaters had once learned of the Great Secret and taught it to the children of Behemat, and as Frost King Borja had invented The Way, they could learn.

And then, there, before Sjarpa's eyes, the Gutbusters were learning that Beastclaw discipline could shift mountains.

'How far to go?' grunted Njal Icebreaker.

The beastrider's monster rubbed shoulder to shoulder with Sjarpa's. Cold radiated off them both. The big ogor slumped over the pommel of his saddle, dragged into a hunch by his own immense weight. He had the reins in one hand, an ice-tipped hunting spear in the other.

'Not far.' Sjarpa was sure he meant it too. His gut rarely lied. 'Not far.'

Skag Vulture-Keeper looked up then and pointed into the swirling snow. He'd been moved, some time ago, to eat the creatures that had earned him his name, but his eyes were still sharper than most.

'Thing,' he announced.

The beastriders of the Torrbad looked up.

An arkanaut crewman showed him the accommodation ladder. Strahl gulped and looked down. The ladder ran down the outer hull through intermittent onslaughts of snow towards the fin keel. About two hundred beard-lengths down. It stopped at a narrow ledge from which a duardin with a sturdier head for heights than his could get into the hold via a wheel-operated side hatch or drop down into the *Bokram*'s starboard gun cupola. The rungs were hoary with ice. The side rails bowed and wobbled, giving off a wounded vibration as the ironclad's own aetherdynamic design blasted it with winds of greater and greater speeds to generate lift.

Strahl held onto the rails until his head stopped spinning. His mother was counting on him. Helmensson was counting on him. And Brigg…

If they couldn't figure out where they were then they wouldn't make it back before the storm wrecked them, and even if they *could* they'd never be able to mine as much of the cloud-seam as they needed without coordinating with the rest of the flotilla. The port would be ruined. Ael would lose it all to the Bankers' Union, and he'd have nothing left to offer as a husband.

Turning, back to the wind, hands fast to the rails either side of the ladder, Strahl prepared himself to back over the edge. Just as he felt he'd built up enough courage to go, the arkanaut clipped a line to one of the utility loops that adorned Strahl's armour.

'Safety first,' he said, a smile in his tone, tugging on the line to ensure it was strong and the clip secure. 'Artycle two, Point seven.' He clapped Strahl on the shoulder, then retreated from the edge.

'Yes, sir.'

It occurred to him only as he was backing out into the *real* storm, his boot sliding along an icy rung, that his mother's letter of marque gave him legal rank over everyone aboard.

A little late to be realising that now.

The wind beat against his side as he clung on to the ladder. It screamed through the various gaps, loops and functional protrusions in his armour. As firmly as he tried to grip, his gauntlets couldn't generate enough friction on the ice. The wind pushed him, cold metal sliding through his fingers until he was hanging off the side rail like a flag. He was acutely aware of every sour breath that rasped through his helmet. He felt somewhat cheated. Being, if not the last, then very nearly the last breaths he'd take, he imagined they should have tasted sweeter.

Marshalling his reserves of stubbornness, he reasserted his grip on the top rung, wrapped his boot around the lower, and descended.

By the time he had both boots on the platform below, his muscles were aching, his heart was beating so hard it was upsetting the spirit levels in his gyroscope. Sweat sloshed around inside his armour, in spite of the crippling cold seizing the plates from the outside. Turning around, back to the frozen hull, he let his gauntlets fall gratefully over the safety rail.

The access hatch to the hold was a little further along. It was barred from the inside as well as requiring a key to unlock from without. The drop hatch to the gun cupola was directly under him. The brass sphere bristled with aethershot carbines in rubber gimbals. It was sitting idle. Had it been occupied, the gunners could've spared Strahl the ordeal, but it was accepted aeronautical practice to keep crew members occupied. There was aether-gold to be mined, and no foes to be fired upon.

After a lengthy battle with his own nerves, he leaned over the rail and looked down.

The *Bokram*'s propellers, a pair of perpetual motion rotors offset behind the keel fin, drummed the air beneath him. The snow was so thick he could barely see them. The mountains, further beneath, were grey humps in an endlessly hurrying white, shades of scale without any sense of proximity or even shape. They could have been anywhere.

They needed to go further down.

He leant over the rail as though he could give the *Bokram* a free yard or two. The ground came into view. It was shapeless and inconstant. Every flake of snow was a white-antlered creature in a huge, disorderly migration.

The *Bokram* descended further into the mountains. The snow thinned.

The ground *was* moving.

At first Strahl thought he had to be looking at an avalanche, until the objects came into clearer view. He gripped the rail in sudden fear as the man-like creatures beneath him came into focus. The *Bokram* was flying perilously low, for individuals within that mass migration to be so cleanly defined. He gawped for a moment, before realising that the error was one of perspective.

The creatures were man-*like*, they weren't man-*sized*.

'Up!' he yelled, pushing himself from the rail, and taking hold of the accommodation ladder. 'Up!' Abandoning the care with which he'd descended, he scrambled back up towards the deck. The arkanaut was still there, ready to relay a message to the conn should Strahl spy a landmark of note. Strahl could see the vari-coloured glow of his helmet lenses through the snow, but no sign that he'd heard. 'Enemies below! The captain has to take us up. He has to–'

His boot slipped on the rung in his haste. It slid out into open air.

With a scream, he slid out after it.

A huge metal belly, girt in lights, descended out of the storm. Three globe-like things hung above it and wreathed it in a weak glow. The shrillness of the gale made its pulsing seem silent, but Sjarpa sensed the urgency of prey that'd caught the hunter's scent. A wave of excited, excitement-starved pointing ran through the greenskin hordes ahead of its wake. There was a crackle of pistol fire and the crude *twang* of Bonesplitter arrowboyz giving chase. Sturmur Rockbelly, at the back of the group knocking the savage orruks' heads together, pulled himself high in his stonehorn's saddle and hurled a spear that fell way short.

'Flying ship,' said Skag.

Sjarpa chewed thoughtfully on his beard. Because he was still learning too, and it'd just occurred to him what the Gutbusters' big guns might be good for.

* * *

Strahl's stomach lurched. He fell, his heart still only halfway to his throat as the safety line snapped taut and banged him hard against the hull. He swore. Pain, relief, terror, and a savage rush of blood to the head left him otherwise at a loss for words.

Hanging from the line, he swung an arm out for the ladder. He slapped the side rail with his gauntlets a couple of times before getting fingers around it and reeling himself in. For several precious seconds he just clung on to it, determined to never again do anything more reckless than breathe.

The arkanaut's shining lenses appeared at the top of the ladder. 'You all right?'

Strahl bit down his preferred retort.

He had the next one lined up when the entire ship shook and an explosion hurled the waiting arkanaut overboard. Unrefined aether-gold that the *Bokram* had already taken aboard burst out through the ruptured plate, turning snowflakes into sizzling droplets of unstable metals that rattled against the hull of the ship.

Strahl cursed and turned his head from the hail. The *Bokram* should've been able to take a hit like that, from that kind of range, but she was packed full of volatile aether-gold and, worse, the cold had made her armour brittle.

Arkanauts rushed to the gunwales. Trained gunners pivoted the aethershot carbines on their pintle mounts to shake off the ice before tilting the guns down. The carbines glowed hot as they spat out aethershot pellets, hyper-accelerated by the strange properties of aether-gold and Kharadron alchemy. The explosive *crumps* of aethercharge torpedoes pushed flat-topped mushroom clouds into weird and unsettling shapes against the pummelling snow.

Strahl couldn't help feeling pride. The *Bokram* had been surprised, separated from her escorts, but she carried firepower enough on her own to flatten a small army.

Air horns situated along the length of the deck blasted out their warnings, and Strahl felt the pull of gravity on his boots as the *Bokram* hauled her prow into an emergency ascent. He screamed as the manoeuvre drew his stomach towards his feet and his hands from the ladder. To make something as massive as the *Bokram* climb was not a straightforward matter. The aether-gold in her endrins could make her lighter than air, but there were still powerful, fundamental forces to be overcome. Strahl gritted his teeth, feeling every one of those forces hard at work on his fingers. He flung his arm over the rung, locking it against the crook of his elbow, and yelled wordlessly into the gale.

His warning for Helmensson was moot now. The captain evidently knew already that his ship was under attack.

Judging from the size and direction of the ogor horde, Strahl had a fair idea of where they were. Chances were, they'd been turned about at some point of their journey and were now above Arik's Pass, the last and largest of the major routes from the southern ranges onto Karag Dawrkhaz. If this migration was to make it to the Gate of Throngs unchallenged then every duardin, whether they lived on the mountain, in it, or under it, would be in peril.

He thought of Brigg. A knot formed in his belly. His intended would relish the prospect of death in battle against a vastly superior horde, but he'd not give her the choice if he could avoid it.

The captain knew what was below his ship, but the knowledge was useless so long as the *Bokram* was forced to choose between tearing herself apart or getting blasted out of the sky. Someone had to warn the rest of the flotilla.

Strahl had to warn the rest of the flotilla.

He looked around for inspiration. His gaze settled on the gun cupola below. Before he could change his mind, he transferred his hands from the ladder's rungs to the side rails and slid to the bottom. His boots slammed into the metal. At any moment he expected the metallurgy to give before his weight, but the Kharadron made their armour light and their alloys tough, and they did their welding right.

Taking a moment to catch his breath, he hurried to the platform's edge. The narrow walkway directly overlooked the gun cupola.

He jumped off, kicked in the roof hatch, and dropped down.

Inside was a pair of reclined seats. The cupola's curvature squeezed them together. Each faced an aethershot carbine and a small window. Ignoring the snow blowing in through the now-open hatch, Strahl slid into one of the seats. The padding yielded to his bulky armour, displacement causing it to flow around and effectively glue him into place. He took the carbine and pulled it towards him.

He didn't turn it downwards. He turned it up.

The *Bokram*'s semaphore array couldn't punch a warning to the rest of the flotilla through the storm, but perhaps her aethershot weaponry could.

The weapon's roar drummed through the cupola's thin shield. Three short bursts of fire, three long, and then three more short, together screaming 'Beware!' in the old miner's Hammertongue that the Kharadron skyfleets had adopted for their own. Tracers of aethershot spat in the general direction of the realm's zenith, accelerated on their way through twinkling rainbows of aether-gold and a rapid succession of sonic booms. He only hoped that there was another ship out there, and that whoever was flying it had been as unsympathetically educated as he had been.

Incoming fire from the ground lit up his window. He ignored it, squeezing harder on the trigger as he repeated the signal, but he couldn't rewrite the rules of aether-khemistry with willpower alone to make the bullets fly any faster, or seek out a Kharadron vessel any better.

He thought of Brigg and found himself grinning, imagining how she would approve.

Bits of hull around him came loose under fire. He saw them as they dropped into his tight visual field, and then out of it again, tumbling towards the distant ground. The ship shuddered once more. He told himself that it was so loud this time because he was ensconced within the cupola now rather than hanging loose off the hull. He told himself this was a good thing.

The shuddering rose into a dying squeal. The drag on Strahl's guts abated. For a few short seconds, he was weightless.

The *Bokram* had stopped climbing.

Strahl screamed, as she began to go down.

Ogors and greenskins alike cheered as the duardin sky-ship came down. Beastriders fired their guns in the air. Those without fire-arms tossed up screaming greenskins, or else just roared. Sjarpa Longtooth watched with interest as the big ship ploughed into the ribs of the mountain. After a lifetime as long as his on the Mawpath, new sights were rarer than aelf meat and just as welcome.

The ship's metal skin rippled, turning to a form of liquid whilst somehow holding onto its basic shape as its rear end continued to drive its front into the slope. Its middle crumpled like a helmet between an ogor's hands. The mountain responded with a shudder, snow shaken loose from the summit already rushing down the slope. It struck the sky-ship side-on and buried it. The snow slip didn't stop there. The jeers of the Kruleboyz and Bonesplitterz nearest the crash turned into screams as the avalanche cut across the rear of the horde and buried them wholesale.

Ulf chuckled. There was a reason everyone called him the Strange. The rest of the Beastclaw just watched stoically.

'More meat to go around when we make it to the Fire Crown,' observed Brogg.

'We eat the duardin only if they refuse us,' Sjarpa reminded him.

'Then we should search it for meat and guns,' Njal suggested.

Sjarpa shook his head, the wind already picking up loose snow from the avalanche and pelting the ogors' faces with it. 'We need fire and shelter. We need it soon. Leave the wreck for the yhetees, we do what the Beastclaw always do.' He turned and snapped the thundertusk's iron-studded reins. 'We go on.'

'The duardin are solid and dependable people, seldom given to flights of fancy. Indeed, if one were so determined to find a slight against them, it would be for a paucity of imagination rather than its excess. How then to explain, always when the light is short and enemies near abroad, the duardin who'd swear to being visited by a white-bearded wanderer from the oldest stories...'

CHAPTER TEN

Guthrun Gorlflaer was an eminently sensible duardin. He rarely topped up his ale ration from his own pocket, seldom allowed suspicious herbs near his pipe, and always took a pinch of salt with scuttlebutt tales of ghost ships, blimp-squigs and siren aelves luring the overly covetous onto metaliths hidden in the clouds. With the tip of his gauntlet finger, the pilot scraped the ice off his altimeter dial and frowned at the nonsensical reading.

Giving up on the dashboard instruments as lost causes, he scanned the blizzard for the faintest sign of the *Bokram* or its fleet. Perhaps another Hammertongue signal, like the one that had just lashed across his bow and almost shorn his gunhauler in half. Snow lashed his helmet. The lenses were back-heated and hermetically sealed, but the snowmelt pooling in the sockets was enough to make a visual search challenging.

He resisted the urge to ease off the pedal and drop speed. The last thing he wanted to risk under these conditions was a stall.

Guthrun had been Grundcorps for sixty years. He'd piloted

gunhaulers for fifteen of them. And that was at the end of a respectable eighty-year career in which he'd crewed on just about every class of ship the skyfleets still flew and a few they didn't. His gunhauler, *Tenker*, was a small craft, comparatively, but sturdily made, and with a powerful endrin for her class. She growled as determinedly as any old sot cheated of a coin in spite of the snow pelting her nose and the gouge across her keel.

He told himself he'd flown through worse. A dozen times, at least.

No particular occasion came to mind.

'Anything?' he barked down.

Yorin Suthur, his gunner, leant out of the cupola, scanning for the ground with an aetheric optiscope trained to his right lens. He didn't appear to have heard.

Guthrun yelled again.

Yorin lowered the optiscope. 'What?'

'Can. You. See. Anything?'

'No, I–'

Guthrun brought up a hand for quiet. Yorin, having flown with Guthrun for the better part of a decade, cut himself short.

'You hear that?' Guthrun shouted.

It was subtle. The *whup-whup* sound of a propeller rotor, a repetitive counterpoint to the steady hum of the gunhauler's endrin. He looked over the side and almost gasped as the box-outline of a Dunrakul gyrocopter hove into view from below. Its pilot was draped in a heavy coat, but wasn't even wearing a mask: just a chunky set of aviator goggles with the adjustable straps flapping loose and a mass of beard. A tough lot, these Dunrakul pilots: Guthrun wasn't sure he'd be half so keen on a head-to-head with gravity if he had to do it in a heavier-than-air steel box with naught but a free-spinning auto-rotor and a crank engine to keep him airborne.

The pilot threw him a thumbs up, then gestured for Guthrun to follow him. Guthrun returned the gesture to indicate he understood.

Yorin took the optiscope from his eye and gave it a whack. He trained it on the gyrocopter again. 'No wonder we couldn't find the fleet. Blasted thing isn't working.'

'He's going to lead us down,' Guthrun yelled.

'What are the Dunrakul doing all the way out here?'

But Guthrun was no longer listening. As the gyrocopter and her white-bearded old pilot peeled off, he pulled on the stick and followed her down.

Borrin Helmstur was also an eminently sensible duardin. Had he been otherwise, when his king had called on the throngs to muster and the thegns to honour their longstanding oaths, he would have protested deafness and remained behind in the city he had grown to love. He missed Azyrheim. Every day, and the nights most of all. The nights in Azyrheim were endless, but they had a beauty that surpassed all splendour in the Mortal Realms and could move even the dour heart of a duardin to the beggarly attempts at poetry he had tried to write. It had never been a warm city, existing under perpetual starlight as it did, but the ale was served warm, the food as dependable as the duardin who served it, and the crimes committed against the king of his forefathers' forefathers had been far enough away for him to forget, if not forgive.

Shivering in the unseasonal cold, Borrin hastened up the winding stairs of his watchtower. At the top landing, he pushed through the wooden door, and out into howling wind and driving snow.

The tower was a stone structure, stuck to the narrow end of the cordwood ranger cabin he shared with his mother, uncle, sister, brother-in-law, and two nieces. The storm blasted in through the open sides. He'd never felt cold like it. It urged flesh to shrink to its bones, blood to surrender its extremities and retreat to its deepest fastnesses for even that scant hope of warmth was surely lost forever.

Muttering, Borrin drew in his hood and crossed to the coal brazier in the middle of the floor. The engraved tinderbox shook in his gloved hands. The few sparks he managed to scrape off the steel with the flint sputtered out before they were able to fall amongst the tinder.

He should've taken his family back to Karag Dawrkhaz when the weather had turned foul and the other rangers had fled. It was bitterness, as much as stubbornness, that had made him stay put. If the oaths of his ancestors demanded his family live in a dere-lict cabin on the outermost arm of the Spiral Crux instead of the quiet terrace he'd owned in Azyrheim, then come storm or foe the cabin was where they'd stay and King Kolram could be damned.

The timber frame of the attached building trembled slightly as the Kharadron sky-ship he'd spotted while out emptying his bladder for the third time that night sailed overhead and disappeared in a flurry of endrin sparks in the direction of Karag Dawrkhaz. Peer-ing through the window in the direction it'd sailed out of, Borrin thought, as he had before, that he saw figures moving. Ogor scouts and their big hunting cats. Moving up through the pass. If he got the beacon lit then those ogor scouts would know for sure that Borrin's cabin wasn't as empty as it must've looked.

But he had a duty. It was a duty he hated utterly, and would gladly die for. He'd not have it said of Borrin Helmstur that he put his kin through three decades of discomfort and penury only to fail in his oaths in the end. Muttering a string of choice curses, he scraped at the tinderbox.

With a prickling sense of being watched, Borrin looked up and around.

His first thought was that his elderly uncle had somehow made it out of bed and up the stairs. His uncle had been a famous ranger in Sigmar's Freeguild, about two hundred years ago, but it'd take more than a shaking cabin to rouse him these days, and more than a horde of starving ogors to get him up the tower's stairs.

The stranger was similarly broad of shoulder and large of girth, however, and had a beard that put his uncle's two and a half centuries to shame. His solid frame was draped in a cloak that was travel-stained and tatty but clearly finer, once, than anything that a duardin of the Helmstur clan had ever owned. The snowy-white hairs of his beard poked through where the cloak didn't quite join in the middle. His face looked lived-in and, though it was apparently not his uncle, Borrin felt an uncomfortable tickle of recognition. As though he knew this duardin, but was equally certain that it could not be who it appeared to be.

Cupping the smouldering bowl of his pipe against the wind, the stranger whom Borrin refused to name offered it up and smiled.

'Light?'

Vulkarl Bloodhammer was dependable enough, but as un-sensible a duardin as they came and proud of it. It was in large part because of him and his fyrd that, in spite of the talk of peace in the air, the Dunr Lodge and the Kharadron who trespassed in his ancestors' hall remained very much at war.

Blood and spittle flecked his beard, his eyes stretched wide with Grimnir's own wrath, as his axes tore at Kharadron armour. An arkanaut swung his pistol towards him. Vulkarl cut through the arm at the wrist just as the duardin squeezed. The pistol discharged as it fell, shooting the Kharadron through his own foot and dropping his neck to the perfect height for severing. Vulkarl roared as blood sprayed upwards like a fountain, and hurled himself after the retreating gun-line.

The Kharadron were a fearsome foe to face at range, but up close, where the work was done with axes and muscle, they vanished in smoke like the paper their honour was written on.

From nowhere, the butt of a Kharadron rifle cracked him on the forehead.

Vulkarl stumbled backwards with a snarl, spitting curses as the rifle butted him again, splitting his eyebrow and landing him on his back. He blinked blood out of his eye and stared at the ceiling, refusing to flinch from the kill-shot. Death meant walking through fire and sleeping in stone. Fighting at Grimnir's side in preparation for the final battle, the *Doomgron*, when Chaos would be overthrown and the Mortal Realms consumed in its flame. There was nothing there to fear.

After several seconds, during which the kill-shot failed to land, Vulkarl scowled and lowered his gaze to the Kharadron standing over him.

His head was helmeted, but the ancestor mark engraved there was uncannily familiar, as though Vulkarl had seen its likeness a hundred times before but forgotten where. The runes adorning his armour, too, looked almost like something that a priest of the Zharrgrim would beat into a berzerker's flesh in the rite of *grundtogg*. It was only the fact that they'd been hammered into metal rather than meat that made them look strange.

And for a Kharadron, he could fight a little.

Under the cool gemstone glow of the Kharadron's lensed eyes, Vulkarl felt his battle-frenzy begin to leave him. With a grunt, he sat up and looked around, shamefaced by what he saw. Fyreslayers and Kharadron warred over the length of the hall. Grand, stone colonnades had been chewed to pieces by Kharadron firepower while, having bought their way up close with blood, fyresteel axes now made a similar mockery of Kharadron armour.

His former foe was watching too.

Vulkarl had never felt shame in his life, and he disliked the feeling intensely, but what he saw in the strange Kharadron's silver mask was the anguish of several lifetimes' worth.

'Come on, lad,' he said, smothering Vulkarl's brawny hand in a large and unexpectedly powerful grip. 'Up you get. It's not too late to make something good of this yet.'

Strahl Aelsson had thought himself a sensible duardin, up until the moment he'd decided his debt to Ael had been worth more than his own life.

Tat-tat-tat.

A dull, metallic knocking rang through the *Bokram*'s twisted hull. Strahl came around slowly, drawn as if from a dream in which he'd been curled up in his own bed with Brigg beside him, whilst at the same time feeling numbingly cold.

Tat-tat-tat.

He looked around groggily, breathing slowly, shallowly, his brain taking its time in recognising the gun cupola from the starboard keel. It had lost its spherical shape. The alloy panels had buckled inwards. Several had been shorn away completely, bits of metal gnawing inwards like animal teeth. The roof hatch was gone. The window was smashed. A rock had driven through it, impaling the seat next to Strahl's. It was thinly dusted with frost, the source of all cold in the Mortal Realms.

Tat-tat-tat.

Ogor cannons. Crash landing. Avalanche. The fool that he was. He remembered it all now.

He fumbled around his waist for the restraint belt release before realising there was none. The adaptive cushion had moulded itself so snuggly to his shape that it was wedging him in place. The thoughts moved slower in his head than his hands pushing against the padding. He was feeling the effects of hypothermia.

He remembered reading about it. Strahl wondered if his complete absence of panic was another of the symptoms.

Managing, at last, to push himself out of the all-body embrace of the gunner's chair, he dropped two feet and *clanged* onto the cupola side, where he discovered the torn panels from the ceiling and the remnants of the aethershot carbine.

The ship had come down on her side. Either that, or the cupola had torn loose in the crash. He allowed his head to rest in the metallic debris. It was cold, but inexplicably comfortable.

Tat-tat-tat.

He stirred, realising he had fallen asleep for a moment. There was that sound again. Like the grip of a hand tool or the butt of a rifle tapping on the skin of the wreckage.

Tat-tat-tat.

It didn't sound as though it was coming from far away.

With a groan, he drew one hand under him, then another, and then pushed himself up onto his knees. There was a tear in the cupola wall that looked large enough to accommodate him. He crawled towards it. It led through to a twisting conduit of mangled hull plating, perforated at sporadic intervals by pipework and rebar and spines of rock.

Tat-tat-tat.

The sound was louder now. Definitely coming from just the other end of the metal corridor. Moving unnaturally slowly, like a herptile in winter, Strahl manoeuvred his armoured frame into the breach and stepped through.

Some parts were large enough for him to walk through. In others, he had to crawl on hands and knees, then to drag himself like a worm, his armour scraping along rock and metal until, with the exception of the repetitive *tat-tat-tat* guiding him to the outside world, it was the only sound left in the realms.

He didn't know how long it took to reach the passage's end

because his mind told him it took forever, but at some point the fingers of his outstretched hand crunched into powdered snow rather than crumpled metal and he realised he was outside.

He looked up. The wind blew snow into his face and it was the most wonderful sight in the Cosmos Arcane. His eyes stung in the sudden, incomparable glare of a sunless winterscape. From somewhere close by, he heard the high-powered whine and sonic *crack* of aethershot weaponry being deployed in wrath. But he couldn't seem to summon the attention that it needed just then.

An elderly duardin set down his axe and crouched down in the snow beside him.

He looked a bit like old Wyram, but even as Strahl tried to focus on his features they blurred like one of his tutors' optical puzzles. His attire shifted too. An archaic mode of arkanaut sky-armour became bare, fire-tanned skin, then the travel-stained cloak and garb of one of the Dispossessed's itinerant kings. For every way in which his appearance changed however, he remained, in some unaccountable way, exactly the same.

'You…' Strahl mumbled. 'You…'

The old duardin smiled gravely, and nodded. 'Aye.'

Strahl felt lighter than air as he lifted his hand from the snow to grasp the elder's proffered wrist.

He heard a shout. Thumping boots. Two pairs of strong, aethermatically empowered hands took each arm, the vibrations of their furnaces shaking him from his daze, and hauled him fully from the wreck.

'Grombrindal,' he mumbled, reaching for the hand that was still offered to him albeit now from impossibly far away.

'Lad's delirious,' said a voice that sounded like Helmensson.

'Suit's got a leak,' said another. 'Cold's getting in.'

'Prototype marks, eh?' spoke a third. 'All grand until someone crashes a Gromthi-class on you. That's when you want a good old-fashioned Makaisson Mark Twelve.'

'Fetch him a sealant kit,' Helmensson barked. 'Go.'

The owner of the third voice tramped off into the snow. Strahl was half walked, half dragged, from the *Bokram*.

The sounds of gunfire drew nearer.

Strahl blinked away the storybook visitation he'd thought he'd seen, and felt his mind coming sluggishly back to itself. When a crewman in battered arkanaut gear returned from the snow, lugging an aether-gold canister behind him, Strahl waved him off.

'Your suit needs sealing,' said Helmensson.

'That's the aether-gold we harvested for my mother.'

'Your first marooning, I'm guessing. Your toes'll fall off before we're clear of the slope, and a fat lot of good the haul will be to Mistress Dunrsdottir then.'

'I'll manage,' said Strahl, pushing away the canister.

From some never-before-explored reserve of inner stamina, Strahl shrugged Helmensson aside and stood under his own, diminished power. Patting absently over his equipment holsters, he found his aethermatic volley pistol and drew it. 'We have to get back to Karag Dawrkhaz. If it's too late to warn them, then to help them.'

'We're one crew, without a ship.' Helmensson shrugged. 'We don't even know the way.'

Strahl looked up. Where the old whitebeard had vanished into the snow.

He'd been shown where to go. All he needed to do was walk it.

'I know the way.'

CHAPTER ELEVEN

Kolram set out from the throne hall for Ael Dunrsdottir's meet with two-score of elite Hammerers, six-score of clan warriors equipped with crossbows and axes, and an entourage of irritable longbeards that nobody had sought to count. They took the Anga-zongi Stair, Kolram maintaining a dour and kingly disposition throughout as Hangrark and three of his stoutest Hammerers manoeuvred the royal litter up the winding staircase.

The Angazongi was the backbone of the Dunrakul's former glories. It began in the treasure vaults of the seventh deep, climbed through the guild halls and craft halls of the middle Deepings before reaching its weary end amidst the gyrobays of the mountain's loft. The shaft cut through twenty miles of rock. There were forty thousand, eight hundred and three steps. Construction had been completed during the reign of Karragin Dunrakul, grandfather to the Last King, having taken ten thousand duardin masons from across the Mortal Realms eighty-one years to accomplish. Kolram was aware, too, of the newly popular endurance sport of *sigstrollen* – which translated into the Azyrite as *stair-running* – and did not approve. He'd learned, however, to show a little forbearance, and tolerated the sport as he did such faddish novelties as Kharadron, free cities, and the proliferation of the aelven races. That season's champion was a Hammerer named Skorn Duzbak who'd managed the round trip in just under twenty hours and just happened to be one of Kolram's bearers today.

Of course, the royal throng had joined the Angazongi at the second deep and were only heading as far as the first on this leg: a climb of a mere three-quarters of a mile over one thousand, five hundred and eighteen steps.

With a bit of shimmying and cursing, his bearers got the litter up onto a landing and turned it around a corner onto the next rise. Kolram muttered admiringly as he was borne under an armorial frieze recording the bloodline of kings, and from kings to gods.

He closed the book in his lap with a sigh. He'd hoped the lengthy journey would provide ample time for reading, but the rough cornering was making it harder to keep his place on the page than he'd like. It was also aggravating the alms maidens' stitching.

'How far have we come?' he demanded.

Hangrark glanced over the gilded handle that lay across his shoulder. The warden took an untoward pride in his scruffy, roots-of-the-earth appearance but, given the occasion, he'd made an effort to give himself some polish: a vision of duardin pomp to impress even Ael Dunrsdottir and her new-money kin. He had even raised the bronze-headed greathammer, Zankeller, from its place in state in the family vault. His distant ancestor, it was told, had wielded it at the Battle of Burning Skies, fighting alongside Sigmar Heldenhammer and the Pantheon of Order in its last stand against Chaos. According to clan legend, it had kneecapped the infernal steed of the Grand Marshal of Chaos, Archaon, himself, and out of respect no duardin had ever wielded it in battle since.

Hangrark would wield it, he said, when the last days of the Dunra-kul drew in about them and there were no duardin left worthy of bearing it should he fall.

Kolram wondered if those days weren't nearer than the warden supposed.

'I've counted four hundred and thirty-two steps,' he said.

'Only one thousand and eighty-six to go,' said Kolram.

Hangrark blew out his cheeks and turned to look ahead. 'Sounds about right.'

'The steps are steeper than they used to be,' one of the long-beards taking up the rear complained.

'That'll be Chaos for you,' said another, to much grousing and widespread tutting.

Kothi and Kurrindorm marched at the back with their elders, either side of Gromrhun, who appeared inexplicably exhausted by the short ascent. Both duardin certainly looked the part of heirs to the karag, in long coats of heavy mail adorned with the runes of the Last King. Their beards, though short yet, were dressed with bronzes, their shoulder-length hair combed back into winged helmets. Their boots were polished. Their gauntlets were jewelled. The proud blazon of the Dunrakul shone from the shields on their backs. Both carried runic handaxes with gem-encrusted handles that had been worn to battle by their mother's father.

Kolram wished he could put his finger on what it was about the two beardlings, aside from their shameless *youngness*, that he found so irksome.

Kothi had taken to wearing a silk cloak in the Azyrite, over-the-shoulder style and in a distinctly wrong shade of red. Kurrin-dorm, meanwhile, had professed a preference for the sword over the traditional axe. The wavy-edged blade that he wore in a scab-bard had been a parting gift from his Khainite weapons tutor and, it was alleged, one-time lover, in Sigmaron. The sight of it there alongside his grandfather's axe irritated Kolram like too much pepper on his breakfast.

They made the first deep about an hour and ten minutes later.

The landing alone was large enough for a throng of a thousand. The ceiling was arched and vaulted, populated by jewelled frescoes depicting the ancestors of the duardin mining, brewing, and warring. Their gods, ten times the stature of any mortal depicted thereon, buttressed the walls, appearing to have simply stepped forth from the rock to aid their descendants in the strengthening of their ceiling rather than having being carved by iron tools.

It would have been a fitting first glimpse of the glories of the Dunrakul Kings, for those rare non-duardin granted passage beyond the Great Hall.

'We'll rest here for an hour or two, and then travel the rest of the way to the port-city,' Kolram said, to much grumbling, as Hangrark and the other bearers carried his chair through the arch.

At once, Kolram sensed something amiss.

The Great Entrance Hall was half a mile wide and several miles long. The Gate of Throngs was itself half a mile high and wide enough for two gargants to stagger in abreast, arm in arm, and with a third sat bestride their shoulders. And in the days of old, such a sight would not have been entirely unthinkable. Now, snow billowed through them, piling up in great drifts against the thick, angular columns of the hall. Even as far back as the Angazongi Stair, the occasional flake fluttered about in the air as though lost. The shops were closed, their stone facades sealed behind heavy chains and runic wards. Karag Dawrkhaz was far from the nearest realmgate, further still from the nearest friendly settlement, and when the trade through the Kharadron's port-city suffered it seemed that the merchants of the Dunrakul suffered with it.

The few duardin present were busily arming themselves, pulling on shields bearing the runic icons of the merchant clans and hustling in their kinbands towards the Gate of Throngs.

Kolram held up a hand.

A snowflake landed in his gauntlet. It melted slowly, turning the metal around it misty. Kolram lowered his hand and looked around, perplexed.

'How long has it been *snowing*?'

The abrupt return of Guthrun Gorlflaer and the *Tenker* had thrown Ael's expensive preparations into disarray. News of the ogor horde scaling Karag Dawrkhaz under the cover of the storm, and the rumoured loss of the fleet, swept through the sky-port like the threat of bankruptcy.

Kharadron filled the corridors, carrying everything they owned or that could be claimed as legitimate salvage in the event of disaster, clamouring for the limited number of berths aboard the funicular. The carriage could safely hold thirty for a one-way trip of about an hour, assuming it dropped them off at the First Deep station to return and pick up more rather than carry them all the way to the terminus at Grimnir's Forge. Others, ready to risk the storm if it meant getting off this sinking venture, had broken through the Grundstok picket and were pouring into the docks.

The *Prospect Shield* was the last rated ship still in port. She was a venerable, single-endrin, eighteen-gun sixth-rate, little more than a post-ship really, under the command of Captain Errn Shiriktorn of Barak-Nar. Errn was infamous for her aversion to risk. She never gambled. Not with her money, not with her ship, and definitely not with her life. This was why, after due and lengthy consideration, she had decided to keep her ship safe in port while the *Bokram* had taken every other ship with it in search of fortune. The latest dispatches, Ael suspected, were a solid endorsement of the captain's choices. Her arkanauts lined the gunwales, knocking back the dockers and guild-workers attempting to storm her sides with brusque strikes from the butts of their handguns. Errn herself yelled for the gangplank to be retracted and the mooring lines cut.

Ael wandered the mayhem in a daze, her own well-paid entourage of Grundstok Thunderers pushing the opportunistic and the desperate alike out of her way. She didn't know where she was going. Or why. She had already lost everything. Her ships. The shares she had already sunk into getting a port established here. The prospects to be found beyond the mapped frontier. The backers she had convinced. Her son too, she belatedly supposed. The lad she'd raised as her own. Not blood, perhaps, but *kin* in every legal and real sense.

What did it even matter now that she'd lost it all? What was wealth and prestige for, if not to pass on?

Someone grabbed her shoulders. For some reason, her Thunderers refrained from caving in the culprit's head. She looked up.

'Mistress. Are you in need of an escort?'

Vice-Admiral Drakksson's dented helm swam into focus. She had left her glasses on her desk. Her eyes took longer than usual to adjust.

'Admiral...' she mumbled. 'Are you leaving on the *Prospect Shield*?'

Drakksson looked offended. 'I've never abandoned a post in my life, mistress.'

As he spoke, the port gave a tortured groan. The deck beneath them tilted, drawing terrified screams from the already panicked Kharadron.

The snow had already as good as buried the loading yards. Fierce winds caused the projecting steel tines of the docking forks to flex and whine. The sound they made was as if the port was crying out in the cold. If only she'd paid proper attention to

Forecastinator Zorek's warnings and less to her desire for wealth. The storm would still have come. She would still be ruined, but there would have been ships to flee on and Strahl would have been with her.

There would have been a slim chance that they could have recovered.

But not now.

'It would have been prosperous.'

'Aye,' Drakksson sighed. 'I think it would've been.'

'I failed.'

'You've got to take the risk before you can fail, mistress. Sometimes we fall and sometimes we ought. Wounds make us stronger and failure makes us wiser.'

Ael smiled, albeit briefly, heartened by the words before she remembered how far a good attempt would stretch with the Usurers' Guild of Barak-Nar. 'It sounds like something Wyram would say.'

'Now you say it, I think it might've been.'

'Have you seen him? I lost him before the news came in.'

'I'm sure he's found his way to safety, mistress. As you should as well. Let me loan you some of my crew to escort you to a gunhauler.'

Ael shook her head. What was the use in running? She was bankrupt in every legally definable way. Why in the name of all her ancestors should she *not* spend what little she had left on the remnants of her people?

Weren't they kin too, after a fashion?

Like Strahl had been.

'I'll take the crew, admiral. And you as well.'

She raised her hand and pointed.

The *Prospect Shield* rocked in her wind slip, running lights blinking on as she drew power from her single endrin and took on buoyancy. The wind lashed her rugged contours with straight, sleeting lines. Snow bearded her grim figurehead. The raw aether-gold that was raging ahead of the snowstorm ignited vivid corposants of purple-and-green fire across her endrin rigging. This was no mere storm. Ael saw that now. Even the rudimentary instruments of her arkanaut suit were picking up the extraordinary amounts of magic in the air.

A more superstitious sort of duardin would have read the numbers on the dials and seen the malign hand of the gods at work. But Ael refused to believe she was cursed. Success or failure was in her own making.

'Mistress?' Drakksson prodded.

'I want to be on that ship.'

The cold burned in Brigg's throat as she rode out through the Gate of Throngs. Her magmadroth, Oxtarn, was a living furnace. Steam rose from the colossal beast's mouth and nostrils, as it did in smaller quantities from the Fyreslayers who marched out alongside her, but not enough. Breath by breath, Brigg felt, the fire in her belly burned a little less hot. Breath by breath, she was sure, something vital inside of her was being quenched. She fought the urge to grasp her axe and draw it, to ignite the runes and to be warm again. Aware of the nervous stares of the Dunrakul warriors who had parted to let the Fyreslayers pass through, she resisted, tightening her grip on Oxtarn's reins until the leather started to come apart in her hands.

She had been outside the mountain many times, but had never left it by this door. She was old enough to remember a time when the Spiderfang had ruled this Deeping, and the Dunr Fyreslayers had come and gone by converted heat-channels that led from the magma-vault to the hearts and ovens of bakeries and guardhouses throughout the outer fortress. It had been thirty years since the Dunrakul had returned to clear out the grots and make the Great Hall their own again, but Braegnar-Grimnir preferred to use the old ways still.

The Dunrakul throng had been fully mustered, their various clan banners raised at precise intervals throughout the mountain-side fort. Brigg looked up, shielding her eyes against the snow, as a large Kharadron sky-ship descended. Strings of lights along the vessel's hull stabbed through the blizzard, briefly, until the thing set down further along the defensive wall and the snow swept across to take it.

Oxtarn continued to tramp ahead. The rest of Brigg's kinband followed in the monster's hot wake.

'Easy,' Azkaharr muttered to them and, raising his hands in a placating gesture meant for the Dunrakul, spoke something similar in the ancestral tongue.

Some combination of his words, his actions, and his world-weary manner seemed to put the Dunrakul at their ease.

'They're heeding you,' said Dremm. The battlesmith sounded disappointed.

'Say what you will of the Dispossessed,' said Azkaharr, 'but they have some respect for their elders.'

'And I don't?'

Azkaharr snorted. 'You have your own special way of showing it.'

Ordinarily, Brigg would have prized any opportunity to escape the confines of the familiar mountain halls and venture outside. Sky above her head. No walls, but those outside of the next mountain, far away, with halls unknown and histories yet to be written. This was no ordinary day. The gold ceilings of the Dunr Lodge, or even the spiderwebbed stone of the Middling Deeps, would have been preferable ceiling to the grey-black churn that roiled overhead.

The Gate of Throngs was the defiance of Karag Dawrkhaz drawn in stone. Its granite gatehouse had been hewn from the rock face in the sullen likeness of Grungni the Great Maker. Its iron doors were his teeth. Batteries of cannon were his eyes. His bottom lip was the castle on which Brigg and the grand fyrd of the Dunr stood dwarfed amidst three thousand Dunrakul warriors. A wall encircled it all. The structure was low, coming only to waist height on the duardin standing behind it, for the mountain slope was a multiplier that turned it into a wall five times as high for any attacker from below.

It was the last one of a dozen.

The kings of old had carved shelves from the mountain's slope, and crafted them into a series of cunning and increasingly intricate defences. The Outer Stair had been abandoned to the blizzard. Assuming that Kolram had restored them in the first place, given that the greater threat to his newly claimed crown had come from within. It was hard to imagine such strength ever being fully restored. Harder still to imagine the fury of Chaos it must have taken to bring such strength low.

A familiar duardin was waiting for them at the wall. He glared up at Brigg, and at Braegnar-Grimnir on his own mount, Firechaser, as though he'd gladly stare down the entire Dunr Lodge alone, and that the half-thousand warriors at his back were there at the beck of some other king. Snow dulled the glitter of his mail and of the thick bronze circlet inset into his helm. It fuzzed the edges of his round shield and axe, but the lines in his face went deeper than all the delvings of the duardin, and deeper even than this curse-winter could smother.

'How's the back, Braegnar?' said Kolram.

Brigg, and every Fyreslayer in hearing, spluttered vengeful oaths at the Dunrakul king's failure to use the proper honorific for a runefather of his lodge.

'Stings a bit,' Braegnar-Grimnir conceded, without apparent rancour. 'The shame of having a scar on my back stings more.'

'My gunners assure me they were aiming for your head.'

The runefather was silent. Then he laughed, hard, and all of a sudden the threat of a kinslaying did not seem so near. Brigg allowed herself to relax. Oxtarn, however, rumbled like a frustrated volcano beneath her.

'And the leg?' Braegnar-Grimnir asked.

Kolram tapped the handle of his axe on his thigh. 'The alms matron says I'll get to keep it.'

'Good.' Braegnar-Grimnir leant over the pommel of Firechaser's saddle. 'Never let it be said that I made you limp back to Azyrheim.'

'Is that what you're here for then? You and your fyrd? Kick me off my mountain, the moment my back's turned.'

The two kings glared at one another. Neither moved.

Brigg looked around for someone who could offer the pair wisdom, but Azkaharr appeared to have wandered off once again and she could no longer see him. As she searched, she became aware of one of Kolram's entourage, one of his sons judging by the rich armour he wore and the royal emblems that adorned it, calling for someone named Gromrhun and peering confusedly about his own ranks.

'I'm glad to see my calls for peace have been so enthusiastically heeded.'

Both kings broke off their staring match and turned.

Ael Dunrsdottir walked along the battlement towards them with a handful of troops who, though few, hemmed her in a wall of guns. There was something hurried in her stride that struck Brigg as somehow *wrong* before it dawned on her what it was: she'd never shared a potential battlefield with a duardin who didn't call themselves a warrior before.

'A pity I couldn't receive you properly in my own hall,' Ael said.

At the sight of Ael, Kolram and Braegnar-Grimnir all gathered together in one place, Brigg felt a tingle of something she couldn't immediately define.

Destiny.

'Where's Strahl...?' Brigg asked. She was there. Kolram's two sons were there. So where was he?

Ael turned from the two kings as though noticing the presence of others for the first time, hearing what Brigg was saying on some kind of a delay as though they were shouting to one another from neighbouring mountaintops.

Before the Kharadron could answer, a horn sounded from somewhere below. Its note was higher pitched and less steady than any duardin trumpet. It was more of a moan, like ice that was being squeezed, just before it split. Duardin of every allegiance fell to muttering.

Something came.

Brigg, Ael, Braegnar-Grimnir and Kolram all moved to the parapet and looked out. Kolram gave a voice to his disgust.

A dishevelled-looking ogor rode up to the wall on a beast that, even from afar, made Oxtarn look slight in comparison. Its bulk was cloaked in dense white fur, and bristling with icicles that tinkled with each stomping footfall. Snow swirled around its curving tusks, billowed from its nostrils as though breath by breath the beast and others like it were generating the blizzard that had crippled and blinded them. Brigg could have believed it. It wouldn't have been the strangest tale she'd heard of the Mortal Realms. Instead, she shivered and wrapped her arms around herself, sinking more fully into Oxtarn's aura of heat. The air had become palpably colder as the ogor and its behemoth mount drew near.

The ogor raised an enormously fat hand to show he was unarmed. Above the other, a bloody scrap of once-white cloth flapped from the broken-off end of a spear.

Brigg peered over him, into the snow. With the ranger cabins emptied, with the Kharadron's sky-ships blinded, there could have been literally anything coming up the Outer Stair behind this ogor. If there was one, then surely there must be more. Were they here to fight? Had they really engineered the blizzard to cover their assault? Or had they simply been driven ahead of the storm?

Brigg supposed it didn't matter. If it was the shelter of Karag Dawrkhaz they were after, then it was a fight they'd get.

'I'm Sjarpa Longtooth,' the ogor announced, in a thick, treacly voice that nevertheless handled the ancestor tongue with reasonable skill. 'I am Blizzard Speaker, and speak now for Frostlord Sturmur Rockbelly of the Oldenguts tribe.' The ogor lowered his white flag. Eyes that were already too beady for the mass of his face narrowed as he surveyed the duardin arrayed across the wall. 'Who speaks for the Fire Crown?'

CHAPTER TWELVE

The weakest part of any ground fortress, or so Ael had read, was its gate, and so with duardin ingenuity the Khazalid Kings had ensured their walls had none. In place of the conventional apparatus of gate, drawbridge and portcullis, passage from one tier to the next along the Outer Stair was by a canal-style lock; an entire length of battlement coming away and descending on rails. As the forebears of the early Kharadron, the old duardin had been blessed with a little craft, Ael had to admit.

She, Kolram and Braegnar-Grimnir stepped out of the lock together.

They might, grudgingly, have set aside their respective grievances for the present moment, but they weren't about to accord implicit honour on another by allowing one amongst them to walk in front. Kolram was trailed by the scruffy-looking bodyguard who had introduced himself as Hangrark and a small cortege of Hammerers holding aloft his standards. Braegnar-Grimnir brought only his daughter, Brigg, whom he allowed to walk at the front alongside him, but only after she had insisted. She kept throwing looks at Ael as though she wanted to ask something, but couldn't bring herself. For her own part, Ael was content with a pair of Grundstok Thunderers on triple pay. She had thought it better to leave Anfrik Drakksson behind, just in case anything happened to her, and to make sure that Captain Shiriktorn wasn't tempted to leave without them.

For the meagre service of ferrying Ael and a squad of Thunderers down to the Gate of Throngs, she had been forced to sign over a sum that should have seen her to the Varanspire and back. Ael wasn't sure why she insisted on throwing good money after bad, but it felt right, and with her prospects in tatters she didn't know what else she was going to do with it.

Sjarpa Longtooth waited for them, alone and on foot. He was enormous, and only became more so as Ael approached and the snow sweeping between them grew thinner. His lumpen head, and even his chest, loomed over the duardin dignitaries. His girth was such that, with the snow falling thickly, there was no position Ael could hold from which she could see all aspects of his belly at once. This was the first time Ael had seen an ogor. The books did the reality a severe injustice. Sjarpa was three times her height, six times her breadth, twelve times her weight even in armour. His arms looked strong enough to lift a gunhauler above his head. A metal plate hung over his belly. It bore a crude rendition of a mouth, picked out with a variety of metals presumably representative of whatever the brute had had to hand at the time. His skin was a flabby, varicose white. The tip of his nose and the ends of his fingers were frostbitten. In poor mockery of the duardin he hoped to treat with, a ragged stratocumulus of beard tore about his chin in the wind.

In rough concert, Ael, Kolram and Braegnar-Grimnir drew to a stop. Their respective retinues fell in a respectful distance behind. All except Brigg, who remained at her father's back. In spite of everything, Ael found herself admiring of the girl's determination to be in the way of things.

If only Strahl could have been more like that.

Longtooth's lips moved soundlessly as he looked them over. As though counting to four was overtaxing the muscles in his head.

'So many,' he said.

Ael glanced to either side, surprised that neither Kolram nor Braegnar-Grimnir had spoken up first, then cleared her throat as she would before delivering her opening summary to a tribunal. 'You asked to speak to the one who speaks for Karag Dawrkhaz. Unfortunately, there is no *one* at this time.'

Kolram grumbled under his breath, but managed to keep his tongue held.

'The Winterbite, too, follow many leaders. The Everwinter hunts them all, but they fight anyway.' Sjarpa lowered his white flag until the broken spear's metal ferrule clanged on the paving slabs. The white scrap of cloth beat frantically against the ogor's mane. 'Sturmur would have me remind them of The Way.'

'Ogor and duardin are nothing alike,' said Braegnar-Grimnir.

Sjarpa lazily held the runefather's glare. 'The Mawpath ends here. Where it began. Borja Kragnfryr was Frost King then.' The ogor paused, looking between the duardin as though he expected the name to bring a reaction. 'He was the last Frost King, grandson of Baergut Vosjarl who once feasted with Gorkamorka before the Great Waaagh!, and grandfather to me.' His rough-edged voice took on a lyrical quality, aided in part by the mythic names he bandied around with ease. Sjarpa tapped a finger on his chest. 'He was *my* grandfather.'

One by one, the entourages lowered their weapons and listened, as talk of old battles and distant ancestors would invariably have a duardin do. For her part, Ael wondered if an ogor could really live to become so old.

'Borja didn't come to fight. Your walls were strong and the Beastclaw have no time for sieges. The Everwinter...' He looked behind him as though he risked summoning a daemon by naming it. 'It follows always. Borja's huskards demanded he attack the Fire Crown, before the Everwinter came, but Borja was wise and knew The Way. He called the king to meet with him.'

With one heavy paw, Sjarpa gestured to the courtyard around them. Its walled sides had ceased even to be hurried suggestions. As though the boundaries of Realm's Edge had shrunk to a few beard-lengths of frigid purgatory and nothing beyond its limits was of consequence any longer.

'At the bottom wall,' he said. 'It was the Age of Chaos, but you were stronger then.'

'Few things are as they once were,' Kolram muttered in agreement.

Sjarpa nodded, as though Kolram and he had encountered long-lost kin. 'Sturmur isn't wise like Borja. But he would learn The Way.'

Braegnar-Grimnir scowled. 'Just tell us what you want. The sooner we can say *no* and get to the fighting, the better.'

'Borja promised your king that in return for shelter, for as long as it took the Everwinter to pass, there would be no fighting and his ogors would eat none of your people. Your king agreed.'

Kolram spluttered. 'Preposterous.'

'I was there.'

'Prove it,' said Ael.

The ogor looked at her. 'What?'

'Prove it.' Her instinctual dislike of the ogor had become a genuine hatred, such as she had never felt even in cases of the most heinous misappropriations of the Code. She could hardly blame a storm for destroying her fleet and claiming her son, but if the Everwinter, as Sjarpa called it, followed the ogors as he had already unwittingly admitted, then she could gladly blame him. 'Artycle eleven, Point four of the Kharadron Code clearly states that in the event of contractual dispute, the burden of proof falls solely upon the aggrieved party. You.'

'Tell us the name of the king with whom you made your bargain,' said Braegnar-Grimnir. 'Give us more than a story, and maybe we'll give more credence to your lies.'

'Korgrun,' Sjarpa growled.

Kolram snarled, making an attempt to throw himself at the giant ogor, and only the combined strength of two Hammerers was enough to hold him back. 'I'll not hear slander against my thrice-great grandfather!'

'Korgrun was weak. Attacked from all sides,' said Sjarpa. 'His choice was to feed us and shelter us or fight us, and he didn't want to fight us.'

'I'd sooner shave my arse and dye my beard blue,' said Braegnar-Grimnir.

'Feed us,' Sjarpa repeated. 'Shelter us. And the pact will stand.'

Kolram calmed enough to shrug off his handlers. The conversation had taken a turn that had diminished him. Even his beard clung more feebly to his wet mail than it had just before. 'If it was sworn...'

'You can let him into *your* hall if you feel your honour demands it of you.' Braegnar-Grimnir jabbed at the Dunrakul king with his finger. 'But I swear to all here present, no ogor will set a foot in Grimnir's Forge with their head still atop their shoulders. Not so long as there's a place for me still waiting in the great fyrd of the dead.'

'Do you deny Korgrun is as much your ancestor as mine?'

'I do deny it.'

'I've been waiting thirty years to hear it.'

'I say he's *more* my ancestor than yours, and that I honour him better by ignoring his poorer decisions.'

Kolram gaped like a cloud-feeding lumprey. 'The Last King is above your judgement, Fyreslayer.'

'Artycle eight, Point three,' Ael went on. 'A verbal agreement carries the weight of a written contract only so long as one of the original parties is present. Otherwise, pursuant of Point four, their contract is to be struck from the ledgers without recourse to tribunal.'

Kolram turned to her. 'I'll not *nitpick* my way out of–'

'I was witness,' said Sjarpa. 'I was there. I answered your question.'

'Assuming that was good enough to satisfy a codewright's first-year apprentice, you're still overlooking Point three.' Ael glared at the runefather for providing such a straightforward test that anyone with a passing familiarity of the region's history could have answered. 'Korgrun Dunrakul is dead. He died...'

'Eight hundred and forty-seven years, six months and twenty-two days ago,' said Kolram. 'By the Azyrite reckoning, that is. He expired in his bed, aged two hundred and five, attended in grief at the Grudges he left to his heirs by his children, grandchildren and great-grandchildren. Which you'd *know* if he was any kin of yours.'

'And,' said Ael, returning to Sjarpa, 'you have already informed us that Borja Kragnfryr is dead.'

'I did not,' said Sjarpa.

'The *last Frost King*. Those were your words. You follow Stur-mur Rockbelly now. And so, in accordance with Artycle eight, the contract agreed between kings Korgrun and Borja, assuming it existed at all, died with them.' She waved dismissively towards the storm and, somehow, without fully meaning to, unholstered her volley pistol and aimed it towards the mess of beard that swaddled the ogor's jaw. Braegnar-Grimnir growled approval. His own hand went to the axe across his back. 'You're not coming in. If this is your storm then you can wait out here and face it. Or you can fight us, if you're so sure you can win.'

Sjarpa looked entirely unperturbed. 'I never said Borja was dead.' Turning away from the duardin, he beckoned to some ally further back in the blizzard.

How anyone could have seen him gesturing to them through the snow, Ael couldn't fathom. She saw absolutely nothing at all of them until they emerged from the blizzard in answer of his summons. Her Grundstok bodyguard immediately tensed, drawing up their aethershot rifles and pulling in close. Kolram's Hammerers and Braegnar-Grimnir's daughter did the same.

When Sjarpa Longtooth turned back and waved for them to lower their weapons, they were hardly reassured.

A pair of thundertusks lumbered out of the snow. Titanic creatures, they made even Sjarpa look frail and small. Coarse white fur hung off them like frayed scraps from a frozen carpet. Tusks glittered blue-green with hoar frost. Their eyes were those of an enamel carving, empty and cold and eternally staring. They had no ogors on their backs. Two more came after them. Then two more. Chains ran out from their empty saddles and into the snow, dragging behind them a monumentally heavy log that turned out to be a column of ice.

Fur-draped ogors trailed after the thundertusks like aelementors of the Hyshian blizzard, detaching the chains and leading the monsters back into the storm.

With only the ice block itself left behind, Sjarpa Longtooth walked towards it. He beckoned for the duardin to join him.

After a nervous look amongst themselves, they followed.

The cold deepened with every step Ael took towards the ice. By the time she was standing over it, it was so intense that she had to flex every few seconds to keep the joints of her armour from freezing. How Kolram and Braegnar-Grimnir endured it, she would never know. Counting on the warranty of her armour, Ael leant over and looked inside.

She gasped at what she saw.

She had thought that Sjarpa was huge, but the ogor frozen inside the pillar of ice was twice his girth and tall enough to knock a low-flying frigate out of the sky. Muscle and fat were indistinguishable on him and both were appallingly abundant. Ael decided that she was looking at either the laziest ogor to have ever gorged his way across the Spiral Crux or the strongest. It might well have been both.

She saw now why it took six thundertusks just to drag him uphill.

'Borja isn't dead,' Sjarpa said again, this time with a slow smile. 'But...'

Ael was at an uncharacteristic loss for words. Eyes of the same smoky blue that sat in Sjarpa's face stared up at her from the ice. She couldn't shake the feeling that their owner saw her and hungered, even as the face they were smothered by remained inanimate.

'He's not dead,' Sjarpa said again.

The colour had fallen from Kolram's face. 'Grungni's beard,' he breathed. 'It's true.'

'Borja led a great Mawpath,' said Sjarpa.

'How did he...?' said Ael, glancing at the monstrosity in the ice. 'I mean, how...?'

'Borja was strong, but greedy. One day his belly got too big for his mouth to fill, too big for any stonehorn or thundertusk to carry. He tired of endless hunts that never filled him. I was young then, but already Huskard Torr and Blizzard Speaker of the Olden-guts tribe. I sent the Icebrow to capture the mightiest beasts in all Chamon to carry him. None were strong enough. I had the cleverest gnoblars build an engine to push him. It failed. So in the end, Borja ate the Icebrow, and the beasts they brought him, and the gnoblars, even though they taste horrible. He ate so much, and so long, that he didn't move again. He'd eat the Everwinter, he told me, as I left him, and maybe then his belly would be filled.'

Looking into that frozen face, Ael did not think the ogor had found satiation in his living death.

'I led the Mawpath here for the one fire in Chamon hot enough to melt the ice of the Everwinter. Free Borja and you'll have your proof. And you'll get to live. Sturmur Rockbelly is more like the huskards of old, though he wants to be more. Deep down, he wants only to eat you all.'

'And you don't?' said Ael.

The ogor shrugged. 'Then there would be no fire waiting the next time the Everwinter catches up to the Oldenguts at the end of their Mawpath.'

The runefather folded his arms over his chest. '*Never*. Any ogor that gets close to Grimnir's Forge is going *in* it.'

'We *must*,' Kolram answered, sternly. 'It was agreed, and a duardin's word is stone. Time alone won't break it. And if this was a deal struck by the Last King then I'd hear of it from this King Kragnfryr's own mouth.'

'You are talking about reviving the ogor so hungry that even his own followers chose to leave him to the winter,' said Ael.

'Yes,' said Sjarpa. 'But he'll teach Sturmur The Way.' As though that was not only a desirable outcome, but the only one that mattered.

'There's no other choice to be made,' said Kolram.

'Well, there are three of us here, Kolram, and as Artycle fourteen of the Code *explicitly* states, in any joint enterprise–'

'And where are your ships now?' Kolram snapped, throwing his hands up as though scattering what was left of his self-control to the winds. 'Where are your warriors? What has happened up in your mountaintop enclave that your people are now filling up the Lower Deeps. Abandoning the mountain's fastness and taking to the skies all those years ago has returned to shame you, mistress, as I've always said that it would. Prince Korn, at last, has been proven the favoured son of the Last King, abandoning his city to preserve its traditions in exile, rather than tinker with lighter-than-air endrins like his brother.'

'His elder brother,' said Ael.

'His *disinherited* elder brother. And who was never legitimately married, I might add.'

'Kolram, you are so absurdly old-fashioned.'

'The Dunrakul will fight the Kharadron *and* the Fyreslayers if you force me to.'

Kolram unshipped his axe. With a clattering and a scraping, his Hammerer guard drew their own weapons. Braegnar-Grimnir and Brigg did likewise, golden runes sputtering as though freshly pressed into the axe-blades. Ael's Thunderers split their aim between both groups. She regretted now having brought only the two.

Sjarpa regarded them all, puzzled.

'I'll not be remembered forevermore in the pages of the *Dunrakul Kron* as the duardin who broke the sworn oath of the Last King.'

'Well, I stand with Dunrsdottir.' Braegnar-Grimnir kicked the frozen Frost King. There was an audible *hiss* and *snap* as rune-heated flesh struck Everwinter ice and came off the worse for it. 'If you mean to haul this lump down the Angazongi Stair towards Grimnir's Forge then it'll be through me and my fyrd.'

Kolram squared up to his opposite number. 'You think I wouldn't?'

'You think I care?'

'Lower your weapons,' said Ael.

'I'll not,' said Kolram.

'Nor I,' said Braegnar-Grimnir.

'Just put them away and stop behaving like children.' Ael slapped her Thunderers' gun barrels until they turned them down towards the ground. Something that Kolram had said had given her an idea. 'The records of the *Dunrakul Kron* go as far back as Korgrun's reign. Correct?'

'Of course.' Kolram lowered his axe distractedly. 'It predates the Conference of Maldralta and the first issuance of your precious Code by several thousand years, chronicling–'

'Then there is a record of this agreement,' Ael interrupted.

Kolram paused, mid-speech. He thought about it. 'If King Borja caused my ancestor any offence in his deal-making then aye, it would've been recorded.'

Braegnar-Grimnir snorted.

'What?' said Kolram.

'It's your ancestor. It stands to reason an ogor would've offended him somehow.'

Ael turned to Sjarpa before Kolram had a chance to think. 'Then, in accordance with Artycle fourteen, Point two, Footnote eleven, the parties are agreed. Lorekeeper Braztom of the Dunrakul will be summoned from his libraries and, pending a thorough reading of the relevant pages, the merits of your claim will be duly discussed.'

'But...' Kolram seemed at a loss for words, torn between his respect for proper protocol and honouring the good word of his ancestor. But if Sjarpa and his ogors wanted to get inside the hold, then Ael was determined to make them fight for it.

'This is a first-hand, evidential document,' said Ael. 'It simply cannot be ignored.'

'There's no time,' said Sjarpa.

'The duardin will not be *rushed*,' Ael returned.

Sjarpa Longtooth stared hungrily at each of them in turn. His eyes were hard and unblinking, chipped ice, shielded from the worst of the blizzard by a heavy brow of bone. It gave the impression of simplicity, but those eyes belied it. Ael saw the evidence of a mind, intelligence of a different sort, and it knew when it was being played.

'The Beastclaw are patient. The most patient of all ogors. But it's the Everwinter that pushes. Not Sturmur Rockbelly and not Sjarpa. Decide quickly.'

With that, he turned and walked away. After only a handful of paces the snow had him.

Borja, Ael noted, had been left exactly where he was.

Sjarpa Longtooth walked to where Njal Icebreaker, Frorgen Maetsgral and Sturmur Rockbelly all waited. They weren't far past the courtyard. Far enough that the Everwinter had hidden them from the duardin completely. They were all mounted and ready. Njal held Sjarpa's reins with his own. A pair of gnoblars in thick white coats and fur-trimmed hats rushed to set down a box by his thundertusk's near foot. Sjarpa stepped up onto the box, took a firm hold of the saddle and, in an act of titanic strength, pulled himself off the ground. The gnoblars, having already taken punting rods from their gubbinz packs, strained their wiry muscles to guide his buttocks into their seat.

Panting with the exertion, Sjarpa leant across and took the reins from Njal. The gnoblars collapsed in the snow.

'Well?' Sturmur grunted.

'They don't honour Borja's pact.'

The Frostlord's teeth made a grinding sound.

'They stall for time,' said Sjarpa.

Sturmur digested that. 'Then we feast.'

Ogors were hungrier these days than they'd used to be, Sjarpa was sure of it. They had less restraint. The wise ogor kept half an eye on the next meal, on the next time, however many centuries it might be, that the Mawpath closed its circle again. But, he supposed, there was always the chance that duardin would return here. That they might forget Sturmur and Sjarpa as they had forgotten Borja Kragnfryr. The Mawpath was long, and it got longer every time.

'I gave them until the Everwinter pushes.'

'It's in the guts of the gods then,' said Frorgen.

Narrowing his eyes against the ever-thickening swirl, Sjarpa leant aside to whistle a mournfang rider. The ogor was wearing a heavy winter coat and had been riding his mount back and forth across the rear of the square at a walk to keep warm. The smaller monster was no swifter than a stonehorn or a thundertusk, but it was easier to turn.

'Ride to where Rump Broadfeast of the Ice Tyrants tribe waits with his Gluttons. Tell him to attack now.'

The ogor snapped his reins, and rode off into the blizzard. Sjarpa allowed his weight to settle back into the saddle.

'What was that?' said Sturmur.

'The Way,' Sjarpa told him. 'The Gutbuster tribes feel the Everwinter's bite earliest. They need to attack first.'

The Frostlord digested that too. He was slow, but determined to master this knowledge.

Njal still looked confused. 'But you let the duardin go think.'

Sjarpa bared his teeth. They were all still learning. 'I lied.'

CHAPTER THIRTEEN

Kolram Dunrakul wept as the first wave of ogors assaulted the wall. He wept as he took his axe to them, tears streaming down his cheeks and freezing before they made it as far as his chin, glittering tracts of silvery warpaint streaking his beard. The shame of it all. *The shame.* He hadn't wanted this battle, had argued against it, but a hefty portion of the blame for it lay in his lap nonetheless. He had allowed the watch forts and cabins over Arik's Pass and the Outer Stair to fall into disuse while he turned his attention to skirmishes over the Deepings. And worse, he'd clearly failed to memorise the many thousands of grudges of the *Dunrakul Kron* as fully as he should have.

So would it be remembered.

The ogors moved up on foot. The *crack* and *bang* of Thunderers' handguns rang through the blizzard like the harsh reprove of Grungni himself. Splashes of scarlet appeared in the whiteout where Dunrakul gunnery struck ogor flesh. Ael's Kharadron had set up a firebase at the north end of the battlement around the fortress-within-a-fortress of their grounded frigate. Its guns and theirs were a flickering scream of gold that punished the ogors for every yard they climbed. But the ogors came on, absorbing gunshots with their own bulk and shrugging off every loss. There could be no bonds of kinship, Kolram supposed, between brutes and cannibals, even if the manner in which Sjarpa had spoken of his grandfather and his great-great-grandfather made him wonder otherwise.

He discarded the thought, baring his teeth in hatred as an Irongut ogor showed his ugly face above the parapet. The brute had a greasy moustache and a few lank streaks of hair drawn over an otherwise bald head. Kolram brought his axe down on the ogor's groping arm. The fine blade clanged off the ogor's scrap-metal vambrace, stinging him into dragging the arm back over the parapet. The Irongut roared, more frustrated than hurt. Spittle froze to his chin.

'Lorekeeper Braztom is still on the Angazongi Stair with his books, you thaggi curs!' Kolram cracked the ogor's jaw with the bronze rim of his shield and, while the brute flailed, another of his kin hauled him from the wall by the shoulder and took his place.

'Dunrakul! Defend your king!'

Hangrark whirled a borrowed hammer overhead. Zankeller was still on his back. The runes engraved across its bronze head held such power as was lost to the smiths of the Dispossessed in Sigmar's Age, but to draw it would be to acknowledge the doom of the Dunrakul. Even with the evidence of that doom pressing upon them, Hangrark was too stubborn to see it yet.

Veteran longbeards crowded their king behind a second wall of wooden shields at the warden's cry. They grumbled about numb fingers and snow in their eyes as the ogors battered them, packed in so close their beards tangled, and the shock of axes hitting rusted plate rang through Kolram's body as though the blows were his own. Kothi and Kurrindorm were close by, the two princes doing themselves fairly proud from inside a knot of Hammerers. The signature weapon of the Dunrakul's elite royal guard required both hands to wield, but left such a trail of broken ogor skulls in their wake that neither lad paused to lament the lack of shields.

Ogor guns barked.

The rampart shuddered under the impacts of cannons wielded as handguns. Snow blasted from the parapet. One of Kurrindorm's Hammerer guard took a hit in the chest. He flew back from the wall, his mail coat blown open, and the survivors instinctively ducked behind the battlement while a glutton swung a war-pick over the wall.

With a roar, the ogor torqued his upper body strength and *pulled*. The entire merlon and a large chunk of masonry crumbled into the second tier to the raucous cheers of the ogors' kin.

Kolram felt wrath shiver through his fingertips and into his axe.

If only Lorekeeper Braztom had been swifter up the stair. Not so that this act of oathbreaking might have been avoided, but so his final act as king of Karag Vawrkhaz could have been to mark that ogor down for Grudgement.

'For shame!' he roared, and his warriors took up the cry.

'For shame!' the longbeards yelled, working themselves into the patient outrage of a thousand years of exile.

'When I led the assault on Stingagit, the Grot King, and his dread spider, Dawidum, did I break so much as a single stone? Did I not keep my cannons' powder dry, even at the cost to me in duardin lives?' Kolram carved an ogor a second mouth and sent his nose flying free of his face. 'For shame.'

'For shame!'

With a panicked roar, the gluttons broke before the furious axe-work and implacable shields of the Dunrakul. To the pounding of drums and the bleak lowing of horns from deeper within the blizzard, they turned from the wall and fled back down the slope.

In spite of the insufferable wrongs done to their great-great-great-grandfathers, the duardin merely muttered to one another as they redressed ranks, reset shields, and limbered their axe-swings as though this were all good practice for the real fighting to come. A longbeard caught hold of Kothi's arm and tutted at the youthful exuberance that might have tempted the young prince to give chase. Gun and cannon fire burst along the length of the wall, pounding the withdrawal of the first wave. Another longbeard loudly blew his nose.

'It's getting colder,' Hangrark observed.

'Battle has aged you,' said Kolram. 'You complain like a longbeard.'

'I can't feel my face.'

'We'll endure. Like the rock beneath our feet.' Kolram looked over his throng.

A ferocious roar went up from the southern ramparts.

The ogors' rout had not been even, and the fighting there had continued until that moment. Kolram watched as they attempted to flee, only to find Vulkite Berzerkers of the Dunr Lodge throwing themselves from the wall they were supposedly defending and hacking into their backs. Braegnar-Grimnir's fire-breathing behemoth, Firechaser, clambered up onto the battlement, and a feeling more bitter than any curse tightened around Kolram's heart. The runefather, bloody-bearded and wreathed in rune-flame, screamed incoherently at his remaining warriors and waved his grandaxe after the fleeing ogors.

'Get down, you rabid *urk*,' Kolram yelled. 'We've barely enough warriors to hold the wall as it is.'

Deaf to him, deaf to all but the fiery ragings of a dead god in his gold-poisoned ears, Braegnar-Grimnir urged his magmadroth to charge.

* * *

With a final shout the ogors Ulf and Brogg, aided by a team of shrill-voiced gnoblars with a tricky set-up of levers and pulleys, heaved Borja and his block of ice upright. The gnoblars cheered, slapping one another's raised hands before quickly falling out over something or other and descending once again to violent bickering. Brogg bent over his thighs and wheezed. Ulf simply sat down in the snow. Even in life, Borja had been too fat for any mortal creature to move. Packed in the ice of the Everwinter, he was too hard to be broken by the finest tools, and too heavy for ogor strength to shift. But the gnoblars were clever.

Sjarpa grimaced as the little greenskins shrieked at one another and threw snowballs. One of them burst against his chest. He looked down at the powdering snow on his front.

Sometimes, they could be clever.

The roads leading up to the Fire Crown were arteries that had become clogged with Gutbuster fat. Frorgen Maetsgral's Fighting Hand ignored them entirely in favour of making their own road. His stonehorn ploughed through the walls, demolished the empty castles, and almost incidentally left behind a rubble-strewn climb more than gradual enough for the Maneater mercenaries, half-tame scavengers of the Icebrow Skal, and eager orruk bands to follow up behind.

Only the Thunder Hand, Eating Hand and a few Kruleboy mobs, waiting to see where the fighting was going to be easiest, were still holding back.

Sturmur Rockbelly was as great a fighter as Sjarpa had seen in a long time. On the back of a stonehorn, with the frost spear that Sjarpa had carved for him, he was as close to unbeatable as any mortal fighter came. But his prowess as a fighter could sometimes be a substitute for his abilities as a leader. Leaving the horde to its own devices, the Frostlord had joined the Fighting Hand with the idea of leading from the front. Deprived of instructions of any sort, Sjarpa could already see his horde starting to break up into its ill-fitting parts.

Orruk boar-riders broke off and spread out so as not to be shredded by grapeshot from the duardin guns. Maneaters dropped off Maetsgral's punishing pace, bawling with laughter as they took potshots with outsize duelling pistols at the Kharadron hiding behind the last walls. Only around Borja, that mighty battle standard of the Everwinter and The Way, did the Thunder Hand wait with some semblance of decent order.

'What more was there to your great secret?' Sjarpa asked his frozen grandfather. A shared enemy? A common goal? He had provided Sturmur with those. Was the threat of starvation and cold, slow death not enough to force a fractious horde into becoming an army? 'I have to do everything myself,' he grumbled.

Then, very slowly, he began to smile.

It was traditional for the Blizzard Speaker to advise, not lead, but now he thought of it he didn't know why he'd never considered it before. Why waste his strength trying to teach an idiot like Sturmur The Way when he could just tell the Mawtribe what to do himself? The power of his revelation was immense. It filled his thick-boned head, swelled in him to fill even his belly and make his guts ache as though needing to pass stool after a hefty meal. The sky flickered white and grumbled.

The Everwinter saw his new understanding and approved.

The next time Sjarpa Longtooth set out into the Everwinter to craft an ice spear for a Frostlord, as his role as Blizzard Speaker demanded of him, it would be for his own hand to hold.

'No more sky-ships,' said Skag, peering into the sky.

'They fall prey to the Everwinter's teeth,' said Sjarpa. 'We chew only on the scraps it leaves behind.'

Hearing what sounded like ogors roaring in panic, Sjarpa looked up. Rump Broadfeast's Ice Tyrants were breaking from the centre and legging it back down the duardin stair. Sjarpa had been expecting them to run, after softening up the defences a little bit for the Fighting Hand and the orruks, of course, but was more surprised to see the Fyreslayers leaving their own positions to give chase. Their more disciplined allies raged at the emptied walls they left behind.

It had never occurred to him that there could be duardin as ignorant of The Way as Sturmur Rockbelly.

He summoned Skag Vulture-Keeper. His head was aching from the knowledge it had taken in already, but he could do nothing to stop the new idea that was forming there.

'Ride ahead,' he said. 'Tell Sturmur that the Everwinter sends him a new path.'

Braegnar-Grimnir howled in berzerker fury as his magmadroth, Firechaser, galloped down the Outer Stair. He clung to the reptile's craggy scales with one hand, hacking down routed gluttons with fizzing swipes of his latchkey grandaxe with the other. His throat was torn from yelling. Bloody lumps flecked his beard and smouldered in rune-fire. Firechaser made a regurgitative noise and vomited up molten rock, burying the fleeing ogors and blocking off half the stair.

Nostrils flaring, Braegnar-Grimnir wrenched his axe from an ogor's back. The runes in his muscles throbbed, so hot they hurt, tormenting him for every moment he spent failing to wield that fire in wrath. The gluttons were in full rout now, and the children of Grimnir would not allow a single one to escape the vengeance of the fire.

'Blood and gold!' he bellowed, a raw, sweet agony on his ruined throat. 'War and death! In Grimnir's name, every last one of them dies!'

It was a short road the Fyreslayers walked: from birth to the final fyrd. Braegnar-Grimnir knew it well, and so found the joy in every step, rarely pausing to consider the next or to look back in reflection at the one before.

Sparks flew from tall helms and crests, from the tinderbox strike of bare feet on duardin stonework, as the grand fyrd hurtled down the stairs on foot to join him. Flames trailed from their weapons as they ran, fire and cold waging a constant war of reckless advances and sudden reversals. In his god-wrought frenzy, Braegnar-Grimnir recognised only the most familiar faces. There was his Brigg, his daughter and heir, guiding her own magmadroth, Oxtarn, and her berzerker kinbands on a rampage that set a mob of Ironjawz to rout down a side stair. And there was Dremm, the battlesmith, belting out a battle-dirge that told of Grimnir's many contests with Gorkamorka and his chieftains of old.

For a moment, he thought he glimpsed Azkaharr too: a flash of white amidst the red and gold, a dazzling arc of axe-work cleaving through shoddy plate, and a clear voice raised in whichever old song the fyrds needed to hear most.

Finding himself in danger of having his charge overtaken by his own karls, Braegnar-Grimnir growled and urged his mount onwards, just as a berzerker came flying through the air and smacked into the wall not far from where he rode. The Fyreslayer's head had been bent fully around. Sparks sputtered, his muscles twitching as his runes tried to force the dead body to get back up and fight, but failed.

Braegnar-Grimnir looked up. A monstrous column was advancing up the stair.

Stonehorns.

The beasts were shaggy-furred and slump-shouldered, a wall of stone forcing the routed gluttons onto side paths or simply grinding them into paste underfoot as they came on. The stair was wide enough for a dozen ogors to flee down and for three dozen Fyreslayers to give chase, but only two stonehorns could walk abreast there. Their heads were armoured in stone. Rocky protuberances erupted from their knees and shoulders, like metal studs on leather armour and a thousand times as hard as either. Tusks and horns left a permanent record of their passage in the stonework to either side. On the back of each, a large ogor draped in furs wielded tough reins and a whip, steam billowing from their hungry maws.

Another Fyreslayer went flying past Braegnar-Grimnir's shoulder.

Crazed berzerkers slapped into the front rank of beasts like mud flung at a shield, utterly heedless of the warriors bouncing off, falling under stone hooves, or being hurled aside on tusks. Braegnar-Grimnir snorted, furious, and yelled at Firechaser to meet the charge.

The right-hand rider of that front rank of two was clad in crudely worked hides and draped in furs. He had a metal eyepatch screwed into the orbit of his eye and was armed with a long, spike-ended chain that droned as he whirled it above his head. The rider on the left was even larger. His armour was metal rather than hide, albeit of mismatched pieces and, aping the stonehorn he rode perhaps, studded with sharpened pieces of rock. A thick grey fringe obscured his face, betraying the icy glint of a blue eye or a snake of tattoo only when the wind deigned to paw it aside. A grisly trophy rack festooned his shoulders, a pair of crossed poles set across the saddle-back flying the standards of a gaping maw and of a round belly struck through with stones. Both flapped stiffly in the freezing wind.

Braegnar-Grimnir knew a warlord when he saw one.

Roaring his challenge, for death against a lesser foe would be looked on unkindly when it came time for Grimnir to muster his final fyrd, he turned Firechaser towards the second ogor. Sturmur

Rockbelly – it could only have been the Frostlord that the emissary, Sjarpa, had mentioned – raised a glittery spear of ice in acknowledgement. Otherwise, he gave no obvious sign of singling Braegnar-Grimnir out for single combat. A charging wedge of stonehorn simply could not be stopped or turned.

'Grimnir!' the runefather roared, as the two monsters ploughed into one another head-on.

There were few beasts in Chamon capable of stopping a magmadroth ancient in its tracks, but the stonehorn rammed the god-reptile out of its path, bending its thick neck awkwardly to one side and shoving it unceremoniously through a wall. The wall shed bricks, stonework crumbling over Firechaser's back and Braegnar-Grimnir's shoulder, and still the stonehorn ploughed on. Bellowing with the fury of the ur-salamander, the magmadroth bit down on a horn and wrenched the stonehorn's head to one side. Their path veered out of the wall and back onto the stair, Firechaser raking his claws down the larger monster's chest while his hind feet scrabbled for purchase on the icy steps.

With flames igniting the ends of his beard, Braegnar-Grimnir brought his axe crashing into Sturmur's spear.

The supernatural frost of the Everwinter warred with the eternal flame of the Zharrkhul. The spark of Grimnir and Vulcatrix bound to the latchkey grandaxe's curving edge guttered and writhed, drawing back from every thrust of Sturmur's spear but refusing to be doused entirely.

With a snarl, Braegnar-Grimnir fought his way up until he was standing in the saddle, the better to match his gigantic rival blow for blow, the runes in his biceps blazing like ingots as they strove to match him for strength as well.

The rest of the ogor beastriders, meanwhile, continued their advance up the stair. Half of the column, led by the chain-wielding chieftain with the eyepatch, continued to trample over the

Fyreslayers' berserk charge. The second half, with nowhere else to go and no hope of slowing down, ploughed into the back of Sturmur's stonehorn and forced it, in turn, onto Braegnar-Grimnir's magmadroth.

The runefather milled his arms and took a stumbling step towards the back of his war-throne. Sturmur Rockbelly's mouth made a jagged gash, eager, but still said nothing. Firechaser bellowed, and belched lava over the horn that the mass of two-score advancing stonehorn was forcing down his throat. The stonehorn bellowed in pain as thick hair turned to smoke and stone skin dribbled away to expose the red blood and raw nerves underneath. The monster stumbled, the injured leg collapsing under it and leaving Braegnar-Grimnir cackling as he struck his axe down into Sturmur Rockbelly's suddenly open chest. The blow dinged the rock-studded metal straps that protected his shoulders and scorched a rough gash all the way down to the belly.

The Frostlord grunted as though he barely felt it.

'Say something!' he yelled in frustration, reversing his grip on his axe to send it back across the Frostlord's gut-plate and this time carve it in two. 'Fight me like it bloody matters!'

At the exact same moment, the wounded stonehorn surged back onto its still-steaming front foot, ramming Firechaser back another dozen beard-lengths and sending Braegnar-Grimnir's axe high over Sturmur's head as he was forced to address his footing. He gave a bellow of defiance, just as he felt the crack of Sturmur's spear butt against the side of his head. The blow was powerful enough to have broken through a castle wall. It dented Braegnar-Grimnir's helmet and set his skull to ringing. Standing in his saddle and already off-balance, he staggered backwards, tripped on the saddlebow, and fell. His back cracked the ice sheeting the Outer Stair.

He made to rise immediately, only to gasp with the piercing

cold going through his heart. He looked down, coughing blood and dying embers over the haft of the ice spear erupting from his chest. Fire and cold raged within him: a constant war of reckless advances and abrupt reversals.

Sturmur pulled out the spear. Snow blew in to fill the hole it left in him, but couldn't muster a cold nearly so great as that which had just been delivered.

Defeat. Death. Even disgrace.

He could abide these things, so long as the battle was worthy and well fought.

Turning his head away, he watched as the grand fyrd of the Dunr Lodge fled back to the fortress with the frenzy well and truly beaten out of them. He sought his daughter and her mount amongst the rout, and felt a moment's panic when he could not find her, but the world around him was shrinking, its edges hardening and turning white. He forced a fierce smile onto his lips, even as he wrapped numb arms around his broken chest and the shudder of passing stonehorns went like knives of ice through the stone steps under his back.

Braegnar-Grimnir was Doomgron-bound.

The messenger, Skag Vulture-Keeper, returned to the court-yard. His thundertusk shouldered through the increasingly thick snow as though it was nothing but a spring shower. The battle for the stair that was being fought between the Fyreslayers and the Fighting Hand was a dull growl behind him, a dim and very distant second to the wild shriek of the wind. The Everwinter was all. It allowed for nothing else.

'Sturmur has killed the Fyreslayer King,' Skag reported.

Sjarpa absorbed the news with a frown. If there was one duardin here who could have bested the great Sturmur Rockbelly and freed Sjarpa to lead the Mawtribes in the proper way then it should have been the Fyreslayer warlord and his god-lizard.

'He's hurt though,' Skag added, sensing that Sjarpa was less than happy with this news. 'His beast too. He limps now after Frorgen and the rest of the Fighting Hand for the walls.'

Shivering, Sjarpa looked over his shoulder.

The Everwinter was on them. There was only one clear way now, and that was to fight their way through the duardin defenders, with the Frostlord or without him, all the way to Grimnir's Forge. No matter what.

He drew the harpoon launcher from its hook on the side of his saddle, then motioned for Brogg and Ulf. The two beastriders were still dismounted, trying to corral the handful of gnoblars that hadn't taken the opportunity to lose themselves in the abandoned fortress the moment the fighting had broken out.

'Fix Borja's chains to our saddles and bring him,' he said, turning towards the fortress. 'It's time.'

The Kharadron weren't going to hold.

The arkanaut crews and Grundstok Thunderers were trained and equipped for repelling boarders. Decksweepers and fumigators, it turned out, served just as well for clearing a rampart as they did the gunwales of a sky-ship, while a well-aimed skyhook betwixt the eyes proved a more than adequate method for felling an ogor. But they weren't going to hold. Kharadron excelled at range where superior technology and sheer firepower provided them the advantage. Most of their shorter-range and close-combat weapons were repurposed tools: aethermatic saws, arkanaut cutters and the like. And against foes as strong as ogors, their heavy armour provided almost no protection at all.

Yard by yard, they surrendered.

On either flank the Dunrakul held on, as stubborn as a mob of troggoths with a loose idea in their collective heads. Their handgunners cursed as gunpowder firearms spat and failed them in the snow, resorting to clubbing ogors with gun butts as the brutes hauled themselves over the parapet and dying horribly for their courage. Aethermatic weaponry suffered no such disadvantage.

But they weren't going to hold, and Ael wasn't going to be the one to make them. The Code was explicit on the principle of lost causes.

They withdrew to the *Prospect Shield*. The frigate had been tied down, unable to take off under the rapidly worsening conditions but still more than capable of laying down a withering amount of fire. The Kharadron at the Gate of Throngs were few, but they packed a punch far in excess of their weight. Captain Shiriktorn's garbled orders echoed through the aftcastle loud-hailer to be snatched up by the blizzard. Recent turns, Ael suspected, had not been proven so ringing an endorsement of the captain's natural caution. As Ael saw it, Errn would have lost her ship anyway once the Everwinter hit the port. Better to roll her dice here, now, and go for bust that the Dunr Fyreslayers and the Dunra-kul could hold the ogors back.

But then Ael had always been a gambler.

With a cry that she hoped sounded sufficiently warlike, she blasted short-sightedly with her volley pistol. The salvo winged two ogors that happened to be standing close together, but only served to enrage them all the more. Anfrik Drakksson finished them off for her, one after the other, with a pair of face-melting shots from a heavily customised vulcaniser pistol. The vice-admiral was giving every impression of enjoying himself enormously, taking advantage of the brief but necessary cool-down between shots to offer up an unhelpful tip or an anecdote from his pre-retirement years plundering the sky-lanes.

'Not half as big without heads on their shoulders, eh, mistress?' he said. 'Reminds me of the time I was forced to winter with a crew of Scourge pirates over Misthåvn...'

Ael let his reminiscence pass over her.

She felt as though she had brought a knife to an aeronautical broadside. She'd read the admiralty field manual, *Olgrimm Grundstok's Mercantile Encyclopaedia*, the second (and definitive) edition of Kolon Dunray's *Steel Triplet Bestiary*. She'd kept herself up to date with dispatches from the frontiers, and attended several lectures in tactics and general strategy by the esteemed Lord-Magnate Brokk Grungsson himself. She had, she was forced to concede, squandered a great deal of money.

Squinting through the out-of-focus blur, and missing the eyeglasses she had forgotten in her wardroom, she took careful aim and placed half a dozen rounds through the mouth of an Ironguts ogor that had been in the process of pulling itself over the wall.

Forgetting all decorum, she whooped.

'A perfect hit, mistress,' Drakksson called out.

Ael grunted. She couldn't deny that she was enjoying herself just a little bit too. Or that there hadn't been a tribunal or two that she wouldn't, in hindsight, have preferred to resolve with six bullets in someone's mouth. Being a berzerker for the day was, in fact, highly agreeable. So long as she had aether-gold in her pistol's cylinder, she could almost forget all that she had lost and how little she was still fighting for.

A pity it couldn't last.

The Kharadron weren't going to hold.

'We should be falling back now, mistress,' Drakksson shouted to her.

'What about Kolram and Braegnar-Grimnir?'

The vice-admiral shrugged. As a retired officer of Barak-Zon, Anfrik Drakksson had a respect for his warrior kin that Ael sometimes failed to show, but not this time. 'If they know what they're doing then they'll soon be falling back too.'

Ael supposed it was only practical. 'Fall back!' she yelled, waving to Captain Shiriktorn and the *Prospect Shield* to pass the order along. 'Abandon ship. Retreat to the Gate of Throngs!'

The ogors were too many. There was no longer any profit to be gouged from attempting to deny them here and, once again, it fell to the Kharadron to be the voices of pragmatism.

Aethermatic air horns cried retreat, disconsolate brass notes sounding their secret shame to the buried slopes. Abandoning the fight for the battlements in enviable good order, the Kharadron withdrew, step by step, punishing the ogors with gunfire all the way. Several Dunrakul clan companies abandoned their positions to join them: proud warriors, battling under the banners of families and guilds, right up to the moment that Ael Dunrsdottir gave a tug on their courage and found it as substantial as aether. Even the Fyreslayers, whom no duardin would dare call cowards to their faces, were streaming towards the wall in full rout.

Kolram's disappointment was immense, but came at least with the vindication of being proven wholly and unutterably right in all things.

'No retreat!' he barked. 'No quarter!' He raised his shield, readied his axe. The longbeards formed into a square around him and his Hammerers. His arm was weary. The cold had made his grip on his axe slippery. But he was duardin: he shirked no toil, whether it be with a miner's pick, a mason's hammer, or a warrior's axe. 'This way belongs to the Dunrakul, and the Dunrakul don't lightly surrender what's theirs!'

'Your majesty, can't you see? This battle is over.'

Gromrhun stood in the second rank of the longbeards. He had his helmet in his hands, a nasty-looking bruise welling up over one eye. He had also taken a deep cut across the cheek. His expression looked graver than Kolram recalled it ever being, his eyes sunken even more deeply into the flesh of his cheeks, his white beard fraying from its tight golden braids and pulling loose in the winds of the Everwinter.

'Where have you been, longbeard?'

'I can be in many places at once, your majesty. When I've the need. But there always comes the time when a duardin is forced to pick his battles.'

Kolram blinked. 'What?'

'I said this battle is over.'

'No. After that.'

Gromrhun pinched his eyes. 'I said more? Then truly, I'm tired.' Muttering what sounded like a gripe against the encroaching cold, the longbeard shook out his cloak. The aura of warmth it put out seemed to expel the cold, and even to push back against the snow for a time, only to see both returned with vehemence, and the longbeard appeared even more diminished by the failure of whatever magic he had sought to bring to bear against it. 'Worth a try,' he said. 'But the Winterbite come again to the end of their thousand-year Mawpath, and I fear it'll take a warmth fiercer than that of the Hearthmother's to hold that which comes after them at bay. The ogors are nothing, majesty. They're naught but the heralds of the real doom that's coming. The Kharadron are leaving and the Fyreslayers are broken. It's time we fell back to join them at Grimnir's Forge.'

'For shame,' Kolram muttered.

'Shame,' his warriors agreed.

'Do you think your ancestors forsook Karag Dawrkhaz because they were beaten?' Gromrhun snapped, and Kolram felt his spirit recoil from that small glimpse of the longbeard's ire. 'They withdrew to Azyr because they *refused* to be beaten. We're duardin, majesty. We're not beaten until we're slain and duardin don't slay so easily.'

'We are the Dispossessed,' said Kolram, finding his own backbone again. 'The burden of shame that that entails us is ours to wear, and wear it we do. No duardin in the Mortal Realms fights harder for what shall never again be.'

'But, father–' Kurrindorm cut in.

Kolram raised a hand to cut him short. 'Go, lad. Go with Grom-rhun if that's what you wish.'

'I don't understand.' The prince's voice rose with his despair, but Kolram refused to turn and see him.

Kurrindorm's last memory of his father would not be of the moment of defeat.

'See that the Gate of Throngs is barred tight and the runes are struck. Let the hopeless dream of the Dunrakul live on. Kothi and Hangrark and I will hold them here, and move not one inch until it's done.'

The longbeards muttered approvingly. For the first time in Kolram's thirty-year reign of Karag Dawrkhaz they found nothing to fault, in his words or in his deeds.

'You're a stubborn fool, Kolram,' said Gromrhun, his expression softening in spite of his harsh words. 'But you're a duardin right enough. For better or worse.'

He offered his hand. Kolram grasped it by the forearm and held it tight.

'If you're set on dying then see that you die well,' said Gromrhun.

The battlement shuddered as though struck by an earthquake. It lasted for all of a second, after which the great wall of Kolram's ancestors came tumbling from the ram-head horns of a stonehorn, its splayed feet making light work of the rubble slope.

Kolram flexed his fingers. His grip was empty, but his axe-hand felt warmed nonetheless. Gromrhun was gone. Kurrindorm was gone.

And Kolram *knew* who he had just seen.

'Stand firm,' he cried. 'Many wrongs shall be made aright this day, and more will be written. Only when the *Dunrakul Kron* is empty is our defiance done.'

The first ogor through the breach, an eyepatch-wearing brute with a lank moustache, raised a blood-tipped spear and growled a challenge.

With a sigh, Hangrark threw down his hammer. He drew Zankeller.

The last days of the duardin were upon them.

Sjarpa would have held back longer, if he could have. If he could have slowed the advance of the Thunder Hand any more, if the Everwinter had not been biting at their backs, then he would have waited until the fighting at the gate was done with and Sturmur Rockbelly either victorious or slain. But the Everwinter was coming, and it was coming now. His thundertusk crashed through and ground over what little the stonehorn had left of the duardin's last wall, crushing everything big enough to earn the status of *rubble* into snowflake pieces of grit. The corpses of mournfangs and stonehorns lay under a thick blanketing of snow. Ogors lay beside them. Some were dead too. Others were simply gorging on their former mounts, with the battle having moved on from them.

There were still duardin fighting by the gate. Defiant to the last.

If he hadn't fought duardin before, it would have been hard for him to credit that warriors so small could have held up the Fighting Hand for so long. There was something of the Beastclaw in them, he thought: it was the same tenacity that made them cling on in spite of a frigid end, that made them *ride* even though they knew in their bones that the Everwinter would always catch them in the end.

'Where are the gluttons?' asked Njal. 'The orruks?'

'Lost in the blizzard,' said Sjarpa.

Or lost *to* the blizzard. It made no difference. The Everwinter was always hungry.

Sjarpa didn't care any more. All he wanted was to get inside the

Fire Crown and eat his way to Grimnir's Forge, where he could thaw the old Frost King and feel warm again.

With a bark for his attention, Skag Vulture-Keeper pointed to a chilblained corpse on the ground. It was Frorgen Maetsgral. Njal and the others licked their lips. Their bellies rumbled loudly. Dead friends meant more meat to go around, and fewer mouths to feed. Sjarpa didn't even need to pretend that he was sad. In the way of the Beastclaw they rode on.

The last bit of courtyard was an upward slope, shallow steps feeding in towards the snow-blown maw of the duardin. The thundertusks would be there in a dozen strides.

Sturmur Rockbelly was ahead of them. The Frostlord was wounded and on foot. His stonehorn was dead beside him, its head obliterated by a single massive blow. A duardin lay crushed underneath it, only the bronze head of a warhammer and the hand that gripped it, the bent wing of a helmet, still visible under the bloody mat of hair. Others lay strewn all over, armour crushed, bodies torn open. Only one duardin was left. His good mail was prickled by snow. His cheeks were blue, vapour huffing from his mouth as his lungs froze. The cold made him sluggish, brittle, but like every stubborn fool that ever wore a beard, he stood.

Sjarpa recognised Kolram. King of the Dunrakul.

Njal hefted a heavy javelin, but Sjarpa raised a hand to stop him. 'The Frostlord needs no help,' he said.

Ahead, Sturmur gave a roar, wielding his frost spear two-handed like an axe, and struck at the duardin king. Despite the cold seizing up his limbs, Kolram managed to lift his shield to block it. Runes flared across the metal rim and, one by one, exploded as its protections were overwhelmed by Sturmur's huge strength and the ice power of his spear. It was a blow that would have knocked out an Ironjaw, and should have been more than enough to kill even a duardin, but with the numbness in his arm, Kolram barely even seemed to feel it. Sturmur stumbled in for a follow up swing. Black, frostbitten scabs pinched over horrific cuts all over the Frostlord's body. Heavy plates hung loose off his rock-studded harness where straps had been cut or knots worked loose by fighting.

But Kolram, as good as dead already when the Everwinter arrived, steadfastly refused to die.

The duardin tottered under the Frostlord's swing and drove his axe hard into Sturmur's stomach. The blow ought to have hit metal, but the sagging gut-plate had left white skin and curling belly hair exposed and Kolram's axe sank greedily into blubber instead. Sturmur roared in pain. Kolram's teeth chattered as he struggled to keep a hold of his axe, sawing the blade backwards and forwards to loosen it. Belly fat, like the greasy lumps that the Butchers skimmed off their broths, spilled out of the Frostlord's body, running down Kolram's arm to dollop over his metal boots. The mighty Sturmur Rockbelly collapsed to his knees, squidging down into his own custard-brown juices, and groping madly for the duardin who was killing him. He missed entirely, his hand instead scooping up a fistful of oozing fat, which he then stuffed into his mouth and chewed, eyes fluttering in contentment even as he died.

Kolram staggered back, appalled by the Frostlord's ravenous death throes, and only then noticing the approach of Sjarpa Longtooth and the Thunder Hand.

Shivering lips drew back from their teeth. He seemed singly unafraid. 'C-c-c-c–'

Sjarpa raised his harpoon launcher. There was no more time for talk.

The harpoon whistled out on its chain, punched through the duardin's mail vest, chest, and lodged its barbed hooks in the wreckage of his shoulder blade. The king grunted as though he'd been pushed in the shoulder, raising the axe in his un-ruined arm as though to hack through the chain. Sjarpa pulled on the hand-crank before he had the chance, triggering the chain to retract back into the launcher and yanking the king off his feet. He slid without dignity across the ice, losing his axe along the way, before Brogg Threeteeth leant casually over to skewer him with his javelin. Sjarpa's thundertusk crushed him underfoot.

And they rode on, Frost King Borja Kragnfryr tottering behind them on chains, as though he was riding home in a chariot of ice, drawn by the champions of his Thunder Hand. Sjarpa could almost hear his grandfather's voice in his head, shouting out from the back, instructing him on what to do.

'The gates are locked,' said Njal.

Ulf the Strange was visibly struggling with a thought. 'The king died so the others could close it. That's... funny.'

Sjarpa shook his head. Sacrificing themselves for others was not what kings did.

With one hard-chewed, ice-splintered fingernail he pointed to the gate. It looked strong. Runes glowed defiantly across the grain of the wood. But it was not, he imagined, as strong as it had used to be.

He gave the one order that mattered.

'Smash it in.'

CHAPTER FOURTEEN

Brigg spread her hands, pinpricks of cold nicking her bare arms and upturned face.

It was snowing.

It was snowing in Grimnir's Forge.

White glitter fell in thick, billowing curtains through the volcano's main vent. Most turned to fog in the furnace heat of the magma lake. Little settled. That it was here at all gave her a shiver of dread, as if the realm had been inverted and the mountain set upside down. A sugary dusting coated the fyresteel chains that crisscrossed the steaming magma chamber, bearded the golden frescoes that had never looked down so grimly on the works of their descendants.

The battle for the Gate of Throngs was over and the duardin were defeated. The war, it seemed, had moved to the very heart of Karag Dawrkhaz.

Brigg could feel the mountain fighting to rouse itself as she led her fyrd across the bridge. Tremors squealed through the piles and bearings. Magma crashed against the high side-wall, singeing her crest, and forcing demoralised berzerkers to duck their heads and mutter about dark omens in the fire. The magmic battle-forges, making up the archipelago of conjoined isles that sat upon the lake, and thickly veiled by local eruptions and ferocious heat, looked smaller now they were clearer to see, naked almost in the encroaching cold. Zharrgrim zealots, dangling over the lake in their gilded baskets, exhorted the fire to burn more fiercely and cast the Everwinter back but, thus far, it did not.

Her magmadroth, Oxtarn, wheezed as she plodded across the bridge. Scaly joints creaked in the cold. Every breath was a huff of steam so great Brigg was certain it was going to be the last. But, like the godbeast that had spawned her, the old matriarch didn't know when she was beaten. Another breath always followed. Another bridge-pounding step. Brigg blessed and cursed her.

The last warriors of the grand fyrd, a dozen or so, traipsed alongside, strung out into a snaking column for some distance behind. These were the warriors who had been slowest in the charge and the quickest to break. They were not mourning the death in battle of their runefather, nor even the defeat of the Dunr Lodge; but their own failure to die was a burden they would find hard to live with.

Brigg knew.

A small kinband of Auric Hearthguard, because small kinbands were all that had been left behind, stood guard at the far end of the bridge. At Brigg's approach, they stepped smartly aside. None of them pulled her over to ask after the battle above. The Fyre-slayers were warriors: they knew what a victory looked like and it looked nothing at all like this.

The magmadroth stepped up onto the funicular platform that, just a few days ago, had returned her from her last, *her final*, tryst with Strahl in the Kharadron's port-city. The carriage had stalled a few yards off its docking clamps. Snow was starting to pile up on the roof and a party of Kharadron had set up camp inside. They had their gloves and helmets off and were mulling beer over an alchemical heater. One of them filled a mug and passed it through cage doors that had been wedged open with a miner's pick to the Fyreslayer standing guard below. The warrior took a sip, smiled, then offered it on to the family of Dispossessed sitting on the floor wrapped in blankets. Brigg found herself heartened by the small display of solidarity, even as the elderly Dunrakul grandmother turned the offer down, too proud to accept Fyreslayer charity.

Distracted by the sounds of a scuffle from one of the parallel bridges, she reined Oxtarn in and turned to look towards it. A large, unarmed throng of Dunrakul were in the process of crossing from the Middle Deeps. A second kinband of Auric Hearthguard had their magmapikes crossed to block them from entering, loudly shouting that Grimnir's Forge was now full, and warriors from elsewhere were hurrying across to shore up their kin.

For a length of time that would shame her later, Brigg just watched. She felt jagged inside, little pieces of grief caught under skin.

What she felt, in the end, was not compassion for her destitute kin, but resignation. Perhaps, if they had all been less ready to fight one another over every last bit of what they claimed as their own, they would not now be together in having lost it all. Karag Dawrkhaz had fallen before, and from greater heights of power than Kolram, Braegnar-Grimnir and Ael had been able to restore it to. There was no shame, then, in suffering the same. Provided the downfall was hard-fought. But the mountain had fallen in a day. If Kolram had not neglected his mountainside forts and ranger outposts... Had Ael kept a keener watch... Had Braegnar-Grimnir not expended all his wrath on bitterness... Could they not then have held the ogors at the Gate of Throngs for longer than a day? Or at least long enough to condemn them to their own blasted Everwinter?

She sighed. 'Let them pass.'

A few of the Hearthguard raised their voices in protest. Brigg wasn't sure she had the fight left in her to argue.

It was Dremm who shouted them down. The old battlesmith limped ahead of Oxtarn, using his icon pole as a walking cane. He was bloody all over. Weary of body. Ashamed in spirit. But his voice still had the power to command.

'Do you know who this is?' he yelled. 'This is Brigg, queen of the Dunr Lodge and heir to the Doomed God.' He smacked the icon pole on the floor, startling several reluctant Hearthguard into lowering their pikes. The aura of the old runefather lingered on him like the fire of the Zharrkhul. 'She speaks, and it's the place of her Hearthguard to fight, to the death if need be, over how best to obey her command.'

Shamefaced, the Hearthguard bowed low and stood aside. The Dispossessed throng trudged through.

'It's not like you to be compassionate,' she said to Dremm.

The battlesmith shrugged. 'You're still young. There's probably a lot you think you know that's wrong.'

The Dunrakul shuffled past them, all that they hadn't already lost carried across their backs. This generally amounted to a small pack, hurriedly filled with heirlooms, and a frightened child. They thanked her as they went by, reaching out to lay a hand on Oxtarn's scaly shoulder as they did. They'd lost a king too. Like the Fyreslayers, they needed someone to fill the impossibly large, empty hole that left in their hearts. Look past the excessive clothing and the rigid customs, and the Dunrakul were really not so different. Even their hair, although worn down and short, tended towards the same reddish gold of the Dunr.

They were kin, after all. Weren't they?

Queen Silveg, Kolram's widow, nodded grimly as she walked past. Her face was stone. Lorekeeper Braztom shuffled a beard-length behind her, back bent under a panier stuffed with heavy tomes and ledgers and pushing him low across the handles of a library trolley overflowing with yet more books. His grief was not nearly so restrained. He was too old, he cried: he had not been fast enough on the Angazongi Stair to fulfil the king's last request and Kolram's fall was his shame alone to bear. Barring the occasional, deeply embarrassed pat on the back from a kindly longbeard, he was ignored.

A duardin that Brigg recognised as Kolram's son left the group to approach her.

'Kurrindorm,' he said, with the faintest trace of an Azyrheim accent, and offered up his hand.

He'd been on the wall, Brigg recalled. To be here now he must have run, as she had, and she could certainly understand that shame. It hadn't surprised her in the least to hear that Kolram had chosen to die for his gate rather than flee. Her father, she was sure, would have done the same. They had been so alike, now she thought on it. Was it any wonder they had fought each other like brothers?

After a moment's consideration, she reached down and grasped the Dunrakul prince's hand.

'Brigg,' she said.

'I know,' said Kurrindorm, letting go.

'Well, this does an old longbeard's heart the world of good,' said an elderly duardin, who appeared to have left the column of refugees to stand at Kurrindorm's side. He wore a red cloak over a long coat of mail, both heavily scraped and dented but, courtesy of the snow no doubt, surprisingly clean of blood and the other stains of battle. His thick, white beard was braided through a number of gold rings and the graven images of the ancestors adorned his vambraces. In spite of the sombre mood and the general atmosphere of doom, there was a sparkle in his eye, as though, however much was lost, something good might yet endure, provided just one duardin remained.

He reminded her of someone else, but it could not have been him. She had last seen Azkaharr beside her father in his fight with Sturmur Rockbelly, and so he was almost certainly lost.

'Have we met before, oldflame?'

Kurrindorm looked over his shoulder, as though surprised to find he had company. An embarrassed look came over his face, and he looked down. 'This is Gromrhun. He's the one who saw me from the battle and helped me to seal the Gate of Throngs against the ogors behind me.'

'It was the king's last wish, lad,' said Gromrhun, patting the prince consolingly on the back. 'You did him proud.'

'Strange,' said Dremm. 'You look familiar.'

Gromrhun nodded sagely. 'I get that often.'

At the sound of a commotion of some kind from further up the line, Brigg looked up.

Ael Dunrsdottir, still in armour and recognisable enough because of it, was leading a small band of Kharadron across the same bridge. With the Dunrakul travelling at a weary slog, the Kharadron had merged with their rearmost ranks and had begun pushing in: hence the irritated grumblings arising from the throng. With her arms out, an open appeal for calm, Ael and a pair of gun-armed guards worked their way up the line towards Kurrindorm and Brigg. The Dunrakul prince made to offer a greeting, but Ael, too, had just noticed Gromrhun.

Fumbling with gloved fingers at her helmet's clasps, she flicked them loose and pulled the helmet from her head. Brigg tried to feel something other than pain at the sight of her. Strahl had been adopted, after all. It was not as if he and his mother looked anything alike. But his face was all she saw.

'Wyram...' Ael murmured.

With the three of them – Brigg, Kurrindorm, and Ael – all focusing their full attentions on him, the elder's outline seemed to turn molten before her eyes. His features burned white, like metal worked over the fires of Grimnir's Forge before settling into something altogether new that, when brought from the anvil for the smith's steady appraisal was really no different at all from what it had been before. Brigg could not even say for certain what about him had changed except that it was *good*. She found herself reminded of the oldest stories she knew. Children's stories. Stories of a white-bearded wanderer who would come to the duardin in their times of plight to remind them of the tools they needed to engineer their own salvation. Stories, she remembered now, that a certain white-bearded wanderer whose name she had never known had once told to her.

She wanted to laugh, but found that she couldn't.

It was an outrageous thing to believe. And yet the truth stood in front of her.

'Azkaharr?'

'Long ago,' the white-glowing duardin said, in a voice that sounded exactly like Azkaharr's and, by some strange magic, like Gromrhun's and Wyram's too, 'the duardin were set onto separate paths. It's made all of you strong, but now...' He gestured at those around him. Everyone, Dunrakul, Kharadron and Fyreslayer alike, had set aside their differences to stare at the myth, the *Ancestor*, that had come to stand amongst them. 'Now's the time to walk a different road, to be strong together as you once were.'

'Who... are you?' said Brigg.

'I think you know.'

Brigg shook her head as though to reject it. 'Then why come in disguise? Why couldn't you just *tell* us of the danger and what we needed to do?'

'You think your father would've listened?' The duardin turned to Kurrindorm. 'And yours?' A glance at Ael. 'And as for you...' He chuckled.

Ael licked her lips as though it would help words slide out. None came.

'No,' said the White Duardin. 'That's not our way.'

'You think that just because I choose not to pray, I wouldn't listen to what a god had to say if he walked into my study?' said Ael, finding the words she'd been looking for.

'I'm no god.'

'You could have told us,' Brigg said again, barely above a hiss.

'I could.' The duardin nodded. 'I could give a thirsty duardin a beer.'

By some runic trick, he did indeed immediately fashion one, drawing a pewter tankard embossed with a golden rune from under his cloak. A strong, hoppy smell rose from the golden-brown liquid it contained. Turning away, he passed it to one of the Auric Hearthguards, muttering a 'Thank you kindly, lad' as the Fyreslayer cupped it with great reverence between both hands. The warrior was too awestruck to even think of drinking it.

'I could do that. But Valaya, instead, chose to teach you how to brew and I'd say that's worked out more-or-less all right. Wouldn't you?' He laid a hand across Kurrindorm's shoulder and squeezed it in what was so plainly a gesture of farewell that the duardin all around who had been hanging on his every utterance moaned in despair. 'You'll do all right.' He gestured to the duardin crowded over Grimnir's Forge. 'You've all you need to weather this storm right here.'

'But the ogors–'

The White Duardin shook his head. 'The Everwinter is a curse that's almost as old as mine. Beyond even the Maker's power to undo, I'd be prepared to wager. Not that it's Grungni's way to mend that which others might learn to fix for themselves. Sjarpa's an old lad, and he's got a head on his shoulders. For an ogor. I remember him well from the last time I was here, in Kogrun's time. I'll help you deal with him, but, as I've said, he's not your real enemy here.'

'He seemed to think Grimnir's Forge could help him,' said Ael.

'Grimnir's Forge hasn't burned at its hottest in a thousand years. The lore of how to do it long lost.' The White Duardin glanced again to the Forge, where runesmiters, aether-khemists, engineers and even a few Ironweld journeymen huddled under blankets. He turned to Brigg and winked. 'Or so they say.'

'Vengeance will be his. When our foes are great, he will return. When the foul creatures of these worlds bay at the doors, he will take up his axe once more and his ire shall rock the mountains.'

CHAPTER FIFTEEN

Strahl Aelsson and the crew of the *Bokram* had by some miracle, if he believed in that sort of thing, made it out of Arik's Pass and all the way to the bottom of the Outer Stair without encountering serious opposition. They had shot their way through a few bands of Kruleboyz and gluttons, most of whom they had found wandering in small groups, lost in the snow, and into the old fortress itself. Most of it was buried under ten feet of snow and Strahl barely recognised it any more. The first thing they had tried to do was follow the stair to the Gate of Throngs, but the snow was too deep and the cold had become too severe even for their arkanaut suits to resist. Captain Helmensson's navigation instruments had lost every landmark and they had been forced into the shelter of an old artillery bastion.

It was somewhere between the fourth and fifth tiers. Strahl was as sure of that as he could be.

The fortification had been so hastily abandoned, and so long ago, that a flame cannon still sat rusting at the embrasure. Strahl wasn't at all surprised to note that it was the exact same design of weapon that the Dunrakul were using today.

The doors had been wooden and were long gone. Snow blustered inside, piling up in a mound on the floor which had since been brushed everywhere and turned to freezing slush by the Kharadron hurrying inside. A rank of corroded storage trunks sat at the back of the room. An opening, similarly doorless, led to what might have been a guardroom. A faint warmth was emanating from it.

If it was a guardroom, then chances were there was a flue there, sealed behind a grille, conveying heat from Grimnir's Forge. Brigg had shown him several that had been widened into tunnels, used by the Dunr Lodge to come and go over the long centuries during which the Gate of Throngs had been occupied by their enemies. But he had no idea where any of them emerged and the chances of just stumbling onto a concealed Fyreslayer entrance were surely too remote to entertain.

As it was, the heat he felt was barely discernible, even with instruments, and Strahl wondered if it wasn't the vague warmth of a memory, a sense of Brigg and his mother on the other side of a hearth grille, rather than something real he could share.

While he stumbled in the general direction of the guard-room, acute hypothermia sending his thoughts into tighter and tighter spirals and marvelling giddily at the failure of his distant kin to innovate a better design of cannon, Helmens-son was ransacking the storage trunks. Looking for cannon fuel, Strahl supposed. Anything that might burn. The captain thumped the lid of the last trunk and cursed. At the same time, a group of three arkanauts busied themselves pitching a foil tent, laying down bedrolls, banking the snow up in the doorway and rigging up a set of thaumic heaters. One of them detached from the group and approached Strahl. He made a grab for the aether-gold canister that Strahl had stubbornly hauled all the way from the crash site on the slim chance that he'd be able to give it to his mother.

'No,' Strahl protested, and pulled it out of the arkanaut's hands.

'We need it to fuel the heaters,' the arkanaut said, and made another go for it.

Strahl stumbled back towards the guardroom door, dragging the heavy canister along with him. The arkanaut made to follow him.

'Leave it,' said Helmensson wearily, looking up from the empty storage trunks.

'But, captain–'

'Just leave it.'

The arkanaut turned his head, some understanding passing between him and his captain, a cypher, known only to the sky-farers of Barak-Zon, encoded in the cold glitter of snow-reflected light on a helmet's lenses. Whatever was said or intuited, the arkanaut reluctantly backed down.

'If Mistress Ael still lives, then maybe she'll find the aether-gold with our frozen corpses and pay out our share to our kin in Barak-Zon,' said Helmensson.

With the arkanaut returning to assist his crewmates with their emergency shelter, Strahl felt the last of the stubbornness he had been holding onto desert him. He slumped back, sliding down the wall, and hugging the aether-gold canister from the *Bokram* to his chest. They were both as cold as each other.

Helmensson squatted down beside him, as if to say something reassuring, but the sound of something large and angry moving around outside drew his attention back to the entrance. Reluctantly abandoning their heat shelter, a pair of Ael's Grundstok Thunderers took up crouching positions either side of the door-less opening and sent rapid-fire pulses of aethershot flickering out into the snow.

Whatever it was bellowed in frustration and rattled the stone-work with arrows.

Strahl watched the door. Perhaps it was the cold-fever creeping up on him, but he would have sworn to the spirits of his own dead parents that he saw a white-bearded duardin in a mail coat and a cloak nod casually to the busy Grundstok fighters and step inside. Shivering gruffly, the duardin drew his cloak in about him and stomped the snow off his boots. A grin progressed slowly across his tired face as he caught Strahl's gawping stare, and then glanced approvingly towards the arkanauts' foil tent and thaumic heaters.

'The Maker would approve, I reckon,' he said, and shrugged. 'Whether you care for his approval or not.'

Strahl reached out. His hand was weak and it wavered in his vision. This time, the elder grasped it firmly.

Strahl almost wept as the fresh stamina that ran through the old duardin and into him brought pain back to his arm.

'On the eight skies and all their riches,' he heard Helmensson mutter.

Feeling more lucid than he had in a day, Strahl realised that he was not imagining things. The White Duardin really was standing over him, and Helmensson and his crew could see him too.

'It's you,' he said. 'Isn't it?'

With great solemnity, and without exactly answering, the White Duardin unbuckled his cloak at the collar and threw it over Strahl's shoulders. Whatever enchantments had been woven into the tattered fabric, they crackled like a low and comforting flame. Strahl felt the thin ice encrusting his armour begin to melt. Condensation faded from his helmet lenses.

'Why...?' Strahl managed to say. 'Why me?'

The duardin shrugged. 'Why not you?'

'You could be helping Helmensson and his crew.'

'I'm helping you all, lad.'

Strahl looked puzzled.

It must have shown through his lenses, because the White Duardin chuckled. 'Duardin. They never change, do they? A Fyreslayer would sell his life and say it was for honour. The Dispossessed would do the same for their oaths and their precious grudges. A Kharadron… well, he'd call it contractual obligation, but what's the difference really? Nothing but words, I say.' He laughed again. A great plume of vapour came out of his mouth. He shivered, folding his muscular arms around his chest. His skin, Strahl noticed, was starting to goose bump.

'You're cold,' said Strahl.

'It *is* bloody cold.'

'But *you're* cold.'

'Ahhh.' The elder nodded as an understanding of Strahl's problem dawned. 'This is the Everwinter, lad. Sigmar himself would go blue if he were compelled to stand out there in naught but his woollens.'

Strahl's firm inclination was to shrug off the duardin's magical cloak and return it to its proper owner. It was too fine a thing for him. An orphan ward of the Union of Conservatories and Associated Compassionate Enterprises. An endless source of disappointment. For some reason, simple Kharadron gold-greed perhaps, sensing the profound value of the object draped over his shoulders and drawing it closer, he did not return it straight away. With the wall against his back for support and feeling returning to his bones, he pushed himself back up and to his feet.

The White Duardin's lips hooked up in an appraising smile, finding something halfway sound in what he saw and making Strahl feel foolish for doubting his worth. It was a warm, self-effacing sense of foolishness, as if the emotion could be shorn entirely from the feeling of shame that ordinarily went with it.

Failure, that smile took pains to say, could be an excuse to punish or it could be an opportunity to learn. Sometimes it could be both, given duardin of good intent.

'I need your help,' the duardin said. 'You and your guns. Consider the cloak a down payment.'

Strahl swallowed. A myth had come in from the cold to ask him for a favour and he had paid for it in advance.

He didn't know what to say.

'We'll freeze out there,' said Helmensson, his usual brash air chastened by the aura of semi-divinity, like a gas lamp turned down low rather than one blown out altogether.

The White Duardin nodded sadly. 'Aye. You've got it worse than your kin holed up in Grimnir's Forge right now, that's for sure. But, with that being the way it is...'

He turned back to Strahl. The smile he was still wearing was no longer mirthful, nor was it even comforting, but for all its grim resolve it was oddly heartening all the same. As though, with two dozen half-frozen arkanauts united in common purpose, there was nothing they could not do. Whatever he meant to ask for, Strahl did not think he would be able to say no.

'What do you say about going in for a pound?'

CHAPTER SIXTEEN

'BREAK!' Sjarpa yelled, as the thundertusk mashed its head into the gates.

Warding runes flared. Hardwood groaned. Unnatural frost clawed through the blackwork and the support frame buckled. Vibrations shook through Sjarpa's belly, fatty rolls wobbling against the cracked leather of his seat.

'IT!'

With a collective roar, mouths packed with snow, fourteen dismounted beastriders of the Thunder Hand fought a tug-of-war to draw the shaggy monster back along the ice.

'DOWN!'

They let go, and this time it was the thundertusk pulling all fourteen of them forward as it lowered its head and slammed its horns into the duardin gate with another spasm of runic magic.

It was taking too long. The door needed to come down *now*.

Reins hanging over one wrist, Sjarpa drew his arms round his chest and pulled them in tight. The hairs on the backs of his arms stood on end. The flesh was dimpled by goose bumps. His fingers were numb.

A Blizzard Speaker of the Winterbite Mawtribe was cold.

Sjarpa closed his eyes and let out a sigh. The eruption of freezing breath made his thundertusk grumble in alarm.

Warmth. He could almost remember what it felt like. He had wanted all the Mawtribes to feel it too. Maybe then they would understand, like he did, that there was more to life than filling their stomachs and see the importance of The Way. Far from the reach of Baergut's curse, safe in the bowels of the Fire Crown, they would have been able to wait out the Everwinter. He would have found the last of the duardin's living rulers, the Kharadron Magnate, and had her write for him the words that would give power over those who came after her: the magic duardin words of a *contract* that would forever say that Korgrun and Borja had a peace and that the Mawtribes would have shelter in the Fire Crown. Now, everyone who had ever disagreed with that ambition or needed regular reminding of it was dead and few of the Mawtribes were left. For the second time in his life he was at the threshold of the Fire Crown, and he found he didn't care much about those things after all.

He wanted to wade into the fires of Grimnir's Forge until the pins and needles of sensation came back to his skin.

Only the door stood in his way.

There were no defenders left, and Sjarpa regretted that. A little hot oil, in particular, would have been welcome. He would have showered under it. He would have turned his face to the ramparts and invited his ogors to join him, mouth open, and guzzled under it.

'BREAK!'

The fourteen released their thundertusk again.

Sjarpa bared the blunted yellow icicles of his teeth as the doors splintered and the runes cut into them faltered. If he was cold enough to shiver then it was ten times as cold as it needed to be for steel to shrink and become brittle.

The Everwinter would break the duardin's gate. Long before it broke the Beastclaw.

With a snarl, Sjarpa commanded the ogors back. Bulging muscles pushed thick rolls of straining fat as the ogors hauled their thundertusk from the gate. Gnoblars hurried in with tools. The shivering greenskins stuck tiny crowbars into the upright crack that the thundertusk had forced between the doors and levered furiously.

'You want a jack for that.'

Frowning at the unfamiliar voice, Sjarpa turned.

There was no one there.

'Down here, lad.'

He looked down.

The duardin stood level with his mount's knees, leaning wearily across the head of a big two-bladed axe and watching the gnoblars with a professional interest. His beard was as thick and white as a fur coat, but the nose that poked through it was a cold-blistered, red bulb. Sjarpa felt his brow furrow in confusion. He wondered if Kolram had come back from the grave to avenge his own killing. The beard was longer. The axe was bigger. But there was a resemblance there if you looked for it. Obviously, it wasn't a real duardin. If it was, he'd have more to show for the cold than a chapped nose.

'Are you a spook?' he asked.

The duardin shrugged. 'After a fashion, I suppose.'

'I know you.'

'We've met before, lad. Aye.'

Sjarpa growled. 'I'm old enough to remember Baergut Vosjarl. I'm no one's... lad.'

The duardin spook tutted and looked up. 'Bit of advice, lad. Let's not turn this into a *who's got the biggest father* contest, eh?'

Sitting up in the saddle, making himself a few inches taller, Sjarpa looked around to see if anyone else had noticed the odd duardin that was speaking with him. They were all too busy with the gate, with their irascible battering ram, with stopping the gnoblars from running away and ensuring Borja Kragnfryr was drawn up the last bit of slope to the gatehouse. No one was looking at him just then.

'I remember Borja, you know,' the duardin went on, amiably, following Sjarpa's backward glance at the frozen king. 'A good sort, for an ogor. I think he genuinely meant well.'

Sjarpa squinted hard at the duardin. He had not known that duardin could live as long as ogors. 'You were there?'

'A part of me was. It's complicated. Maybe one day I'll tell you the story of it.'

At the promise of a new story, Sjarpa felt something stunted and innocent in him wake up, its eagerness almost enough for him to forget the cold and his hunger. He licked his numb lips. 'Tell me.'

'Later. Perhaps. Suffice to say that I counselled the Last King, Korgrun as you knew him, in the dark days of the Age of Chaos. Ogors walk in circles, I told him. Big circles, granted, but circles just the same. Give them an inch once and your descendants will be forking out miles until the realms are cold. Borja won't be around forever. Boot the lot of you off his mountain, I said, but alas, he didn't listen. Those were dark times, as you rightly recall, and Karag Dawrkhaz had been weakened by too many wars. He was too eager to avoid another if there was peace to be had. It was his hold, after all, and his descendants who would have to live with his choice. Borja was true to his word, aye, but there wasn't much of a hold left by the time his ogors moved out. They'd eaten almost everything that wasn't a living duardin, and the hold fell not long after.' The duardin spread his hands in an expansive shrug. The snow was so hard and deep that his axe, sunk in by the haft, stood up on its own. 'So here we all are again, just as I warned we would be, but perhaps Korgrun was right after all. It's all worked out all right, I'd say, as I've found it generally will if you leave duardin to muddle through on their own.'

With a light tug, he pulled his axe out of the snow. Taking it two-handed, he gave it a couple of practice swings, his voice still conversational, to the extent that Sjarpa had no clue yet if they were about to fight or not.

'Korgrun's descendants have been needing a boot up the back-side for the last thirty years. So, nicely done, lad. Nicely done. But I'm afraid you've come as near to Grimnir's Forge as I'm going to let you get.'

With a snarl, Sjarpa pulled his harpoon launcher from its saddle holster and pointed it down. It already had a bloody harpoon in the rack. 'I'm not afraid of spooks,' he said, just as the duardin struck his axe into the thundertusk's knee.

The sound of it was like that of someone trying to headbutt a glacier. Sjarpa dropped his aim and laughed. A thundertusk was made of the same stuff as the ice encasing Borja. You couldn't break it with an axe. But then he heard a noise that he didn't think he ever had before, and didn't realise what it was until he was tipping sideways. It was the sound of a thundertusk trumpeting in pain.

The monster crashed onto its side with force enough to shatter the flagstones and bring snow cascading down from a thousand places amidst the abandoned forts. The impact threw Sjarpa clear and slid him across the ice. He saw the thundertusk's severed leg on the ground, decorated with blueish jewels of frozen blood. The thundertusk itself was still alive, but far too massive to have any hope of getting itself back up again. It bellowed uselessly as the duardin walked round it.

The rest of the Thunder Hand now definitely noticed. The fourteen dropped their chain and went for their weapons.

Their thundertusk, no longer restrained, thundered towards the gate with the space to build up real speed. The gnoblars working on the gate dropped their tools and shrieked in terror, tripping over each other in their haste to throw themselves out of the monster's way. Bloody splats, like squashed tomatoes, marked those that ran too slow or didn't dive far enough, and when the thundertusk hit the weakened door, it gave at last in an explosion of woody splinters and broken runes. The ogors around the gate, including half of the fourteen, gave a hungry roar and, regardless of what they'd been doing before or what Sjarpa had told them to do, dropped everything to run after the charging monster. Those gnoblars who had survived the thundertusk now met an equally sticky end under the stampeding Beastclaw.

The seven beastriders left behind were Sjarpa's closest allies and strongest fighters. He had fed them well over many years. Most of them, he had snatched as infants and reared almost as his own.

With Njal Icebreaker leading, they charged towards the strange duardin.

Njal threw a fist the size of a gargant's mouth at the duardin's head. The warrior sidestepped and let the punch sail over his horned helmet, burying his axe in the groin of Ulf the Strange. The ogor pawed at the snow and mewled before folding over and lying still. The duardin stumbled back in order to get the stricken ogor off his blade and block Brogg Threeteeth's pulverising downswing. The ogor's favoured weapon was a club, modelled on the one that had once smashed his teeth out, made from a chunk of Everwinter ice wedged into a piece of wood to serve as a club. It hammered into the duardin's block like a falling castle and sent him skidding back across the ice.

Njal rejoined the fight. Bending over with a grunt, he wrenched up a piece of gate and hurled it into the one-sided melee. The duardin barely needed to duck, but did, and the flying door hit Skag Vulture-Keeper in the mouth. Brogg Threeteeth laughed riotously at the sight of another ogor's teeth flying out of their mouth. Skag roared in outrage, forcing the duardin to dive out of the way of his stagger, and swung a punch that took Njal in the head.

Getting up off the ice, grumbling at his fighters' ineptitude, Sjarpa drew a deep breath and exhaled the Everwinter. The icy blast swept between Skag and Njal and threw the two ogors aside. It hit the duardin full in the body, and booted him like a gnawed bone through the ruined gate, where he skidded into his people's hall.

Brogg Threeteeth, who by this point was the nearest ogor who was not either dead, wrestling with one of his supposed comrades, or torn between eating his own guts and pushing them back in, tightened his fist around his massive club and turned towards the gate. There was a sudden *crack*, like metal passing its brittleness point, and a quizzical expression crossed the ogor's small eyes. He reached up to touch the smoking hole that had appeared at the back of his head and grunted in annoyance, even as several more holes burned into the lighter flab on the ogor's back.

With a tinny roar, Kharadron came flurrying out of the snow behind them.

The manifest impossibility of their presence there stole Sjarpa's ability to count them. There was no other people that weathered the cold like the Beastclaw, and no Beastclaw that could bear it so long, so willingly, and to as great a profit as the Winterbite Mawtribe. For him to be attacked *from behind* was so unthinkable as to be absurd. Golden pellets spat from their rifles as they charged, and for the longest while as aethershot blistered the air around him, he stood with his mouth open and did nothing. Brogg Threeteeth took several more hits that he tried ineffectually to swat on the back of his head before finally conceding to being dead and falling over. Another slumped over the top of him, as though shielding the ogor with his own bulk, but just as dead, his body riddled with burning shot. Gnoblars ran everywhere, screaming, mown down by Kharadron gunfire.

Halfway across the courtyard, the Kharadron slowed their charge and divided up into cover, splitting their fire between the various ogor mobs still standing around in confusion. A duardin in a red cloak took up a position behind Borja Kragnfryr and sent a hail of buzzing rounds singing across Sjarpa's body.

Then, he stirred.

Gesturing angrily towards Skag and Njal, who were just then pulling themselves up, horrifically frostbitten down their left and right sides, respectively, but not completely crippled, he directed them towards the Kharadron while miming the tearing of meat.

'Deal with them,' he barked. 'And then follow. I will deal with the spook myself.'

He stomped in through the broken gate. The duardin was still there where Sjarpa had put him, groaning on the floor while trying ineffectually to get up, his limbs encased in Everwinter ice.

Forgetting the harpoon loaded in the rack, Sjarpa swung the launcher overhead like a club and mashed down where the duardin lay. The strange fighter forced an arm to move and blocked it. The metal launcher had been cobbled together from gnoblar scrap, but it, like all ogor gear, was built to last. The solid frame buckled around the duardin's golden vambrace, but he gave a satisfying cry of pain as his arm flopped, weirdly jointed now, to the flagstones.

The duardin kicked him in the shin. It was like being rammed by a charging rhinox. Sjarpa ignored it as he would have ignored that, and kicked the wounded arm out of his way, drawing another cry out of the duardin's mouth as he bent down. He grabbed the duardin by the collar, a fistful of beard and mail, pulled him up and headbutted him. The duardin's frostbitten nose burst. Blood splattered Sjarpa's face. The duardin hit the ground and skidded until the roof of his helmet *thunked* against the wall.

Shivering, panting, Sjarpa wiped blood from his face on the back of his hand and licked it off. Good eating. For a spook.

'I never saw a duardin fight like that.'

With his back against the wall, the duardin sat himself up. 'I could tell you... some stories... lad.'

Sjarpa wavered across the threshold, torn neatly around the middle between leaving the duardin to freeze and making for Grimnir's Forge himself and *stamping* on the duardin's head until everything above the neck was a smear on the ground. With a hundred ogors and his wisdom to lead them, he could sack this place. He'd endure the Everwinter. He'd bully the local grots into joining him on the Mawpath until he could find more ogors to teach The Way. That would have been the thing to do. But the sight of the duardin still trying to get up after the thumping that Njal and the rest had meted out filled his belly with a gurgling rage that wouldn't be ignored.

He took a stumbling step towards him.

He wasn't sure why he was stumbling. Now he thought about it, his legs were numb below the knees. He held to the wall to steady himself and, leaning his shoulder into it, walk-slid the rest of the way down to where the duardin sat propped up against it. The gunfire and the shouting from outside seemed very far away.

And then, for no obvious reason he could think of, they just stopped.

'Gonna... kill you,' he said. 'Then... gonna eat you. Then... gonna find... the Forge.'

The duardin raised a hand. Sjarpa blinked at it, puzzled. His thoughts moved so slowly he could almost feel them crossing from one side of his head to the other.

'Wait,' said the duardin.

'For what?'

'What's the rush?'

'The rush…?'

Sjarpa felt his eyes cross. His fist lowered itself to his side. As soon as he noticed it going down, he tried to make it go up again, but the muscles were stiff and wouldn't let him. He tried to wiggle the fingers. They ignored him.

'Huh,' he said.

The duardin raised a smile, ice snapping off between the hairs of his beard and tinkling over his lap. 'Don't you want to hear the story?'

Sjarpa tried to shake his head. 'I know… all the stories.'

'Not this one, I'll wager. Aside from me there's only two gods who know how it starts, neither one of whom has been around much of late, or belong to what you'd call the sharing kind. So, what do you say? Do you want to hear it or not?'

Almost without meaning to, Sjarpa let himself go limp. His knees finally gave out under him, pitching him into a sideways slump that left him in a heap against the wall by the duardin's side. His breath came in shallow, ragged gasps. In and out. His mouth didn't move for it. His chest hardly rose. The work of living was being done deeper in, where there was still just enough warmth left to make it happen. He tried to *make* his jaw move and failed. It was frozen rigid. He should probably be scared, but in the complete loss of his body to the Everwinter there was peace, and quiet of a sort. It felt, almost, like the freedom he'd been chasing all his life.

He wasn't hungry any more. He wasn't even cold. All he wanted was to hear the story.

Maybe *that* had been Borja's secret all along.

'T-t-t-tell me,' he managed to say.

'Well,' said the duardin, as the Everwinter rolled into the Great Hall and took them. 'I suppose it all begins at the deathbed of a High King...'

Sjarpa listened. And for the first time in his unnaturally long life, he knew peace.

CHAPTER SEVENTEEN

Brigg kept her watch for weeks after the battle had ended, but Azka-harr, if that was even his name, did not come back. The sounds of fighting from the tunnels, relentless until that time, died away. It was so cold. The Upper Deeps must have been frozen over, and even those Beastclaw that had made it through the Gate of Throngs had stopped coming to die on the Dunrakul Ironbreakers' shields. The residual heat of Grimnir's Forge, the volcano's turgid heart, was all that was left keeping the last of the duardin alive. The flues and channels that had been dug in ages past to channel the heat of the Forge to the industries of Karag Dawrkhaz, had been reversed now, turned into a web of funnels for the Everwinter's cold.

Brigg recalled the warriors and sealed the ways. Portcullises of rune-hardened steel, proof against any invader but this one, slammed shut over the tunnels' entrances. The wind, however, raided freely through the magma-vault of the Dunr and chilled whatever it touched. The rumour of its passing set the net of fyre-steel chains and devotional icons festooning the magma chamber to jangling. Where it gathered its strength and struck in force, the lava seethed and geysered, and duardin scrambled to find deeper shelter amongst the battleforges.

What power lay behind the Everwinter, Brigg wondered, that it could lay even the volcano low? What could the ancestors of the Beastclaw have possibly done to earn its ire, and what crime had the duardin committed against it to attract the curse upon themselves? Where was the realmgate to Vostargi Mont that, the legends claimed, was buried under the magma lake? What use were all the prayers spoken in anger by the runesmiters to the Zharrkhul and the Brokkfoor since their ordeal began? Would the duardin still be suffering now if they had united earlier, as Azkaharr had sought to persuade them to do, rather than as their last resort when the hold was already lost? If they had confronted the ogors in strength as they had spilled from Arik's Pass would the storm have passed them by, or would it, too, have been unable to resist the lure of Grimnir's Forge?

Magic, particularly when it was old and exceptionally powerful, could assume a sentience of a sort. She knew this. Those who made a life from working with ur-gold or hunting Endless Spells across the Spiral Crux had tales in abundance to attest to the uncanny malevolence of the most powerful magic. What then was the Everwinter, Brigg reasoned, but the most ancient of Endless Spells. She would be surprised, given what she knew and what she could suppose, if the Everwinter was not intelligent, perhaps even godly, in some predatory, elemental way.

And if that were true, then even if the ogors had all been slain, and far from Karag Dawrkhaz, it was likely that the Everwinter would have sniffed out its cornered prey in any event and sought them out of sheer malice rather than simply break.

Maybe *this* was always the most that Azkaharr had hoped for.

Snow buried the highest platforms, sturdy fyresteel bridgework groaning under the unaccustomed weight. The wind ripped its way through the bridges as duardin fled them, abandoning the Zharrgrim itself, for the warmth and shelter of the lakeside. All that remained of the proud population of Karag Dawrkhaz, fewer than a thousand doughty Fyreslayers, Kharadron and Dispossessed, withdrew to the volcanic archipelago of Grimnir's Forge.

Brigg opted to remain on the outermost isle. Its magmic battleforge portrayed Grimnir in his aspect as the eager apprentice, he who would learn that fire was hot only by burning his hand: the aspect of himself he had shown when freed from the Iron Mountains by Sigmar and returned to the Realm of Metal for the first time in an age. Its island was currently the coldest. It was the one the Everwinter would overwhelm first, and the first that Azkaharr would return to. If he could endure the Everwinter, and pass through a rune-warded portcullis.

For some reason, she did not bet entirely against him.

And so the days passed, and she continued to watch, but Azkaharr did not return.

With the Zharrgrim emptied, its runemasters and runesmiters spent the hours of their days hurling prayers at the Everwinter. They stood before the blazing battleforges and chanted, feeding the furnaces with ritually prepared coals inscribed with runes of immolation, and thrusting at the leaping flames with blessed pokers to goad them higher. After many days without success, the priests found themselves sufficiently resigned to allow their Dunrakul cousins a closer inspection of the sacred battleforges. Blowing the dust off of yellowed manuals, the blacksmiths and engineers muttered amongst themselves as they returned their counterparts to older rune combinations and ratios of fuel.

Brigg wondered if it was her imagination, or if she *did* actually feel a little warmer after the engineers had been allowed to do their work?

Before too long, Kharadron endrineers and aether-khemists were adding their heads to the throng about the battleforges. Scaffolding grew up around the belligerent edifices, mounts for a new proliferation of semi-arcane instruments to regulate airflow, administer peculiar-looking fuelstuffs, and calibrate temperature.

Brigg watched them. Days went by. But she never tired of watching Kharadron at work.

Massive as a house, Oxtarn curled up around her and snored. The magmadroth had not moved in weeks. Her breaths were epochal, each one marking the end of an age and the beginning of another. The cold had penetrated her scales, permeated her: it had found the godfire in her belly and chilled it. A gaggle of nervous youngflames sat on the floor around the beast's gigantic mouth – Fyreslayers, Kharadron and Dispossessed, all mingling freely in the innocence of childhood – watching for the occasional cinder that would gust from her craggy lips. Brigg smiled, despite herself. The sight of them, she was sure, would have warmed Azkaharr's heart.

'Is she going to wake, Fyrequeen?' Queen Silveg of the Dunra-kul asked.

Sensing, perhaps, where the power had gone to after Kolram and Braegnar-Grimnir's death, his widow had opted to remain with Brigg. She knelt on a blanket that had been spread for her before the mouth of the battleforge, where the coldest isle remained at its mildest. Another lay across her lap and a third over her shoulders. Kurrindorm was there with her, holding her hand in his, as was Lorekeeper Braztom and his beloved books.

Brigg patted the slumbering magmadroth's craggy thigh. It was cold under her hand. Like stone. But the fires ignited by Vulca-trix, the mother of all salamanders and the slayer of Grimnir, were the hottest that had ever burned and the source of all warmth in the Mortal Realms. It could never be quenched entirely, not even by this accursed winter. She was merely sleeping, as the volcano itself was, ready to revive again once the Everwinter had passed. She would wake up, even if the rest of them never did.

'Don't call me Fyrequeen,' she said.

'Is that the wrong title?'

'It's just… too soon.'

Silveg pursed her lips, but nodded understandingly. 'After Braegnar-Grimnir's death.'

Brigg shook her head. 'My name is Brigg, daughter of my lodge, until the runemaster unlocks my father's legacy chest and reads the oath-plaques he left for the Dunr. If he thought me worthy enough to name his heir, *then* I will have earned a new title.'

Silveg thought on that for a moment. 'Very proper.'

'Meritocratic,' Ael added.

The Kharadron sky-mistress, too, had decided to stay. She claimed not to feel the cold, but Brigg had the feeling that she fancied herself some kind of a wise counsel to the new crown. Why everyone was so insistent that she be in charge, she didn't know. Behind the other woman, a helmeted aether-khemist was holding up a briquette of a gold-like substance he called Grungni's Breath and lecturing a huddle of undersmiters and engineers on its combustible, high-burning properties.

'And documented,' Ael went on.

From under Silveg's blanket, Lorekeeper Braztom was nodding approvingly, but absently.

'I had no idea that the Fyreslayers could be so…'

'Literate?' Brigg suggested.

Ael's cheek twitched to allow for a brief smile. 'Orderly.'

'The children of a runefather compete for glory, and for his approval. Those that fail, and don't even fail hard enough to die in the attempt, are expected to exile themselves for the good of the lodge. Sometimes, it pays to be orderly.'

'It does,' Ael agreed. 'Sometimes.'

'You are lucky then,' said Silveg.

Brigg frowned. She didn't feel it. 'How?'

'You were an only child.'

Brigg made a fist, wanting nothing more than to hit the Dunra-kul queen, then breathed and let it out in her lap. It would solve nothing. She doubted it would even make her feel better.

'Yes,' she said. 'In that, I suppose I was lucky.'

'It doesn't surprise me,' said Ael quietly. 'To learn that we're so alike. We are kin after all, and I have dealt with other duar-din many times. It is *how* we are alike. It's not the ways I was expecting.'

'What were you expecting?' said Brigg.

Ael sighed. 'The age is fast coming, I am sure of it, when wealth and education are the only traits needed in a leader, but if all of *this...*'

Her hand waved about her like an exhausted moth in a gesture that nevertheless managed to affect the entirety of the Forge. From out of the huddle at her back, a pair of Dunrakul engineers wearing thick gloves, heavy goggles and flame-retardant aprons were tossing their golden briquettes of Grungni's Breath into the battleforge. Zharrgrim priests raised their voices in prayer while the aether-khemist barked at them to get their heads down.

'If all this has shown me anything, then it's that we're not there yet. My city has been pulled from the side of the mountain. I have one gunhauler and a grounded sixth-rate to my name. My son is lost.'

Ael paused. Brigg yearned to say something, to share in whatever the Kharadron was feeling, but in the moment it felt selfish to impose and so she let it pass.

'Doing things by the old ways is what makes Barak-Thryng twenty times poorer than the next poorest sky-hold on the

Geldraad – or so we say in Barak-Nar – but you don't just throw the old away out of hand.' She smiled. 'That's Artycle nine, Point five, by the way. Karag Dawrkhaz had a single ruler once. I think it should again. And I think it needs to be you.'

'Kurrindorm is King Kolram's heir, and a descendant of the Last King,' said Silveg. She didn't say it with any conviction. Not even Kolram's dourest longbeards had shown any great appetite about pressing for Kurrindorm's elevation to his late father's crown. It was Brigg, and to a certain extent Ael, who had been ordering the tunnel-fighting around Grimnir's Forge.

'I don't want it,' Kurrindorm muttered unnecessarily.

Brigg laughed. '*I* don't want it.'

As far as she was concerned, Kurrindorm was welcome to it, but she had always known this day would come: the day when the small amount of reckless adventure expected from the child of a runefather would need to be set aside for her duty to the lodge.

'You are both unmarried,' said Silveg.

Brigg and Kurrindorm looked at each other.

'No,' Brigg said, very firmly.

Silveg cleared her throat, and said nothing more, but Brigg felt sure that if they lived through the Everwinter then she had not heard the last proposition for a marriage union between the Dunrakul and the Dunr.

She smiled ruefully. At least there was still death to hope for.

'My son was to marry,' said Ael wistfully. 'He had presented me with the contract just before I ordered him to depart aboard the *Bokram*.'

In the quickness of a flash, Brigg saw Strahl's face in front of her. She had been so quick to certainty that he had never asked her, so sure that his courage had burned out in the time it took to walk from his bedchamber to his mother's trommraad. She had never been more pleased to be proven wrong, never more deeply hurt. Perhaps there was more of Grimnir in his heart than she had ever given him credit for.

'Did he...' Brigg licked her dried lips. 'Did he tell you who?'

Ael shook her head. 'To my shame, I did not want to look at the contract at the time. It was only after.' She looked up then, fixing Brigg with a stare so firm she was certain that somehow she *knew.* 'I must have read the Code ten thousand times. The original Maldralta Treaty. The Gorak-drek amendments. As a rulebook for diplomacy and trade, which is the purpose for which it was always intended, it is a masterpiece. But there is so much on which it has no wisdom to impart. We duardin have to muddle through on our own good intentions and the spirit of the Code. We adapt. We learn. We do what we think is right. Do you understand?'

'I...' Brigg was not sure that she did. 'I think so.'

'Seize the moment,' said Ael, and then chuckled ruefully. 'At least, I think that's what I'm saying.'

A sigh that wasn't quite her own, but which rumbled through her as though *she* was somehow *its*, rattled the golden ringlets of her dress. She turned, looking over her shoulder, unsure what she was expecting to see, just as the gathered youngflames leapt up and shrieked in overexcitement and terror. Oxtarn lifted her head off the ground on a creaking neck and yawned. Fire flickered from her nostrils, blasting out embers like hatchling fireflies that the youngflames near fell over themselves trying to jump up and catch in their bare hands.

'She's awake,' Silveg murmured.

'She's awake,' Brigg agreed, astonished.

Iridescent fire roared through the magmic battleforge's chimney and blew off the grille mouth at its front, sending the fyresteel teeth of Grimnir the Apprentice flying over Brigg's head and sizzling into the lava off the far shore of the island. Rendered into the most basic of charcoal-drawn line-figures by the inferno behind them, the runemaster of the Zharrgrim grudgingly offered a hand to the Kharadron aether-khemist. They shook. Under-smiters and Dunrakul smiths mobbed them both with slapped backs and *whoops* of unrestrained joy.

Snow began melting before it had the chance to land. Steam started to rise off the platforms. Brigg looked up and began to laugh as, behind her, Oxtarn uncurled from hibernation and luxuriated in the fire's return.

They had done it. The duardin had done it.

The Everwinter was in retreat.

CHAPTER EIGHTEEN

The arkanauts took one side. The Dunrakul clansmen took the other. Both looked back. Depleted furnaces made the arkanauts' lenses dull, the bronze edgework and ringmail worn by the Dunrakul glittering more brightly in the dim light from the surviving glimstone sconces in the walls. They awaited Ael's command. She took a deep breath and, with a curt nod, gave it. Together, the warriors of Karag Dawrkhaz heaved open the gates of the Angazongi Stair. Snowmelt sloshed over the lip of the doorway. A few of the Dunrakul carried torches, preferring them to the brighter and more efficient aether-fuelled lanterns carried by the Kharadron, and the fire danced in the warm air as it rushed up out of the stair to displace the cold.

Ael followed it, stepping over the threshold, her plainly armoured boot sinking up to the greave in slush, as she looked around the Great Hall of the Dunrakul.

It was raining. Water dripped from every sill and beam, pattered over flooded stones, rattled on the stone awnings of shop fronts and drizzled from their sloping edges, drummed mutedly on Ael's armour. Everywhere, the Everwinter announced its surrender. Everywhere, it was in retreat. Where it persisted it was in the beards of frost that coated the lintel beams of doorways and the windowsills of the shop fronts. It was the spiderweb glitter of the farthest corners and the crystalline jewellery that embellished the abundant statuary. It was almost beguiling in its serenity, in its beauty, though it struck her that the ice did not appear to be melting evenly.

She told herself she would concern herself with that tomorrow. Or the day after. She refused to be worried today. There was, she had decided, no problem that the ingenuity of the Kharadron, the stubbornness of the Dispossessed, and the intensity of the Fyreslayers could not come together to solve.

The wet *slap* of footsteps echoed through the hall. Brigg hurried to catch up.

Ael had advised her to remain behind. The first responsibility of a captain was to their ship, after all, as Artycle one clearly stated and, to quote Point seven, with a new ship and an untested crew, it was an unwise captain who took his hand off the wheel and his eye off the hold.

Brigg, of course, had ignored her completely. She wanted to be the first to step outside.

At the Gate of Throngs, they all slowed, pausing in a spontaneous gesture of respect. The doors had been torn completely off their hinges. The Dunrakul clansmen, a few carpenters amongst them, muttered darkly until Ael shushed them.

'They'll be rehung,' she said. 'And made even better than before.' If anything, the duardin grumbled even more loudly about that, but Ael ignored them. She refused to be worried today.

Under the ruin of the door, two blocks of ice lay. One was smaller, about the size of a sarcophagus for a duardin, while the other was gigantic. Leaning in towards the smaller, she almost choked on her grief. It was clearly Wyram, his expression peaceful. Turning to the larger block, she leaned over and spat on it. Her spit froze in an untidy lump between Sjarpa Longtooth's frozen stare. 'Good riddance to you,' she muttered aloud, just as a cry of what sounded like dismay rose outside of the gate.

The Fyreslayers, of course, had decided not to wait.

With a curse, she left the frozen ancestor to rest a little longer and pulled the volley pistol from its holster, turning towards the Fyreslayers' shout. Outside, she stumbled to a halt, blinking in the watery first light of spring.

The first ring of fortifications had been turned into an ornamental rockery of ugly, eerily delicate statues. There were ogors, orruks, smaller greenskins, even a few Kharadron too, though Ael had no idea how they had got there, all of them frozen and twinkling in the pale Azrilruf sun.

A single Kharadron was limping out of the snow, stiff with cold, but somehow, impossibly, still alive. He walked like a duardin in a daze, as though he had never walked before or, perhaps, a duardin who had once walked, long ago, but had allowed himself to forget the skill, expecting never to need it again. His footfalls were heavy, and Ael realised that his aether-furnace must be spent. His armour was cracked in the cold. The armour's make was familiar, but draped in a long red cloak stitched with golden runes that emulated the appearance of flame and made her feel warmer just for looking at them, even in ignorance of what they meant. As she watched, her mind still trying to reason through the impossible, Brigg issued a second cry and rushed ahead to crush the unfortunate Kharadron in the rune-empowered strength of her embrace.

The Auric Hearthguard who'd insisted on coming with her milled around the frozen dead with postures of acute embarrassment.

Ael opened her mouth, but before the words could form in it,

Brigg broke off her embrace and everything around her ground to a stop. Her breath. Her thoughts. Her beating heart.

Stopped.

She was Kharadron. She didn't believe in miracles.

But it was Strahl. Caught outside in the Everwinter, trapped without shelter for over a week until she and Brigg had unsealed the doors to the Angazongi Stair, but somehow, *miraculously*, still alive.

Brigg pulled off his helmet and kissed him fiercely on the lips, then put an arm around him and led him back inside through the Gate of Throngs.

Ael watched them go. *Nothing to worry about*, Wyram had told her when she'd been fretting about the betrothed her son had chosen. She smiled to herself. He had been right about that, as he'd been proven right on everything else.

'What should we do with this one?' said one of the Hearth-guard who had been left behind. He had a familiar look about him that Ael could not quite place, a streak of white through his long, reddish hair and a knowing smile on his face. He was also, she noticed, wearing a very fine red cloak. He pointed towards a singular large column of ice, the very one that Sjarpa had presented to her, Kolram and Braegnar-Grimnir before the Battle of the Gate. The huge, eternally hungering features of Borja Kragnfryr, last Frost King of the Winterbite Mawtribe, stared down at her.

'Take him inside.'

'You're sure?'

'We had a contract, didn't we?' said Ael, and smiled as she met the old Frost King's helplessly furious gaze. 'Take him inside. The duardin of Karag Dawrkhaz may have their differences, but we are no oathbreakers.'

ABOUT THE AUTHOR

David Guymer's work for Black Library includes the Warhammer Age of Sigmar novels *Kragnos: Avatar of Destruction, Hamilcar: Champion of the Gods* and *The Court of the Blind King,* the novella *Bonereapers,* and several audio dramas including *Realmslayer* and *Realmslayer: Blood of the Old World.* He is also the author of the Gotrek & Felix novels *Slayer, Kinslayer* and *City of the Damned.* For The Horus Heresy he has written the novella *Dreadwing,* and the Primarchs novels *Ferrus Manus: Gorgon of Medusa* and *Lion El'Jonson: Lord of the First.* For Warhammer 40,000 he has written *The Eye of Medusa, The Voice of Mars* and the two Beast Arises novels *Echoes of the Long War* and *The Last Son of Dorn.* He is a freelance writer and occasional scientist based in the East Riding, and was a finalist in the 2014 David Gemmell Awards for his novel *Headtaker.*